Firebird went rigid, her mind a battleground for foreign powers.

She had no weapon to bring into this battle but her Turn, a thing of powerless agony. But Firebird could not lie down and die. She dove inward, imagining the wall, and swept through.

The intruder followed. His point of presence seemed to glow with delight as he perceived the death march of her imagination. He *wanted* her to destroy herself. The visions fed his strength. They intensified . . .

In agony, she flailed for the gleaming cord of epsilon energy deep at the core of her horrors. Deeper—deeper—

With her last effort, she touched it.

Bantam Spectra Books
Ask your bookseller for the titles you have missed

FUSION FIRE

by Kathy Tyers

BANTAM BOOKS
TORONTO • NEW YORK • LONDON • SYDNEY • AUCKLAND

To Linda Peavy, Jo Sykes, and Jane Yolen,
My first teachers.
Thank you.

FUSION FIRE

A Bantam Spectra Book / November 1988

ISBN 0-553-27464-3

Published simultaneously in the United States and Canada

Bantam Books are published by Bantam Books, a division of Bantam Doubleday
Dell Publishing Group, Inc. Its trademark, consisting of the words ''Bantam Books''
and the portrayal of a rooster, is Registered in U.S. Patent and Trademark Office
and in other countries. Marca Registrada, Bantam Books, 666 Fifth Avenue, New
York, New York 10103

PRINTED IN THE UNITED STATES OF AMERICA

O   0 9 8 7 6 5 4 3 2 1

Contents

The ideal condition
Would be, I admit, that men should be right by instinct;
But since we are all likely to go astray,
The reasonable thing is to learn from those who can teach.

Sophocles

эп

Chapter 1

The Lost of Auria . . .

tema
theme

Firebird Mari Caldwell had been a pilot, once.

And will be again, she vowed. Standing on an outer walkway that led to the main dome of Thyrica's major military base, she watched as a pair of elegant black intercept fightercraft screamed over her from behind. One day, when she was no longer grounded from military flying, she would shamelessly use her husband's pull to get on the pilot-training list for those beautiful, deadly fighters.

A second pair closely followed the first: the light, quick, killing birds of the Federacy. She'd flown against these dual-drive, space-and-atmosphere fighters once. It had been a strategic disaster.

Never again. You're a Federate, now.

All four fighters vanished over the line of gray clouds that swirled against the Base's weather-control zone, and Firebird sighed. The gray-and-green, soaking wet world of Thyrica had its lovely moments, but it was not her home.

Well. She would make it her home. She had no choice. *We have no choice,* she corrected herself, and one of the twins kicked agreement against her ribs. After half a day struggling to write a sonata for the small N'Taian harp, she was coming to meet Brennen for dinner.

Brenn. At least you've still got m-flight clearance.

She never would have believed she could so miss a person she lived with. This was the down side of pair bonding: She no longer felt whole when she was alone. Something inside her felt drained, emptied—stolen.

The sky shone deep, clear blue overhead, but dampness squeaked between her fingers and made her loosely belted Thyrian skyff cling to her legs. Thyrica's huge ocean had given the planet life, but like some primeval god, the sea also drove its weather. Man could contain it, but never master it.

Firebird shivered and hurried on.

She slipped inside the dome's reception area, where a smoked glasteel ceiling curved high overhead, letting fading daylight bathe the broad reception quadrangle. On her left, two workiers in green coveralls pushed a service cart between them toward a corridor; from her right, a husky, dark-haired man approached. He wore the four-rayed shoulder star of her husband's kindred, Thyrica's telepathic minority: the Sentinels.

Her heart sank when he came close enough to recognize. *Oh, glory,* she groaned. *Not Terrell. Not now!*

Like other telepathic Sentinels, Staff Officer Bosk Terrell could not use youth implants without crippling his "epsilon" neural system, so he looked his age: midforties, a little out of shape from twenty years of desk service, hair freshly cut. His hands worked constantly, as always, down at his sides.

Terrell turned a wide, charming smile toward Firebird and made a small bow. "Mistress Caldwell. How good to see you." Two of his fingers twitched into a half-fist. "You're well?"

"Yes. Thank you." A chill seemed to suck warmth from the quad. She stepped aside.

"How goes your composition for the clairsa?"

Leave me alone, she thought, and then blanked it quickly, hoping Terrell maintained a normal cloud of emotion-shielding epsilon static. Rude though she felt, she didn't want him to pick up her antagonism, but even with shields down, the Sentinel could not have picked up her vocalized thought unless he was probing, and Firebird knew the subtle, invasive sensations of mind-access. Terrell was keeping his epsilon energy to himself.

Firebird planted her feet squarely. "I'm . . . stuck on the middle section."

She glanced at his hands. That constant restlessness hinted at energy that was barely controlled, ambitions that had escaped his grasp. "It wants to shift back into major too soon," she went on, "and I'm afraid I'll have to rewrite the whole passage."

Abruptly she realized she had never run into Staff Officer Bosk Terrell with Brennen along. She would have to remember to ask Brennen what he knew about Terrell, when she saw him—

Which had better be soon. Glancing down at the lights on her wristband, she feigned surprise. "Oh. Excuse me, Officer Terrell. I'm late."

"Of course, Mistress."

She did not look back as she strode to the clearing desk that guarded the office pod at one corner of the quiet quad. A slender captain in Thyrian-blue shipboards sat busy at a computer screen. Firebird touched one fingertip to the woman's long desk of bright, red-grained ironbark. "General Coordinator Caldwell?"

"One moment." The clearing captain wore a line of patches and cords on her sleeve that chronicled an honorable career in Thyrian service—and told Firebird she was not one of the telepathic few, who wore only the Star. She glanced up as she reached across her desk toward another console. "You're looking well, Mistress Caldwell." Her long fingers tapped a series of panels on her left.

Easing sideways toward a deep white chair in the waiting area, Firebird exhaled her frustration. *Oh, yes. I look wonderful. A tank looks wonderful when you need groundside defense, but that doesn't make it pretty.*

She had been slender, a few months ago, small and slight. A long curl of her auburn hair fell over her shoulder as she leaned forward, and simultaneously she was punched soundly from inside. She straightened. Another pair of intercept fighters came in low.

The captain glanced aside at Firebird. "You may go in."

Firebird was grateful the Thyrian woman did not stare. Six months pregnant, she felt as if she were waddling in a two-gravity simulator. She didn't like wearing ringlets, either, but in this alien dampness it was easier to let her hair have its own way. Behind the captain's desk, a smooth black door slid open, and she walked through.

Wholeness: contentment: union: strength: Firebird sensed Brennen's presence before she saw him, the moment she passed inside his range of telepathic projection. Eight months ago, when he had pair bonded with her in his people's way, their emotions had become indissolubly linked, and now, though she was no Sentinel and never could be, she read his feelings as plainly as another Sentinel would discern them, whenever she was near him.

And he was glad to see her, no matter how heavily she walked;

as he tucked a stylus into his left cuff, his feelings of completeness echoed hers and built a resonance between them. Was that relief he felt, as well? She'd interrupted something, something that disturbed him. Brennen stood beside his desk, a slender, middle-sized Thyrian who looked even slimmer wearing the deep midnight blue of the Thyrian forces. On his right shoulder gleamed an eight-rayed Master Sentinel's star.

A second Sentinel stood a few steps to his right. Taller, blond, more heavily muscled than the typical Thyrian, he wore the four-rayed Sentinel's star. "Air Master Dardy," she exclaimed. "You're back."

Dardy inclined his long body slightly, his broad, whole-hearted smile making the thirty-year-old look ten years younger than Brennen. "I understand today is a celebration, my lady. Congratulations on the occasion."

Firebird laughed. It was just like Damalcon Dardy to call her by her N'Taian title, on this anniversary in N'Taian years of her birthday.

"Twenty-four on the *real* calendar." She tilted her chin and smiled up at him. Way up—her head did not even reach his shoulder height. "I'm aging well, don't you think?"

"For nineteen *Standard*." Dardy reached down for her hand and held it.

Firebird laughed again. "Actually, at present I prefer the old Thyrian calendar over either Federate *or* N'Taian. By that one I'll be pregnant only seven months."

Brennen stepped backward, smiling on the inside (she could feel it), a lock of light red-brown hair dangling over one dark brow. From where she stood, the squadron of gold-sealed training certificates on the wall framed his face and shoulders—a nice effect, she thought, if a little overdramatic.

"I didn't mean to interrupt you," she said.

Dardy shook his head. "Not on your birthday, Mistress. There's no need to dampen your mood."

"My mood?" She glanced over at Brennen. "What were you talking about?"

Brennen hesitated only a second; then, evidently sensing her annoyance, he smoothed the errant strand of hair. "Tell her what you've been telling me."

The tall blond man dropped her hand and crossed his arms. "I've just returned from Ixthic, Firebird. Minor system, off the usual trade routes, but under Federate protection because its third planet is inhabited by a small, semi-intelligent race."

Firebird set both hands on the back of the large black chair beside her. She hated to sit all that way down if she were just going to get up again, but her legs were so tired.

"Pruupae. Small, pink-eyed, gray-furred creatures." Brennen sat down on a desk corner. "Mentally primitive, but sentient. All the same, they haven't risen to ante-Federate technological levels. We protect them anyway."

"From the Shuhr, I suppose," she said quietly to Dardy, "if you're involved."

Dardy nodded and leaned one shoulder against the warm-toned ironbark paneling. He belonged to Thyrica's small group of Alert Forces, who kept watch on the starbred families' renegade relatives. Psionic outlaws. The Shuhr.

"The Shuhr raid Ixthic," Dardy said, "to kidnap pairs of the little creatures—the pruupae. We thought we'd tightened our security adequately by leaving a patrol at the major settlement, but the patrol was wiped out and half the young population gone."

Gray-furred creatures, pink eyes . . . The hormones of pregnancy made her emotional, Firebird knew. She sank into the chair. "What do the Shuhr do with them?" Stretching out her legs, she flexed her ankles. "Do you know?"

Brennen rested one hand on his desk. "We've found crippled adults left behind after raids, sometimes." He kept his even features relaxed, his emotions under Sentinel-trained affective control. "Apparently the Shuhr keep a breeding population, amputate the pups' limbs, and give the pups to their own children for practicing psychic domination."

A soft tone sounded at one corner of Brennen's desk. He turned his head. "Yes?"

"Message for you, sir." The desk spoke in an excellent imitation of the clearing captain's voice. "Captain Kinsman, on 'personal.' "

Ellet. Startled, Firebird glanced aside in time to see a smile crinkle Dardy's lips. Then Brennen's head-turn snagged her peripheral vision, she caught a glint of his blue eyes, and a caressing inquiry touched the edge of her awareness. Guiltily, she tried to suppress her jealousy—

"Ask if it can wait until morning, please," Brennen told the desk.

Firebird bit her lip. When would she learn to control her reactions? She'd prefer to be present any time Ellet spoke with her husband. Ellet Kinsman had wanted Brennen, had once deliberately endangered Firebird while assigned to protect her. And Ellet, like Brennen and Dardy, was a telepath. Pair bonding might last for life, but the depth and ease of communication Brennen shared with other Sentinels was something denied Firebird. It made her —*yes*, she admitted, letting the feeling rise again: *jealous*.

Mentally shaking herself, she saw Brennen and Dardy stare-locked, communicating while her attention wandered, but the instant she focused her attention on them, they broke off the stare.

Brennen was nothing if not well trained.

Dardy rubbed his chin. "I think I know what she wants. You're mentioned in the monthly report from Federate Regional Command."

Brennen swiveled on the desk's slick top. "Yes?" He maintained a casual pose, but Firebird felt his conflict of inner feeling at the mention of his former superiors.

"It identifies your new position," Dardy said. " 'Lieutenant General Brennen D. Caldwell, formerly of Special Operations, has accepted a position with the Thyrian Home Forces, as General Coordinator, serving as a liaison between the Sentinel College, Aerospace Academy, and Home Forces.' "

Formerly of Special Operations, Firebird echoed to herself. She didn't even try to mask her bitterness, though Brennen would feel it. *Ten years of Federate service. The best intelligence officer they ever had, and they let him go. All because his superiors wouldn't admit that my people were about to create a terrible disaster.*

Brennen flicked one hand, and a stack of papers slid aside. "At least they acknowledge that I exist, again. For four months it looked like I had permanent deep-cover here." Firebird caught his glance. A man with intelligence and initiative, rising quickly in the ranks, was bound to tread on someone's toes, and last year Brennen had done it—though Firebird and Dardy (and who else on Thyrica?) guessed the Federates' acceptance of his forced resignation was temporary, and would one day be rescinded.

Dardy touched his own four-rayed star. "We're going to have a Sentinel on the Federate High Command some day, Caldwell, and you happen to be the best candidate this generation."

Firebird snorted inwardly. Sometimes Dardy sounded like Ellet Kinsman. He certainly shared her convictions regarding the ascendancy of Sentinel ideas; even Brennen admitted tiring of his friend's ultraconservatism.

"Time to get home." Dardy picked a pair of scan cartridges off Brennen's desk and slid them into his papercase.

"Good to see you, Dardy." Firebird clasped his hand.

After Dardy had gone, Brennen bent down behind his desk.

"Mari?" When he straightened, he held his hands cupped. "Something for you. He walked slowly around the desk, then bent down in front of her and opened his fingers.

Between them nestled a lily. Eight intensely blue-green petals framed its yellow center, and its heady, honey-rich odor made her blink. "Brennen." She looked up. "It's beautiful. What's it called?"

"Remember the mira lilies at Hesed?"

At the Sentinels' pastoral sanctuary world, they had been married, eight months before. They hadn't stayed long, but comforting impressions of Hesed always lingered below the surface of her mind. "Aren't mira lilies white?" she asked.

"The blue lilies are rare, but look how this sets off your coloring. It will stay fresh indefinitely in this climate, if you give it enough light. It only needs air and a little moisture."

He tipped the lily off his hands onto hers. Gingerly, she examined the delicate blossom. Behind the bloom curled a short, pale green root, covered with a network of brown lines.

Brennen reached into a pocket of his wide belt. "If we're careful, you can wear it in your hair." He pulled out a silver clip, took back the lily, and wove its succulent root through half the clip. "—For special occasions, such as your birthday dinner."

Firebird held her breath while he pinned the bloom over her left ear. "There." He arranged her long red-brown curls about her shoulders and then stood back.

She felt his wash of approval and returned gratitude . . . and arousal. He knew—he *felt*—her response whenever he toyed with her hair. He offered her a hand up out of the chair. "We'd better go. Our reservations are for ten minutes from now." He waved off the room lights.

As Firebird passed out into the central quad, now illuminated by a series of shining strips where light-colored walls joined its ceiling, she caught sight of . . .

I don't believe it. Terrell, again!

Brennen, ahead of her, saluted in midstride. "Tomorrow, Terrell," he said casually.

The husky officer smiled steadily at Firebird. "What a beautiful blossom. Hesedan, isn't it?"

The clearing captain beckoned to Brennen, who stepped over to her station.

"Yes." Firebird touched the flower. "I'm told that it is."

Why did it have to be this way, that the only Sentinel who seemed to take a personal interest in her—other than Brennen and Dardy—disturbed her so deeply? But there it was again: her niggling premonition about Bosk Terrell. There was death in his keen brown eyes. Whose death? She didn't know.

Holding a pair of scan cartridges, Brennen rejoined her, and she caught his sidelong glance. "Did she tell you it's her birthday?"

A net of smile lines sprang up around Terrell's dark eyes. "Congratulations, Mistress Caldwell. You're a lucky man, Caldwell. Good evening to you both."

Seeing Terrell step toward the elevator, Firebird paused to examine a gold-hued glass sculpture that lay on a table between two waiting couches. It was a relic of the plague-scattered Aurian race, the Sentinels' telepathic ancestors, brought aboard their transport of last hope across the light years.

When she looked up, Terrell had gone.

Brennen touched the small of her back. "You're agitated. What's wrong?"

She laid her arm on his. "Staff Officer Terrell bothers me, Brennen. It's difficult to explain, but I always have the impression that . . . there's something not quite focused about him, not quite true. He's one of the strong ones, isn't he? Why doesn't he wear a Master's star?"

His dark brows arched. "He's only a Staff Officer. Not particularly strong, an A.S. forty. I rather like the man."

Firebird started. "Really?"

Brennen barely nodded. "Why not?"

"He treats me oddly." Firebird stared at the sculpture. "And he feels strong. When he talks to me, it's . . . it almost feels like an interrogation, as though everything I said needed . . . No, I know he's not using mind-access, but . . ."

"He's a good officer," Brennen said blandly.

"At his age, he's still only an aide? Someone else has taken a disliking to him, I'd guess."

The pair bonding had helped them through many of the misunderstandings of new marriage; each always understood precisely how the other felt, and it had proven a blessing many times over, as she and Brennen—raised on different worlds, in very different cultures—tried to forge a relationship that would endure the lifelong commitment.

"Mari, I know the man. I work with him. He's good enough at what he does. Maybe he has refused promotion to keep a position he likes."

His protest rose at the back of her perception, carried by the pair bond, then abruptly vanished under a wash of epsilon static.

Pained, she met his stare. She knew how much effort it cost him to hide his feelings from her. Heartily she wished Terrell had left the complex ten minutes sooner.

Touching the mira lily in her hair, Brennen shook his head. Probably he wished the same. The emotional resonance returned in a slow, careful crescendo. She reached for his hand, and a flicker of his epsilon strength stroked her thoughts. "Aren't you hungry, Mari?"

Firebird's stomach grumbled. "Always," she said.

Chapter 2

... Will Find Her People ...

moderato sussurando
moderately, whispering

In a pleasant, slowly awakening haze, Firebird lifted her cup of steaming cruinn and breathed deeply. She'd paid dearly in Federate gilds for two kilos of the N'Taian beverage, and she meant to savor every whiff. The heavy, sweet scent brought back such a swirl of memories: all she once had been, images of her rooms in the Angelo palace on Naetai, friends she missed dearly—and unpleasant memories, too, the constant weight of impending martyrdom for her homeworld's honor. She had been so proud to carry that weight, to expect to die young.

Firebird raised her cup and toasted the memory, then sipped. It was good to live free of that weight. To carry life. Some small limb punched her insides. She felt like a dance hall, sometimes. Her life had turned canard-over-tailfin during the war, but adjusting to pregnancy was the most challenging task of all. Never in her life had she hoped for children.

She padded on soft slippers to the dining table. A Thyrian dekia, ten days, had passed since her birthday. Against the long sweep of windows that made the north wall of their home, Brennen sat finishing his breakfast. Built into the side of Trinn Hill by a retired messenger captain who'd spent too much time in a tiny *Brumbee* courier ship, the house's expansive upper story centered on a decorative stairwell that was half-walled in glass and densely grown with vines, and its northern windowall overlooked Soldane, when the area was scheduled for sunshine.

As Brennen ate, he eyed a small bluescreen on the tabletop and occasionally jabbed at its keyboard. Here on Trinn Hill, in the hillands between Soldane city and the forbidding, coastal Dracken Range, Brennen had invested all his Federate severance pay in the most secure location he could find, then seen to it that the home's sec system was the best available, to protect them both —and their children, soon—from Shuhr, and other enemies Brennen had collected in ten years of service. All approaches could be monitored from terminals in every room, and a person indoors could dispatch an intruder at any entrance.

Firebird glanced over Brennen's shoulder at the bluescreen. He was using the terminal merely to access the home database and preview his day's work. Cradling her cruinn cup, she sank onto the opposite chair and gazed out the window. Rain—still. The region's dry dekia would not begin for another twelve days. Their home was spacious, though, and she could escape to the coastal Base when she ached to see the sun. Beyond the security-gridded glasteel kitchen wall, little puddles collected on an ironbark deck and dripped between slats onto mossy ground below. Watching the rain made her sleepy again—she took another sip of cruinn —but watching Brennen was far more interesting. Already smartly uniformed, he stared thoughtfully at the screen, pressed a key, then lifted another bite of smoked fish to his mouth. The bright blue light of the screen gave his face an odd cast and shone wild and bright in his eyes: an alien look.

Did he imagine an alien when he looked at her, too? Or just a once-slender, small-featured woman, whose body now swelled with his sons?

Firebird swirled the cup and slid into memory again. Apprehension had nearly kept her from marrying him. He had been a Federate officer—an *intelligence* officer, Thyrian and therefore alien in her homeworld's view—and she had been taken prisoner. Naetai might one day forgive her for accepting the ideals of its Federate conquerors, for the Federates had ruled Naetai well and fairly these months, but marrying a Thyrian Sentinel?

Unthinkable.

She had been warned that marriage with any of Brennen Caldwell's kind would mean an intimacy far beyond the physical, a linking of souls at appalling depth. For days after the wedding,

Brennen had remained the center of her consciousness. Tenderly he cared for her until she emerged from bonding shock, a separate entity again.

She recovered fully, but remained keenly aware of the change that had taken place: a kind of emotional stereo programmed permanently into her perception. The pair bonding had proven far different from the dehumanizing continuous telepathy Firebird had dreaded. The best of it came at night, for he knew exactly what pleasured her. . . .

What would be on that screen now? She took another sip. She knew he had found the overseeing of procurement and maintenance people tedious, but occasional inspections and test flights enlivened the cycle of personnel duties. He was working full-schedule at a half-time shared position, learning the ropes and accruing leave time, because he intended to stay home for at least a month once the twins were born. Revising Provost Dankin's flight-training program absorbed more of his interest and consequently more time, but she suspected other projects, too, and conscious of military security, she kept her peace when she could.

"Brenn?" She stared past him into misty forest. "Dardy mentioned yesterday that Staff Officer Terrell wasn't born on Thyrica. Where *is* he from?"

He curled his fingers around his kaffa mug. "He's offworld born, but his family relocated while he was still young enough to be tested and Sentinel trained."

"But where—"

"Bishniac."

Firebird waited for him to explain. Perhaps she should have opened conversation on some other subject this morning, but she sensed no irritation in his response. "Where's that, Brenn?"

"Griffin region, just south-spinward of Caroli. There's a small Thyrian enclave there."

She slid downward in the chair. "Brenn," she said carefully, "I caught him looking at me yesterday, staring, the way Vultor Korda used to do. But as soon as I opened my mouth he changed. It was as if I'd sneaked a glimpse around a barrier. There's power in his stare, Brennen. He's so much like you, yet . . . Oh, I don't know."

"Mari, we've been through this before." He fingered the rim of his mug.

"He tests only forty on the Aurian Scale. A.S. forty: solid but not exceptional," she quoted the guide he'd given her. "No, Brenn. I mean . . ." She groped momentarily to control her resentment. "I know this sounds pretentious, Brenn. I'm not trained in Sentinel ways and I know it, but would it be possible to deliberately test lower than your true potential?"

Brennen blanked the bluescreen, and the eerie light in his blue eyes flickered out. He looked at her solemnly: a man's face, man-colored. This was no alien, regardless of what her people thought. "Lower? Mari, everyone tries to test high, to increase his eventual rank and influence."

"Yes, of course. But would it be possible? He looked . . . so intense. Do you think a person might conceal his A.S. potential, try to lower his score, if that could reveal his identity?"

His mouth crinkled, and he didn't try to mask his amusement. "I suppose it's possible."

Firebird grasped both edges of her chair and scooted upright again. "Oh, all right, Brenn. I'm sorry."

Leaning forward, he stared into her eyes in a way that made her wonder if he saw directly into her soul without using his epsilon-energy skills. "I do understand, Mari. You see our system from the outside. All that's been drilled into us for years, you still question. That's good, so long as you respect it, too. Never try to defeat that side of your nature." He folded his hands. "Because you questioned your people's traditional right to sacrifice you in battle, you're here today." His eyes smiled. "With me."

That sense of approval in him—already she was addicted to it. He knew how happy he made her, and her joy pleased him, and she felt his pleasure: the emotional resonance of pair bonding.

"All right, then. Let me have the touchboard for a minute." He slid the little console her way, and she pressed several keys. "Look at this, Brenn."

He rested his elbows on the table's white surface. "Terrell's service record. What am I looking for?"

"Nothing. That's just the point. Nothing outstanding at all, neither positive nor negative. Almost blatantly average in every way, as if he were avoiding notice."

"Don't you trust average people?" She felt his amusement rise again, but satisfaction took its place. "I'll guess you'd be easier in your mind if I talked to the testing chief. He would probably let me try to lower my reading on the sensors, just to see if it could be done." He rose, took a platter in each hand, and from across the room he sailed them dead into the 'washer slot. "I might even have time after my meeting this morning. What would you say to that?"

"Thank you, Brennen—show-off." Hoping he felt how sincerely she meant her thanks, she stood and shuffled toward the vine-grown greenwell at the center of the living room.

Testing chief. Firebird stopped short at the edge of the glass enclosure.

Before they had been married a week, Brennen had sensed epsilon energy rising behind her own consciousness. The mystery of Naetai's sonless royal family was solved by a simple blood test: she carried the hereditary, male-specific antigen of the Aurian plague, or makkah; she, like Thyrica's starbred, was distantly descended from the plague-scattered Aurian race. Apparently, a small Aurian crew had made planetfall on Naetai, and one Aurian's bloodline, secreted among the aristocracy, had not died out. How Firebird had wished for access to a N'Taian historical bank when she found *that* out!

Treated now, she carried sons. Sons. She still had trouble believing it. Angelo women did not bear sons. The plague had left the Aurians without sons, too, a dying people scattered to the stars in a last search for pockets of humanity. Five hundred years ago, a colony ship carrying twenty-seven survivors had made planetfall on Thyrica. The plague had left a legacy of spontaneous termination of male pregnancies—until the cure was found, and the Aurians' great-great-granddaughters bore sons at last.

She bent forward. A baby kicked—or shoved—or butted—and she straightened. Brennen laughed softly behind her. He wouldn't have felt the kick, but by now he would most likely identify the mixed emotions she felt when either baby moved.

I'd like to know more about the testing. Maybe he'd take me with him. Would there be time before my appointment with Master Spieth? Distracted from her concern with Terrell, she almost spoke.

No. She pressed a palm against one clear wall. *Don't bother the testing chief. Ask Aldana Spieth.*

They flew inland together, Firebird piloting up the cleft in the jagged Drackens—one thing she could still do nearly as well as before she'd become so heavy. She'd do it again in battle someday, too, but this time on Brennen's side. Imagining the nervous pressure of a carrier landing, she used only a quarter of the College's breakaway strip to set down.

Brennen helped her down the stepstand in the parking loft. "Not bad, Major. You're almost due for a promotion." Then he strode off to seek out his colleague in aerospace training.

A young man wearing unadorned midnight blue and the narrow gold ring of a student-apprentice Sentinel, or sekiyr, walked Firebird to the Medical Center, the highest and blockiest building on the grassy grounds. It was a peaceful campus. The lines of every structure seemed to harmonize with those of every other: a small cluster of rounded, red stone buildings, the cumulative effect of its network of architecture, lawns, and waterways more calming and otherworldly than she could explain.

After painful decades of distrust, these part-Aurian telepaths had made a secure place in Thyrian society by binding themselves with a code of ethics so stringent that the nongifted had no need to fear manipulation and by establishing this College, where they were rigorously trained. Centuries later, the starbred Sentinels now constituted a major force in the Federacy: in medicine, in education, in intelligence.

In the skylit, glass-walled central atrium of the medical center, her guide found Master Aldana Spieth. The silver-haired woman sat either asleep or deep in thought on a stone bench, below a huge, brown-boled tree hung with ferns and vines. Firebird's guide motioned her forward.

She stepped up confidently. It had been different, the first time she met Aldana Spieth. She had come for treatment, a series of protein injections and low-frequency irradiations, to clear her ovarian tissue of Aurian makkah antigen. That time, her delighted awe to be standing in the Sentinels' College had been balanced by apprehension, a sense of isolation, and dread.

Now, as she crossed a steaming, faintly sulfur-scented pool on broad stepping stones, the Master opened her eyes and stood, shaking down one full white pant-leg that clung to her calf.

Firebird heard the youth step away behind her. "Am I disturbing you, Master Spieth? I know I'm early."

Spieth adjusted the belt of her tunic. "Not at all. You are gladly expected. Come along."

Firebird followed her out another door cut through the glass walls of the misty, otherworldly atrium, and into a very ordinary gravity lift.

When Spieth finished the second-trimester examination, including a blood test for plague antigen remaining after her treatment, she motioned Firebird to a dark green chair in the office end of her station. Firebird still stood, however, at the edge of the slick laboratory flooring.

Spieth, like Brennen, wore a Master's star, hers closing the shoulder of a pure white medic's tunic. "You are more comfortable standing, Mistress Caldwell?"

Firebird stepped onto the shortweave carpet and took the seat. Very well, then: she had come to know Spieth well enough to hazard her question. She settled her hands in her lap. "Master Spieth, this is very awkward for me, and perhaps out of line, but might I ask you a question in professional confidence?"

After a brief silence, Spieth barely smiled. "Master Brennen is not to be included in this?"

Firebird glanced at the diskfiles behind Spieth. "It's not that." No, that was a mistake. She must be as honest with Spieth as possible. A Sentinel could always sense deception. "Maybe it is. But, you see . . ." She trailed off.

"Kaffa?" Master Spieth reached for the thermal carafe on the end of her desk.

Firebird nodded and allowed the ritual of hospitality to make the office less foreign, more homelike. After a long sip, she began. "Master, exactly how can you people evaluate something so nebulous as a human being's mental abilities?"

"Ah." Aldana Spieth set down her cup. "I hear a very curious mind, Firebird, and questions deeper than the one you have spoken."

Firebird met the silver-haired woman's steady stare. "Is it permitted, then, to discuss the question?" Ellet Kinsman, she recalled, had consistently sidestepped questions of this nature during her brief guardianship. Firebird had to leave Spieth an "out." She had learned that much Sentinel etiquette.

"In normal cases, no. As you have noticed, we tell outsiders as little as practical about the phenomena that set us apart. But yours is no normal case. As an outsider bonded to Master Brennen, I believe you have a right to be trusted with some facts. What has he told you about the testing?"

"Very little, very vague. I ask you rather than pressing him."

Aldana Spieth reached down to her desktop terminal, speaking while she touched keys. "Thoughtful. I can tell you these things, Firebird. When a child is screened for epsilon strength, he has invariably caught the attention of those sensitive to the phenomenon. The epsilon wave functions as a carrier, by which other impulses are transmitted. You are familiar with radio theory?"

"Yes. Brennen and I have discussed the phenomenon that far."

"Then you know the human mind operates in a fashion similar to that carrier-wave phenomenon. A child with a strong epsilon function, broadcasting indiscriminately, is easy to detect.

"The screening test utilizes resonal scanning circuits, lest a human tester show prejudice regarding a candidate. If the scan indicates high potential, he is then allowed to appear before a testing committee.'' Spieth pressed another key. ''The numerical score finally assigned combines these findings on the Aurian Scale of a hundred. Your Brennen tested exceptionally high in all areas of practical application, as you know, but since we speak in the confidence of this office, let us understand that I have known others who seemed to possess more native strength—but only in background potential, which is impossible to quantify. We can calibrate only strengths for which we have developed a use and a test.''

''Oh,'' Firebird answered quietly, filing more information than she had seriously hoped to be given. Why was Spieth telling her so much?

Spieth touched the panel again, then sat back, her expression professionally sympathetic, revealing none of her thoughts. ''And you have been told, Mistress Caldwell, that you descend from the Aurians as well, and that you show surprising mental strength, and you cannot go on without asking if you too could be tested.''

Firebird felt her cheeks warm. ''Yes, Master. I live among a people to whom a 'twenty-five' is a poor cousin and a 'ninety-seven' such as my husband a creature to be held in awe. Is it wrong to wonder?''

''Only natural, child. But consider this. The connaturality that drew him to you, the similarity of your souls, is a function of spirit, not carrier. You cannot hope to match his ninety-seven, and I read you as a competitive person. Does that make you hesitate?''

Firebird shrugged.

''Among us you are unique, Firebird, unquantified but vital in your role as shamev to the 'Lost of Auria shamah.' I would hate to see you lose the confidence of that prophecy's mystique.''

''Mystique.'' Firebird wrinkled her nose. ''What about our children? Won't they be disadvantaged, with a mother who cannot do for them what a Sentinel mother could do?''

''Many children we train have one or even two parents who were ineligible, Firebird. That is not a concern.'' The elderly Master stared solemnly across her desk. ''If I test your carrier strength and background potential there will be no word of numbers to anyone, Mistress. I promise that. Do I have your vow in return?''

Forgetting the risk of being kicked, Firebird leaned forward. ''Absolutely.''

''To my knowledge, no one has ever screened a bonded individual, nor a pregnant one.'' Spieth steepled her fingers on the desk top. "It is always performed on the young and unwed. What influence that might have on the resonal circuits, I have no idea. It should not affect your potential." She paused. "And it will not harm the babies."

"You're certain of that?"

"Absolutely. The apparatus acts as a highly effective receiver: it transmits nothing," said Spieth. "There is a facility available this afternoon. I can perform a preliminary scan, if you are still eager."

Knowing Spieth would sense her elation, Firebird wondered if she should try to speak calmly.

Spieth stood and extended a hand. "You are. Come, then."

An hour later, Firebird tried to relax in a soft lounger and ignore a faintly nauseating sensation originating in the pad at the small of her back and the lightweight, splayed-finger arrays Spieth had pressed gently over her ears—a sensation of "otherness" like what she felt when anyone but Brennen attempted mind-access. It seemed to last forever. The vibration pulsed, throbbed, and changed minutely with each burst. She tried to blank her thoughts as for sleep, as Master Spieth had directed, but her habitual alertness prevented it, and despite the assurance she had given Spieth, she literally trembled with the desire to score well.

Abruptly the pulsing stopped. She blinked hard.

Spieth appeared behind her and pulled the arched headset away, then helped Firebird upright. Anxiously, Firebird examined the lovely old face for clues to the test's results. It betrayed no flicker of expression. Frustrated once more by the Sentinels' absolute emotional control, Firebird slipped down off the lounger and resnugged the wide blue web belt over her red skyff.

Once the apparatus lay nestled in its cubby, Spieth inclined her head toward the passway. As stealthily as they had come, they returned to Spieth's office several levels above.

The Master Sentinel poured two fresh cups of kaffa and settled in her deep chair. "I am sorry, Mistress," she began slowly, "to renege on an unspoken promise. I cannot speak of numbers even with you, for reasons I am bound by my vows in the Word not to explain. We walk the very limit of permissibility today. However." She struck the desk with one fingertip. "That Word, in its broadest sense, encompasses all the Godhead's creative expressions, and their relationship back to their Source. No matter how small a part of creation you think yourself to be, it is a crime that you were not screened as a child. Whatever your discriminate potentialities, you would have been eligible for committee testing on the basis of epsilon strength alone, and that is no inconsequential matter.''

Frustrated at one breath and elated at the next, Firebird groped for words. ''Is there nothing I can do with what I have?''

Spieth clasped her hands on one knee. ''It would take time to undo your habitual patterns of action: time that must be invested in the young, the malleable. Even if a trainer could spare the time, the result would not be complete. The most basic skills, the foundational abilities, can be mastered only by exquisitely plastic personalities. I mean nothing derogatory by the term. In our parlance, it connotes a mental habit that can be changed but will harden permanently into its new conformation.''

''But on my own? Perhaps . . .'' She opened both hands.

Spieth's expression changed abruptly to the startling intensity Firebird had seen occasionally in Brennen, when challenged on his own ground. ''No. Nothing is ever done 'on one's own.' Training is not granted on the basis of epsilon potential alone. Character is tested, too, and stability: more factors from the alpha matrix than you might expect.

''So. We deny training to almost half our eligible children because of personality flaws.'' She was speaking quickly now, and Firebird felt small in her chair. ''If they could unlock their abilities outside our supervision, what hope for order on Thyrica? They live subject to penalties for misuse of their gifts just like those whom we train, although with them we try to be more forgiving, for only with the training comes drilling in the Privacy and Priority Codes. Certain medications, injected directly into a cranial artery, block the synaptic transmission of epsilon energy, and offenders must report for bidekial treatment. . . .''

She unclenched her hands. The controlled abruptness of the change irked Firebird. ''I apologize for digressing. It is enough if you understand how rigorously we must enforce our codes, the reasons for secrecy, and why *no one* is allowed to develop these skills except under authority. We intend nothing sinister. Caution is the best protection for others—and for us. Surely you see that.''

''Yes. I—I do see.'' Firebird sat hard on her suspicion, and the temptation to plead passed. In five hundred years, these people had undoubtedly learned too well the responsibilities of their talents. It occurred to her, too, that perhaps she was being tested now. She stood.

"I understand, Master. As Brennen has said, my alpha matrix is too well established. But I thank you. I'm sure you realize what knowing this means to me."

"I do, child. Rest easy in our secret."

Across the College, Firebird found on the message board that Brennen had changed his plans and now expected to stay late in conference. She sought out a monopod—a one-man repulsor craft, available for hire at the College—pressed the ID disk given her at Regional Command, Alta, into its template, and then thumbed its checkpanel to verify. The disk gleamed faintly. A green flash on the program panel confirmed the debiting of the rental to their household account. She touched in a program that would return her to Trinn Hill. Scarcely noticing the forbidding peaks of the Dracken Range as the autopilot craft negotiated the route through the deep cleft between Efferdale and Soldane, she stared ahead. In memory, she retraced the conversation with Aldana Spieth. Reviewing their words, she became increasingly certain that the Master Sentinel had managed the entire interview, and at the last her curiosity had been subliminally squelched.

She reached Trinn Hill in a vile mood.

Brennen returned late. Deferring dinner, he plucked a crimson blossom from the distrugia vine in the greenwell and tucked it behind her ear.

"It was a good idea, Mari, but not one of us was able to lower his epsilon reading. Cristod Harris tried, and Thurl Hoston, and I worked long after they'd given up and gone home. But it seems impossible." She followed as he ambled to the bathing room, pulled a towel from the steamer, and buried his face in it. "If you honestly feel Terrell is a threat," came his muffled voice, "I'm willing to keep a personal watch on him." He tossed the towel into the sterilizer and reached for another, but caught her glance before pressing it to his face.

All her frustration melted away at the sight and sensation of his sincere concern. "Thank you, Brenn," she whispered. She reached up and clasped her hands behind his neck. He dropped the towel. A shiver slid through her, caressing memory and sensation. Burying her face against his chest, she murmured, "I wish I could do that for you."

"But you do, Mari." Brennen held her close. "Don't you think I feel your pleasure?"

Firebird squeezed him.

She shuffled to the kitchen, programmed the warmer to assemble and cook the evening meal, and slipped out onto the deck. By then, Brennen stood at the rail, stars brightening above him. Cold, still mist rose toward their level, swallowing a stand of weeping rustilian trees and carrying the scent of Soldane: resinous and vaguely sweet, the odor of damp kirka bark.

He spoke without turning. "I also spent some time with Master Spieth. She called just as I was leaving the College."

"Oh?" Alarmed, Firebird focused her thoughts and feelings on her pregnancy.

"She asked if I would allow her to read your personality through your bonded imprint on me. Naturally I submitted. I believe she's concerned about your . . ." He hesitated. "Your maternal instincts."

"Or lack of same."

"No, she reads you as very concerned, and asked me to encourage you."

Then Spieth *had* kept the secret! Firebird leaned on the railing beside him. "I never claimed to enjoy pregnancy. Did you see Terrell?"

"Not to speak with him." He kicked a kirka cone off the deck and watched it bounce away downhill. "Have you checked the newsnet this afternoon?"

"No. What happened today?"

"They think they've caught a Shuhr operative in Kyrrenham, applying for an apartment. He had just arrived from Alta, he claimed, but was carrying illegal weapons. They'll be probing him at the College tonight."

"Without you?"

"No. I'm going back. Don't wait up."

The kitchen timer rang twice and they slipped back into warmth. Firebird sat and let Brennen serve. "It seems to me that carrying illegal weapons is begging to be caught," she said.

"That's what I thought." He laid out the platters, then took the other stool. "He could be a plant."

"To distract attention from someone? Will there be any kind of a general alert or calling Sentinels in to be reevaluated?"

"No, Mari. We don't like to see suspicion cast on the innocent."

How Federate, she thought, spearing a forkful of shredded vegetables. *How trusting. On Naetai they'd already be interrogating.* "Be careful, Brenn."

"I am always careful, Mari."

Chapter 3

Phoena's Choice

marcato
each note stressed

The Queen of Naetai's birthday was celebrated annually in Sae Angelo with parades, exhibits, and a ball. The palace ballroom, floored in black marble shot with gold and curtained in crimson velvric, was lined with elaborately carved furniture and statuary. For Princess Phoena the ball had always been the highest point of her year, for at the Queen's Ball she could dress in her finest and dance again with every nobleman on Naetai, young and old, from all ten noble families, receiving their homage. This year the Ball honored Phoena's sister instead of her mother, but that made no difference. Also this year, a slightly jealous husband hovered nearby, although he always offered some delicacy and a friendly word for her dancing partner. In two months of marriage, Phoena had found that respectability had drawbacks. Undoubtedly, Tel loved her—he behaved beautifully, almost pitifully anxious to please—but she was lovely, and loveliness should be shared. She knew the way her honeyed complexion affected men, and she could unnerve the most noble Duke with a flicker of hot brown eyes and a toss of pale auburn hair.

She shook out the full gold-toned sleeves of her gown, a dramatic contrast to the slim fit of the pale orange bodice and triple skirt, slashed layer by layer to reveal the tiers of shimmering fabric beneath, and took the arm of thin-faced young Baron Reshn Parkai

to promenade with him onto the floor. At one end of the ballroom,
a full orchestra sat installed upon the dais, and below triple ranks
of chandeliers she stepped into another dance. Here, the aristocracy
of Naetai ruled a crowd sprinkled with only the wealthiest of
commoners and not a uniformed Federate in evidence: Tonight,
this did not look like an occupied world. Through the press Phoena
caught a glimpse of a small, slender male figure, and she smiled
slightly. Tonight Phoena would surround herself with courtiers
and revel in the attention of the nobility, and if her husband, the
new Prince Tel Tellai-Angelo, chose to enter the merry circle she
gathered, she would allow it.

The orchestra played superbly. A pity Firebird couldn't hear it,
Phoena observed as she whirled in step with Baron Parkai. Music
had always affected her Wastling sister in a way beyond Phoena's
comprehension; it swept her away, altered her moods, brought out
the perverse inner strength Phoena found so inexplicably threatening, requiring great energy on her own part to keep Firebird in
her place. Unquestionably little Firebird had hoped to displace her
in the succession—had had the talent to try it, had she dared.
Phoena had almost hoped Firebird intended to come home for the
ball, to try to present her Thyrian filth to the nobility. After all,
she'd been married nine months without showing her face. She
would have discovered quickly what happened to a Wastling who
flaunted authority and tradition, even with a conjuror to defend
her, and Phoena would have been freed at last from her own
greatest fear.

Phoena and Parkai bowed correctly to one another as a line of
trumpeters rose with a flourish on the dais steps. As the fanfare
echoed across the ballroom and called the crowd to assemble and
toast Queen Carradee Second, Phoena fetched her small, dainty-
faced Tel and joined her elder sister and Prince Daithi on the dais.
Servants in scarlet livery circulated with goblets on trays. The
Queen's future would be saluted by six people, and then Carradee
would answer. Phoena, asked to toast, had declined. Any woman,
she had reasoned to Carradee, would rather be saluted by a man
than another woman! And Carradee, who seemed to trust almost
everyone, had believed. "Carradee the Good," and "Carradee
the Kind," Phoena had heard her called.

Carradee the Federate Toady, Phoena pronounced to herself.

First Lord Bualin Erwin stepped forward, then knelt at the dais's
foot. "It is my sublime privilege . . ."

Phoena gave her nails a quick buff on her sleeves and displayed
her "public" smile. She had long ago mastered the art of feigning

gracious interest. If her mind dwelt more on the speaker than the speech, no one would know. Beside her, Tel posed for the crowd. She laughed to herself. How he enjoyed parading in the fringed, formal sash of his new rank!

She turned her attention to her sister. Carradee, she admitted reluctantly, looked lovely tonight, though Carradee was not known for *her* beauty. Why tonight? It couldn't be the simple blue gown, although that did set off Carradee's pale gray eyes and camouflage her tendency to heaviness, nor the all-too-conservative sweep of blonde curls below her jeweled crown. Carradee had no imagination in clothes. But she was enjoying herself. That was it: She was happy, glowingly happy, about something.

It would be lovely to be Queen at the Queen's Ball, figurehead ruler of all the N'Taian solar reach and its two buffer systems. At Hunter Height Phoena had reached for the Crown and missed, and in time Carradee had forgiven her. But another chance might come, so Phoena endured her month of house arrest, then turned again to guiding the Loyalist movement that hoped one day to throw the Federates off Naetai. Meanwhile, she would remain the paragon of correctness.

Carradee rose in her turn, made elaborate offers of thanks to each man who had toasted her, and drained her glass. Before signaling the orchestra to begin again, she raised a hand for silence. ''One other thing.''

This is it, Phoena observed smugly, shaking her shoulder-length hair, which tonight she wore loose in perfect waves. *Whatever has her so tickled, it's about to come out.* Maybe she's pregnant again. Phoena glanced aside, but Tel, brushing dust from his black sateen jacket, remained oblivious.

''I have the privilege,'' Carradee continued, clasping her hands before her, ''of making an announcement no other Queen in the history of our great people has made, and I do singularly feel the honor, the delight, and the hope that this is only a sign of things to come in the years ahead, as Naetai takes its rightful place among the great systems of the galaxy.''

Hm. Well put, for Carradee.

As Carradee's gold-jacketed Prince Daithi stood at attention on the dais steps, his brown curls for once slicked smooth, Carradee slow-stepped along the dais's edge. ''We have entered a new age of greatness and great hearts. And so, Noble Electors, gentlemen and ladies, the rumors that circulated two months ago were true. Our youngest sister, Lady Firebird, who was formerly a Wastling, expects a child in three months.''

For several seconds, if a greenfly had landed everyone in the ballroom would have heard. Never had a Wastling gone so far. Tradition barred even Phoena, the second-born, from bearing children. Carradee beamed, while other faces showed shock or disbelief or delight. Then a wave of sound splashed the banner-hung walls, as everyone began to speak at once.

Everyone but Phoena. Scandalized by Firebird's crime against the family and tradition that should have meant more to her than life itself, she stood motionless until Carradee reached her and spoke quietly against the clamor. "I tried to reach you alone, earlier, but you were at the tresser. I want you to know that, insofar as the Crown is concerned, you and Tel are welcome to have children of your own, too. 'Heir limitation' has outlasted its usefulness. No estate is worth preserving at the cost of our children. I believe that. Don't you?"

Phoena eyed her scornfully from coronet to blue leather dancing slippers. Her monarch, the Head of the Electoral Council—the Federate puppet!—approved of Firebird's disgraceful actions. She offered a chance to commit the same crime with impunity. She needed to be shown that Phoena was made of finer stuff than that. Once again Carradee proved that she did not deserve that beautiful, sparkling crown—with the extra chins it gave her.

"You'll see what I believe," Phoena answered in a low voice like poison. Carradee belatedly signaled the orchestra, and as the players struck up another dance medley, Phoena gathered her skirts and whirled from the dais, trailing Tellai behind. Dodging dancers across the marble floor, she left the ball.

At three hundred that morning Phoena lay awake, irritated to the core by Tel's soft, regular breathing. He had admitted he felt glad for Firebird. *Glad! The little slink!*

Too much was changing on Naetai, too much power slipping from the hands of the rightful nobility, and somehow it had to be set right. The Loyalist movement remained strong, but had been stymied by Carradee's unprecedented appointment of several commoners to the Queen's Electoral Council. *Another of her sycophancies,* Phoena fumed. If she were Queen, with the support of her own Electorate, she could repair much of the damage. But she couldn't challenge the Federates who stood around Carradee, between herself and the throne.

No, but by Ishma and Delaira and the littlest moon Menarri, she knew who could! A few outlaw Thyrians had abandoned the Sentinel organization over the years. They and their descendants were building a real power, a strong one. She and an offworld acquaintance had discussed them months before, and she had scoffed. But she had seen their cousin Caldwell's abilities now, and now she believed. She'd considered seeking their aid for the Loyalist movement for a week now, and this . . .

This was the final straw.

She sat upright in the octagonal bed, thinking hard. The Naetai she knew would be changed forever, unless someone were willing to make a bold throw to save it, to dare—and risk losing—everything. She would show them all. She had the courage. Generations hence, the nobility of Naetai would recall Phoena's choice and stand in awe.

In the freshing room she slipped silently into an unostentatious traveling suit with a face-shading hood, then gathered up a few bits of feminine trivia for her shoulder bag.

Tel stirred. Phoena stood motionless, waiting for him to speak, but he rolled over and sank deeper into sleep. She found a warm black coat. Should she leave him a message with her personal girl? No . . . He'd try to stop her, and she didn't want to be followed. He would know soon enough that she had left.

And she would not return until she came as Queen.

By stealth and luck, Phoena left the palace grounds unobserved by the House Guards, the Federates, and even a team of Thyrian aides, whose watch was focused at the critical moment on a minor disturbance at the front gate. She made her way through the darkened streets on foot, to a place Vultor Korda once had told her she could find offworld help in his absence. *If only the man is awake,* she thought, as footsore and shivering she knocked rapidly on the faded door of the ground-level apartment. Some night noise made her look back into the street to see if the Federates had trailed her.

The door slid partway aside. "Yes?" asked an unfamiliar voice.

"Penn Baker?"

"Just a minute." The door slid home, and she exhaled sharply, containing her pique. Korda had warned her to watch her temper with Baker. She pulled the black coat tighter around her body.

The door slid slightly open again. "Who is it?"

"Princess Phoena Angelo," she hissed. "Let me in."

Two men sat inside: Penn Baker, a doughy-figured man with watery eyes, and a dark-haired man with long, bony limbs he introduced as "My guest Astrig Tulleman, a traveling merchant."

Pleased to find them up, evidently talking late, she tried to defuse a strangely eager hostility in Astrig Tulleman's stare with a polite question.

"You're here on business?"

"Call it that."

She disliked Tulleman's dark smile, almost a sneer. She decided to ignore him and deal with Baker.

It took only a few words to explain what she wanted.

"Of course, I'll represent you to them." Baker stirred sugar into his cruinn. "I'd be deeply honored. No one knows you've come to me?"

"No one. I'll thank you for not asking questions, and for concealing my presence here until I can take reasonable precautions for my own safety."

"Naturally, Your Highness. I would be honored. More than you know."

For a week Phoena showed Baker her public smile, wore borrowed clothing, and endured the waiting. She eased her boredom by laughing over the lack of word concerning herself on the newsnet station. Carradee would be frantic but too proper to seek public help for some time yet.

One evening Baker slipped back to the apartment. "They will deal favorably with you, Your Highness. Your proposal delights them."

"As well it should." She sniffed. "Very well. I have made my arrangements. Let us be gone."

At the heart of a colony known to the Shuhr as Three Zed, Regnant Eldest Juddis Adiyn increased the flow of epsilon current into his shielding cloud of static to protect the sanctity of his thoughts. A messenger walked slowly across Adiyn's long office, a small man in blue and gray, emanating the kind of dread Adiyn had found to portend news of the worst kind, news that could cost a messenger's life if delivered clumsily. Huffing in unwilling anticipation, Adiyn lounged behind his ebony-micarta desk and tapped a stylus against its surface. Spyce Hender stopped below the desk—maintaining his shielding moderately well, Adiyn observed with a glance to his right, where his young second, Testing Commander Dru Polar, waited at relaxed attention, openly eager for bad news. Tall and muscular-slim with black hair long over the red collar of his shirt, Polar stood surrounded by the dense epsilon cloud of his own shields. Adiyn could almost see them, they deflected so strongly. Polar, for one, seemed untouched by the inbreeding weakness this small colony had to fight so rigorously.

Adiyn dropped the stylus and turned aside, sending his point of awareness to float in a holographic projection tank twinkling with tiny star-dots. The sensation soothed him, sang to him of vastness and his sphere of power. Then, with a flick of a thumb, he signaled the messenger to let his shield diffuse.

A torrent of information coursed into his conscious alpha matrix, so badly scrambled with Hender's defensiveness as to be virtually undecipherable. Adiyn leaned forward and ran a hand over his graying dark hair. *Sit down, Hender*, he ordered in succinct subvocal thought patterns, ignoring Polar's subtle, wryly projected suggestion that he deliver the expected insult and speak aloud. *You are babbling. Organize your thoughts.*

Eldest. Spyce Hender accepted a hard black chair.

Adiyn watched Polar stop beside Hender as if on guard, black eyes narrow in his long face.

Word is out on Thyrica, Hender sent, his alpha matrix in better order now, as he began to regain presence. *One of the Caldwells has married an outworlder. Less widely known is the fact that the woman carried the Aurian makkah. Our close operative says you will know what that means.*

Indeed he did. If the woman carried the Aurian plague, the makkah, she carried Aurian genes. And according to the eleventh Thyrian Shamarr's prophecy, *this* Aurian line they must *not* try to breed into the small Shuhr population.

Adiyn clamped down hastily on his alarm. Thoughts could be either sent or shielded, but emotion broadcast itself for all to read who were not static shielded themselves, and must be controlled at its source. Young Polar should not sense fear in him.

The 'Lost of Auria shamah.' Dru Polar cocked an eyebrow and probed. *Where?*

She was from Naetai, sir.

Where is that?

Hender took control of a blue indicator dot in the projection tank and swept it off Three Zed's gold-glowing sphere into the nearly starless reach beyond the Federate Whorl of the galactic Arm. *Naetai, mine elders*, he projected into their matrices, more confidently than before. The blue dot superimposed itself on a yellow-white star. *Small independent sector, until absorbed by the Federacy only last year. One primary system with twelve planets, five of them colonized, and two subjugate 'buffer' systems.*

Feudal government. I stress that because apparently the new Mistress is of the ruling family, a matriarchy.

Adiyn nodded. In an untreated Aurian strain there would be only females. But a ruling family? *Ah*, he thought privately, *that will make its descendants easy to locate. Bluebloods so typically advertise themselves.*

Matriarchy. Polar echoed Adiyn's thoughts. *Matrilineal? Or no males?*

Insufficient data, sir. We have checked the current Federate registers, however, and that news is both conclusive and encouraging. Caldwell's woman—the name is Firebird, if you will believe it—is the youngest of three sisters named for native birds. Only one has children—

"Daughters?" interrupted Polar. Approvingly Adiyn noted Polar's attentive shift to the rising generation. As Testing Commander, second in colonial rank only to himself, Polar's responsibility was to mold the young generation of Unbound that would succeed them, by selecting the most fit and eradicating all others: a difficult position, and Polar filled it well.

"Yes, Commander. Two daughters." Adiyn smiled in a shielded corner of his mind at Hender's verbal reply to Polar's verbal question. "Apparently no other relatives stand closer than the third degree, and none claims descendance from the royal line. Something about a tradition of 'heir limitation': only one heir is allowed to reproduce, and any extras are killed."

Really! Adiyn widened his smile and sent satisfaction for the others' scanning. *That's not many. Go on. Naetai.*

Yes. Its status shifted recently to Federate protectorship because of a conflict over a Federate colony world, VeeRon. The Naetai government apparently overstepped: the Feds have only conquered three other system-states since—

"Irrelevant." Polar spoke aloud again, contempt ringing in his tone. "Is that the pertinent data?"

Adiyn felt Hender's instant quailing. *It is. Commander.*

"Down," Polar ordered.

The courier pleaded wordlessly, but Adiyn glanced away. When he looked back, Spyce Hender drooped on the plastene chair, sunk into self-willed tardema-sleep.

Naetai. Adiyn winced. *How ironic. A little independent sector out on the eighty-six rim.*

Was independent. And the location makes it all the more plausible. Our Ancestors did come from beyond the rim. Dru Polar sat down on Adiyn's desk, hung a leg over its side, and sent the blue spark spinning around a globular cluster of stars above the galactic plane: the mystery-shrouded home of the extinct telepathic Aurians, whose human-mingled, "starbred" families now included both Shuhr and Sentinels. As certain as fate, one of those branches would one day rule humankind as its logical successor, in the name of Progress—and of Protection. The Whorl had been conquered by aliens before, and those aliens remained a threat. Somewhere, they waited.

Adiyn did not rebuke Polar for taking liberty with his desk. It was inevitable that Polar would eventually eclipse him, though he intended to keep his young subordinate penned for several years yet. Polar had been singled out already by the Chad-negiyl, the Shuhr overlord who guided their evolution, and wore the aura of his touch. He could now accomplish the near-impossible: link his epsilon energy with Adiyn's and wield both together.

Out of habit Adiyn drew his boot dirk and toyed with it, below the desktop and out of Polar's view. *We should have started sterilizing those fringe systems the day we heard that bedimmed prophecy.*

Polar twirled the sleeping messenger's chair. *Too expensive.*

Now we have the Federates to contend with.

Polar formed the epsilon equivalent of a sneer. *When have they ever been a factor?*

Certain individuals in the Federacy could pose a threat, and this Caldwell is one of them. Adiyn considered, briefly, the other large Shuhr colony—his rivals for power, and the other half of the breeding pool. *I intend to contact Tulleman and the brood at Echo Six.*

Polar almost laughed. *The danger worries you?* he asked.

Adiyn's distinctive gift was exceptional clarity in his glimpses of the elusive shebiyl, or paths of the future. There, he had seen his own death too many times, in too many ways, to maintain Polar's dry confidence. *Echo Six is also affected,* he sent, maintaining a callous texture. *We plan carefully, we strike suddenly. A shamah can be subverted. It alerts us to danger and allows us to direct our forces effectively. Contact our people on Alta and return word to Thyrica; activate the clandestines and continue the watch on Caldwell. Carefully.*

Polar stared back at him, his lashless eyes unblinking.

Naetai is as soft as a tarr's belly, though. We can strike there as soon as we choose. The 'lost' Aurian line won't be a factor for long.

We should blockade Hesed, if we can find enough ships.

Adiyn continued to fidget with his knife. *Yes. If the Federate Sentinels were to strengthen their sanctuary there, we could have trouble getting to it. But we've kept track of Caldwell long enough. He'll attack, not run. We need only draw him out. He knows he's talented. We'll show him he's not invulnerable. He has never dealt with us in numbers before.* Adiyn silenced Polar's rising objection. *Yes, but Mazra was a Tulleman operation, and he had the advantage of surprise. This time he'll find that we—we, Polar— have the advantage of choosing the time and place. We may have to sacrifice a few agents, hopefully Tulleman's, but when we're ready . . .*

Before Dru Polar could react, Adiyn's dirk skimmed Polar's shoulder, sliced across the dim room, and slit the precise center of a geometric wall print.

So much for your original Scurrly. Polar's own fighting blade pinned the helpless messenger through the throat to his chair. *So much for the 'Lost of Auria shamah.'*

You didn't need to do that. Adiyn furrowed his brow and looked away. *Did it gain you any pleasure?*

Polar shrugged.

Chapter 4

Daughters of Power

duo senza amore
duet without love

The following week, Polar and Adiyn held council in Adiyn's office, correlating reports sent in by Federate agents. Preliminary research for the strike at Naetai pleased Adiyn. According to the Federate register, they faced two women and two infants, guarded—if one could call it that—by a ring of groundside personnel and a "no-flight" zone: so simple an elimination that he would be able to choose his method for its emotional effect on the survivors rather than simple, efficient murder.

The fielding-approach alarm sounded unexpectedly, signaling an unscheduled spacecraft. Dru Polar activated the audio transceiver on Adiyn's master console. Intercepting the exchange between patrol and intruder, Adiyn listened with growing disbelief and final incredulity to Penn Baker's identification of himself, his passenger, and his mission.

As he keyed off the transceiver, Polar laughed weakly. *This is unbelievable, Jude! Why weren't we notified? What do you suppose motivates the woman?*

It doesn't matter. She's here.

Adiyn pressed against the back of his chair and activated its massage unit, watching as Polar drew a slender rod from his blue sash belt and checked its charge. A dendric striker, the rod was a prize from Polar's first raid as a full adult. A touch of its probe would stimulate every nerve ending within twelve to eighty centimeters; with it, he could distract a subject resisting mind-access with a burst of pain, or kill in agony or in an instant, depending on the charge he used and the proximity of his contact point to a nerve center. That and a small fighting dirk were the only weapons Polar chose to carry.

He tucked the striker away.

Princess Phoena could hardly wait to debark from Baker's DS-350. Three endless days in quasi-orthogonal "slip" space had weakened her resolve. Years before, Firebird had scornfully labeled her a "groundhog," and there had been miserable, claustrophobic moments on this trip when she wished she too had adjusted to space travel: the oddly vibrational sensation of slipstate, with the molecules of her body turned at right angles toward normal space so that the craft could exceed lightspeed, the terrifying awareness of light-years of vacuum just outside the thin alloy skin of the craft, the knowledge that something—some unknown infinitesimal something—could go wrong. She remained short of breath for most of the journey.

She didn't spot the colony until the last minute before landing, when with a pudgy hand Baker pointed out mammoth shielded entries, incongruously smooth strips along several edges of an irregular dome that crouched among crags on an airless lump of a planet.

"Not everything on Three Zed that looks like a mountain is one," he remarked, then busied himself at the controls. She didn't understand the maze of dials and glowing panels on the display, nor did she care to. As inhospitable as that crater field below them looked, she ached to stand on solid rock.

One entry barely opened, and they glided through. Penn Baker grounded the craft at the center of a small hangar. "We'll pass through into the main bay when we have air," he warned.

As Phoena walked down the craft's landing ramp a minute later, she felt her first qualm about coming to these people. Her suit smelled musty, and she doubted their first impression would be as regal as she wished. Resolutely wrapping her fingers around her shoulder bag, she strode to meet ten men who approached at a slow walk down a corridor between rows of service machinery.

Two stopped just short of her and Baker; the rest passed by toward the ship. She eyed the pair. Tall and slender, both had dark wavy hair and cold, distant brown eyes in nicely masculine faces.

"Your Highness?" The one on the right wore an edging of gold on the collar of his deep gray-green jumpsuit. He barely bowed.

"Yes. I would like to speak with someone in authority."

"Those are my orders," he answered. He gestured toward a door near one corner of the bay. Baker offered Phoena his arm, and as she stepped out, the others paced a few steps behind.

She followed down shiny-walled corridors with an unnerving number of branches, some at right angles and others curving like tetter tunnels, to a large open room. At its far end, near a holographic star-map tank, two men stood behind a desk. The stocky one seemed about fifty, with short graying hair, and the other looked so much like her guards that she guessed abruptly the degree of inbreeding among the colony's population. This taller man had grown his hair longer and wore sapphire blue. In his black, lashless eyes she recognized the singlemindedness of a kindred spirit, and she understood her peril. If he could be shown that she could serve his ends, they might meet on common ground.

"Your Highness, welcome. I am Juddis Adiyn, the Eldest, and this is Testing Commander Dru Polar." The older man bowed as he spoke, but Polar merely blinked his dark eyes. "Your presence on Three Zed honors us deeply." Adiyn flicked one hand.

She heard footsteps behind her and turned to see Baker and the other two men exit the room.

Phoena stood as stiffly as she spoke. "Gentlemen, let me state my business without unnecessary formalities. I believe that we face a situation as intolerable to you as it is to myself. Some sort of a quasi-religious prophecy has evidently been made, concerning some threat posed to you by a union of a Thyrian family with some other bloodline—which has been postulated to be my own. I do not accept that insulting supposition, gentlemen, but I recognize the fact that others do. Have I made it clear to you that I am no friend of Thyrica, nor of the Federacy?"

"Admirably so, Princess, and with few words. Please, won't you sit down?" Commander Polar held a tall black chair for her.

When they had seated themselves around Adiyn's desk, Phoena felt some of the suspicion in the atmosphere turn to conspiratorial quiet.

"My youngest sister," she said in clipped words, "has married a Thyrian, an ambitious man who means to use her position for his own gain."

Polar and Adiyn shared a quick, oddly intense glance. She wondered if she could possibly have surprised them with that information.

"In doing so," Phoena continued, "she has committed a crime of the most blatant sort against her nation and her family. I am of the impression that you would like to see her eliminated because of that marriage, and I have come to offer my assistance in that effort."

Polar leaned over the desk, his face devoid of expression. "Surely, you expect some favor in exchange."

Emboldened by his prompting, she spoke quickly. "Yes. Another sister and two nieces stand between myself and the throne. The little princesses . . . perhaps they could be assimilated into *your* culture? They are lovely girls. I could give you information that would help you with those endeavors."

"Then we put you on your throne?" Polar asked drily.

"Of course. I am no . . . murderer," she said delicately, "but Carradee and her people are gravely misguided. Something must be done, for the sake of Naetai."

Dru Polar turned to Adiyn. Again she saw them stare into one another's eyes that puzzling way.

"I have, of course, left messages." Phoena detected a hint of forward slouch in her posture and corrected it. "Should I fail to return or send word within a month—N'Taian calendar, of course—the *Federacy* will come for me."

A very long silence followed. When she thought she might shout just to break it, Dru Polar stood and offered his right hand. "I do not fault your measures for your own defense, of course. I believe we can reach an agreement. Let us discuss your offer in council and return a final word to you. Meanwhile, you must consider yourself my guest. I shall have you shown to our best visitors' rooms, where you may rest while we explore all aspects of your proposal. And . . ." He dropped her hand, and as his lashless eyes looked down into hers, she felt a sharp, compelling sensation she could not identify. "Thank you for coming," he said.

Phoena followed the man with the gold collar to a suite that seemed dreadfully stark. Although she was willing for the time to accept the proposition that this outpost could offer no better, she thought it had rather the look of a prison cell.

There was no cooking facility, not even a servo. Still, the blue-walled receiving room had the basic appointments, and the darker blue bedroom seemed spacious enough for comfort, even if its slick walls looked, smelled, and felt like plastic. The lack of windows disturbed her, too, but she steeled herself to living underground for a time. If this were her road to the throne, she could endure a few minor inconveniences more easily than another slip through space.

She wished to bathe but had brought no extra clothes. Rapidly, she searched compartments in a wall of the back room, but she found nothing. Very well, she would go buy something. Surely there were shops, and she would be extended credit as part of their hospitality.

As she crossed the sitting room, the door opened. A voluptuous woman with perfectly straight black hair and Polar's proud eyes stepped inside. Young—much younger than herself, Phoena judged—but possessed of a firmness about her full lips that suggested rank.

"You'd like some clean clothes," the girl said blandly, and she signaled behind her with a hand controller. A service cart glided into the room. "Penn Baker says you brought nothing along. That was wise. You are about my size." She looked Phoena up and down. "Commander Polar asked me to loan you some things."

"Thank you." Phoena stood for a moment. When she realized the girl expected her to unload the cart she reached for it quickly, as though she had anticipated nothing else. She piled one armload on the lounger. It smelled faintly of strange sachet.

"Are you related to Commander Polar?" Phoena asked between loads, when the silence had become uncomfortable.

"We're all cousins of one degree or another. Can't you tell?"

"I had noticed a resemblance." One compartment lay empty of blouses and jumpsuits, and Phoena began on another. Although the girl's indolent slouch peeved her, she was so glad to find dresses in the second compartment that she said nothing about the slouch.

"You look like your sister, too." The black-haired girl's tone conveyed no open insult, but her stare suggested she knew perfectly well it would be received as no compliment. "My name is Cassia Tulleman. I was born on Echo Six, our *major* colony, where my own father is Eldest. I've been here a week. One of the joys of the Unbound life is that all females are shipped to the other colony soon after acceptance as full adults, to improve the gene pool."

Oh. Daughter of power. Tulleman was the name, Phoena noted. Astrig Tulleman, then—Baker's friend—would be a member of the hierarchy as well. Cassia seemed bitter. And was that look on her face jealousy? Phoena unloaded the last items onto the lounger, and then Cassia left with a cool, "I'll be seeing you."

Phoena chose a likely enough ensemble of pale yellow lace and then treated herself to a long, delicious warm vaporbath in her tiny freshing room. Once dressed, she decided to explore while the men finished talking. She walked to the outer door.

It had no handle.

She pushed.

It didn't budge.

Phoena stepped backward from the entry, bumped into the lounger, and sat down, fighting fear with reason. They would soon finish their council, no doubt, and they wished to be able to reach her immediately. Meanwhile, no servants had arrived. She would put away the clothing herself.

A few minutes later, hearing footsteps, she ran to the outer room. Testing Commander Polar stood inside, his loose blue shirt bright against the sitting room's pale walls.

"Well?" she asked.

"We have accepted your offer, Your Highness. I am certain we will be able to make effective use of your help. We want everything you can show us concerning Lady Firebird, her personality, habits, and history. We need to be able to predict her most likely responses to several paths of attack we have considered. Then we will evaluate Naetai. I'm sure you know Sae Angelo well, the layout of the palace, and the routes most frequently traveled by the Queen and her children."

"When I'm Queen, you'll be able to keep a close eye on me as well, won't you?"

"We're not worried about keeping eyes on you. We will have other concerns."

Mollified, Phoena took a seat on the long brown lounger. Polar pulled over the smaller of two mock wooden chairs and sat down almost knee-to-knee with her.

"Have you experienced mind-access before?"

Phoena pushed away. "Commander, I have every intention of answering your questions. There is no need for interrogation."

"I believe that, Your Highness." He reached for her hand, and she knew from the heat of his fingers that hers had gone cold. "But at this point we don't know where to begin. I can do a quicker, more thorough job this way, and you will notice very little discomfort."

She snatched back her hand and sprang to her feet. "This is entirely unnecessary, sir."

"Sit down," he said with a queer quiet tone in his voice. Phoena found herself obeying.

"How dare you," she breathed.

"I am told your sister was not eager to be accessed either, when Caldwell first breached her. Cooperate, Phoena. Those were the terms. You'll do as we say, and we'll see you well rewarded."

The throne, she reminded herself. The Crown, the Federates banished from her homeworld, and that Fire-brat settled forever.

She raised her eyes to his, and he began.

Phoena came to herself lying on the lounger with the emptiest stomach she had ever suffered. Her awakening impressions were of peace and safety, and those feelings, stronger than any she had ever known, remained.

Cassia Tulleman entered, bringing warm, fruit-scented pastries and kaffa and an exotic flower in a crystal chalice, and without even rising from the lounger Phoena set to. "Oh, Phoena, one thing." Cassia laid paper and a stylus on the end table. "Your husband must be worried sick about you. I think you should let him know you're safe."

Despite her lack of respect, the busty little creature was quite right. Poor, loyal Tel would be frantic by now. "Thank you, Cassia," Phoena said. "That's a good idea."

Carrying a scribebook to study, Adiyn walked with Polar toward their apartments down a long, glossy corridor that curved with the dome. *I can't believe the naiveté of the woman,* Adiyn subvocalized. *What makes her think we owe her anything at all, let alone a throne? She hasn't a guess where she's been these days. I never saw a mind more amenable to memory blockage.*

Polar shrugged. *The youth implants have already ruined her epsilon system. If she thinks she's more to us than bait in a trap, let her think it. And it's good to have a DNA sample from her line, even if we don't dare clone and use it. For now, the Chadnegiyl is well pleased.* He paused. *You do think the Sentinel will come?*

He has no reason to help this one. She's been no friend to him. Adiyn halted outside his quarters and palmed the lock, wishing he were not so weary.

I think you misjudge the man, Polar answered. *For one thing, he can't resist a challenge. Never could. And another: So long as Naetai lies under Federate protection, the royal family does, too. They'll want to send someone as long as they think she's alive, and you know who is most likely to be sent. He'll be here, sooner or later. Pride and his conscience will bring him in.*

You're forgetting he's gone to Thyrian service, Adiyn sent calmly.

He'll come, answered Polar.

You'd care to bet on that?

Certainly. They'll release him. We're talking about Thyrica, for Zed's sake. Their forces are stinking with Sentinels. Polar transferred his scribebook from one hand to the other. *If I'm wrong, you can do as you like with this Angelo princess. But if he comes, after he's been rewarded for all the trouble he's been to us, I'll kill them both myself.*

His genes, we could use. You could, ah, perhaps incorporate his potential into your antipodal fusion work, as well?

Adiyn chuckled then, for his casual suggestion incited a surge of eagerness and the hint of a smile on Polar's usually fixed features. "Yes," Polar murmured.

First we must bring him in.

He'll come, Polar repeated.

Chapter 5

. . . In Spirit and in Flesh . . .

rubato
in free tempo,
not strictly

". . . so we were hoping the two of you would join us at Peak. It would mean so much to Mother."

The dark-haired, pleasant-faced man had very familiar eyes, chin, and cheekbones, and no wonder. Dr. Tarance Caldwell was Brennen's brother.

Firebird leaned a little closer to the tri-D set in the downlevel master bedroom. "Tarance, we'd love to. Would you know if the Base goes to minimal staff for Planetfall Day?"

"He's General Coordinator. He can get the time off. He—" Tarance's head turned. "Excuse me, Firebird." The screen went silent as he drew away. Beside him, Firebird saw a girl of about ten talking earnestly. Firebird stood beside the comscreen, one hand on the bureau, and kept her end of the line active. Brennen's relations with Tarance had remained awkward ever since the brothers were tested as preadolescents for epsilon ability, and Brennen, the younger by two years, was inducted on the spot into Sentinel College.

The girl, then, would be her niece by marriage. Blonde, with a delicate chin and intensely blue eyes, she'd be a beauty some day.

A soft hiss from the speaker indicated that Tarance had reactivated his line. "Firebird, this is my daughter Destia. She'd like to be introduced."

"Destia." Firebird made a meeting-dignitaries-at-the-palace half-bow. "I'm honored." *Maybe through the niece and nephews I could help bridge the gulf between Brennen and his family.* She knew the keenly sensitive side, now, that hid beneath Brennen's trained emotional control. Tarance's standoffishness must have hurt him deeply. How many years had Brennen passed offplanet with the Federacy without celebrating Planetfall, the festival commemorating the Aurians' arrival?

Destia vanished, and Tarance's head and slender shoulders filled the screen again. "You can reach Mother at her lab, if you can't get me. We'll take care of the pavilions and food; all you'd need to bring is yourselves."

And gifts for Destia and her brothers. Firebird suddenly remembered an advertisement she'd seen on the newsnet. Planetfall was *that* kind of holiday. "We'll do our best, Tarance. Thank you for including us."

He gave her a dark look, then said stiffly, "Of course you're included. I look forward to meeting you in person, Firebird. Take care of your health."

"Thank you again for calling." The screen went dark, and Firebird cut the transmitter. "Take care of your health"—Brennen's family might have taken offense at her before, as an offworlder not entitled to marry into the Caldwell line, but now that she was pregnant . . .

Yes, and now that the Lost of Auria shamah had been thoroughly discussed on the newsnet . . .

Well, she told herself, *it gives his relatives their own touch of notoriety. We were silly to try to hide it from the Shuhr, if their intelligence is worth anything.*

Planetfall Day. It did sound like a good chance to go through the formalities of introduction, and she would enjoy seeing Peak, where Brennen had spent his childhood.

Would it be anything like Name Day? she wondered, remembering Sae Angelo riotous with flowers and filled with music from a hundred small, informal choirs and ensembles.

Vaguely homesick, she made her way through the distrugia vines up the spiral stairwell to her music room, which lay just off the spacious living area. A small, windowless side room walled in natural wood, she guessed its original owner had meant it for —storage? A studio?—but Firebird, hearing its acoustics, had begged Brennen for it. He'd hurried to agree, asking only that she leave the door open when she practiced.

Cradled on a special hook high on the wall, her clairsa hung beside a new, smaller instrument: a Thyrian kinnora she'd found in Soldane. An ancient instrument like the clairsa, the kinnora looked small, broad, and plain next to the clairsa's long, ornately carved, wire-strung triangle of high-grained leta wood, but the kinnora's pastoral tone had enchanted Firebird, suggestive of wild, well-defended Hesed.

Hesed. She touched the instrument. Sometimes she wished they had stayed. They'd been encouraged to remain at the sanctuary for safety, because of the shamah and the Shuhr. All that complexity, and their mutual desire to stay in military service, had broken their peace too soon.

Too soon, she sighed, recalling the ecstasies of the first tender nights. She lifted the kinnora off its cradle and sat on a corner stool, resting it on one leg, since she no longer had a lap. Running her fingers up the strings, she smiled at its odd tuning. She always startled at the missing notes; it was a very old scale. Exclusively a folk instrument, a part of Brennen's heritage—

Firebird gripped the little instrument in sudden inspiration. She would learn a piece on the kinnora for Planetfall, as soon as she could get back to that shop near Kyrren Fjord and ask the owner about suitable music.

Rehanging the kinnora, she took down her clairsa, the last and most precious of her N'Taian possessions. Clavell's Sonata would warm up her fingers for new music, and she hadn't practiced Clavell in far too long. Hastily she corrected the tuning and then swept into the opening arpeggios. The notes rang sweetly—and unevenly.

Firebird halted, shocked. Always before, she had been able to spin off arpeggios as smoothly as anyone on Naetai.

She berated herself for going so long without hard practicing. *You've been busy,* she reminded herself. *And soon you'll be busier. If you don't want to lose your technique altogether, you'll set up a practicing schedule.*

Fifteen minutes later, she was still trying doggedly to work that annoying gallop out of the arpeggio when the entry alert gave a shrill call.

A busy day on Trinn Hill. Firebird rehung her instrument and stepped to the closest control center, high on the near wall of the living area, gray shaded by thick fog outside the long window. The midday alert seemed odd. Surely anyone wanting Brennen would go to the Base.

On the silver panel just above her eye level no light burned at low center, so the caller had not passed into the security entry. *Obviously*, she told herself. *You locked it*. She pressed a key to slide open the outer door, counted a slow ten, then asked, "Who calls?"

A small bluescreen lit at the left of the panel. On it she saw a young man: he stood in the entry, clutching a parcel under one arm. His tunic appeared pale blue on screen, but it could have been white, and it looked damp. He wore a star on his right shoulder.

"Mistress Firebird, I bring this at Master Spieth's request." He swung up the small, square parcel and held it toward the monitor.

That seemed queer. The vis-pickup was virtually invisible from inside the entry. How had he seen it, to look up that way?

"She instructed me to give it into your hands only. It is specifically not for Master Caldwell."

Firebird stared hard at the small image. "What is it?"

"I was not told, Mistress. Only to give it into your hands."

It occurred to Firebird that Master Spieth had no idea of the security system at their home, and an innocent messenger could have been sent from the College's Medical Division. From the underside of the control panel she unhooked a tiny remote. Palming it in her left hand, she walked to the inner door.

"Open," she told its pickup. She held the module tightly. A touch on the central indentation would activate an immobilizing electric grid the length of the security entry.

As the door slid aside, a wisp of cool, damp air swirled into the house. The young man in white took a step inward.

"Would you mind staying where you are for a moment?" Firebird stood with her toes at the edge of the vestibule and extended a hand.

The man presented his parcel. Wrapped in a rough fabric cover, it felt heavy for its weight but evenly balanced.

"Did she send any message?" Firebird asked.

"Yes, Mistress. I was to refer to your last conversation with her, and to recommend you open and consider this alone."

Last conversation? When she tested . . .

Now thoroughly puzzled, Firebird pocketed the remote and examined the mysterious package, turning it over and over. "Thank you. Tell the Master I am well."

"Mistress." He strode through the outer door of the security entry.

"Close," she murmured to its pickup as she turned back toward the greenwell. To be truthful, she didn't like the way the man rushed off. But if this had come from the Shuhr . . . certainly their methods included nothing so simplistic as drop-and-run poisons or explosives. Furthermore, the instruction to open the parcel without Brennen would never have come from anyone who wanted Brennen dead, too.

The Redjackets? She drew a deep breath. Her lifelong guardians and enemies on Naetai: Could the Wastlings' watchmen finally have come to see her Geis Orders carried out? A Sentinel's star might not be too difficult to counterfeit, and plenty of shops sold medics' uniforms.

She hurried to the com center nearest the music room and punched in Master Spieth's code, then stood waiting, fingering the parcel's fabric wrapping.

The Master, she was informed by a pleasant recorded voice, sat in conference. Did she wish a return call?

Firebird's glance flicked from the control panel to the package. *Well?*

"No," she told the voice. "Thank you."

Sliding down onto the floor, she berated herself for a foolhardy child and slipped off the package's covering.

It was a book.

On its cover, satin-finished in midnight blue, a golden star with four points was embossed and circled in gold. A slip of paper lay inside. She propped the book open and read the note.

Mistress Firebird—

I feel you can be trusted, which my consultation with Master Brennen only confirms. The fact remains that I cannot spare time to help you with this. Begin at the beginning and see what you can accomplish on your own. I will evaluate any progress you are able to make and help you as I can when we meet for medical reasons.

You must attempt nothing but P'nah until I have approved your progress, for you could harm yourself and others by proceeding carelessly without supervision. For the time, my authority will cover you. I know you will read ahead; read with my blessing, only try nothing further.

Keep the book in its wrapping. I doubt you need the warning.

Firebird reminded herself to breathe. The developing neural system of the fetus, Spieth had said, required a particular amount of oxygen at all times, and she carried two. She lifted the paper and eyed the first page.

Aldana Spieth's name, scribed on the coverleaf in a young, flowing script with midnight blue ink, was the text's only preamble.

One. P'nah, The Turn.

The release of mental energy onto the modulated epsilon carrier presupposes the ability on the pupil's part to identify and locate epsilon energy arising in his own body and to separate it from background sensory imagery. Turning inward to sense one's self at the primal level is therefore the beginning. Proceed with prayerful caution.

At the moment before falling asleep, when thought is stilled, there occurs an inward-chasing of the mind's natural pattern that will lead in sleep to dreams. To consciously follow that chase inward has proven the most practical beginning in this course of study. . . .

Firebird skimmed to the bottom of the text, then began to flip pages. After "The Turn" came "The Epsilon Harmonic," then "Securing the Carrier," and the slim volume ended with "Four. Shield and Pulse Modulation," and a solemn reminder of the consequences of "capricious or selfish use" of any skill taught therein.

There must be any number of these volumes, Firebird reflected, awed. *How many has Brennen, hidden away in the study?* She saw no charts or illustrations, but—she paged back to "The Turn"—nothing sounded too dreadfully difficult. Thank the Thyrians' Word that as a Wastling she had never been entitled to youth implants! Eagerly she studied the P'nah section. Then, leaning against a riffled wall crosslegged on the carpet, she closed her eyes and relaxed toward sleep—or tried to.

The next hour surpassed any day spent with Phoena for sheer hellish frustration. The simple act of quieting her mind to Turn her focus inward seemed utterly beyond her. Thoughts of food, faces she had seen, common, irrelevant matters kept distracting her, although she thought, once, almost . . . but her startled leap toward the odd momentary sensation brought her alert and silenced the faint touch under a chorus of mental comments. Exhaling

deeply, she let her head droop. Maybe she should ask Brennen
for help.

No. Master Spieth had trusted her with a secret, and Brennen
had told her repeatedly, though gently, that he believed she could
do nothing, even with his help, because of her age. As a matter
of principle, she should do it alone. Perhaps she had missed some
clue in the text.

The clairsa hung close. *Back to Clavell.*

Brennen came on Base very early the next morning to meet with
his friend Air Master Dardy, Corporal Claggett of the Home Forces,
and Cristod Harris of the College, whose preliminary research into
the possibility of developing a long-range projector for a Sentinel's
skills had caught his attention. He found them in Claggett's office,
in the sixth level below his own.

After hurried greetings, Dardy leaned over Claggett's desk,
rolled out a wide sheet of scribepaper, and subvocalized, *This is
RIA: Remote Individual Amplification. It's not on computer; RIA
must not be tapped by the Shuhr, under any circumstances. So
far as we know, they haven't yet discovered how this feedback
amplifier cycle can be operated by a single individual.*

Dardy articulated it as *Ree-a*, Brennen noted. His glance traced
the rough schematic sketch twice, from its input, drawn as a simple
headset, through several circuits and transmatches, and finally to
the series of projecting antennae. *You said it takes a surprising
mass of machinery.*

*Yes. The wave-matching simply can't be miniaturized effec-
tively. We're trying to develop a ship-mounted module. Here are
some of the problems.* Dardy stroked the paper with one finger.
*The input filters aren't quite selective enough to eliminate back-
ground alpha energy, which tends to cancel out the motivating
epsilon type. Then here, at this toroidal juncture, putting a single
epsilon wave into phase with the DeepScan carrier will require a
more delicate adjustment. The projecting system is similar to basic
planetary fielding—*

Faster-than-light capability, then?

And range roughly equivalent to DeepScan. Dardy raised one
eyebrow. Brennen scattered the cloud of epsilon static that normally protected him from emotional noise. As he expected, Dardy
was disappointed by that range.

When it's perfected, put in Harris, a small man of cocksure
stance.

Dardy nodded.

So. Short range, and that only eventually. Brennen leaned closer. Interspersed with conventional electronic symbols, he saw others marking currents of the projectible epsilon energy that arose only in the starbred.

Expensive?

Moderately so, answered Claggett.

Dardy shrugged. *Comparable to a low-end particle shield. That's a small investment, if we can make it work.*

Dardy had a good sense of practicality: His work with Thyrica's Alert Forces had closely paralleled Brennen's with the Federacy's Special Operations. Brennen asked, *Do you have a working model?*

Once again Dardy layered his projection with a wry undercurrent. *One that should work, but doesn't.*

May I see it?

Claggett turned toward a wall and raised one hand. A long panel slid upward to reveal a bank of machinery, circuit boards exposed. *Nothing simple, of course.*

Firebird relaxed in the passenger seat of their little jetcraft and stared down into rain forest. Planetfall had been a success. Destia and her brothers begged to play the kinnora and the clairsa and in return read her ancient Aurian holy tales. She'd felt comfortable with them, even loved.

Well, liked. She yawned and stretched. A good day. A silvery river snaked past, far below, and she traced its twisting line up to the horizon.

She'd watched Tarance with his children, too, and Brennen's mother relaxing with her grown sons. The casual interplay of intercepted thought and interrupted speech looked so comfortable, so right. She rejoiced to see Brennen at ease with his own people, though the glimpse into a loving family reminded Firebird painfully of something she had missed.

The elder Mistress Caldwell even took her aside, warned and encouraged her as to life with the tiny and talented, obviously wishing Firebird had the epsilon skills to nurture the babies.

Firebird wished it, too, more now than ever. If she were trying to raise a child for musical talent, she would sing to him constantly, whistle to him, play symphonies for him. How could she do less for a child with extraordinary epsilon potential?

At least they'll have their father to teach them epsilon games, she thought. And then: *But if I can learn to Turn . . .*

• • •

The following day, Brennen returned to the house set into Trinn Hill. Alarmed by the intrusion of his perturbed, chastened uneasiness into her evening calm, Firebird hurried uplevel to meet him.

In the kitchen she found him still in uniform, standing beside the long counter and pouring a glass of pale yellow Carolinian wine. Now her unease rose to answer his. Like most Sentinels he generally avoided depressants, and he had purchased it to help her sleep. She paused in the archway and called, "Brenn. Is something wrong?"

Raising the glass, he saluted her with it, then drank half. "Working at College today—research Dardy and I have on the side—we discovered a way to lower our epsilon readings. We can do it, Mari. It is possible after all."

She stretched out a hand and leaned against the arch. "It's no fluke?"

"The resonal scanning circuits are easier to deceive than the Access specialists, and it is hard to consistently land the same score, but I improved a little with practice." He reached for her hand as he drank again, and she stepped closer. "Hoston and Dardy tried, too," he said. "They're both in the seventy-five range. Hoston couldn't bring himself to make a serious effort, but Dardy brought his reading down to sixty or so. I took mine once to fifty-three, but it gave me such a killing headache that I declared my point proven and stopped trying."

"So the higher your potential and the harder you work at it, the better you can falsify?"

"That seems to be the case. And I—" He set down the glass. "I don't like the implications at all. If this is a skill practiced among the Shuhr . . ." He flicked the wine bottle. "It will be a subject of intensive study at College, now. Dardy and the Alert Forces will be particularly interested."

Bosk Terrell, she thought. *Terrell could either be a legitimate forty, as his records show, pushing a hundred, or off the scale.* "What can we do?" she asked.

He considered the oval of clear liquid at the bottom of the glass. "Each of us is theoretically subject to periodic rescreening, and some random checks occur each year simply to keep us all on line. I've put Terrell's name in, anonymous but Security I. He will probably be called in a day or so. I'll stay clear of it, but the minute there's news I will alert you."

Startled by his instinctive leap, which looked for all the worlds like mind-reading but this time was not, Firebird nodded. "Good, Brenn."

She spent most of the next day trying to Turn. When Brennen came in that night, she sat alone in the master bedroom, cupping the blue-green mira lily in her palms. He sank onto the bed beside her without asking how she felt. (He knew. Besides frustrated, she felt trapped. Fat. Ugly. Seven Standard months pregnant, and with twins.) He handed her a thin parcel. "This is for you, Mari. It was delivered today."

"What is it?"

"Take it."

Gently Firebird replaced the lily on its crystal plate, then lifted the parcel's pressboard lid. Inside, a spiraling ebony handgrip protruded from a black yest-skin belt sheath. She tipped the dagger out of the box, caressed its beaded pommel, and whispered, "Brenn." The grip felt made for her holding, and she knew it was. Then she drew the blade; it too was finished in flat black, for invisibility at night. Just longer than her hand, it tapered gracefully from narrow waist to symmetrical point, with a wicked double edge.

"It will split paper." He smiled down the blade. "I tried it." He stood and took a few steps toward the room they called the "study," which lay on the master room's windowless side, built into the hill. "Now let's see if you remember what I've taught you."

She groaned.

"They're still out there, Mari. A small woman must be able to kill. You'd get no second chance in a confrontation."

He was right. She might look and feel like a cruiser, but the enemy took no pregnancy leave. "All right." She slapped the dagger into her palm and followed him in, pulling the gather-panel snug at the so-called waist of the loose Thyrian skyff that had become her uniform.

Brennen pressed a panel on the far wall of the long, narrow storeroom they'd converted for weapons practice. From the case that slid open, he selected a dulled training dagger, then he pulled off his tunic and skinshirt to face her bare-chested. "I'll match you. No rest periods until that blade has blood on it, Major."

He began to circle to his right on the springy blue mat, his face perfectly blank.

Firebird drew the black dagger and tossed its sheath toward the wall behind her. How to draw blood without really injuring? He had given her a short course in Carolinian dagger-play, beginning back at Hesed, where he'd proven he could slow his reflexes to just faster than her own: a display of self-control that baffled her, because it got him hurt.

He can block pain, she reminded herself. *But be careful.* A flesh wound would satisfy him, over his ribs, if she could get inside his reach, and arms constituted fair strikes, but never the hands, not in practice. Glancing at the taut tendons on his tawny hands, she faltered. Her arms hung limp. "Not tonight, Brenn. Somehow I can't bear the thought of blood. It must be these maternal hormones."

"Mari." He crouched in a wide stance. "This could mean your life one day. Unlikely, but possible. Trust me, if I see myself in real danger . . ." He gave her a one-sided smile. "I'll react. As you'd better—"

He lunged. Automatically she pulled away, surprised by the quick reaction of her body to his dull dagger. She swiped for his arm but missed. Instantly he spun and cracked her forearm.

"Come in *short*." He glared. "You deserve the bruise. That N'Taian sword-thrust will get you killed."

All right, then. She warmed a little to the fight, to the knife's nubbly grip heating in her hand and the ebony blade quivering in front of her. She changed direction and circled left. Brennen countered immediately. If only she had his reach. Again the thought of blood, Brennen's blood, made her swallow hard.

He sprang. She saw the opening and sent the dagger low, across his ribs, under his arm. She felt no resistance against the blade and wondered if she'd missed again.

But he raised a hand. "Call. Check."

Now she saw the red trickle on his side. "Are you all right?" she asked hurriedly, holding out the black dagger. On one side of the tip gleamed a thin damp curve.

"It's not deep. Don't worry."

She fetched the medical kit from its locker and snatched a biotape spool off its spindle as he sank onto a short bench. Gently she wiped away the blood, then pressed a strip of the pale gauzy fabric to his side. The bleeding stopped.

"I'm slow," she muttered. "Heavy."

"You're trying. But you're tense."

"I hurt you."

Straddling the bench, he twisted his body around to coil a strand of her dark red-brown hair on his hand. "Do you know, Mari, I find it much more unpleasant to blood you than serve as your target. Even though I've trained others to first blood, even though it is imperative you learn how quickly biotape works so you'll fear wounding the less, I find I dislike hurting you, dislike it very much.''

She fingered each edge of the tape to ensure its absorption into his skin, then pulled back a little to examine her handiwork. "Because you feel my fear, I suppose, or because I can't block pain."

"It has nothing to do with either. It comes more naturally to defend you than train you. Does that offend you?"

"Not if you don't mind my defending *you*. There. Thank you for the dagger." She cleaned its blade on a spare strip of damp paper gauze and then kissed his forehead. "I like fighting with steel."

"Of course you do. Steel is intimidating. A blazer can miss entirely, but a blade nearly always cuts something—unless you're fool enough to throw it."

"Is that why the Sentinels still carry the crystace?"

He had removed his, in its wrist sheath, but she rarely saw him without the Aurian relic: a weapon with a sonic activator and crystalline blade. That blade hid inside the gray grip until its molecular bonds were excited by a resonant pitch.

"Intimidation is a factor," he said. "Also, few blades so long can be concealed—and in skilled hands it's the best known defense against moderate laser fire." He smiled. "As you've seen. It has a certain ceremonial value as well."

"Well." She sighed. "How many openings did I miss?"

He shrugged back into the thin black skinshirt. "How many did you see?"

"One." She adjusted the skyff's draw panel.

"I gave you four. Stand over there, and we'll go through them."

Chapter 6

Born an Angelo

vivace expressivo
lively, expressive

"Whatever she is now, sir, she was born an Angelo." Carradee Second paced the carpet of her sitting room. Erect in a row of waiting-chairs sat three members of her Electorate: Count Wellan Bowman, Baroness Kierann Parkai, and His Grace the Duke of Claighbro, Muirnen Rattela. As she reached his end of her course, Rattela shifted on his slender-legged chair and lowered dark, manicured brows. Carradee chose not to notice. She was the Queen.

"Born an Angelo," she repeated. "I will not move that she be restored to the succession, but that she be restored to citizenship, Noble Electors. The Assembly's review of her conduct at Hunter Height was conclusive. Lady Firebird took no unnecessary action, spared life when possible—from the standpoint of self-protection—in short, defended herself and her . . ." it felt awkward to say this, glad though she was for Firebird's happiness, "and her husband, from harm. And whatever our views regarding the permanence of the Federate presence here, Princess Phoena's motives and actions at the Height can only be considered dubious."

Carradee eyed Muirnen Rattela as sternly as she could, with the glance she had inherited from Queen Siwann and practiced in front of her boudoir mirror. She had been furious—furious!—to learn Phoena had established an illegal weaponry lab at Hunter

Height, the family's lovely old vacation home, and she knew now Rattela had been a prime instigator. She did not hope Phoena's secessionist movement had died at the Hunter Height incident, nor did she imagine Phoena left it leaderless when she went . . . wherever. Surely its new leader sat before her, opening a tin of after-dinner mints, his sateen-swathed bulk resting uneasily on the delicate chair.

"She took Federate transnationality, Majesty." Rattela flicked a mint under his tongue, pocketed the tin, and then folded both hands across his middle. "Renouncing her N'Taian citizenship. You would give it back after she flung it away?"

"Causing who-knows-what blight on her own conscience." Carradee had vowed she would not back down. Loyal, proud, determined to fulfill her martyrdom and earn a glorious place in Naetai's history, Firebird had gladly offered her life in battle. *That* was how Carradee would choose to remember her youngest sister. It hadn't been Firebird's fault she was captured.

She pulled a white blossom from the bouquet on the end table beside Rattela and rolled its stem between her fingers. She held nothing against the Federates any more. They were far better administrators than she had been led to believe—ordered to believe—at Queen Siwann's deathbed.

"Madame." Wellan Bowman tapped his brass-tipped walking stick against the leg of his chair. Frowning, Carradee held the notum bloom to her nose and peered at the black-haired nobleman over its petals. "If the survival of Lady Firebird confused the succession, how much worse now that she carries the heir of an offworlder? A Federate, a—Sentinel? What status must her daughter be given? Shall we give that halfblood-N'Taian citizenship, as well?"

Carradee had anticipated the question. "No, Bowman. If, by any stretch of fortune, the Electorate and the Assembly chose to restore Lady Firebird even to the succession, then, and only then, would we consider the matter of her offspring. For what other circumstance would she be restored to the succession, Noble Electors, than that of need?" She lowered her voice. "There is no need. Our Princesses are nearly of an age to be confirmed."

She strode up the center of the long, high-curtained sitting room. They hadn't asked the one question for which she had no answer, thank the Powers: What of these Shuhr? What if they truly meant to wipe out the bloodline, as Firebird had warned in that terse communiqué Carradee received last week?

At the end of the chamber nearest the dark fayya-wood door into the outer hallway, she laid the blossom on a butler's tray. "Noble Electors, we shall make the motion tomorrow. We would be pleased to count on your support." *Not that I expect it from any of you,* she thought, but she never would have dared say it aloud. "I ask only for her citizenship—as a token, my friends. Only a token. If she had meant to harm us, to damage Hunter Height—" Carradee collected their stares and held them a moment. "In a tagwing fightercraft such as she escaped in, she could have done so, as I think you know. Whatever her loyalty, she is a fine pilot and a skilled markswoman."

She tapped the door twice, and it opened. One by one and silently, Parkai and Bowman left the chamber.

Carradee paced to the nearest window and gazed out. This room faced the front, public gardens of the palace, which lay brown with winter; under bright lights, only the evergreens retained their color. Two long, white ground-cars pulled slowly toward the curb to receive Baroness Parkai and Count Bowman.

Her dependable support in the Electorate consisted only of the four commoners she'd appointed. Others seemed to waver between disdain and reluctant assent. Phoena's poor, lonely husband, Prince Tel, would vote with Rattela. The other younger nobles followed similar patterns of influence.

That wasn't the way Mother's Electorate voted. The Crown was a figurehead once again.

Fingering a yellow curtain—she despised jeweled windowfilters, and had had them all replaced with antique sheers—Carradee sighed, then turned.

Rattela still sat.

"Majesty." His pale green eyes narrowed beneath thin, plucked brows. "What do you intend to do if she turns on us again?"

"She won't." Carradee stopped the warm pool of a lamplight. "Have you—heard from Her Highness, Rattela?"

"Princess Phoena? No." The Duke shook his head, sniffed loudly, then strode out.

Feeling rebuffed, Carradee retreated through the east door of the chamber into her private apartments. Prince Daithi sat in pale mauve pajamas, propped against several pillows, reading a scan cartridge on a glowing viewer, on the bed in his own room. "Daithi?" she asked softly.

His eyes, soft and dark like a brownbuck's, blinked twice. Brown curls lay carelessly tumbled on his head. Tall, gentle—though eight years her senior, he had the caring heart of a child.

Sometimes he seemed like the younger brother she had never had: the younger brother no Angelo had ever had.

"Would you sleep with me tonight?" she asked.

He laid the viewer on his brown velvric coverlet. "Of course." She rested one hand on his right shoulder and touched his smooth throat. He smelled of leta-wood soap. He'd bathed a second time today, as usual, in case she made that very request.

She passed through his room into the adjoining double boudoir, and there changed into her nightgown. In mid–brush stroke, she smiled at Daithi as he passed by. "I'll warm the sheets," he said.

Carradee nodded as the chambermaid followed him through, carrying a bundle of blankets. She sighed contentment. If anyone could help her relegate Rattela to the zone of forgetfulness, it was Daithi.

Hours later, she woke perspiring. His Grace the Duke Muirnen Rattela had stalked her dreams, challenging and belittling her. He wasn't *really* like that. She stumbled out to the boudoir. Examining her scalp, she thought she detected a hint of oiliness. *A hundred strokes would do it good—and wake me out of this dream-daze.*

In her drawer she found the pulse brush. She set it for low speed, held its vibrating bristles to the crown of her head, and shut her eyes. Then she set to brushing.

At the ninetieth stroke, terror seized her. She dropped her brush. The sensation was so strong, so irrational—

It's coming from another mind. The thought flashed fully verbalized into her consciousness.

Sentinel? she answered it. She felt distant, scornful laughter, and groped for a rational anchor for that sensation.

Shuhr? She had ignored Firebird's warning message. Now the thought rang so loudly in her mind that her lips moved.

A *crack* echoed behind her. The walls groaned, then gave a grinding crash. The world flew to pieces around her. Screaming, she flung up her arms to protect her face. Something struck her from behind. She tumbled from her stool, clutching long tufts of carpet. The floor heaved once beneath her, and small rattling noises trailed off into silence.

The explosion—it had come from behind her—Daithi! She pulled her hands off her face. The boudoir had gone totally dark. Her legs and torso ached under some immovable weight. By pressing with her arms and shoulders, she could raise her head, but it smacked something hard.

She lay back down. "Daithi," she moaned.

For some time she drifted in a faint, then erratic crashing and crunching noises roused her. Perhaps someone called her name, perhaps not. *Shuhr? No,* she thought. *Sentinels?*

And if they're in league?

Pain sliced into her legs and lower back as the weight on them shifted. "Hello," she moaned. "I'm here."

"Majesty." The male voice sounded breathy and frantic. "Majesty, keep talking."

"I'm at the dresser," she began. "It's dark. I think my legs may be hurt, and my back—"

A light flashed in her face. "You can stop now, Majesty." When it moved aside she saw two faces, one a comfortable, familiar face. "Doctor Zonderma," she murmured. Four masculine arms heaved a long timber off her, and she tried to crawl out of the trap that had held her. "Daithi. He was in my bed. Find Daithi."

The doctor pressed a hypodermic against her arm. "We will, Madame. Lie still."

Governor Danton was good to come to her hospital room.

Carradee shifted on the bed, and its contours shifted underneath her. Doctor Zonderma assured her the bone damage was reparable, that with therapy she would soon walk again. But Daithi . . .

He will live, she reminded herself. *Be grateful for that, and wait to see what the doctors can do.* She gulped back a desire to let go and weep on the shoulder of this Federate governor, who had been kind to her from the beginning. With whom she had never had to fight, the way she had to constantly fight her Electors. But she must not weep with him. She was the Queen. She must make him see it that way, although every instinct screamed her personal anguish: it was her fault Daithi had lain in that bed. She'd invited him.

"If," she said steadily, "you can get Iarlet and Kessaree to a safe, unknown locale, do it. Please. Do it quickly." Then her reserve began to crumble. "Up until this point, sir, whenever we have spoken I have spoken as Queen. Now I am a mother. I cannot explain how these instincts swell up in me. For my own safety I will be answerable, but I would never be able to live with myself if there were anything I could have done for my daughters, and through my not having done it, they were harmed. Do you understand, Lee?"

The Federate governor fingered the cleft in his chin, and fading afternoon light gleamed in his blond hair. "I do, Majesty. I had three children of my own. Lost one. Between us, Madame, I have dreamed of her—monthly, sometimes. I understand well. Now, there are several possib—''

"No." Shutting her eyes, Carradee pressed her head back into the pillow. Her mouth tasted queer from some medicine. "I don't want to know where, Governor. If your suspicions are correct— if what I felt just before the explosion was some sort of psionic dart, meant to inform me of my killers—if they come again, and can read into my mind—I want no knowledge of where my daughters are sent into hiding." Grief tugged her heart. "That is, not now. You can tell me later, but you cannot unsay anything you tell me now."

She opened her eyes. Danton was nodding.

"They want us all dead," she whispered. "They do. Firebird was right."

The Federate governor swung one dark-trousered leg over the other. "You are well watched, Madame. Perhaps it will comfort you to know that we have enlarged a special guard for you and your daughters from the Special Operations branch of the Federate forces, including a number of trained Sentinels. Any Shuhr agents on Naetai will have to be very quiet, very careful. I doubt that they would dare try anything against you now."

"But you will see to the other matter?" she asked.

"Yes, Madame."

"Yes," said Wellan Bowman. "But if she is . . . disabled . . . for a time yet?"

Muirnen Rattela took two steps along the long colonnade and stopped, running a fleshy hand up and down the smooth white marble of a pillar. Fortunate that the ancient palace still stood. Only two internal walls had collapsed. Danton was wrong about precision explosives; the virtue lay in the ancient N'Taians, who had built for strength. The palace: the Electorate: the Crown.

Fortunate, too, in a way, that Carradee had not been able to press the issue of the Wastling's citizenship. Carradee tended to forget that Lady Firebird still stood under a sentence of execution for treason.

"She will be," he said. A chill breeze fluttered his collar ruffle; irritated, he smoothed it. "Emotionally, she will be unable to participate in government for several weeks at the inside. This is according to her own physician, mind you. Psychosomatically, she is distraught over the Prince's injuries and must not be given authority until his condition stabilizes. So. The Crown needs a regent, with authority to act at Electoral meetings. Emergency powers only, of course," he added, "but there is no need to set a limit on his term of service."

Count Wellan Bowman rapped the column with his walking stick. " 'Iarlet's accession, at her majority,' would make a logical phrase, should any of the new-faction press for a limitation," he said smoothly.

"Yes." Rattela drew out his tin of mints. "Yes, it would."

Rain. Again. Firebird rolled over in bed as far as she could, stared out the bedroom window, and groaned. Brennen had left for work already. She shut her eyes, yanked the coverlet over her head, and dozed.

Beside Brennen, she stood before the Federacy's Regional Council, on Alta, beneath the high, gray ceiling and white arches carved of sparkling Altan gypsum. From the midnight-blue robe she wore, she identified the occasion: They had returned to Alta from Hesed, just after being married. This had been their first audience since slipping, against the Council's orders, to clean out Phoena's rebel's nest at Hunter Height.

Whispers broke out in the gallery on the chamber's far side, amplified in her dream to the rush of river water.

How long could they walk a path on this silver-flecked stone, between Thyrica's wishes and the Federacy's?

She woke shivering. She never wanted to go through that again!

Brennen had tried to explain, without making public the newly discovered matter of the shamah, how he sensed in the intimacy of bonding Firebird's own flicker of epsilon strength, and her kinship with his people.

The lost of Auria will find her people, claimed the prophecy, *will unite with Thyrica in spirit and in flesh. From new life will spring death, a pyre for the enemies of Thyrica.* It was necessary they find a more secure place at which to begin a family, as quickly as possible.

He'd explained, too, that his act of apparent insubordination had rested on the necessity of following his Sentinel vows—despite Consular Orders.

"What of the Federate Fleet?" General Voers of Bishda had snapped. "Special Operations? What of Delta Squadron, the strike group you have so painstakingly built and wielded?"

"I leave Delta Squadron regretfully, hoping it will continue its tradition." Brennen stood at attention and spoke calmly. "I hope to return one day to Regional Command, Your Honors. I did not foresee this development."

"And then the High Command?" The dark hostility in Voers' voice startled Firebird. "You are not yet eligible for indefinite furlough, General Caldwell. Are you certain it is not a half-time paternity position for which you wish to apply?"

Firebird flushed. Brennen's rapid rise to the Lieutenant Generalship did place him in an odd position, without some privileges usually accrued by one of his rank; and the High Command, the council that coordinated the vast Regional fleets of the Federate military, she knew to be a longtime goal of Brennen's.

"Alta is too dangerous a place for us to live, Your Honor," Brennen said, "too open to offworld commerce, which the Shuhr could use to bring in their agents. Cannot an exceptional furlough be granted in my case?"

"Will any so move?" Tierna Coll, head of the Council, swept her gaze up and down the table's arch.

Voers leaned forward over his folded hands. "Even should he resign altogether, General Caldwell can look forward to a noteworthy career—among his own people. I feel that he should stay here, with Special Operations, if he intends to remain in Federate service."

And Voers prevailed. Vividly she recalled the sensation of shock rising in Brennen when Tierna Coll denied his request.

"Then," he said, "I must ask that you accept my resignation from the Regional Command."

"From Federate service," General Voers amended. "Distinguished Service category."

Brennen turned to Tierna Coll for confirmation, too intent on the Council now to control his feelings of betrayal. Firebird slid her feet farther apart, resisting dizzying disorientation, fighting cold fury of her own.

Tierna Coll nodded.

"I do not wish to resign from Federate service," Brennen said in a low voice. He paused and glanced at Firebird. Over his fine chin and cheekbones his skin had gone pale. She pressed her lips together. How could they do this to him? What could she say? She had given up her own homeland for him and his Federacy, and now stood ready to sacrifice her future as a military pilot for his people and their shamah. One highest priority, he had insisted, or she could never be a whole person.

"I have a mission now, Your Honors," Brennen confirmed her

thought, "and a hope, that in our line the threat of Thyrica's greatest enemies might be ended. Because . . . by doing so . . ."

Firebird felt his resolve waver, then harden.

". . . I hope to serve the Federacy in a way that I could not on Alta, I do ask that you accept my resignation—from Federate service."

A baby started kicking. Firebird sat up on the bed, seething. After all he had done for the Federacy!

She had to shake this mood quickly, or it would color her day as gray as the endless rain. Hurriedly she dressed and headed for the Base and sunshine.

Soon she perched alone on a stool at one corner of the Base ranging tower's deck, gripping a glassite railing and peering down at breakers that nibbled the stony beaches below the cliffs. Awe of the vast Thyrian ocean had freed her from the tyrannical vividness of that dream; now, perhaps, it might quiet her thoughts enough to catch that elusive Turning. In a week of sporadic effort she had not succeeded. But neither had she given up, nor told Brennen of her efforts.

The onshore wind tied her hair into auburn knots, but its sting in her face felt so clean and invigorating that she didn't mind the tangles. Far to her left perched Shanneman's atop its tower, the restaurant where Brennen had taken her for her birthday dinner. Northward, to her right, the sea-beaten cliffs bent westward into another fjord and then faded into haze.

"Mistress Caldwell?" A young blond guardsman with only one fine stripe on his midnight blue sleeve stepped out into the sea wind. "General Coordinator Caldwell asks if you could come and speak with him."

Surprised, she slid down from the stool and walked in to catch a lift.

When she slipped into Brennen's office, immediately his agitation made her fidget. He remained in his desk chair. "Sit down, Mari."

She took one of the black chairs. "Yes? Bad news?"

"Phoena," he said. "She vanished from Sae Angelo two to three Standard weeks ago."

"What? Why are we only now hearing about it?"

He slid a hand along his desk top. "The Occupation has just found out. Danton is maintaining secrecy for the Palace, for a suspected Shuhr operative named Penn Baker disappeared as well."

Brennen sat silently while she absorbed the news and its implications. *A Shuhr operative . . . and Phoena?* Firebird clenched her hands in her lap.

"Yes," said Brennen. "She could have been kidnapped. She'd be an easy one to lure in with promises of power. But I have other news, worse. Carradee has been involved in an explosion in her rooms."

"No!" Firebird glanced up. No wonder he felt agitated.

"Carradee's bed was literally blown to splinters in the middle night, but Carradee wasn't in it. She was injured by a collapsing wall in the adjoining boudoir. The Prince's condition is serious but stable. The palace staff has been detained en masse for questioning; meanwhile, Sae Angelo is in an uproar."

"I can imagine," she muttered, fingering one long, tangled curl.

"Governor Danton is sending Carradee's daughters off planet to a safe locale."

"Hesed?" she asked. Certainly two carriers of the lost Aurian line would be allowed access to the Sentinel sanctuary.

"He didn't say. His message concludes: 'We ask, with all respect for your abilities, if you have considered seeking sanctuary yourselves.' "

Staring at his desktop, Firebird slowly shook her head.

"General Director Kindall came in shortly after I had the word about Carradee. He wants me to take furlough and is offering to keep my position open while we're gone. So it's public news."

"And you said . . . ?"

"I said, 'We refuse to spend our lives running.' " He slid back his chair and stood. "Lunch? Home?"

"Certainly," she whispered, dry-mouthed, and he helped her up.

They headed across the quadrangle and down a passway. At last Firebird felt certain of her voice. "Right at the heart of the palace."

"An expression of contempt, I think, and a symbolic blast at your heritage."

"How much of it was damaged?"

"Two non-structural walls collapsed."

"The precision that implies, Brenn, the intimate knowledge of the palace . . ." She stopped in midstep. "What if Phoena wasn't kidnapped? What if she went to them?"

"It . . . could be. I had thought of it."

"Phoena!"

"Hush, Mari. They might have killed her already, whether or not she went willingly."

She kept walking. "Do you think General Kindall believed you, then?"

"I think he is inclined to. If we must run for sanctuary, the better convinced the Shuhr are that we intend to stay here, the better chance we will have of catching them flatfooted. They do expect defiance from me, particularly since my pride is supposed to have been shattered by Regional Command."

Supposed to? she thought. She passed an open door. Hearing voices, she fell quiet until they boarded the elevator. As they rode downward Brennen touched her hand. "Have you heard any more about that rumor," she asked, "that Regional is considering a strike at—"

"No. I have not." He planted his feet a little farther apart and studied the chamber's metal-panel ceiling. "We're all concerned by the indications of cooperation between Three Zed and Echo Six. Their rivalry runs deep, though. They may fail utterly as a unit."

"I'm so sick of waiting for something to blow up. I'm not complaining, Brenn, but I'll be mightily glad when this, especially, is over." She splayed a hand on her belly.

"You're the one who's determined to hang on here," Brennen said as the lift stopped and the doors parted.

She walked off. "I carry two potential heirs to the N'Taian throne, and the Electorate will demand witnesses to their parentage."

"Didn't you intend to give all that up?"

"Yes, for myself. But I want my sons to have all the options."

Brennen paused just outside the parking hangar. "You don't need witnesses to prove parentage," he said gently.

"They'll have enough trouble with the Electorate without my ignoring *all* the traditions."

"That's not like you."

She pressed her lips together.

The earnest expression on Brennen's face matched the determination she felt in him. "You must not forget that their safety, their survival, must remain our highest priority."

"I know," she muttered. He would never force her to run for sanctuary unless absolutely convinced of its necessity, would he? She stepped into the parking bay and found her path blocked by a stocky form. Bosk Terrell.

Not now! she moaned as she halted in midstride.

"Mistress." He spread his hands. "You seem agitated. Is all well?"

"No. My sister has been hurt. Carradee, the Queen."

Terrell extended a hand. "I'm so sorry."

Firebird had to accept his gesture. As his fingers closed, prickles danced up her arm. She pulled away as quickly as decorum allowed.

Brennen stepped closer, and she caught his sidelong glance. He had sensed her recoil and her attempt at control, she guessed, and now shielded her in his own cloud of epsilon energy static, less to protect her than to save himself from embarrassment. "Not good news," he remarked. "An explosion in the palace. But she's said to be mending quickly."

Terrell rubbed his fingertips together. "Terrible. Please convey my wishes for a speedy recovery." Shaking his head, he slipped by them into the corridor.

"Brenn," Firebird whispered, leaning in his direction. "I know what it is about him. He treats me *too* politely. Like someone who's not supposed to live much longer. Like a Wastling."

"Too politely?" Brennen stared up the passway after Terrell. "He's clean. He passed his retesting and security review."

"I know he did. I trust him all the less for it. If he has lowered his A.S. rating, he could fool the review board, too."

Chapter 7

Waste the Man

sinistro
sinister

Juddis Adiyn watched Polar stalk across his richly carpeted office. Polar was bristling and not bothering to conceal it. *That woman. That woman!* He raised a hand to flick at the new light sculpture on Adiyn's wall, a glowing, three-dimensional work of art replacing the geometric print Adiyn had sliced. *Gold-plated guano! I've never seen such arrogance! You should have seen her, pulling the ears of that pruupa pup Tulleman culled, and trying to force it to look into her eyes. As if she could do anything to it.*

She had the epsilon strength, you know, before she took a vanity implant.

Polar extended his shield again, dimming the heat of his presence from Adiyn's scanning. *Of course,* Adiyn felt him subvocalize on a tight wave. *And if she's an average for the line, the sister could be dangerous. But they're deadheads. Untrained. I would almost rather put our Princess into stasis than humor her. All she can talk about is 'When will we send her back in triumph?' She'd be better company frozen.*

Think of it as a training exercise, Polar. Adiyn lit his comscreen. Polar wandered back toward the star-filled projection tank beside Adiyn's long desk, his black mood enveloping him like a vacuum suit.

The office door slid open and a girl of about nine Standard years, one of Polar's subadult charges, entered with fresh kaffa and flatcakes on a warming tray. She set it on a corner of the desk and turned to hurry out.

"One minute, Millia."

Adiyn glanced at the girl. At the sound of Polar's audible, contemptuous voice, she stiffened.

Adiyn watched passively. Someone had to eliminate the substandard children, of course. Polar showed a genuine warmheartedness toward the little ones, most of the time. But the children learned quickly to avoid Polar's temper, knowing what it stirred in him. Even a child would sense it now.

Polar glided forward to tower over her. "Your Phase Three evaluations were less than perfect, I hear. What was that about a refusal?"

Your son Jerric got in my way, Commander, and I feared to cross him. She stumbled back a step.

"There is another blot on your record already. Can we remove those blots? Or must we eliminate a child who shows too much weakness?"

Adiyn shut off the comscreen. "Kaffa, Polar?" he asked in a soothing voice.

Certainly. To the girl, Polar said, "Let us do this. Go down to my offices. Access the computer, bring up your life file, and enter the termination program. In a few minutes we shall determine together if it will be carried out."

The girl's cheeks became paler yet. *Sir.* She fled the office.

Polar took a cup and lowered himself onto the chair. *I don't know. Millia has tried very hard to overcome her shortcomings. I would miss her, I think.*

Adiyn shrugged. *Do your job: whatever is best for the Unbound.* Inhaling the kaffa's warm scent, he offered the tray of cakes. Rage lingered just below the surface of Polar's control: Adiyn felt him struggling with it as he shook his head in refusal. Adiyn set down the tray.

Polar lifted his cup, sipped, and then slammed it down, sloshing kaffa onto the desk top. *Scorch the girl! If she can't do something so simple as serve kaffa at the proper temperature . . .*

He stood. Adiyn felt his anger escape, and with it rose his distinctive greed. Somehow he had come to cherish deep contact with the doomed and dying, sharing their moment of supreme terror. Polar reached into his sash for the striker, paused, then shifted his hand and drew a bootknife. *Sometimes, these little things make all the difference.*

An hour later, Phoena laid down a fine-bristled brush and patted her waves of chestnut hair into a frame around her face, admiring the straight line of her nose, her clear complexion, her perfectly symmetrical lips. Tedious though her days at Three Zed had become, with only a few scanbooks for company in this blue-walled pair of windowless rooms, by night she had made a study of a new sort of prey. Dru Polar mystified her, cold but strong, a masterful contrast to her spineless little prince-of-convenience. On Naetai the attention of every eligible heir had been hers to appropriate since she could remember. But this new, heady game intoxicated her with victory as his defenses began to crumble before her beauty, her perfection and regality. Last night, after a week's play, she had finally allowed him to hope for conquest. She laughed silently. The idiocy of the notion, that anyone might hope to rule *her!* And what a feather in her cap this would be, to claim the second-in-command of all the Shuhr for her lover!

She lowered her eyes and blinked coquettishly at the attractive image in the mirror, then started. Two images gazed back at her, the second, that of a long, black-eyed face, expressionless and compelling.

"Drat you, Dru!" she scolded his image. "Don't you know better than to sneak up on a woman like that?" She whirled on the stool and thrust a long finger up toward his face.

He caught her hand, bowed his head slightly, and pressed her palm against his cheek. "Don't be angry, Phoena. I have had a long afternoon, very tiring. I hoped your lovely smile would open a more pleasant evening."

Abruptly devoid of indignation, she decided she rather liked the situation. "You have nice enough manners, when you remember them," she said with a particular toss of her head she had found irresistible to N'Taian nobles. "Perhaps dinner, then, to begin that evening?"

Some time later, they sat leaning against one another on the cushioned lounger in her outer room, sipping a sweet exotic tea from Sabba Seven-Gamma or some such world. Drowsy now, she held the plastene cup as delicately as if it had been her gold-edged porcelain at the N'Taian palace. "Dru," she sighed. "When have you last had—had . . ." She found herself stammering.

"Yes?"

"I . . ." This inexplicable confusion interfered with her contentment. "I forgot. I'm sure it wasn't important."

Nodding, he laughed softly, knowingly. Not a nice laugh at all, but she liked it.

She combed the ends of his glossy black hair with her fingers. Finding a tiny clump of something that looked like dried blood, she pulled it free of his hair and flicked it aside. "Dru?"

"Your *Royal* Highness?"

How she loved the sound of that. She set the cup beside her on the squat end table and pulled her legs up onto the lounger. "Tell me when you'll make me Queen."

Polar lifted his chin. "Soon, little bird. Soon you'll be queen of all you can see. All Naetai will bow at your feet," he added with a sweep of his fingertips.

She sniffed.

"That's what you wanted to hear, isn't it?"

"I want the truth."

"Ah, the truth." He stretched languorously and slipped an arm onto the lounger behind her. "Would you *truly* like to know what concerns me?"

She nodded.

"Some day, Phoena Angelo, that megaterrestrial government that calls itself a Federacy will tear itself apart, world by world. Mind you, the unbound starbred will have had a hand in that. It is quick and easy to seize a freighter, give its crew to space and bring its cargo to Three Zed or Echo Six, or to neutralize an isolated world. But to bring our own men, unsuspected, into positions of authority within an institution the size of the Federacy —ah, that takes time. And care. At the least suspicion we must waste the man. But Phoena, we are growing stronger than we ever have been. One day soon we will take the hate and fear the common human has for the Sentinel. And we will *twist* . . ." One-handed, he grappled with some invisible force. "Who better to do it? In terror, the Federacy will shake itself free of them. Then *we* will have the Federacy. World by world, as we choose to take it. And we will keep it, safe from alien intrusion."

"Safe." She stared at his open hand. Wouldn't he touch her? "And you? What will you . . . You've never really explained to me what you do here, Dru. What *is* a, a 'Testing Commander?' "

He barely smiled. "I am a guide in evolution, my dear Princess. I believe you might enjoy certain aspects of my duties. I will show you, one day soon. But not now. Now you will sleep. I am tired."

The last thing she saw before waking the next morning was that pale, blue-veined hand, as he reached toward her forehead.

Ten floors below his own office, in the main dome of Thyrica's Home Forces, Staff Officer Bosk Terrell sealed both ends of a silvery message cylinder, then set it on the desk of the unoccupied cubicle. He let his shielding cloud of epsilon static diffuse and remained in a position of mental silence, alert, attuned for eavesdropping, but sensed none. He was undetected still.

Eyeing the cylinder, he frowned. He hated to send it. *They* would not like the news.

But other news, public enough for Them to hear of it, necessitated this. If They didn't hear first from him, They'd suspect insubordination.

Tucking the cylinder under his arm, he slipped out into the passway.

He had his contingency plans. He wasn't finished yet. He guessed what his next assignment would be: no more waiting, watching, or listening.

There would be a strike.

At last.

Six days later, deep below Three Zed's dome, in a vast cavern lit with true-wavelength lamps, Dru Polar halted in midstride and touched one finger to his belt. Beyond him, the huge pittena he had tracked nearly to the kill bounded away, parting an aisle through tall grass. *Of all times Adiyn would call*. "Polar," he said aloud.

"News," said the Eldest's voice in his belt speaker. "Private and important. Come up."

So much for vacation. "I'm on my way," he said, with a last glance after the fleeing cat.

Without explaining, Adiyn played Polar the coded disk, rerecorded at Bishniac from Terrell's message. When it ended, Polar stomped away. The deep, red-gray carpet of Adiyn's office absorbed the sound of his footfalls, but even in dim light Adiyn could see open anger on Polar's face.

He knew better than to waste a messenger this time. Adiyn chuckled.

Polar did not look over his shoulder. *Who in chaos could have requested his rescreening?*

Adiyn shrugged. *His cover was perfect, absolutely perfect. Twenty years clandestine and not a quark of a suspicion. Now this. At least he reported the rescreening.*

Dechow would've if he hadn't. Terrell isn't stupid.

He claims, Adiyn sent, *the retesting could be random, it proceeded with absolute consistency, and we're not to worry. But I think he's under suspicion. Someone spotted him.*

Caldwell?

He's the only new arrival in Soldane who could have, I think.

Blast Caldwell to atoms, Polar subvocalized hotly. *So Terrell's cover is gone. What now?*

I'm ordering him to attempt a personal attack. He's the best we have. If he fails . . . Adiyn shrugged again, observing that Polar's rising temper boded ill for someone. *There are others. He's no good as a clandestine any more.*

Not too soon. He'll be watched. Suggest he not report for several dekia: deepest cover, until other concerns crowd out any of their suspicions. According to Phoena's impressions, Caldwell's Firebird will be entrenching and getting ready to scramble for power, even to head back for Naetai, perhaps, so her newborn will have a chance at the N'Taian throne. They think they need a N'Taian witness of birth, for some reason. Have Dechow keep her penned until Terrell judges it's time to strike. At least two months, three would be better. Above all, don't let him jump too early.

And Caldwell?

The girl first. She's their weak link.

Not so weak, perhaps, sent Adiyn.

Oh, come. Against Terrell?

Chapter 8

Tellai

risoluto assai
very resolutely

A week later, the administrative affairs of Base One were winding down for the afternoon when Brennen saw a light pulse twice on the communications panel recessed into the left margin of his wide desk. A message from Captain Frenwick, just beyond the wall at her station in the quadrangle, followed in five seconds.

"Man to see you," said the desk. "No appointment, claims urgent."

Brennen pressed the ACKNOWLEDGE panel, then with a flicker of epsilon energy channeled through one hand he cleared a spread of papers, some into a scribebook and some, committed to Sentinel-trained memory, into a sonic shredder. The desk assigned him matched the copper-hued ironbark that lined his side of the walls, and like the office, it was almost embarrassingly expansive. He glanced up as a silvery frigate roared over on low approach.

Without hurrying, he pressed another series of panels—NAME BUSINESS QUERY?—then stared again at the frigate, now parting two squadrons on afternoon drill.

"Tellai-Angelo, Tel. Homeworld Naetai. Won't state business. Shall I spell the name?"

Tellai? Brennen reached for the touchboard quickly this time: AUDIOVISUAL CONFIRMATION QUERY?

Captain Frenwick's husky voice filtered through the com console's speaker. "Look this way, sir, for an identity check."

On the small screen inset into the desk's near corner, Brennen saw the silhouette of a slight-figured man, standing as near the dome's curving edge as his height would allow. Then the man stepped closer, into the indoor lighting. When Brennen saw the face, round, small-nosed, almost girlish, with large, soft eyes as dark as his hair, he knew him.

Brennen pressed his transmit key. "Send him in." He heard a clatter as Captain Frenwick replaced her vis-pickup in its slot, and then, "The door on the right, sir."

Brennen had cleared his desk completely by the time Tellai stepped through the door. "Please sit down, Your Highness," he said, dispersing his cloud of epsilon static to read Tellai's emotions.

Prince Tel Tellai-Angelo took the deep-cushioned black chair nearest the door, and Brennen watched him catalogue the curved ceiling of smoked glasteel, the glossy ironbark walls, and the recessed filing compartments. His long-lashed eyes stared up at a crossed pair of silver daggers, surrounded by a squadron of gold-sealed training certificates, with the framed Federate Service Cross flying lead; then down at the desk itself with its twin recessed touchboards, multiple com center, and glass and leather surface. When finally Tel faced him, Brennen acknowledged that the office's designers had succeeded. The young popinjay had been taken down several levels before he'd even spoken, and by then Brennen made a chilling guess.

"Have you heard from Princess Phoena?"

"Yes." Tellai groped into a breast pocket and drew out a folded scribepaper, but he held it tightly. "Your Excellency . . ." He cleared his throat.

"I have resigned that post, Your Highness. 'General,' please."

"General, then. I read this to Governor Danton, and he sent me to you. It is from Phoena, in her own scribing, but something's wrong with it." Brennen read a curious mixture of fear and disdain in him. "He said if anyone in the Whorl could help me, you could." He shrugged. "So I've come. I suppose I owe you an apology, if I mean to seek your help."

Help? Brennen controlled a smile. He would have liked to refuse outright—but he had an obligation to Danton, at least. "All right," he said quietly. "For the present, we'll forget your politics. I'll do what I can for you, with one condition."

He met and held the stare of the proud brown eyes. "I can't simply trust you, Tellai. You've started poorly. I must be certain that you aren't here to murder me—or Lady Firebird."

"I understand that."

"Good. Then you'll allow me mind-access, to confirm your motives?"

Tellai blanched.

"Didn't you assume I would want that?"

"I did. But I hoped you had better manners than to ask. What guarantee do I have that you won't do more than that, once you have me?"

"What are you hiding?"

Tellai looked away, and Brennen waited silently. A squadron of intercept fighters buzzed the dome, and Brennen wished heartily that he were flying one of them rather than watching this weak-willed N'Taian aristocrat squirm in a black jassethide chair. He fingered the smooth leather of his desk top.

The Prince probably had plenty to hide, for Tel Tellai had supported Phoena's plotting for the throne since before Naetai had fallen to the Federacy; still, their power games interested him less than Tellai's frame of mind. Tellai posed a new threat to himself and his family, a threat that had to be canceled quickly.

The silence wore on. Finally, Brennen spoke again. "Do you want my help or not, Your Highness?"

"Yes," Tellai mumbled. "What must I do?"

"Look this way."

Brennen caught him, held him, and probed gingerly at the surface emotional layer of Tel's alpha matrix. He confirmed the hostility to and terror of himself, dominant in a web of plans and dreams that was utterly tangled and uncontrolled. Tellai did not know his own heart any better than when Brennen had first probed him, back in the Lieutenant Governor's office at Sae Angelo. Something in Tellai's misplaced pride recalled the labyrinth that had once been Firebird's emotional state.

Then a foreign image flew through the back of his awareness, one of the rare flashes of insight he had been trained to catch and hold. Although too misty to visualize, it left him with the impression Tel Tellai held a pivotal point in his own future—but neither how nor why. Startled, he paused in his probing, then withdrew, brushing delicately at the fear and suspicion to calm Tellai.

Tel shook his head as if trying to throw off the probe Brennen had already withdrawn. "That's all the time it takes you?"

Brennen closed his eyes for a few seconds, then said, "I know what I need to know about your motives and very little else, in that time. Now tell me why you came, and I'll help you if I can."

"Thank you, General. I never thought I'd be glad of your abilities, but they've saved me a long, convincing speech. Here." He handed the paper across the desk's black scribing pad.

The normal, momentary weariness was passing. Brennen unfolded the sheet to book-page size and pressed it flat against a rectangular glass inset. "I'd like to duplicate this for my records."

"Granted," Tellai said stiffly.

Brennen turned the sheet over, pressed a concealed panel with his knee, then picked up the letter again.

Darling Tel,
 I am safe and can write you now. We have friends at Three Zed with the power we need to accomplish all our aims. Keep Carradee calm—don't let her go rushing off to Danton. She needn't.

She was alive, then, but in Shuhr hands. Brennen glanced up. "How *is* Her Majesty?"

Tellai fidgeted with a silver jacket button. "She's nearly well. It's Daithi they're worried about now—or, that is, when I left Naetai."

"Yes?"

"He's . . . that is . . . Carradee's not saying, but no one has seen him since the explosion."

Brennen read on.

They are treating me respectfully, so you needn't worry. Soon we'll be together, and Naetai will be put to rights again.
                                          Till then,
                                          Your love,
                                          Phoena

Brennen rested his chin on his hand. Even though he and Phoena had avoided one another scrupulously since the aborted cease-fire negotiations over Naetai, he had occasionally dealt with her in his role as temporary Lieutenant Governor for the occupation. This letter's tone was all wrong. "Have you anything else in her scribing? Something older?"

Tellai blushed vividly. "I do, sir, but it is extremely personal."

"I won't copy it, then. But I need to see it."

Brennen stared up into Tellai's eyes. Having just held him under access, he could read his emotions with greater sensitivity, and Tellai struggled transparently between hope and indignation. Brennen waited. One man would emerge from this meeting the acknowledged dominant.

Finally, the slender nobleman drew a tri-D from his pocket and slid it across to Brennen. It was a portrait of Phoena in tiara and robe, and its calligraphic message was personal indeed, accepting his proposal of marriage and promising revenge together on the Federacy and several other enemies, including Firebird. Ignoring the contents of the texts, Brennen placed them side by side and compared scripts.

"Come around, Tellai, and let me show you something." Tel hurried around the desk to stand by his shoulder. Brennen pointed to several short words that occurred in both texts. "Can you see the difference in the rhythm of her strokes? The hand is the same, but the cadence has changed significantly."

"Didn't Phoena write this, then?"

"I believe she did. If it's a forgery it is superb, but I think we can assume she is alive."

Tellai rested a trembling hand on the desk. "Have they done something to her mind, Caldwell?"

"It's likely, I'm afraid. That would account for the changed cadence and for the tone of the letter, which reads 'not Phoena' to both of us. I don't think she's been brainset, nor irreversibly altered, but they've probably lulled her to keep her under control."

Tellai swallowed hard and pocketed the portrait. "Then I'll tell you what I think. I think she went to them out of anger, when we all thought it was rather nice that Firebird was having a baby."

Brennen started. "You did?"

"Well, yes, Carradee and I both did. I'm afraid that Phoena does intend to help these people kill Firebird and . . . Carradee, too. But I don't want to see either of them hurt. And—Phoena has a bad habit of underestimating other people. These Shuhr . . ." Shrinking from his speculation, Tellai walked away. "Once they have taken what they want from her, will they keep her alive and leave her be?"

"They might, if they think she could be of some use to them."

"Make her a puppet queen?"

"Possibly." But even as he said it, Brennen guessed the Shuhr had no need of a symbolic ruler for Naetai.

Tellai halted with his back turned. "Danton thought you might be able to help."

"I might," Brennen returned carefully. "One way or another."

"Would you help me try to get her away from these people? I have resources—the cost of fuel would be no problem. . . ."

"Why did you come to me?" Brennen pressed both forearms against the edge of his desk. "You could have joined Phoena. Why do you think now that they're dangerous and we're safe? What made you change your mind?"

Tellai addressed the diskfiles across the room. "That's not easy to answer, Caldwell. It's more a matter of what you haven't done than anything you have. I know more about you Sentinels now, and you in particular, and all I can say is, you've played things very quietly, compared with what you could have done. I can't side with you, but I do respect you—as an opponent." He wheeled suddenly. "And I need your help. Suns, Caldwell, isn't it enough that I've swallowed my guts and come to you? They're going to kill my wife if you won't help me!"

"I've told you, I'll help if I can. But I will do nothing for Phoena that endangers Firebird. Maybe you aren't aware that we're at risk ourselves."

"I understand that." Tellai slumped back into the chair. "How is she?"

"She's well."

"How long now?"

"A month and a half, Standard, if she carries full term." He felt Tellai's spirits sink as he spoke.

"I suppose you'll want to wait here for that."

"Most likely. There will be other factors to consider, as well. I have professional commitments." He drew a deep breath. "It would take time to decide how to move, and whom to leave with Firebird when she's most vulnerable. *If* I were to leave Thyrica."

Tellai folded his delicate hands on his lap. "Can you find me a place to stay?"

That, sir, is exactly the problem. "You'll have to be guarded, Tellai, and I'd prefer to know precisely where you are. But I don't relish the idea of having you locked up." Brennen considered the risks, the advantages, and his wavering glimpse of the shebiyl. "I'll make an offer with a price."

"Offer away. I can probably afford it."

"The price is a deeper access. I want to know how you stand in this intrigue, and why. If you can convince me you're not a danger to us, you may stay at our home—if Firebird approves. You can assume she and I always go armed, and we have an extensive security system in the house. The only alternative I can see is protective custody here on the Base."

"Nothing else?"

Clearly Tellai hated to put himself under his supervision—and control. Brennen shook his head. "That's all I can offer."

"You have all the cards." Tellai laid his head against the back of the chair and stared at the ceiling. "Which would you prefer?"

Brennen stood and walked around to a chair beside the abashed young Prince, then sat down, close enough to touch him. Tellai blinked rapidly. "I know how to keep secrets, Tellai, and a very strict code of law controls my use of anything I learn."

"No brainsetting. No—what did you call it, 'altering.' "

"None."

Tellai covered his face with his hands, still struggling.

"They've been in there for over an hour, Damalcon," said Ellet Kinsman.

Air Master Dardy plunked one foot on his desktop and shrugged, smiling with all his facial features and his alpha matrix.

Leaning back on the cushion of his extra office chair, Ellet examined her fingers. "Of all the complications we don't need." *Another Angelo,* she thought behind her static shields. *I would to the holy Word they had all been smothered in the cradle.* What right did they have to meddle in the affairs of the Sentinel kindred?

She felt an answering sweep of comforting frequency and glanced back at the tall man behind the desk. Damalcon Dardy, like Brennen Caldwell, was a gentleman.

Yes, there was the shamah. If indeed the popular interpretation was correct, the Angelos were a necessary pestilence. Still. If Prince Tel Tellai–Angelo made enough of a pest of himself, Brennen would wish he'd taken Ellet's advice. She had tried her utmost to prevent all this. Brennen was reaping the harvest he had sown back at VeeRon. He hadn't simply married First Major Firebird Angelo. He had wed into a turbulent family in a position of power, something he should have considered far more carefully than he seemed to have done. He'd been blinded by a connatural matrix. . . .

Pair bonding might last until death, but Firebird Angelo was not the kind of woman to enjoy a long life. She'd take the wrong risk, someday. Hopefully, someday soon.

Dardy levitated a stylus and passed it from one hand to the other. *They may all have to run for it before long.*

True enough. The Shuhr could be following Tellai. *They shouldn't have left Hesed. Not Firebird, at any rate, if they were truly concerned about the Lost of Auria shamah, about uniting the bloodlines in safety. About Brennen Caldwell's genes.* She looked over at him, abruptly curious. *Are they planning to go? What do you know about it?*

Dardy touched the stylus to his forehead. *If they were actually planning, and if I knew anything, it'd be confidential, Ellet. But I'm not in on all Caldwell's confidences. There's deep water in that sea.*

I understand. He feels much too cordial, she thought in the quiet, shielded corner of her mind. Could he be building toward a connaturality probe?

She shuddered, deep inside, at the notion. For one man only, she was prepared to wait half a lifetime, if necessary. Not Dardy.

The texture of Dardy's presence abruptly changed. *Quiet*, he urged.

Surprised to mental inactivity, Ellet felt a subtle, eavesdropping tendril of energy slip away. She should have sensed *that*. Was she so distracted by Dardy's attentions as not to notice . . .

How strange. It tasted of *Terrell*. Now, why would he—

Dardy reached for his intercom unit and pressed two keys. "This is Dardy, Terrell. You wanted me?"

After a moment's pause, a synthetic voice answered. "Staff Officer Terrell is not in his office at present. Should you wish to leave a—"

Dardy stabbed at the desktop, and the voice cut off. He raised one eyebrow.

"He could be looking for me." Ellet pressed up out of the chair. "Key over to my office."

She walked around the desk and stood close beside Dardy as he punched in another numerical code. "Captain Kinsman," began the simulated voice, "is not—"

Ellet rapidly pressed numbers on the keypad. After a moment's pause, the desk spoke again. "No messages, Captain Kinsman. Thank you for checking in."

She drew away from the panel, and from Dardy's leg, which she had been unconsciously leaning against. "I wonder who he *was* looking for," she said.

Chapter 9

Outsider

schietto
sincerely

The comscreen's persistent whistle interrupted Firebird's best session yet on the blazer simulator. Holding the portable firing unit, she hurried through the empty nursery to the master bedroom and keyed the console over onto "answer" mode. Brennen's face appeared.

"Mari?"

She sat down on the white-covered bed. "Brenn. What is it? Someone for dinner?"

"No. Tellai is here. He has fled Naetai."

"Here?" she gulped.

"He came to ask my help for Phoena."

"Any confirmation on where she is?"

"Yes. Alive, but with the Shuhr. Of her own accord, it appears."

Firebird groaned. "He's serious?"

"Yes. I took him under access, and he means us no harm. He loves that woman with a kind of selflessness that borders on idolatry. He's in the waiting area now. Would you be willing to take him in, until I decide whether or not I can give him any actual assistance?"

Dangling the mock pistol off one finger, Firebird laughed. "Say that again, Brenn?"

He did.

She shook her head. "Do you mean to let him live with us?"

"I don't think you have reason to fear him. He actually seems rather devoted to you. But he's terrified for Phoena's sake. He has reason to be."

"Of course." Sweet-face Tellai, Firebird snorted silently. The only man on Naetai fool enough to give himself to her bloodsucking sister.

"Are you all right, Mari?"

She glanced back up to the screen. "You offered him a place?"

"I did, contingent on your approval."

She was glad Brennen sat too far away to pick up her scorn. "If you've offered him a place, I can't turn him away. I'm as much a Tellai as he is; his grandfather was my father Irion's elder brother. Look at Tel. Small-boned and short. Just like me."

"We can reprogram the sec system if he would worry you."

"I trust your judgment, Brenn." She brushed her hair back from her face. "And your ability to Command him, if necessary. If you say he's safe, he can come."

"Thank you, Mari. I'll tell him."

"I'll set up a place in the extra bedroom." She touched off the screen and then sat awhile, staring into Thyrica's mists and shaking her head.

Brennen breakfasted with Tel and Firebird the following morning. When finally she sent him off to his University Advisory Board briefing, it was with a touch of irritation at his hovering. He had never hovered like that before.

The jetcraft's roar died away, until she could hear only the dripping of mossy trees. Firebird returned to the table by the long window, sat down across from Tellai, and folded her hands. "All right, he's gone. You have other questions, don't you?"

Tellai brushed a speck of dust from his black sateen knickers. He'd come to them without a tailor or a dresser, poor thing. "Well, yes, I do. Especially about him."

That N'Taian accent—it sounded so "right." She wondered if she had begun to speak like a Thyrian. "I know," she said. "I've been there."

"Has he—has he twisted you, Firebird? Forced your mind—brainset you . . . ?"

She took a deep breath. "Tel, Brennen spent months waiting for me to settle my own mind about the Federacy. The Sentinels are forbidden to impose their convictions on other people, with the death penalty if they're caught in disobedience." She wrapped

her hands around her cruinn cup. "That's the chief difference
between Sentinel and Shuhr, as I see it: One group obeys a strict
system of authority, even as the other seeks to destroy it. Brennen
gave me reference materials, he willingly answered questions, but
he never, never forced." Of her original struggle with him, and
her more current secret search into Sentinel ways, she said nothing.

"But he trapped you." Tellai's voice trembled. "We all know
that. He met you, and *zzt*, he wanted you. That's not natural,
Firebird."

How did Tel know that? She sighed. "They call it 'connaturality,' when two individuals' minds work the same yet their personalities balance each others' strengths and needs. They're trained
to stay alert for connatural individuals simply because they can
marry no one else. Only the highly connatural can pair bond, and
Brennen's nature is not quite like most of the starbred. He was
unable to find a mate he wanted near his own age among them."

"What did you think of all that?"

"He frightened me. But he offered something very tempting."

Tel arched one eyebrow.

"Life." Firebird stared into the green shadows outside. "Life
with honor, and a cause I found I could believe in. And now, an
enemy to fight together."

Tellai pulled his hands into his lap at the mention of that enemy.
"Do the Sentinels really believe in this—folk prophecy?"

Firebird gave a short laugh. "This particular shamah was made
by their eleventh spiritual leader, or Shamarr. Some Sentinels can
glimpse the future—they call what they see the shebiyl, and it's
a matter of extremely high talent to be able to catch it at all—so
you see, because of their skills they *must* believe in it."

"Oh. Ah. I suppose General Caldwell sees it, then."

"Occasionally, yes."

He rested an elbow on the table. "These Shuhr, then. Who are
they, Firebird?"

"Aurian-Thyrian starbred like Brennen, with mental abilities
like his, but who have left the Sentinels to use their talents against
others. Outlaws, and their descendants. What I know is pretty
grim, Tel. Are you sure you want to hear it from me? I can access
the Federate Register from this terminal."

"Would you, Firebird?"

"Just a minute. I'll refill the cups."

As she made her way toward the kitchen for the cruinn pitcher,
she recalled a conversation over kaffa, at a reception given when
Brennen arrived on Base.

• • •

"There *are* basic flaws in the way the Shuhr operate." Air Master Dardy had looked away from Brennen and fingered the rim of his cup. "They always seem reluctant to set events in motion themselves, taking advantage rather of others' mistakes: seizing others' unguarded goods, playing on variables others have deemed important. Perhaps they see that as less random, more certain. We *have* heard that they breed for talent. The birth rate on Shuhr colonies is reportedly ten times that of Thyrica, but their population does not increase. Their child mortality rate would be astronomical."

Firebird hadn't heard that before. "Genetic problems? Inbreeding?"

"Yes, and eliminations. Only a few would be allowed to survive to adulthood. Rumor says that all their children gestate in wombbanks, and only those who eventually pass the eliminations learn whose genes they carry." Dardy gave Firebird a significant look.

So he knows about N'Taian tradition. They probably all do, and they're just too polite to say anything. "And those who survive the eliminations perpetuate the system?" she said. "You're right. That's not so different from what our aristocracy practices. What effect do you think that would have on a parent, bringing a child to existence intending only to—to . . ." To her surprise, she could speak no farther.

Brennen sat down beside her. "The practice of heir limitation is outlawed now," he said firmly. "Naetai is a Federate protectorate."

How solemn he had looked. Firebird cradled the cruinn pitcher with both hands and walked back toward Tel, wondering if she could ever make him see Brennen as she knew him.

"All right." She sat down across from him and punched up the Federate database. "Shuhr."

That night, she settled in beside Brennen on the bed. The rosiny smell of soaked kirka trees mingled with the faint, seductive scent of her mira lily on its dish at her bedside. Two small, red eyes gleamed briefly in the darkness outside the window and then turned away, as fogwater dripped steadily. Firebird shivered. Groundside evolution on Thyrica had gone little higher than the oozy nightslugs. They might be as safe as Brennen claimed, but she could not match his blasé lack of concern when she confronted one of the arm-length creatures.

He made room for her between his arm and bare chest. "So you spent the entire day at the terminal?"

"All day. It was a real awakening for Tel." She hesitated. "He's actually not a bad sort—he cares more about his family's hospital than its Tiggaree River farm holding. And you should have seen his face when I showed him my lily. I'd forgotten how fond he is of flowers." She laid her arm on Brennen's chest.

He reached across and opened his palm on her belly. "Well, watch him," he said.

"I will." She thought for a moment. "It's a pity he got entangled with Phoena."

"He already regrets it, although he won't admit that to himself. He was young and envied power. She needed to distract Carradee from the Hunter Height scandal, and he offered her a wedding. But he's loyal. He'll still defend her with his life if I'll give him the chance."

"He's afraid of you."

A baby kicked under Brennen's hand. He laughed softly. "Ninety percent of the people I know fear me. I've learned to live with that."

It would bother him. But there was pride in his complaint, too.

"I trust you to gentle him for me."

"He's a child," she answered.

Brennen arranged a long curl down her throat and between her breasts. "He's growing up fast, in the face of this crisis."

"Do that again," she whispered.

He was already plucking up another curl.

The following day, Tel prepared breakfast. In return, Firebird tucked a shock pistol into her belt and invited him into the "study."

He hung back as the door slid shut, closing them into the broad, well-lit corridor floored with springy blue mats. Coincidentally, they matched the lace on his shirt front. Firebird crossed to a cabinet and palmed its locking panel. The door rolled upward and vanished into the wall, and hearing Tellai step up behind her, she moved aside to let him peer in.

"Are those weapons?" he murmured. "But they're all different."

"Of course. If Brennen was to work in different regions of the Federacy, he had to be familiar with different sorts of hand weapons. Most of these are basic energy-pulse blazers." She hefted one with an awkward, cubic collimating chamber. "But not all are easy to draw. I thought this collection would interest you."

Tel examined a tiny, bluemetal projectile gun that nestled with room to spare in his long hand. "Where did he get them? Surely these weren't all issued to him."

"You're right. He'd have had to return any issue weapons. No," she said thoughtfully, "I think each of these has a different story. Some I suspect he claimed from their late owners."

Tel nodded slowly, laid down the gun, and stepped away.

She pressed a touchpanel just inside the cabinet to drop and lock the slatted door. "Come to this end, Tel." Stepping lighter on the practice mat than on most floors now, she led him to a computer terminal with a particularly broad screen and unusual touchboard. On the soft, slant-back chair before it, she sat and then pressed a series of keys.

The screen lit in greens and blues. "Do you recognize those cliffs, Tel?"

"I . . . ah . . . no."

"Soldane spaceport."

"What is this?"

"A flight simulator." She ran a hand over the touchboard. "Federate standard console, on loan from the depot for my sake. And now yours. Sit. First lesson."

He picked at his cuff. "No, wait, Firebird. . . ."

"I know." She pointed at him. "You'd rather sit at the uplevel terminal and read history. The protocols of Federate aristocracies?"

"History was my field, Firebird. When Father died, my schooling ended."

"Well. You never know when you might need to be able to handle a Federate craft. Particularly," she added in a gentler voice, "if you're hoping to try to find Phoena."

It was difficult to find time alone to try to Turn now, with Tel in the house, but Firebird kept trying.

Midway through that month, after the treasured final day of the dry dekia, Brennen made a surprising request over dinner. "I have asked several military Sentinels to meet here this evening, Mari." Holding his empty glass in both hands, he eyed her closely. "But it is a security matter. Would you—and Tel . . ." he nodded toward the slender prince, who sat across from her, watching shreds of a breaking fog swirl past, "mind remaining downlevel for an hour or two?"

"That would be fine," Firebird answered hastily. "Tel? You've been promising to teach me another tile game."

Settled some time later on the master bedroom's floor, she was just beginning to feel that she'd caught the hang of "Fourth Stack High" when the comscreen whistled. She twisted around to reach it. "Excuse me, Tel?"

He rose quickly and backed through a door into his own room. Then she touched a panel. "Yes?"

"Can you come up, Mari?" Brennen's voice asked. His face did not appear on the screen.

"They're gone already?"

"No. It seems we could use your help."

She felt suddenly cold and didn't know why. What could be sinister about talking with a group of military Sentinels—other than learning things she should not divulge?

He knows I've been trying to Turn.

Would that be a security matter?

She couldn't answer. She didn't know.

All this flashed through her mind in a second, and then immediately the rejoinder: If the game was up, she would accomplish nothing by hiding downlevel. "Yes, I'll—I'll be right up."

Then: *Terrell*, she thought. *He could be here, now. Why was there no picture on screen?*

She had found a wrist sheath for her dagger, an old leather one Brennen no longer used for his crystace. Hastily she buckled it on, took up the dagger in her left hand in such a way that her wrist would hide it, and then with only a few words of explanation, locked Tel into his room and headed uplevel.

She chose the greenwell staircase rather than the lift to gain a few extra seconds' composure. Sliding her right hand upward along the long spiral banister, she brushed aside tendrils of distrugia vine. When she rounded the second spiral, she caught the scent of something sweetly smoky, and between the dimmed luma globes saw a number of dark forms scattered around her living area. There sat Ellet Kinsman, leg-to-leg with—was it Damalcon Dardy?

Ellet's hawk-faced cousin Thurl Hoston, a historian, perched close to them on the darker of the long tweed loungers, and she spotted General Director Kindall, Brennen's coworker, between Hoston and a stooped but pleasant-faced woman. Two others, one sitting and one standing, she guessed she should recognize but did not. The older man beside Brennen smiled, his full lips parting to release a stream of pale smoke, as he pulled out his pipe and slid aside to make room for her. But no Terrell. Relieved, she gave her wrist a twist that bedded the dagger in its sheath.

Brennen beckoned her to sit beside him, with the pipe smoker. "Firebird, before we speak I must ask your permission to perform a shielding on the memory you will carry of this conversation. Shall I explain what that means?"

She glanced quickly around at their right shoulders. A minor constellation: Sentinels, all. Squelching the apprehension she knew they would feel in her if any had dropped shields, she said, "No need," and turned coolly to Brennen, determined to behave as correctly as at a royal reception and not shame him.

He smiled slightly, and she felt well repaid for the concession. "Thank you. Then let me explain something that has been proceeding on Base these months: a concept called Remote Individual Amplification, or Ree-a. RIA would enable a Sentinel to extend his range of epsilon influence many times, limited eventually only by the external power source."

Firebird listened, first only glad this would not concern the Turning, and then with keen interest, as Brennen and a small man standing behind the other lounger explained the theory of RIA design. Her few questions met silent smiling refusals to answer, so she never truly understood how such a thing was designed to work. Talk of epsilon carrier, though, perhaps she understood better than they thought.

Air Master Dardy slid an arm behind Ellet's shoulders. His boyish face looked uncharacteristically grave, half lit by the globe hovering over his end of the lounger. "Now suppose you explain the difficulty, Caldwell."

Brennen pressed his fingertips together and eyed her seriously, reminding her suddenly and vividly of the powerful stranger who had interrogated her a year before . . . a year? Could it have been such a long time—or so short? "I'll begin, but each of you should express your inclination. Mari, make no effort to silence your feelings, positive or negative. It is important that we know your reactions."

Their shields were down now, she knew. A queer little contraction rippled across her belly. Hoping no one had seen, she nodded and crossed her ankles.

"Thus far," Brennen said, "we have concealed the practicability of the RIA design from outsiders, Federacy and Home Forces alike, lest the nongifted worry that too much influence might make us untrustworthy. The maxim, 'Power destroys its user,' speaks well for the attitude we face."

"But we must build it now." The small design engineer peered down between Ellet Kinsman and Damalcon Dardy, and Ellet drew away from Dardy to eye the engineer. "We cannot be certain of security. Who among us is absolutely confident that no agent of the Shuhr might have probed him unaware? Even if we do not build RIA, the Shuhr eventually will."

A shiver of apprehension played Firebird's spine like the strings of a clairsa.

"Yirring." Brennen spoke past her to the pipe smoker. *Vice General Yirring!* she admonished herself. *Bosk Terrell's supervisor!*

Yirring pulled the pipe from his mouth and considered its narrow bowl. "RIA is our own. I too hesitate to allow word out. Once the Federacy knows of it, we can never recall that intelligence, and we might be forbidden to continue. I for one would feel compelled to comply with such a stricture." He looked up. "May I add, also, that my aide might be able to shed light on the subject if allowed into the RIA circle, as I proposed at our last meeting."

No! Firebird glanced at Brennen. *Oh, dear,* she thought. *Now they all know how I feel about Terrell.* Brennen ignored her. "Kindall," he said.

General Director Kindall sat forward and sent a long sidelong look past Hoston to Air Master Dardy before he spoke. "But we have built a reputation of trust over the decades, of openness on which the Federacy has come to depend. The moment word of RIA escapes, the High Command will want to know why it was not informed of the existence, even in theory, of such a weapon. We cannot consider it anything else. RIA is a weapon."

Firebird nodded slowly, wondering what conclusions the Sentinels might draw from her conflicting emotions: a thrill at RIA's potential for good or ill—concern at the clouded, vaguely hostile glances she was fielding from Ellet Kinsman and Thurl Hoston—a moment's fond salutation as some pushing limb wedged itself against her ribs—and behind all this, twin apprehensions: *What has Terrell learned about this from Yirring,* and *What are they going to do to my memory?*

"Yet the timing seems remarkable," said Thurl Hoston. "The implications of RIA to the shamah intrigue me. Perhaps the Shuhr will eventually fall to the fruit of our RIA research, if not in this generation then in the next." The white-complexioned historian waved a hand toward Firebird and Brennen. "The research must be allowed to proceed at maximum speed. For that reason I feel it should remain secret, unaffected by outside influences."

Brennen rubbed his chin. "And you, Harris?"

The engineer pushed up off the lounger to stand straight behind it. "I designed RIA with Federate service in mind. I had hoped to offer it to all the worlds of the Federacy in the trusted hands of the Thyrian Sentinels, to enhance the services we already offer: intelligence, protection, enforcement."

Dardy stretched. "Caldwell, you haven't told her how you feel."

"I'm neutral. That is why I suggested we meet here."

"You waver." Hoston stared down his aquiline nose. "We can all feel it."

Brennen nodded, picking at a tuft of upholstery, and Firebird felt doubly uncomfortable: for both of them. "This is hard, Thurl. You know how many years I spent in Federate service and where I had based my hopes for my future. But several months ago, I was unexpectedly thwarted by distrust, because I was born starbred and trained a Sentinel."

"Tierna Coll," Ellet whispered. "She wouldn't believe you, nor Firebird."

"You were no help." His irritation rose with Firebird's. "We nearly lost Naetai, and Alta—would have lost them, if Firebird and I had not intervened, against Tierna Coll's orders and your advice. At the cost of my position."

"I have apologized," said Ellet. Firebird was certain Ellet sensed their doubled, silent retort. "But your experience supports my conviction."

"Mistress Caldwell." The stooped woman beside General Director Kindall broke in. "You see now why we have called on you. Raised an outsider but bonded into our kindred, you can show the reaction of others to the situation without our breaching secrecy."

Ah. Firebird remembered her now. Mistress Kindall. "I cannot react for all outsiders, not even all N'Taians," she insisted.

"Of course, Mari. Only yourself. But vocalize how you felt, learning this had gone on without your knowledge, without even a hint from me."

"A little indignant," she admitted, "but only a little. I expect you to keep secrets from me, when they are of military significance. I felt very curious: I wanted to know how it would work. But a year ago, I might have asked if nothing could be done to suppress these people."

"You see?" Ellet's short black hair framed a glowering face. " 'Suppress.' The word is hers, Brennen, your own Mistress."

"Anything else, Mari?" Brennen asked calmly, not quite looking her way.

Firebird thought back to her early impressions of the Sentinel kindred. "Has it occurred to you that no Sentinel sits on the Regional Council? This Federate Region includes Thyrica."

"And twenty other systems. We know that." Dardy smiled tolerantly and managed to look a little less charming. "We prefer to maintain middle rank when we serve the Federacy."

"But why?" She tried to straighten her back. "Does something keep the Federates from trusting a Sentinel with power? We're told you virtually founded the Federacy. But has there ever been a Sentinel on the High Command?"

"No," said Brennen.

"Why not? I have wondered if Sentinels avoided positions of such authority to prevent the kind of accusations you're trying to rule out now. But if you people have not brought about this absence voluntarily, perhaps you should reevaluate just how deeply the Federacy trusts you. You could be mistaken."

"Yes." Brennen's voice trailed off to a sigh. She sensed that she had stirred his emotions deeply; pride was involved, and the depth of his commitment to his people, but also his ambition, and an odd feeling of a-job-not-done.

And these were out in the open for all his brother and sister Sentinels to see.

"What else, Mistress Firebird?" asked General Director Kindall.

She took a long breath of the smoky air. "We all fear what we can't control," she said quietly. "You Sentinels have struck an extremely delicate balance over the years simply to maintain acceptance among the Federates, your allies."

After a long silence, Brennen spoke. "Any other reactions, anything at all? It will be impossible for you to speak of this later, unless I remove the block I am about to place."

Firebird hesitated. The curious part of her wondered how the epsilon carrier might function in that operation, even as apprehension gathered again. Working in her memory . . . what might Brennen discover about her Turning . . . before all these witnesses?

Wresting her feelings back to the matter at hand, she searched them carefully.

"No," she finally said. "That's all."

He reached toward her. "You will remember," he said in his calmest voice, misreading her alarm. "But if you try to speak, or if anyone outside this group tries to probe the matter, your memory will divert the query." He pressed a finger to her forehead and closed his eyes. She felt nothing, waiting silently, scarcely breathing.

A minute later, he straightened and leaned back against the lounger. The only resonance she caught was his continuing unease, most likely concerning the RIA question. "Thank you, Mari. You have been a great help."

"Yes," said General Yirring. "As you were in calling attention to the matter of reducing one's A.S. rating. We are glad to have you among us, Mistress Firebird."

Coming from another man, that remark would have eased her urgent need to find a niche in this society. As it was, she felt chilled. Was his aide what she feared?

She rode the lift this time, still wondering if Brennen had found in her memory the work, the frustration, the study she had already invested in his people's ways—or if he even realized she had shut him out of that field of effort.

A silvery message roll lay at the corner of Brennen's desk when he reached it the next morning. Before examining the cross-space cylinder, he touched up his day's schedule on screen, ran a check on Bosk Terrell's duties, then carefully noted all times of probable contact. He had done this every day since Firebird voiced her suspicion.

Then he reached for the cylinder—and glared. A long-familiar row of letters and numerals gleamed on one retaining ring, and Regional Command, Alta, had little reason to contact him any more. Brennen slipped a finger into the mechanism, automatically thumbing the slick security seal. The roll opened along one seam, and he pulled free a sheet of translucent paper. A golden Consular crest flared at one corner.

He scanned the sheet hastily, laid it upside down on the black scribing pad, and then sat motionless, resisting a sinking sensation and anger he did not want clouding his faculties. Mentally, he scanned the summons again.

General Coordinator Caldwell, Greetings.

Regarding: The disappearance of Her Highness Princess Phoena Angelo of the Naetai Protectorate System.

Certain of our scout stations confirm the passing of a subspace wake matching that of a craft posted to us by Governor Danton of Naetai, and its course toward the Zed system of the Shuhr.

If Her Highness has indeed been abducted by that people, repercussions among other Federate-protectorate peoples could be disturbing. "Protectorate" status implies enforced safety for a people under our shield.

Lady Firebird's status remains dubious with the N'Taian people, and measures have been proposed in some quarters to petition the Federacy again for revocation of her citizenship. Technically she remains under "protective custody," as you well know, as the Surety for her conduct.

Because of your intimate knowledge of the N'Taian aristocracy, the Regional Council requests that you assist Special Operations in the matter of Princess Phoena, as an independent operator. Our reciprocation would include your restoration to full Security I privileges, and also to eligibility for use of Federate facilities, even should you remain in Thyrian service.

Admiral Jay Madden
On Behalf, F.R.C.

Chilled despite his control by the implicit threat against Firebird, Brennen turned the paper and fingered the familiar crest. So Phoena's whereabouts were public news now—but not the fact that she had gone to the Shuhr of her own accord.

He understood the Federacy's tenuous state of affairs, trying to confirm its ability to protect citizens of its subjected state, and yet to avoid premature conflict with the Shuhr. But his own position had abruptly become more delicate still. Scanning the final sentence, he confirmed its unwritten, underlying message: If ever he hoped to return to Federate service, requisition a Federate ship, or use Security channels . . .

Still, he felt confident he *could* pull off a rescue. He'd managed more difficult things before, and to get back on track for the High Command, the risk might be worth it.

He eyed the cylinder once more, hoping to find reply passage prepaid. It was not. They did not request an answer; he was simply to go, secretly and without overt support. If he failed in the effort, Mari would have only this sheet of paper to prove Regional's request for his action. He had seen Federate pensions granted on such evidence to widows and widowers with dependents. He slid the paper toward the copying panel.

Then he hesitated, one hand over the touchboard.

What would she say to that? He pursed his lips and watched a transport soar over his slice of the smoked glas :el dome. Firebird would accept no pittance from Alta. He would not mention the message, neither to her nor anyone else. But neither would he tell Alta he did not feel inclined to comply—yet.

He shifted his hand over the touchboard and keyed his "at-station" code to Captain Frenwick outside, then turned his attention to his schedule, dropping the translucent sheet into the shredder.

Chapter 10

. . . From New Life . . .

> *stringendo*
> pressing, becoming faster

Particles of the Federate communiqué were settling in Brennen's waste bin when, back on Trinn Hill, Firebird straightened and took a long, deep breath. Something like a strong hand seemed to grip her belly and squeeze.

She set her morning cruinn on the kitchen counter and stared out into the rain. *Is that you?* she asked the twins. *You're awfully early.*

Because Brennen's mind was reaching toward her in sympathy, he felt her flicker of realization and dread. And—what was this?—a flickering sense of danger streaked across the back of his epsilon matrix.

Something's going to go wrong.

He touched up his clearing captain on the desk console.

"Sir?"

"Captain Frenwick," he said in a deliberately modulated voice. "Cancel my appointments, please. I'm wanted at home."

College, he told himself as he hurried to his parking area. *Spieth will help her. Twins often come early.* That glimpse of the shebiyl . . . was probably entirely unrelated.

• • •

Spieth had warned Firebird that labor, unmedicated as was the Sentinels' way (to prevent damage to the infants' epsilon potential), would start slowly and accelerate—and that Brennen would not be allowed to help block the pain until she was well progressed toward delivery. Walking a secluded, epsilon-fielded area of the College grounds on his arm, Firebird began to sense the acceleration. Before night fell, her labor established in earnest. Each contraction started like a jab in her lower back, then her muscles tightened around her sides, ending with the girdling stricture. Each grew just slightly harder and longer.

"All right, love?" he whispered.

The pressure eased. "Still fine."

"It's almost too dark to see, Mari. Let's go in."

"One more. Please. It may be a while before I'm out in the fresh air again."

An hour later, he insisted; then she walked with him in the medical center's misty atrium below moss-hung trees, wishing for the white stepping stones and turquoise-lit sides of Hesed's rippling pool. Controlling sensation with the skills Master Spieth had taught her, she concentrated, too, on closing out the emotional surges that originated in her body's involuntary tumult.

Breathe, she commanded herself. *Focus—relax* . . .

She clenched Brennen's arm, and she felt his deep concern. "That one hurt," she admitted.

"I think you've done as much as you should alone. I'll send for Spieth."

"No." She rested her head on his shoulder. "I . . . I'll be all right a little longer. Let her sleep."

"Too late, Mari." He touched her hand. "She's awake now."

"The contractions begin . . . how?" White hair neatly combed as if she always rose just after midnight, Master Spieth laid a thin blanket across the second tiny cot in a broad, white-walled room.

"Here." Firebird rubbed the small of her back as the precious few minutes passed between contractions, when she could speak.

At the edge of her vision, Brennen reached for a glass of water and then leaned against a long windowbar to drink it.

Spieth folded her wrinkled hands. "A woman's labor proceeds as it will. This, however, appears to be the kind that becomes long and difficult. I'm so sorry. Still, you are here, and safe."

"I wasn't supposed to have children at all." Firebird felt tender muscles tighten convulsively again, and she looked to Brennen.

She was trapped. This time Brennen stepped in. The discomfort diminished to a manageable level. Perversely, she tried to shake off his help. She ought to face the anguish, let it take her, ride through it. Clutching a high-backed chair, she rocked back and forth, and the pressure became pain as she lost control. "The Redjackets execute Wastlings who become pregnant—or abort them—"

"Stop talking! Breathe—focus—breathe, Firebird!" Startled by the Command in Spieth's voice, Firebird obeyed.

"That's better," the Master said softly when the contraction passed. Spieth came around beside her, glancing at dials on the room's side wall. "Be reasonable. Let Brennen close out the worst of it for you now. —You're doing perfectly," she said to Brennen. "Hold on." She massaged Firebird's back.

"Has Tel been sent for?" Firebird gasped. "Brennen, you must send for Tel. The Electorate will demand a witness to their parentage."

Brennen began to knead her shoulders. "He's down a level from here, reading, under guard. Quiet yourself. Review the calming pattern, quickly. Close your eyes. . . ."

Firebird complied. She dismissed conscious thought and focused her attention, as Spieth had taught her, on the image of a white wall, bare and clean and flawless. It was working!—driving her will out of the grip of pain, forcing her emotions to react to that mental picture instead of her physical turmoil. She rode through an entire contraction without Brennen's help.

Opening her eyes at its end, she grinned her triumph at him.

As hours passed, however, as night lightened to morning and then afternoon, the work became dull, wearing repetition that grew slightly more difficult at every recurrence. Firebird knew she must maintain conscious focus, but her strength was fading, her mind beginning to wander. Brennen's help eased them, but the contractions became still more painful.

Night fell a second time. Master Spieth helped her up to a sitting position on the bed. Firebird stared around her, vaguely disoriented.

"Transition phase," Spieth had announced a few minutes earlier. "Thank you, Brennen. You must let her go on alone."

Firebird had been warned. Now she must remain aware of the changes ripping through her body, so Spieth would know when delivery approached.

Whether from stress or exhaustion, all her senses had diffused, fading into a state that was not sleep—the pain rising again confirmed that—but was something less than full consciousness. Had she lapsed into a link with these frightened twins who would have Brennen's strength? Was such a thing possible?

Brennen's voice, though close at hand, sounded faint, and Spieth's lined face blurred. Only Firebird's anguish seemed real, and the image of the wall, flawless and impenetrable, that separated her from that pain. No—was it pain behind that wall, or was it her self? Where had her senses fled?

Scarcely aware that she had fallen back on the bed, Firebird closed her eyes and tried to force her will through that wall. It resisted. She pressed harder. She was through! And there on the other side, she found . . .

Terror.

She reeled back from a shifting, spinning phantasmagoria of death, but could not draw away. Figures, misty figures, lay in a tangled agony ahead of her, and the distance between her point of consciousness and theirs shrank inexorably.

All around her women died in ghastly ways, and all the apparitions were—herself.

Horrified, she tried to flee outward, to raise the wall again.

Another contraction mounted. The physical pain fed her terror, drew her into the spectacle, and joined her point of consciousness to . . .

. . . She lay face down. Cold stone pressed against her cheek, and the warm blood pooling under her chest smelled heavy, nauseating. The knife slice across her throat throbbed as each pulse deepened the sticky puddle. . . .

. . . Her vision shifted. Stars gleamed cold in the black of space; her skin shrieked with cold; she could not breathe out any longer. At any second her body would decompress, exploding all the softest membranes. . . .

. . . Shift again: The half-gloved hands of a man literally twice her size tightened slowly at her throat. The world spun and went black. . . .

. . . Then she stood at the north wall of Hunter Height, facing the traitor's fate she had so narrowly escaped ten months before. The searing disintegration began: her skin and flesh burned away as the D-rifles of the execution detail remained steady on target. . . .

She understood dimly that she had passed out of reality, that these were images she had created, over years of nights spent lying awake in her silent palace suite. She had forced herself to dwell on death and pain on those nights, had tortured herself with visions of dying lest terror reduce her to cowardice when her time came.

That part of her life was over, left behind with her Wastling fate, yet in this recess of her mind the images lived on, unforgotten and fleshed.

That recognition gave her enough presence of mind to wrench free from the center of the horrors. Battling the pain of a contraction now, too, she felt her point of perception pull out of the images' consciousness, but this "point" that was her self began to shrink as the pictured welter of images swelled.

She was dying, then, really dying this time. For what other reason would she feel as if she were vanishing, fading out of life entirely?

She would never see her sons.

Blackness spread around her. Silent it was, still and featureless.

Sudden anguish assured her that she lived. Another contraction took hold of her muscles. She heard muttering voices but didn't dare open her eyes, lest the hallucinations thrust themselves into the outer world and show her one last vision of death, a real one. If she could only shut it out, perhaps it would not claim her! What welter of evil memory had she brought into the psychic peace of the Sentinel College?

Brennen's voice, close in her ear, urged, "Mari! Firebird! *Breathe!*" He drew away. "Spieth! She's . . ."

As she gathered herself in automatic response to Brennen's cue, Firebird heard Master Spieth's voice approach. ". . . blood oxygen is dipping dangerously. Keep her awake, or we'll have a genuine crisis. . . . No! You must still stay *out*."

Awake.

The word jogged her memory to a phrase from Spieth's book: "The inward-chasing of the mind toward sleep. . ."

P'nah.

She had Turned! *Surely* she had Turned. It had been no hallucination—she had seen her inner self!

"No!" she shrieked. Her voice came shrill, choked. "Brennen!" she screamed as another clench of pain began.

Someone seized her hands. Clutching back, she endured the pain, unable to regain control.

When it passed and she dared to open her eyes, she saw both Brennen and Master Spieth, and Tel hanging back behind them. The time was close, then. A pair of ashen-faced Sentinels stood at the edge of her vision. Unfamiliar medical equipment had been moved into the room and loomed close by.

"Do not let that happen again." Spieth too looked gray-faced.

"You have only a few moments before the next begins. Prepare yourself."

Brennen let go of her hands and slipped a chip of ice into her mouth. "You cannot afford to lose control like that, Mari. I can keep you conscious, *if* you maintain control."

She swallowed the precious drops of melted ice. She must have been panting for hours. "But, Brenn! During that last contraction, I—"

"No time. Look." He motioned toward a monitor close to her head, gleaming green on a black wall. "It's beginning again. Face it!"

Despairing, guessing the effort would finish her this time, she closed her eyes and obeyed. Control returned. Again, her senses faded.

The wall rose before her, massive, spotless. For an instant she hesitated and almost turned away. But—if this were some bizarre visualization of P'nah, then on the other side of that wall, past the terrors, must lie the epsilon carrier. She flung herself through.

The visions reappeared. Facing them but holding distance around her point of awareness, she reached inward and outward and in all directions in an attitude of prayer. She held to that for support and examined the roiling tumult.

When by sheer concentration she thrust aside one rushing, swelling image, it retreated without fading into the others. She struggled to shift her perception, to see deeper, find the epsilon carrier.

Woven around and through the figures of the nebula was another tangle, lines of strange, flickering energy like gleaming cords that kept the imaginings bound deep inside her, so the terror of dying could not reach her consciousness.

Could that be the carrier?

What else could it be?

She shook off exhaustion that threatened to quash her within sight of fulfilling her quest. Fearing that if she lost sight of the glimmering lines she would never see them again, she pressed deeper still, farther from consciousness. A new image sucked her perception into deep, slime-covered waters. Weights gripped her ankles. Light faded; the rippling surface vanished overhead.

A blaze of pain exploded in her face. Brennen's distant voice commanded her to breathe. Dark waters swirled, hiding the glowing cord.

No!

Fear of drowning and the terror of failure doubled her strength.

Lungs all but bursting, Firebird groped under the murk toward a faint, blue-white line of illusory force shimmering through slime.

She seized hold. It writhed under her touch, grew and shrank like some kind of alien creature. Again the pain burned her face, then pressure as if the waters would force themselves into her lungs. She clung, closing her airways against death itself, and struggled to wrench the knotted coil free of the phantasm it bound. Longer than she could have believed possible, she held her breath. Like a tickling touch on a limb she did not have, the sensation of contact with this energized entity grew keener.

But her strength was fading. Unable to twist it loose, she tried to shrink her point of awareness again and press it into the cord.

It slipped her grasp. Other visions whirled around her. Cold air stabbed deep into her lungs. New pain rose and seized her, tearing pain that sucked her deeper. Deeper. She felt hands seize her, many hands, hands that squeezed, hurt like claws. . . .

Spieth's face focused in her eyes, and she felt the "otherness" of the medical Master's epsilon probe drive into her consciousness. All shreds of illusion fled. "Hold there, Firebird!" she shouted. "Brennen: now!"

Firebird tried to shake Brennen's hand off her shoulder. He mustn't see the horror, mustn't touch the cord—

Roughly he turned her to face him. "Mari." He caught her stare and held it by the force of his will. "You are in my strength now, Firebird. Yours is gone. Hold! Only a few minutes more . . ."

Pain! Firebird gave a last startled cry and then surrendered to Brennen, unable to move or struggle or even think. She saw only his eyes, blue and unblinking, felt only the Command that held her. Longer, longer . . . she was turning inside out. . . .

Without warning, he released her. She gave a little hiccupping gasp, saw the startled look in his eyes—and fainted.

She awoke much later to see Spieth's iron-gray eyes hovering where Brennen's had been.

Firebird recoiled as memory returned all at once, and with it understanding of what had transpired. Caught up in the illusion of drowning, she had refused to inhale, might even have suffocated her unborn sons moments before they would have breathed of their own accord.

"You fear me?" the Master asked quietly. A delicate probe flicked at the fringes of Firebird's memory.

She choked. "Master, are the—"

"Be still." Spieth took the probe in deeper. Holding down her defenses, although the deep touch brought up a wave of queasiness,

Firebird waited out the access open-eyed. Movement at the corner of vision caught her glance. A blue-skirted sekiyr approached, both arms laden. The oblong mass on the girl's left arm yelled vigorously, but Firebird's attention, forcibly held, could not focus on it.

After a minute, Spieth averted her stare and withdrew. For a while she did not speak. She sat erect at the edge of Firebird's bed, as Firebird fought back tears of embarrassment and lingering pain.

"This is incredible," Spieth said at last. "Now I see why you struggled so. I would not have thought such a thing possible. But had you been alone, we surely would have lost you—and both your sons. You were that near death."

Both? An awful fear gripped Firebird. Apparently the Master sensed it. "They live," she answered before Firebird could ask. "Both are healthy, in the nineties on the response tests."

She glanced at the sekiyr's squalling burden and returned thanks. Then she whispered, "Brennen. Where is he?"

"Gone to rest, Firebird. I put him down myself; he was distraught. You will see him soon." Spieth pressed a hand against Firebird's forehead.

It felt cool and satiny. "Will I be able to touch the carrier again? And without . . . ." Firebird faltered. "It seemed as if I *was* . . . dying."

Pity broke through on Spieth's face like stars out of slip-state. "Try it and see. Try now, while you recall the sensation and the focusing technique vividly. You are rested. I am here, and I will not let you come to any harm."

Firebird closed her eyes and focused inward, remembering the wall and the horrific tangle, and followed recollection down to experience as Spieth's presence hovered at the edge of her consciousness, observing. Her reluctance almost thwarted her as she searched for the faint, tickling sensation contact had brought, while trying desperately to shut out the awful hallucinations. If Spieth recognized the visions for what they were, she would almost die of the disgrace. Spieth had thought her brave, a fighter!—not a terrified child fixed on the idea of her own dying.

At last she succeeded, but the touch brought up a shriek of fear, as if she lived all the visions at once. Unable to stop, she flung away the contact like hot iron and escaped outward.

Spieth sprang off the bedside but did not go far. Gripping one hand with the other, she stepped close again. "Excellent." She nodded, but Firebird saw her lips pressed tightly together. What kind of thoughts were passing across the Master's mind, concealed by affective control? "Very, very interesting. Not only have you achieved P'nah, but recognized and secured the carrier. That is a second-level skill. I am surprised. You may yet surprise us all, Firebird. But—you have other business now. Linna,'' she beckoned. ''Firebird . . .''

Firebird turned to the sekiyr and reached for the child on her arm, the source of the wailing that had gone on at the edge of her attention. Trailing blonde hair over the infant like a blanket, the sekiyr laid him in Firebird's crooked elbow. She turned back a thin warming blanket to reveal a purplish head crowned with soft brown hair, wrinkled from forehead to chin in fury. ''This is the second-born,'' the girl whispered.

''What's wrong?'' Firebird clutched the tiny, shaking thing. He smelled of disinfectant. ''Is he all right?''

''Hungry, I would guess.''

Firebird wished she could escape the source of shrieking, or at least silence it, but beneath that tension flowed a deep, awestruck joy, the peace of utter conviction that at last she had done something absolutely, inarguably right.

She peered at his brother, who lay quietly on the girl's other arm. Linna fingered the blanket away from his face. This head wore a faint sheen of fair hair. Glancing down to confirm the unavoidable comparison, Firebird ran a finger across thick, dark curls. ''Kinnor,'' she whispered. ''Little warrior. You have cousin Tel's hair. How did that happen?''

''Kinnor—kinnora. That's lovely.'' Spieth stopped pacing behind the sekiyr and reached onto a repulsor cart for something Firebird could not see. ''Ah.'' She tilted her head back. ''I feel young. Younger and more energetic than I've felt in years. Perhaps it's the shamah, starting to operate already.''

Firebird pursed her lips. She had never seen the Master so animated.

''And that one?'' The sekiyr's gaze followed as Spieth took the elder twin and held a nursing bottle to his mouth, rocking her body from side to side. He lipped disinterestedly, sighed, and then fell back asleep. Firebird found that she could not look away from his gently squared, fine-featured face.

''Kiel,'' she murmured. ''Brennen chose the name months ago, to follow my family tradition. It is a N'Taian hunting bird. Kiel Labbah, after Brennen's father. And Kinnor Irion, for mine.'' She felt her chin quiver. She still couldn't look away. ''Oh, Master Spieth. Kiel looks so like . . .'' She gulped. ''*So* like . . .'' She struggled to finish the sentence. ''So like his own father.''

Then she wept without hope of controlling herself, clutching Kinnor to her breast. *What is he going to think of me?*

An hour later, after Firebird tried to feed both twins and then surrendered them to the sekiyr's care, Brennen came down. In the door of her chamber, he stood motionless for several seconds. She let his emotional state wash over and through her. He was deeply shaken.

Letting the door close behind him, he came in and sat beside her on a chair.

"Have you spoken with Spieth?" she asked.

He bent toward her. "Briefly. Mari . . ." He leaned away. "She confirms . . ." He lifted his chin and looked directly into her eyes. "Mari."

"I Turned."

"I felt it."

He did not approve. And now that it had happened, she was not certain *she* approved. She stroked her smooth, cool sheet. Several excuses she might offer rose to mind, but none seemed adequate to ease his distress.

To her surprise, the door swept open and Spieth stepped in. Firebird felt Brennen's irritation, and then all foreign emotion cut off. Which Sentinel was shielding her perceptions?

Brennen lifted one foot and studied the sole of his boot. "We'll have to go to Shamarr Dickin, while we're here at the College. He has to know . . . what has happened, and how the established patterns of your alpha matrix are reorienting. It could drive you mad, if you tried to continue. You must believe me. But Aldana—"

Firebird opened her tired eyes wide. She'd never heard him call the Master by her first name.

"Dickin could order . . . what happens to Mari?"

"No," Spieth said calmly. The medical Master seemed herself again: quiet, professionally confident. "Not yet. She's not strong enough to face a deep access during the period of maternal bonding. I will approach Shamarr Dickin. Brennen, congratulate your Mistress." Spieth pointed at him. "She has accomplished what no other in her situation has ever accomplished before."

"I do," he said softly, and Firebird thought she saw sincerity in his gaze, although she could not feel it. "Mari is the strongest woman I have ever known, Master."

Spieth gave Firebird a tiny, triumphant smile. "And time you admitted it, Master Brennen. Now. The deed is done. We can do nothing to change it. Firebird.'' Spieth's lips curved down once more. ''You *will* do nothing about Turning again, until I speak with the Shamarr. You haven't the strength for it, and at any rate, Brennen is correct. There is the risk of madness, with this great an upheaval in both your alpha and epsilon matrices.''

''All right.'' Firebird rubbed her fingers against her palms.

''I'm glad you consent, but you may as well know you didn't have a choice. I've put you under Command for a full day. And Tellai, and the sekiyr Linna, too, until I release them, Brennen. They will not tell anyone she has Turned—if they even realize it. For now, it is our deepest secret.'' She took a step backward. ''Keep it so, Brennen. You are the only one who is free to talk.'' Another step. ''Besides myself.''

She hurried out, and once again, Firebird sensed Brennen's disquiet.

He seated himself on her bed. ''What is this between you and Master Spieth? I think I have a right to know.''

Sighing, Firebird regathered her poise. ''At my request,'' she said, ''Master Spieth agreed to do a resonal scan. Two months ago. She didn't tell me anything concrete, Brenn, but—'' Her spark of pride flared. ''She did say it was a crime I had not been tested as a child. And she encouraged me, lent me a training book.''

''Spieth did?''

Firebird leaned back on the pillow, feeling weak and miserable. ''I wanted it . . . for myself, but also . . . for the babies' sake. I wish I'd never done it, Brenn. You can't know. What I saw—''

Gently he took her hand. ''Tell me,'' he said. ''If you can. No one wants to access your memory for it, but we all felt your terror release, when you fainted at the end. We thought it was only the pain of childbirth, but it seemed abnormally intense even to Spieth.''

In a faltering voice, she told him about the spectrum of deaths, and the nights she had spent sleepless, creating them.

When she finished, he kneaded her wrist and hand. ''Oh, Mari. Mari, I'm proud. Proud as I ever have been. But I'm afraid for you, too.''

''Why?''

It pained him to speak—she felt it—but he met her stare. He spoke softly, almost in a whisper. ''With that epsilon carrier convolved inward with images of death . . . if you try to use it . . . what will it do to you? How could anyone control it, even with training?'' He shook his head. ''No one knows how to train you. No one has ever . . . ever . . . experienced this kind of a Turn before.''

Chapter 11

. . . Will Spring Death . . .

appassionato
impassioned

As if to try the fit of his musical name, Kinnor sang mercilessly that night, insisting on her undivided attention. At dawn, Spieth's assistants took both twins away, and Firebird slept the dreamless sleep of total exhaustion.

For days she remained too tired, too occupied, to think beyond the two tiny shilyaha, heirs to the shamah. Vividly she remembered her Wastling upbringing, and the mother who could not afford to waste affection on a child tradition marked for early death. Firebird had known little warmth, except from the palace staff—and now she gradually learned to touch and love Kinnor and Kiel.

From the first day, their personalities diverged. Kiel remained quiet, patient, almost serene, every little movement purposeful; but Kin complained lustily at the slightest provocation. During her days at College, several Sentinels and sekiyrra came quietly to her rooms; each brought a single flower to Firebird, paid respects to Kiel and Kinnor, and then stole away.

Tel had been told how the Aurian plague had robbed the Angelos of male heirs. "But I really didn't believe it, until they came." He gathered up little Kin, speaking softly despite the child's squalling. "I had of course assumed your heir would be a girl. And you never did tell me you 'waited twins, though I might have guessed it from the size of you."

Firebird resisted the urge to snatch back her baby. How odd that the Thyrians called Kiel firstborn, while Naetai would claim Kinnor as her heir. As second-born of fraternal twins, Kin was considered first conceived by a tradition medical science could neither prove nor disprove.

Sensing their father at the door, she turned her head on the pillow. "Brenn." She cradled Kiel with her arms and body as Brennen tiptoed to the bedside. "He—seems comfortable with me. Can you imagine that? A baby?—with me?"

Kiel stared steadily at her with Brennen's unearthly blue eyes. Brennen glanced aside at Tel and Kinnor. Tel bounced him vigorously, and Kin quieted. "Huh." Brennen shook his head, staring at his son. "It worked."

Tel grinned up at Brennen. "My friend Rattela's children were difficult, too."

Soon she returned to Trinn Hill. A long month passed there, forty days of numbing routine, little sleep, and tense waiting for a pronouncement from Shamarr Dickin that did not come. The best she could claim was that she nearly had her slender figure again, and a bounce in her step.

One afternoon, after a satisfying hour of serious practice downlevel in her bedroom while the twins slept, Firebird laid her ringing clairsa on the bed with the uncanny feeling of being under surveillance. She heard no sound of Tellai, locked in his own room away from Kiel and Kinnor. But someone stood at the front entry, and she urgently needed to let him in. She smoothed her red skyff, adjusted the mira lily in her hair—she'd taken to wearing it, to keep her spirits up—pulled on her shoes, and then hurried toward the hallway lift.

In midstride she stopped and blinked the afterimage of bronze strings from her eyes.

That was wrong! No one stood at the outer door—the windowside bedroom monitor, activated for street watch, showed only sheets of rain—and the entry alarm had not sounded, so no one could be inside the security entry either, except someone like Brennen, who was rarely stopped by locks—

Oh, no.

Let him in, came the compulsion again, stronger than before, and Firebird knew that an enemy stood inside the walls of her stronghold, and if she unlocked the voice-coded inner door, the Shuhr would have her life.

At one corner of the bedroom's security panel was an activation tab for the inner lock. She didn't need to go to the door, nor even uplevel. If she held down the tab and spoke a word, he would be in, and all would be well.

No! It would not!

She breathed hard, fighting the foreign impulses. Tel was so close—but he was locked away—and what could he do to help? And was his mind, shieldless as hers against this kind of attack, under its influence as well?

She took two steps toward his door and then stopped as though tethered. The intruder would not allow her away from the control panel.

Press the tab. You do need help. You need *him* to come in and help you.

She managed another step toward the foot of the bed. Beads of perspiration welled on her forehead from the effort of fighting the inner promptings; she had to take five more steps, and she hadn't the strength.

A glance at the tri-D of Kiel and Kinnor hanging on her wall gave her the will to step once more. *He doesn't want just me,* she admonished herself. *He'll kill all of us, and all our hopes.*

But her legs remained stiff. She was growing dizzy, and feared that if she fainted he would take control of her body. Brennen had intimated that it was impossible to put an unconscious person under Command, but this intruder was controlling her from a distance beyond Brennen's limit.

Terrell?

Yes. He's a friend, let him in. The push felt commanding and reassuring.

No!

She could walk no farther, but she could crawl. She dropped to hands and knees and crept around the bed, half the remaining distance to Tellai's palmlock, before collapsing prone in tears of frustration.

"Tel!" she managed to cry, then regretted it. He could never deactivate that lock from inside.

"Firebird?" His voice filtered through the steel door.

She tried to answer, but her tormentor held her so firmly that she could only squeak again, "Tel?"

"Are you all right?"

"No." There. At least he was warned. But what now? And could the invader read her as easily as he could direct her?

"Let me in, Firebird!"

She groaned and rolled over. Tel might try to force the door, but it was tamper-proof. The security engineers had seen to that. For the babies' sake.

"I . . ."

Go back to the control panel.

No!

She could kill the intruder with a word if she touched the right tab. But touch the wrong one and . . .

". . . can't."

"What *is* it?"

As she tried to struggle in too many directions, her mental control slipped. She rose off the floor and retraced those agonizing steps with ease. Before she could stop, her arm reached for the security panel. She watched horrified as her hand touched the lock activator and held it down, overriding the lethal "dispatch" circuit.

Now speak.

She bit down on her tongue and tried to wrench her finger away.

May I enter now?

No! she wanted to scream.

Speak!

Although she could not move away, not all the com center's defensive circuits were overridden by the lock tab. Before Terrell could read and respond to her inspiration, Firebird hit the alarm panel with her thumb. Seventeen minutes away at Base One, a light would pulse at Brennen's desk.

Was he there?

Seventeen minutes. Almost forever.

Let him in. Speak.

Tellai pounded on the door.

Brennen yanked the little jet's hatch closed and fired its engines with the kind of speed he would have used going into battle. "Caldwell," he snapped into the craft's transceiver. "Clearance. Please."

Rapid engine check, control check. He'd do her no good if he crashed halfway home because of an equipment malfunction. "Clearance granted, General Caldwell," crooned the voice on the speaker.

He took the inland breakway strip at max. After that, he could do little more than set the controls for automatic, because he always took this run at full speed.

Seventeen minutes.

Only half watching airspace, he stretched his focus toward Trinn Hill.

That faint but unmistakable sensation touched Firebird. Between the pair bonded, shallow contact was possible over this distance, but Brennen could do little more than confirm that she was in danger. Concentrating on the sensation of his quest-pulse, clinging to it like a lifeline, she pulled away from the control board, struggled around the bed and across the room, and smacked the palm-panel on Tel's door.

Tellai sprang through, horribly pale. "What is it?"

"Someone at the upper door," she choked. "Don't—" The claw caught her tongue again.

Tellai pulled her to the bedside and sat her down, then stood over her and wiped her forehead with his silken handcloth.

"Brenn's coming." She pushed out the words. "Don't let me touch that control board. It's a Shuhr. A strong one. Get my—"

Abruptly the compulsion to bring in the stranger became a self-destructive convulsion. Tellai seized her hands. Brennen's probe rose to meet the attack; he felt closer now, stronger. Firebird went rigid, her mind a battleground for foreign powers.

She had no weapon to bring into this battle but her Turn, a thing of powerless agony. But Firebird could not lie down and die. She drove inward, imagining the wall, and swept through.

The intruder followed. His point of presence seemed to glow with delight as he perceived the death-march of her imagination. He *wanted* her to destroy herself. The visions fed his strength. They intensified. . . .

In agony, she flailed for the gleaming cord of epsilon energy deep at the core of her horrors. Deeper—deeper—

With her last effort, she touched it.

"Now, Tel?"

Brennen stood beside the long windowall, exhausted. He had found his wife collapsing in Tellai's arms, her consciousness flickering out like a spent glow lamp, very nearly dead—and she would have died, if he'd been just a little later. He arrived barely in time to lend his strength to her failing nervous system.

But she had not revived.

What had happened?

Now she lay unconscious, pale-cheeked, her hair spread on the pillow like dark flames. In the next room, Kinnor wailed. Firebird's clairsa lay on the floor beside their bed, and Tellai pressed his hands against the sides of her throat. "Pulse still steady," he answered softly. "She's too tough to fade on us, Caldwell."

Brennen gave the slender nobleman as much of a smile as he could muster.

"I've called—" The tone of the uplevel alarm interrupted Brennen. "That will be Dickin," he said. "Please stay with her, Tel." Brennen ran to the main entry, two stairs at a stride, and activated the tab. Simultaneously, the inner and outer doors slid wide.

Dickin must have seen the dark-haired body lying inside the entry the moment Brennen saw it. Brennen knelt on the stones. "Terrell," he whispered. Hastily he extended a quest-pulse toward his motionless coworker. No flicker of mental activity remained in the body.

Still kneeling, he glanced up at the Shamarr. *I came in through the service port and didn't see him,* he subvocalized rapidly. *I suppose—* He stood. *—we'd better leave him here, for now?*

One hand on his white tunic's breast, Shamarr Dickin touched the arm of one of the uniformed Sentinels beside him. *Loren, stand guard outside.*

Brennen stepped aside at the edge of the inner door. *Not necessary, Shamarr. This is a security entry.*

Dickin raised one white eyebrow and eloquently glanced down at the corpse.

As you say, Master. Come. Brennen led the older man and his two remaining companions to the household lift, trying as he went to compose himself, shielding with epsilon static his absolute confusion.

In the downlevel bedroom, Firebird lay on the broad bed, Tellai at her side. The young prince stood and bowed when the Shamarr entered.

Dickin nodded toward Tel but walked briskly to the bedside. "Not a flicker here, either," murmured the Shamarr, throwing off his cloak. "Friesst. Caldwell. Assist me."

"Tel, would you see to Kinnor?" Stiffly, Brennen sank onto the bed. Gently he pulled the crushed mira lily from Firebird's hair, and he dropped it toward the floor. It caught on the strings of her clairsa.

Blue.

Blue everywhere, a vast firmament, a wide sea.

Could she be swimming? No: Shifting, she felt solid warmth under her. She blinked hard.

Blue again.

She lay on her back, and Brennen held her in his stare. Her arms ached, stretched taut under his weight.

"There," he said, and she felt an intense inner release of tension. "That's done it. Tel, get a glass of water."

A shiver of euphoria shook her. The attacker had failed. She was alive!

Brennen released her arms and sat back. Her wrists hurt. She rubbed them. Had she been struggling to hurt Brennen, under the invader's control? "Brenn, I'm—"

Then she saw the others. It took her only a second to recognize the Shamarr. Not a large man, Thyrica's spiritual hierarch still had so potent a presence that Firebird wanted to rise and curtsey. His snowy hair and white tunic drew attention to the only contrast he wore: a gold star on his shoulder, eight-pointed like Brennen's, but set with a single sapphire and circled in silver.

"Brennen, what—"

He touched a finger to her lips. "We need you to be still and not ask questions. We'll tell you what we can."

Tellai returned with the water. Barely rising on the pillow, Firebird took the glass. *Tel could have killed me,* she reflected as she sipped. *Brennen read him right. He's with us.* Tel walked to the foot of the bed and sat down past Brennen, looking frightened but determined. *And I nearly killed Tel, at Hunter Height.* She gave Brennen the empty glass.

He remained hunched over her on the bedside. "The problem, Mari, is that your alpha matrix has been manipulated. We're not certain what else happened, but we must assume that everything you see, hear, or verbalize is telegraphed to the Shuhr. Shamarr Dickin has brought you back—Mari, you must just lie quiet for now."

"But . . . how could I be in link? I don't feel anything."

"This is not like access. We do not use it. But we know it can be done."

She shut her eyes and shook her head. Glory! Why had they ever left Hesed? Chaos take her ambitions—and the N'Taian succession!

"We must assume," he whispered, "but it may not be so." He stroked her cheek. "Rest for a while. I must speak with Dickin, alone."

"All right, Brenn." She let her head fall back. Brennen stood and strode from the room, followed by the Shamarr. A second Sentinel walked slowly to the sweep of windows and peered out into the downpour, an unreadable expression on his face. *All right,* she thought, *if anyone's listening.* Angrily she told the Shuhr what she thought of them, with a vicious string of vituperative she'd learned in the N'Taian Planetary Naval Academy and never spoken aloud.

The Sentinel beside the window turned to face her. "We did what we could in this brief time, Mistress. Shamarr Dickin has urgent business this afternoon."

A cry sounded in the next room. Tel straightened and hurried out.

Firebird watched him go, then looked up at the Sentinel. "Thank you for coming." She ached to say more. Were the Shuhr listening? Minutes stretched away, and the downpour droned on.

At last the other two men stepped back into the bedroom, Brennen deferring to Shamarr Dickin. Firebird had never felt Brennen so dismayed, not even before the Regional Council.

Shamarr Dickin offered a hand and pulled her to a sitting position. "We must see you again, Mistress." He studied her with keen, pale blue eyes. "But it must not be soon." Dickin gathered his escort with a nod, and they swept out together.

Brennen sat down beside her. "You still mustn't ask questions, Mari. We hope you're free, but we're not certain."

"Can I ask if anything's been done about catching Terrell? It was *him.*" The moment she had asked, she wondered who else might want that information.

"You honestly don't know."

"Know what?" She tried to open to the touch of his feelings, but his emotions had been forced down deep under affective control, where she could barely touch them. What had Dickin told him?

Wearing a bleak expression, he took her hand. "Mari. I can't tell you. Not now."

"I understand. Then—let me tell *you* why Terrell fooled you for so long."

"Oh?" He fingered the tab of his left cuff, where his crystace lay hidden.

"He knew you were watching for danger. He put a lot of effort into hiding from you. But he never guessed I . . . would read him." She sank back into the pillow. All her body ached. "Tel's with the children."

Brennen shifted on the bedside. "Yes. Listen, Mari. I will tell you one reason why Shamarr Dickin reacted so strongly to what just occurred. It is a secret I have kept from you but not intentionally, and if the Shuhr hear, it will do us no harm." He dropped his emotional blocking and freed a surge of sheepish pride. "We simply don't discuss these matters. When I won my Master's star I was young, my lady. Much too young for that kind of authority and responsibility. Yet the College did not deny it to me. Instead, when the time came for me to be vested in the Word, I was given the shock of my lifetime." His pupils shrank, and he seemed to see something far away. "Shamarr Dickin himself stood to sponsor me. I almost burst with pride. Then he explained at great length, before all the Masters in attendance, that this was no honor but a dreadful burden. I was to answer to Shamarr Dickin as to my spiritual father." He smiled ruefully. "That cooled my wild streak. No more raids without orders, as I had done on Gemina. Not until you and I left Alta for Naetai, in fact."

She sensed Brennen's inner turmoil. Perhaps, at last, he had serious doubts as to whether he had made a mistake in bonding her. "Is he angry with me?" she asked in a small voice.

"No." He looked down at his hands. "With me. For risking the future of Thyrica."

"How?"

"By leaving sanctuary with you when I should have known better," he said quietly. "He has recommended me for discipline. Deferred, I hope. But he's not displeased with you for following the independent pattern of your connatural mate. Nor am I. He is alarmed by . . . events. So much that he has laid a . . . prohibition on us."

"Can you tell me?" she whispered.

"Why not?" She felt bitterness in him. "I am not to touch your mind, Mari. No Sentinel can. I cannot now, nor tonight when I come to bed."

"Brenn," she whispered, aghast. Not in lovemaking? Clearly that was the gist of Dickin's prohibition.

What had she done?

She dared not ask, dared not mention the fact she had Turned, not with the possibility of Shuhr listening in. Why had the Shamarr waited so long to react this strongly?

Brennen walked to the inner door and tapped gently. Tel's head poked through. "Yes?"

"Are they still asleep?" Brennen asked.

Tel nodded.

Without a word, Brennen slipped through into the nursery.

"Are you all right?" Tel walked out to Firebird's bedside.

The gravity of what Brennen had just told her held her down.

Not to touch the depths of him . . . how could she live that way? She glanced up. Tel stood close by, concern plain on his childish face. "I think so, Tel," she said. "Thanks . . . for your help."

"Oh. Ah. Heavens around, Firebird, how could I have done any less?"

A minute later, Brennen reemerged. The two men helped her rise, and silent by unspoken agreement, they all headed for the main elevator. Firebird stumbled twice between her bed and the lift cubicle.

Brennen made kaffa, and they sat on the lounger near the green-well drinking it as loud rain outside the windowall darkened from soft gray toward black. Firebird fought a hungry rumble in her belly. Brennen's feelings seemed tumbled and discordant, as though he were arguing with himself, oblivious to her.

"Brenn?" she ventured. "I'm hungry. Aren't you?"

He uncrossed his legs and shifted on the lounger. "Some fresh air would help you get over this. Would Shanneman's suit you?"

"Of course. But I can cook." She rose wearily. "I'm not that far gone." A wave of dizziness crumpled her onto the lounger. "Oh." She tried to force levity into her voice as she pressed back into the cushions. "Maybe I am."

"I'd like to go out," put in Tel. "To get out of the rain, if such a thing is possible."

Firebird felt that perceptible tip of Brennen's emotions smooth out in decision. She pushed curiosity out of her mind. "What about the children?"

"We'll take them along." Brennen got up off the tweedy lounger and strode across the room. Tel offered Firebird his arm. Gratefully she leaned against him, and together they stood.

"Brenn?" Firebird called. "Would you mind bringing my cloak?"

Brennen stepped into the lift. "No. I'll be a minute, Mari. I must make a call."

Chapter 12

Two-Alpha

trio bravura
for three performers,
demanding all their skill

Shanneman's was filled with diners fleeing the storm in the cliff-
side clear zone, and a knot of uneasy-looking offworlders, including two amphiboid Oquassan aliens, sat cliqued together at
midroom. On the way to a windowed seaside alcove, Brennen
brushed by a tall, uniformed officer Firebird only half saw, for
she had half closed her weary eyes to savor Shanneman's warm,
exotic odors.

"Oh, sorry, Caldwell." The straw-blond man had Air Master
Dardy's voice. Firebird opened her eyes in surprise.

"No problem, Dardy. Tell Claggett we're here." Brennen bent
down and laid the deeply sleeping twins on the inner curve of an
unoccupied booth. So innocent they looked, far below uncon-
sciousness in the barely living state Sentinels called tardema-sleep.
Firebird had been reluctant to bring them this way, but Brennen
had insisted they'd take no harm from it—this once. Tel took her
deep green cloak and draped it over an unoccupied booth.

"Right away." Before Firebird could speak, Dardy hustled off.
Disappointed, she raised a hand in greeting toward the
offworlders—certainly she understood their nervousness, surrounded and outnumbered by Thyrians—then sat down and turned
her attention to the menu embossed on the tabletop.

She convinced Tellai to try resta filli, an Altan specialty. The food came quickly and tasted wonderful, but midway through the meal, she began to sense that Brennen was elsewhere. He sat staring, toying one-handed with a small, heavy, golden bird-of-prey medallion. Tarance had given it to him twenty years before, he'd told her, and he had carried it everywhere he went during his years of Federate service.

Once again his feelings hid behind that cloud; chilled, she realized that he suspected the link with Shuhr agents remained unbroken. Brennen could not hide the tautness of his nerves from her.

So she ate her spicy resta filli and half of his, and blocked the resonating tension from her own mind by singing a very old, cheery song in her memory. She was recovering from her afternoon terror, full now, and she'd fall asleep with her head in her plate if she didn't try to stay alert.

As they finished kaffa and brittle, buttery Destonian kdee wafers, a pair of intercept fighters, deep shadows whose long T shape made her catch her breath, skimmed the rim of the cliffs in beautiful unison. Sight of the craft Brennen had taken into battle at VeeRon did more to rouse Firebird than any number of cups of kaffa.

Brennen seemed to sense that. He dropped the medallion into a pocket of his wide web belt and said, "Mari, it's been a long time since we did any night flying. So long as we have the babies in t-sleep, would you like to take Tel up above the clouds?"

Firebird swung around to stare at Brennen. "I'd love it—if we can do it."

Tel straightened and glanced toward all corners of the restaurant. "Do you think it would be safe?"

"No worse than going home." Brennen emptied his cup. "We still don't know that Terrell was working alone. We'll simply take a ship that can shoot back."

"HF-117." Brennen identified the craft, then stepped aboard, carrying Kiel.

As Firebird climbed the stepstand after him with dark little Kinnor, her cloak flapped at her ankles. She gripped the rail tightly with one hand, delighted to board a Federate military craft at last. Far down at the end of the line of identical gray ships loomed a single deeper shadow: one intercept fighter. It had been so long since she'd flown a N'Taian tagwing, even counted in Thyrian months! If only . . .

No. They'd never all fit. Squeezing once with Brennen into a N'Taian fightercraft had been difficult enough.

With Tel close behind, she ducked through this bulkier craft's hatch and eased between the padded, brown rear bench and front seats, then over—between—down onto the first officer's chair. She found and touched the striplight waker on the bulkhead beside the hatch, then carefully laid Kinnor—so limp and quiet—on her lap. The white glare of spacefield floodlights vanished as Brennen secured the entry, and a sucking whoosh tickled deep into her ears as the sealed cockpit began to shimmer with blue light.

"The controls are set up just like a *Brumbee*! Except this. . . ." She waved a hand over one end of the silvery console that curled around both forward chairs in a dotted patchwork of screens, panels, and gauges. Tellai peered over her shoulder at the display, his brow furrowing in a valiant attempt at comprehension. This board was far more complex than the simulator's.

"That's an advanced energy-layering system." Brennen handed her another limp little form and reached for a cargo net between the seats. By searching out mirror-image controls, she found the other. In half a minute, netted securely, Kiel and Kinnor slept unmindful of their strange bedroom.

Brennen activated the generators. "The HF-117 is the best-shielded craft in the inventory."

"You should know." As she pulled off her cloak and folded it carefully, she felt his emotional blocking slide away. "No checkout?"

"It's been fueled and checked for us."

He hadn't called ahead from Shanneman's, had . . . ?

She gripped the edge of her seat, scarcely daring to realize what he meant. What if They were listening? Brennen lit the navcomputer screen and charged the ordnance banks, then opened the interlink. "Two-Alpha coming up." His feelings lay poised between determination and desperation, precisely as if he were going into battle. A tremor slid down her arms.

Brennen turned to her as the six external sensor screens took up a pale blue-gray glow. "I'm sorry, Mari, but it must be this way. We run or die, all of us, this time."

"Shebiyl?" she blurted out.

"Yes. But *Dickin* saw it. He was angrier than I've ever seen him." As Firebird choked on the idea of the Shamarr commanding Brennen off the home world, he glanced back over his shoulder. "Tellai, you know something about weapons. But have you ever flown in a fighter?"

Tel's face went deathly pale beneath the blue striplights. "No. And I'm not really a speed lover. Motion sickness."

"Then strap in snug and keep your hands off the panels. I'm sorry, but this will be rough. Help him, Mari. Can you?"

"But we have nothing with us!" Tellai clutched the edges of Brennen's seat back.

"We have rations in the compartments and clothes on our backs, and that's enough." Firebird twisted around and pulled the black webbing across his pale blue velvric shirt. Though her eyes were adjusting to the odd light, he looked green. "Brenn, do we have any trisec?"

"Under your seat. And you take about four stims. You need to be able to act, now. You can rest later." He slid a lever back. The ship rose smoothly and began to glide forward.

Bending, she stretched her arm as far as she could to reach a little shelf between metal struts and eased out several strips of wafers in clear cellopaper. "Here, Tel. Take two of these now." She sorted out a sheet of green triangular tabs and tossed it back over the seat. "And the rest if you need them. They'll keep your dinner in you." She looked down at the little passengers webbed snugly into their cradles. *Tardema-sleep.* She shook her head. *He knew what was coming, all right.* The twins would remain in that state, needing no care, until wakened.

And he'd brought along the medallion, too. The clues had been in plain sight.

She swallowed her bitter, red stimulant caps dry-mouthed.

"Thanks," Tel said weakly, and tore open his packet.

Firebird dropped back into her seat, strapped in, and clipped on a headset. "But if they're scanning in on me—"

"We can't worry about that now. The simplest infrared detector would have spotted a flight of this size. They've been waiting out there for us to do just this, and by now they'll have had a report from . . . Terrell's coworkers. They know who we are. They don't know our ships, though, nor our pilots. We may surprise them yet."

"But, Brenn—"

"Only your *vocalized* thoughts." He touched another panel, and the engine's pitch rose. "Those uppermost in your mind, the ones you slow down and think in words."

"Oh," she muttered, adjusting the webbing on her seat.

"Listen, Mari," Brennen said softly. "I can't promise we'll get away. Even Dickin is scared. You know I wouldn't force this if it weren't our last hope, but it's a poor one. They have fast ships and talented people, and I've never flown against them in these numbers before. While we've dawdled they've gathered their forces.''

''How many are there?''

The interlink interrupted. ''Flight two, stand by.''

Brennen reached up and flicked a switch. ''Two-Alpha, on taxi.'' As he answered Firebird, voices continued to echo from the receiver. ''We don't know. I had hoped we could break for it alone if it became necessary to run, but they're watching for us. They sense you, particularly. You can't shield your presence from them, and I'll be too busy to shield you.''

She nodded and eyed the readouts in front of her. One ready-light began to blink on the panel.

''We can assume there will be a fight.'' Brennen reached down beside his seat and pulled a lever. ''But the escort takes the brunt. We stay out of it if we can and slip quickly. If too many of them close on us for the escort to handle and we're engaged, we'll split the controls as before. You shoot, I keep us far enough from them to protect all of you from . . . I don't know what they might send at you, but I'm certain they'll try. If they do, keep your hands off the ordnance board.''

She ached to ask if his research had yielded anything helpful, but because of Tel's presence and the possibility of Shuhr eavesdropping, she didn't dare. She hunched over the orange ordnance board near centerline. Controls for six energy guns, twenty heat-seekers, and two Nova-class drones: enough to keep four crewmen busy. She adjusted the guns' tuning slides randomly to cover a variety of slip-shield wavelengths.

Movement on the sensor display over the weapons board caught her attention. Their ship had skimmed to one end of the breakaway strip, but she hadn't realized they were being followed. Now she saw a full double squadron arrayed behind her: fifteen more ships in a long, narrow diamond. So, not all Brennen's late hours had been in research. Some had been in preparation for this very need, and his friend Damalcon Dardy had been in the thick of the plot, while she was kept ignorant. Tonight she was grateful she'd not known the plan, to betray it to Terrell.

Brennen diverted full power from the generators into the propulsion system. All across the board, lights came on. The engines roared. ''Go limp, Tel,'' he warned.

Suddenly the sensor screens came alive. A mass of ships swept in from behind. Firebird choked back a cry.

Acceleration smashed her into her seat before the pursuers appeared on the curving visual screen overhead; then she saw they were Thyrian, another double squadron of gray heavy fighters spread wide in mass delta formation. She felt the rumbling shock wave pass over.

They lifted. Brennen pulled in below and behind the fifth echelon of the upper group. The flight swept high over the sea, into the thick cloudbank. Above her, the curving visual screen glowed eerily, a ghost cloud illuminated by landing lights of craft above her. Gradually Brennen pressed forward until their ship nestled below and between the third and fourth echelons of the upper formation, and like a flock of kiel hunting along N'Taian cliffs, the flight banked again, broke through the storm, and soared over atmospheric blueline.

Firebird glanced back. Kiel and Kinnor slept on; Tellai's breath came shallow and irregular. She drew a deep breath and spoke against the heaviness of acceleration to Brennen. "But what about the house?"

"I've left Kindall a message," he answered tersely.

Firebird pressed a resolution panel, extending their beyond-visual B-V sensors' range a hundredfold. The squadrons shrank from a majestic flight to two small diamonds dashing outsystem across a wide, exposed field of space.

Her conscience protested. Those other pilots were offering their lives so that she and her family could escape.

"They are all Sentinels in the other ships," Brennen answered before she spoke. "I chose them out of the ranks because they could keep the plans shielded away secret and defend themselves against Shuhr. Most of the Alert Forces are here. All had the option of staying. Not one took it. It's the shamah they're defending: not us, but the prophesied defeat of the Shuhr."

The engine thrummed below her seat, the ventilator hissed beside her. She watched the sensor display silently, anxiously.

"There they are!" Tellai cried, just as she spotted the blips.

Three ominous oval shapes, surrounded by an insectlike flurry of escort fighters' speckles, emerged on the port B-V screen from behind the ball of Shesta, one of Thyrica's companion planets. Twelve ships of the upper diamond peeled away to engage, as the rest of the phalanx wheeled sharply starboard.

"Laying in a slip course is going to be tricky," she said.

"Shouldn't be too bad, if that's all there are," Brennen returned. "That's far fewer than we expected."

Firebird bit a fingernail; it split, leaving a long rough edge.

They had reached only point-one *c*. The heavy craft accelerated far slower than the little DS-212 messenger *Brumbee* she'd ridden before, and until they left the interference of Thyrica's magnetic field, there could be no jumping for the safe, quasi-orthogonal space beyond lightspeed.

"Oh, dear," she murmured, rubbing the ragged fingernail against her seat cover. Another cluster of pips appeared on the starboard screen, cutting them off.

Then a third formation came into sight on the edge of the fore sensors' range: a hundred blips, some surely drones the others controlled, spreading like the vanes of a fan to close them in.

Firebird's sense of humor did not desert her. *This is what you wanted when you married him,* it reminded her as she steadied shaking hands against the ordnance board and swallowed a wave of nausea. *Fighting at his side!*

And if we ever reach sanctuary again, she answered it, *we stay!*

Ellet Kinsman sat eating a late dinner at her servo table when a message alarm whistled across her modest apartment's main room. From the tone of the database's call, the message was Priority I, from College.

Such messages always had the utmost importance to Ellet Kinsman. She dropped her fork, bite and all, and stepped across the room.

GENERAL SENTINEL ALERT, read the bluescreen above her small reading desk. PRESS ID PANEL AND STAND BY.

Ellet complied, curiosity piqued, but disappointed. She'd thought it a specific message for herself.

And then the screen lit.

ALL FORCES: SHUHR ALERT. AN ATTACK HAS TAKEN PLACE ON THE CALDWELL RESIDENCE. OTHER RESIDENCES MAY BE TARGETED AS WELL. OBSERVE ALL PRECAUTIONS.

Ellet's pulse quickened, and she glanced back over her shoulder at her windows. When she looked again at the screen, there was more.

MISTRESS FIREBIRD MARI CALDWELL HAS BEEN PLACED ON *AVOIDANCE* STATUS. DO NOT APPROACH; MAINTAIN EPSILON SHIELDING IN HER VICINITY.

A-status? What in Six-Alpha—?

Ellet stared at the message for a full minute, trying to somehow fit those two paragraphs together. They made no sense. Who had

attacked whom? Had Firebird herself proved to be Shuhr? Had
They done something to her? What could make her such a deadly
threat to all Sentinels as to be put on A-status?

And what about Brennen's children?

Dardy. She snapped her fingers. Damalcon Dardy would know.
Leaning over the touchboard, she hastily punched up his access
code. *Not only would he know,* she told herself while waiting for
relay to his database, *but he'd want me to know as quickly as
possible.*

Two minutes crept by. *He's not home.* Peeved, Ellet slipped
off the stool. Aimlessly she wandered away from the desk. *He's
involved, then.*

Sudden memory swept her back in time. . . .

. . . She sat in his office. Tellai had just arrived. She asked if
the Caldwells might have to leave Thyrica, and Dardy touched
his stylus to his forehead. "If I know anything, it's confidential,
Ellet." She felt again the tingle of his epsilon static, something
he normally did not use in her presence.

Dardy. He was involved. He was *gone.*

He was closer to Brennen than she'd imagined.

Hesed. They were on their way to Hesed House, in the secure,
Sentinel-guarded Procyel system.

How can I get to Hesed?

Her glance fell on her uneaten dinner, still lying on the servo
table. Quickly and efficiently, she dumped the cold leavings into
the recycler and her dishes into the 'washer, then returned to the
reading desk's stool. The message still glowed on her bluescreen.
She stared.

If Firebird had been placed on avoidance-status . . .

What was Brennen going through?

Was there a chance of . . . freeing him . . . now?

The alarm pulse rang again, directly in front of where she sat.
Unruffled, she touched a key.

REPORT MAXSEC, ALTA.

That was the entire message. No explanation followed, no further order: it must be confidential, then, and important. She was
needed at Regional Command.

Ellet grimaced. She wanted to go to Procyel, not Alta!

Instantly she disrupted her protest and clamped down her affective control. It would do her no good to form careless aggressive
habits. She *had* control.

Before rising from the stool, she acknowledged the message by
pressing ten keys at once.

Chapter 13

Echo Six

allegro energico
quickly, with energy

Another pair of Thyrian fighters broke off the formation and charged a gap in the Shuhr snare, trying to destroy the symmetry of the enemy's front. But like heatseekers, the renegades had locked onto their target, and the arc began to close around the Thyrians' defensive half-globe, Shuhr catchfield ranges overlapping, cannon lighting. Firebird slid into hypnotic accord with the sensor screens, translating two-dimensional readouts into a three-dimensional battle.

"Ready, Tellai?" Brennen accelerated with the escort as Firebird poised both hands over the board. Tel groaned. Another gap broke open near the edge of the Shuhr formation below them. Firebird spotted it as Brennen vectored in.

"Cancel formation. All ships to fighting pairs. Two-Gamma, pull in with me." A companion closed with them until their forward energy shields overlapped. Aft, other ships paired. Forward, the gap narrowed rapidly. Could the Shuhr read strategy from her mind? No time to worry about it. They had flown into cannon range. Firebird raised slip-shields as the eighteen Thyrian ships dove for the wall.

Scarcely aware of the familiar quivering in her body as the slip-shield took hold, she felt the ship reel with energy unevenly absorbed. Three enemy fighters closed inward on them. Brennen brought the HF stable again so she could target ships on the screens. She fired the port gun twice at the closest, then sent two heatseekers down the beams. Brennen's glance flitted from fore to visual screens as he pushed the fighter toward escape velocity.

"Blast," Firebird muttered, as the enemy caught her heatseekers in midflight and sent a flurry of missiles in return. She clipped one an instant before it passed on her wingman's side.

"Thanks, Alpha," came a deep male voice on the interlink.

"Any time." Enthusiastically she picked away the rest of the swarm with the port laser cannon. They could have been deflected by being particle-shielded, but that would drain the generators' output. Brennen needed that output for speed.

The ship lurched sideways. Firebird glanced at the screen and saw only empty space on her right where that wingman had been. Her insides sank.

"What was that?" Tellai's voice quivered.

"They got Gamma from the other side," Brennen said tightly. "We're on our own." He rotated upper-starboard and gave Firebird a clear shot at the ship that had destroyed their wingman. Betting the enemy pilot would also avoid using particle shielding, she sent him a missile and counted three. One pip on the screen abruptly vanished.

As metal hail swept by she doubled the particle shields, which briefly arrested their acceleration. A brilliant light charge passed just before the nose of their ship, atomizing a candescent trail through debris and momentarily blinding her through the overhead visual screen. Firebird bit the tip of her tongue. If they had been just quicker, just farther along, they would have been overloaded—and dead.

Which we still could be at any moment. She drummed her fingers. *Without shield overlap.* Brennen raced into the gap left in the wall by the disintegrated enemy ship. She felt him accelerate again, with one hand over his directional stick and the other thumb covering the throttle while four fingers flew on the navcomputer.

"I'm afraid it will be worse than this, trying to get down at Hesed. If they could send DeepScan signals over that range, we'd never make it."

She fired another burst of energy aft at the Shuhr ship chasing them like fury. Ahead waited open space. "Can we jump for Hesed on this course?"

"No. Wrong heading. Have to make an intermediate jump. Anyone still with us?"

She stared hard at the compviewer readout. "It looks like . . . four ahead and about five aft that haven't quite broken through . . . and that first pair is around."

"I can cross-program them from here." The ship pitched as they were hit from behind. The lunge, forward and down, tested the clasps on her harness, but the particle shield held. "But only the ones that are clear to jump. You fly."

She seized the flight controls before her, and as he swiveled away to the sideboard she kept accelerating evasively, with one hand on the stick and the other at the shields.

Suddenly she had an idea, so crazy she almost dismissed it. "Brenn, do we have power and life support enough to hit Echo Six and still reach Procyel?"

"What?" He lifted one hand off the sideboard.

"Could we draw off some of the ships waiting for us at Hesed by hitting one of their home bases and then running again?"

He scarcely moved. "Yes!—But . . . Yes, that may be the one thing they wouldn't expect us to try. They've probably pulled their forces from Echo Six to gather this fleet, too." For a moment, he bent back to the computer keys. "We can do it," he declared, "and it's in this slip quadrant." He programmed a sequence, then called into the link, "Jump in forty seconds. Who's clear?"

She had not missed that pause. *"But,"* what? Hastily she squelched the thought and tried instead to raise the old careless song to the crest of her awareness.

Ten ships answered. After he touched ten panels in rapid succession, he hit a bar to cross-program and activate.

The jumplight pulsed. One kick and they would be free.

"Be ready for anything when we break," he called to his escort. "We're headed for Echo Six."

It didn't matter if the enemy heard him. That was his intention. They would arrive long before any lightspeed communication, and not even RIA could send an epsilon wave that far.

The computer took over the craft and hurtled it onto course vector. With slip-shields already activated, the translight drive engaged, and Firebird faded into her seat.

They were away. The blank screens gleamed steadily.

Firebird let out the breath she had been unconsciously holding. Brennen presented his right hand with a smile that delighted her. "Very professional, Major."

She pulled him close and kissed him so hard her teeth hurt. Slip-state, and safe for a while. They had fought together at last.

In a minute she remembered Tellai. She drew away from Brennen and pulled off the headset. Massaging her scalp, she twisted around to see how Tel had taken the battle.

His eyes shone as big and round as Triona's twin moons. Focused as though hypnotized on the sensor display, they gleamed with tears.

"Are you hurt, Tel?" she asked softly, pressing a control to recline her high-backed seat.

"I guess not." He cleared the gravel from his voice. "I was thinking about Phoena. Those are the people that have her. Was that a major battle? That is, compared with . . . you've both done that sort of thing before."

Brennen rubbed his palms on his thighs. "We were hit. If our shields had gone we'd be dead, just as in a full-scale war."

"I'd never make a soldier," Tellai groaned.

As Firebird dried her own palms, the ragged fingernail scraped on her skyff. Brennen pulled a packet of gray concentrate cubes from below the console and shared them around. Firebird crunched and swallowed, stretched, and pushed the seatback farther down.

"You should sleep, Mari." Before she could protest, Brennen touched her forehead and drowsiness reached up for her. She fell asleep in seconds.

When hunger woke her, both men slept. Tel curled toward the aft bulkhead; Brennen lay with his head rested against the back of his seat, looking as if the slightest change in attitude would wake him, and to her surprise, a tear tracked down one cheek. *Gamma*, she remembered. Brennen knew those crewmen. Firebird located her own cache of flavorless gray concentrates and washed down a double handful with a packet of vaguely tart electrolyte drink, wondering if she should awaken either of them. The break indicator showed over a day remaining on the jump. With a glance down at Kiel and Kinnor, who lay like small duffels stowed between the seats, she loosened her harness, pulled up her cape, and tucked it around her, for comfort more than warmth. Curling toward the starboard side of the hull, she let the thrum of the superlight engine and the odd slip vibration lull her back to sleep.

Carradee Angelo stepped anxiously into her long, lamplit sitting room, where the Federate Governor sat waiting. He rose to greet her. Last week, he'd brought the horrifying news that Iarlet and Kessie's shuttle had vanished. They'd been sent into hiding, true enough—but no one had intended that they disappear.

At least, that's what he had told her. *You're dealing with a telepathic enemy,* she'd decided. *The Sentinels would want you to think they'd vanished, even if they hadn't.*

She extended a hand to the sandy-haired Governor. "Your Excellency," she said in a soft voice. "You wished to bring news personally, and not through my acting regent?"

She seated herself beside him beneath a darkened window, and he returned to his chair. "Yes, Madame. I am sorry, I have no word as yet on your children. This is official news of Firebird's."

"Has she named the child, then?"

Danton shifted on his seat, and she saw that he wanted to smile. "Your sister has borne twins."

"Well!" Carradee laced her fingers. "There's no twinning in *our* family."

"I'm told," Danton said, "that Sentinels are able to manage such things for their wives, if the women want to have all their childbearing over with at once." He crossed his legs and leaned back.

"Oh." Carradee straightened her skirt. *How unnatural. But nice, I suppose.* Then she had a second thought, which she hurriedly dismissed: *If Brennen Caldwell could give her twins, what else could he do for her that a normal man could not?*

"Fraternal twins." Danton smiled openly, now. "Two sons: Kiel Labbah, and Kinnor Irion."

Carradee's hands fell on her lap. "Sons. You did say sons."

He beamed. "I did say sons, Majesty. You recall, perhaps, the Sentinels' insistence that the Angelo line descended from a carrier of the Aurian plague?"

Carradee rose off her chair. Scarcely noticing that Danton stood, too, out of protocol, she walked a few steps down the patterned carpet. "She was treated. I remember you saying that, and Phoena nearly dying of rage at the very suggestion."

"Yes, Madame." He stepped to her side.

"When Daithi is . . . better," she said, blanking the image of her beloved paralyzed on his bed, "perhaps I, too, should be . . . treated. Quietly." She turned to him. "Can your medics hold their tongues?"

"Of course, Majesty."

"I cannot decide now. Later. Thank you for coming, Governor. Is there any other message you wish to give me?"

"No, Majesty."

"Is there no . . ." She hated to sound frightened, but she was. "No more sign of Shuhr activity here?"

"None."

She extended a hand again. He touched his lips to it. Still smiling, he left the chamber.

Carradee paced to the far end of the long, dim room. Sons of an Angelo. Aurians. Sentinels.

Iarlet!

Kessaree!

And then, more deeply anguished . . . Daithi!

She slid a hand up and down a slender lamp pole. Danton did not know—could never be told—that the finest medics on Naetai had barely kept her husband alive. He lay sleeping now, in her new, temporary chambers, sedated as heavily as they dared keep him. Quietly, with Rattela—whose work as her temporary regent, until she could settle her familial concerns, had been irreproachable—she had agreed upon the desirability of trying to conceive again. For the sake of the Angelo family, she needed another heiress—quickly.

But the act was impossible, and Electoral law would disbar any heir medically conceived.

Daithi did have moments of painful lucidity, granted by the doctors who felt even the safest sedatives could not be administered continuously. Daithi understood the situation. If this went on, he would feel it his duty . . .

No. He can't, she wailed to herself.

. . . to suicide, and leave her free to marry again.

With Iarlet and Kessie missing, Phoena was left *heir pro tempore*—but, appalled by Phoena's defection, Carradee had eliminated Phoena from her mental list of potential heirs. Publicly, she doubted she could afford to do so (*not in front of Rattela, certainly!*), for that would leave only—

Carradee stopped in her pacing. Firebird had sons. Sons. An incredible occurrence in the Angelo line. If they were confirmed as heirs . . . even one of them, Kinnor, the elder . . .

For Daithi's sake . . .

She raised one hand to touch the ornate frame of a glowering portrait that hung between high windows. *Could I have it done?*

Rattela would oppose it, of course. But what of the others? *We do have more male than female Electors. Perhaps they would support a Prince.*

She certainly didn't feel alien. If they could be made to understand that the Angelo line was part . . . Aurian . . . already, and had ruled them well for six centuries, then the Electors could not consider Caldwell's heritage alien.

Glancing up at the glaring, long-dead Grand Duke, she drew her hand away from the portrait's frame. *Oh, yes, they could!*

They could even strip the throne from the Angelo dynasty. That privilege was reserved to the Electorate.

No. Not after six hundred years. Her sense of history and heritage rebelled at the notion. She stepped to a window and gazed out over the lights of Sae Angelo.

Painfully she recalled her mother's masterful way with her Electors. The throne *was* legally a figurehead, and Siwann, as a real ruler, had been the exception. Only once in Carradee's experience had an Elector dared to countervote Queen Siwann. That stubborn young Elector had been Firebird, on the occasion of initiating the tragic VeeRon War.

Firebird had been right. But that was water downriver.

Carradee drew herself erect. *I will be strong. I must.*

Eventually Firebird, Brennen, and Tel held a shipboard council of war. "Of course, this could very well be a trap." Brennen hooked one leg over a stabilizer bar. "I wish I could look at your mental fiber, to see if that Echo Six idea was your own or if they sent it at you."

"You could tell that?" Tellai asked. Firebird saw in the set of his brows that he only half believed.

"Maybe. But I can't, now."

A-status. She felt his disquiet.

"So it could still be a trap." Tel took his drink packet from the empty seat.

"It could. As I told the squadron, we must be ready for anything."

He spent the next hours evaluating Tellai's progress with Federate console design. Firebird climbed into the back and listened, pleased by her pupil's progress.

But with weaponry, he had to begin from zero. Once, in frustration, he turned on her. "There must be easier ways to die."

"Oh, yes. I recall two Wastlings who simply disappeared. Maybe they died easy, but I doubt it. You may know more—"

"Mari."

Abashed, she hushed her surge of Wastling spite for the Heirs of the ten noble houses, disappointed to find she had buried her own deep-seated prejudices alive. Prince Tel Tellai-Angelo had come to them, a Wastling and a Sentinel, for help. He could not be held responsible for the traditions of the N'Taian aristocracy, nor the cruelties of other Heirs.

"Sorry, Tel."

"No, don't be." He rotated back toward the ordnance panel. "I wonder how much Naetai has been disadvantaged by some practices I've always condoned."

"Good." She glanced at Brennen. "Brenn, should we wake the twins, do you think? Does it affect your energy level, to keep them in t-sleep?"

"Not at all. Dickin put them down at Trinn Hill for just that reason. I can wake them at Hesed."

Firebird gave him a sidelong look. "You people thought of everything, didn't you?"

They wrung precious hours of sleep from the time in slip. Nerves and anticipation had to be silenced. Whatever awaited, it would be better faced rested than overwrought. Now the glowing green digital break indicator approached zero. Firebird sat erect and full of fight, with one hand at the gun controls and the other firmly clenching a stabilizer bar, waiting to be thrown forward and thrust into battle. The final seconds counted off under the blue striplights. Glowing digits melted, accompanied by a soft but irritating warning buzzer.

Then came the pitch of deceleration. Drop point: Firebird raised the particle shields instantly, praying the feared trap might not exist, then stared transfixed at the sextet of sensor screens, watching for minute anomalies or moving objects anywhere near the plane of the binary Echo stars' planetary system below them. The screens showed ten other ships in a loose, roughly oval group, moving with theirs down toward the ecliptic, and nothing else.

"Looks good," she said hesitantly.

Brennen leaned back. "I think you're right."

She switched off the shields and felt the ship accelerate. On the curved panel overhead, distant stars had focused out of chaos while she watched the screens. Huge, yellow Echo Alpha shone near its small red companion star, and just beyond the Echo system, a weirdly glowing, pale dust cloud filled much of her field of vision. Like an aurora, it pulsed and shimmered, and when Brennen opened his interlink, the speaker roared like a small engine.

"One-Beta, do you copy?"

"Copy, sir," the receiver replied with a basso that rumbled far below the crackling din.

"One-Epsilon, did you make it?"

"One-Epsilon, standing by." That was Dardy's voice!

Brennen too gave a silent laugh of relief. "Excellent," he said.

"Beta, take the squad insystem and make all the trouble you can, while we check the outer bases and try to scare them into recalling their Hesed fleet and leaving the sanctuary unguarded. But be careful. This could be a trap. This interference is ridiculous. How's your copy?"

"Eight-over-six, sir, but I've never heard such noise on a link."

"Then we'll lose audio contact as soon as we break formation. Laser-pulse would be too dangerous to use, this close to a Shuhr base." Brennen checked the screens again. "We'll try to rendezvous in twelve hours near Seven's orbit. That will give you some time at Six. Maybe you can take down their heavy shields and neutralize any attack ships. Use your own discretion. I'll signal on four-two-zero-zero-point-nine when we come in to rendezvous. Did you copy?"

"Yes, sir." The deep voice repeated the order.

Brennen changed course slightly, and Firebird watched the other ships pull into a tight wedge. The RF interference might prove to be a blessing. A minimum of radio-frequency interlink transmissions would stray toward the Shuhr colony, and their chances of striking effectively would increase with the element of surprise.

Soon the phalanx looked small on the screens. "Why didn't we go in on the raid?" Tellai sounded almost disappointed.

"Besides mass detectors, they'll have mentalic fielding, similar to the perimeter we use to guard Hesed." Brennen pulled away from the console. Firebird sensed a relaxing sigh that he did not express but felt deeply. He *had* been concerned that they'd planted that idea in her. "You see," he continued, "no one can pass a certain zone undetected. His mental activity reveals his presence to a trained sensor. Anyone they won't pass, they can force to land and surrender or drive insane. You would both be affected at a far greater range than those Sentinels, though these two—" he leaned down and touched each of his sons, "in tardema-sleep, they're virtually invulnerable. So we'll hang back. If the others destroy the fielding, we can get in on the strike, too, if there is time enough before their Thyrian ships catch up with us."

"How is the fielding projected?" Firebird asked.

"Some day I will show you. If we reach Hesed."

They sank on the plane of the system, decelerating only slightly. Two of Echo's inner planets lay near alignment with outermost Eight, about fifteen degrees from Echo Six. When Firebird checked the computer's screen and then the externals, she saw Brennen was setting a course toward Eight.

A few uneventful hours' flight at barely sublight speed put them close. Firebird, maintaining a wide scanning sweep on the link, began to detect signals at the low end of the band. "I think," she said slowly, "someone's about to pick us up."

"Good," Brennen murmured. "Let's go in."

He decelerated hard. Within minutes a trio of scout ships appeared. Firebird took one immediately, and of the remaining pair, one broke off and hid behind the small icy planet, while the other gave her and Brennen five minutes of tumbling gun-and-shield. Firebird finally ended the duel with a lucky hit on her opponent's stabilizer vane during a flicker of his slip-shield.

They gave chase after the other. Still fearing a trap, they pressed even Tellai onto watch, and it was the Prince who saw the silvery speck vanish into the dust cloud.

"Hm." Brennen pursed his lips. "That's a hopeful heading. He could be running for the Alta sector, and Hesed is very close."

"Shall we take care of whatever they've built down there?" asked Tellai, releasing his snugger with off-handed ease that showed he was beginning to learn the ropes and anxious to prove it.

"I think so." Brennen spoke seriously, but Firebird felt his amusement.

Planetside, a beacon guarded a few buildings. Tellai tried his hand on the last run, wheeling the fore cannon from the rear seat controls and missing as much as he hit, but grinning like a sim-gamer on a hot streak. He did show a surprising talent long stifled by his fear of speed, as his graceful "Tellai hands"—so like Phoena's—tapped the panels. Firebird was tempted to sit on her own: the Angelo hands, wider and shorter-fingered, "for clenching the reins of power," as some derided. She had never minded them before. Why now?

Because Kinnor has them. Wistfully she glanced down at her "touchy" twin. He still slept.

They turned in toward Six. Echo's two stars glowed brighter than before, just off center on the visual screen. Two hours remained before their scheduled rendezvous on the interlink. Firebird caught a concerned look from Brennen and spoke quickly. "I feel fine." She stretched. "But maybe I could catch one more nap."

While she slept, they bypassed the orbit of Echo Seven. She was dreaming about Phoena, an endless chase around a small, sweaty-smelling black world that was supposed to be Three Zed, when Brennen began to react hard and quickly to some threat. Instantly she came awake.

The fore screen glittered with ships converging on Echo Six.

Within the swarm clustered a smaller group; the rest of their squadron would shortly be trapped near the southern pole by the descending mob.

"Well, you were lucky," Tel said through clenched teeth. "That must be the gang that was waiting for us at Thyrica. We beat them. And you're still free to jump."

"Not without them." Brennen accelerated toward the planet.

Firebird found the prearranged frequency on the transceiver. "Flights One and Two, this is Two-Alpha," she said, clearly detaching each syllable from the others. Her repetitive signaling was answered only by overriding static.

"Set a tone," Brennen suggested.

She switched on a G above middle C and keyed the signaler to a lively, syncopated rhythm.

"Aren't we getting out of here?" asked a small, frightened voice behind her.

She glared at Tellai. "Those are our people," she cried. *Aristocrats!* "And, besides—"

"Mari," Brennen said sternly. "Keep your mind on the present. You don't know who's listening, and we're coming into range of a scan team."

Frantically she squelched her words and thoughts of escape to Hesed, of the need to draw off its Shuhr blockaders, and the futility of trying to run that Hesedan blockade alone. She'd had no sensation of access, but she had to believe in the danger.

As Brennen's fingers danced across the board, the globe swung on their screens until its southern pole lay dead ahead. Below, the swirling battle abruptly slowed. A wave of hostility washed into Firebird and slowly ebbed. "Brenn—"

"I felt it. Don't touch the board. They could try to make you fire on our own ships."

The pattern on the ventral screen changed. Against the orbiting spirals of Shuhr craft struggled a tight wedge of fighters, slowly rising free as the enemy shifted focus onto Firebird and Brennen.

"Mari!" Brennen cried.

Startled, Firebird pulled away from the console. She had been going for the ordnance controls, against all reason.

"Get in back with Tel. I can't help you now. Tellai, hold her."

"But I can't help you as well from—"

The ship lurched as Shuhr firebolts grazed their shields. For the first time in Firebird's experience, raw anger flooded the bonding resonance. She fumbled hastily out of her harness and squeezed between the seats and over the babies, almost landing on Tellai.

"I can do some shooting for you, Caldwell," Tel offered with an edge of determination in his voice.

"Only if you hold her, too."

Tel grappled Firebird's hands in one of his own, then reached for the sidehand ordnance board. From her uncomfortable position stretched across the bench, Firebird watched. *Thank the Powers Brennen gave him a little weapons training!*

The Thyrian ships had nearly cleared the swarm of Shuhr. Brennen fought his way toward them as they began to drive through the secondary swirl attacking him. Finally the last aggressor was shot away, and the Thyrian squadron englobed him.

Firebird's arms ached. "Is it safe to move now?"

Brennen turned around, then leaned close and looked sharply into each of her eyes. No emotion passed his shields. "Let her go, Tel. But watch her."

She twisted her body one way, then the other.

"Two-Alpha, this is One-Beta. Are you all right, sir?"

His glance flicked to the interlink speaker. "Good enough. Report on your attack run."

"It was undermanned. Even the fielding was down."

Brennen interrupted. "Fielding down?"

"Confirm, sir," answered One-Beta's deep voice.

"Then who's harassing Firebird?" Tellai hissed.

Brennen covered his microphone and whispered, "I'd guess a fielding team on one of their larger ships knows her alpha profile well enough to target her. That would explain why they've left *you* alone."

One-Beta continued his report. "We flattened the ground level on the first flyby and were going back to clean up with the Novas when guests started arriving."

"That's all right. We may need those drones." Aside, he added for the N'Taians' ears, "Their civilians can dig themselves out of the lower levels. Eventually."

"Women and children?" Tellai sniffed. "Look who they're trying to eliminate: you Angelo women and your babies."

. . . and children, Firebird's inner voice echoed. She leaned down to stroke Kinnor's silky, strangely cool cheek. *Even among the enemy there are lives worth saving, children who might have grown up noble and good if they had been born on Thyrica.*

On a Shuhr world that kind would die very young, she decided.

"We could take another run on the colony," the voice on the speaker was saying. "These new shields are taking it well."

"I'd like to, but there aren't enough of us." Brennen kept

his stare fixed on Firebird. "We had best make a fast jump to Alta for reinforcements, if we hope to finish this tetter's nest."

Alta. Firebird nodded. The Fleet, and safety. *They couldn't refuse us help—could they?*

Brennen addressed the interlink. "Disengage and make ready for a jump, Alta quadrant, as fast as you can get clear."

The Shuhr ships above began to pour missiles into the Thyrian sphere at an unprecedented rate of fire. Firebird reached automatically for the guns.

Tellai dove over and seized her arms. "Stop it, Firebird!"

She choked off a frustrated retort and let him pull her down onto her face. With her eyes closed, her other senses became sharper. She felt the guns fire, then the missiles. The ship gave a coughing groan, and Brennen's feelings changed to anxious waiting. She opened her eyes and pressed up slightly. Tellai's fingers tightened on her wrists.

"One of our Novas," Brennen said quietly. Then they waited again.

The visual screen flashed, and Brennen whooped. "Took its reactor! The biggest ship, Mari. Hold tight to Tel."

Wildly the HF tossed as waves of debris began to slide around its doubled shields, expanding in concentric globes of destruction through both fleets. Firebird pulled upright and stared awed at the instrument screens. Along the perimeter of the outermost wave, the less massive Shuhr fighters, whose shields could not turn the metal storm, came apart and became part of the wild, brilliant chaos.

Then, on the dorsal screen, a flight of surviving Shuhr ships peeled away, headed for open space. Caught in the maelstrom their missile had created, the Thyrians lagged, helpless to pursue.

The Shuhr flight vanished. A second drew away.

Brennen glanced aside. "Alta heading," he announced grimly. "Unless we slip quickly we'll never beat them."

Firebird shut her eyes and rubbed her face angrily against the rough fabric covering the bench. She had telegraphed again.

A double arc of renegade ships stood between the Thyrian fighters and the sanctuary of space. Again they drove at it, but the Shuhr fleet commander tightened it around them. Two ships at the rear of Brennen's formation were destroyed by missiles from astern.

"Oh, no!" Tel pointed toward the overhead viewscreen. "There's their Hesed blockade fleet!"

Out of the shimmering radio cloud emerged fifty more ships, bearing down on the battle.

"It couldn't be!" Firebird squeezed Tel's fingers. "Not yet!"

"You're right," Brennen muttered. "It couldn't. All ships, arm drones," he called into his tiny microphone.

Tel released Firebird's hands to wipe perspiration from his forehead, and immediately she found herself reaching for the other ordnance board. Disgusted, she twined her fingers into a double fist and clenched it between her knees. Then realization struck her. "It *was* a trap, Brenn! These came from somewhere else! They simply didn't know how fast our ships are!"

Brennen accelerated again. She pressed deeper into the seat. "Prepare to fire," he said in the singsong of ordering sequence. "All remaining drones."

She tightened her legs to hold her rebelling hands.

"Now!"

The drone hold coughed. Brennen followed the huge missile briefly, then pulled away.

"Tighten up," he ordered his pilots.

The squadron of drones sped forward and the fighters banked aside, and Firebird knew each cluster of blips would look much like the other on enemy screens. Some renegades gave chase. Others closed in on the Novas.

Half a minute later, the first drone found a target. The visual panel splashed with new light. Attuned over Brennen's shoulder to six pale screens, Firebird felt the squadron ride broadside along waves of debris that had been Shuhr ships, accelerating away from the ecliptic as the second fleet closed its trap.

The jumplight flashed. Brennen turned to the computer and made a minute course alteration. "Correction in heading," he announced to the interlink. He hit the bar one second before the indicator zeroed.

The ship spun and accelerated past lightspeed, and as the stars turned pale and vanished before her, Firebird felt a scarcely tangible slip away.

She slumped forward. Once again she had betrayed her people. The Shuhr were undoubtedly racing toward Alta to head them off. The Thyrian ships had proven they could outrun the Shuhr's; this time, though, it would be terribly close. Brennen had said so.

Brennen turned his head, laughing crazily as though exhausted, and returning triumphant apology for her guilt.

"I'm sorry I deceived you, Mari. But it worked."

"What?—You tricked them," she breathed.

"With your help. Think clearly, now that you can. They couldn't beat us to Alta. I'm sorry for playing with your matrix. They may cause some trouble at Alta, but I am sure Regional will manage. Meanwhile, I think we'll have an easy time getting down at Hesed."

Of course, she thought. Then, recalling that last humiliating audience with the Altan Council, she wondered if perhaps Brennen struggled with spite of his own, and would be amused to see Regional stirred up by a Shuhr strike in his absence. "Brenn . . . ?"

He unharnessed, then flexed his hands. "Yes?"

"No." *That's not Brennen's way.* "Forget it."

Chapter 14

For Phoena's Sake

offertorium
presentation of the offering

No Shuhr blockaders challenged them at Procyel, and under falling darkness with lights out, they glided silently in on Hesed's landing strip. Half the original escort had engaged the Shuhr at takeoff and retreated to Thyrica; others' shielding had failed. Only nine heavy fighters remained.

Onto the scorched field Firebird stepped, carefully holding little Kiel close to her. Grimy and salty, she was anxious to see him awake again.

Near the foot of the boarding ladder that had been floated up to the craft stood two familiar, poised figures: one man tall and lean, whose pale yellow hair and white belted tunic almost shone in the fading light, and one feminine, slender, erect, with hair that hung far below her green belt: Jenner Dabarrah, Master of the Sanctuary, and Mistress Anna.

Anna Dabarrah smiled warmly and held out her arms as Firebird drew close.

Firebird carefully gave Anna the child. "He's in tardema," she said, then wondered if she needed to explain that to the Sentinel woman.

Holding him tenderly, Anna pushed the blanket away from his face. "He's beautiful," she said, and Firebird felt warmer despite the evening breeze.

Tellai followed. Last down the steps came Brennen, carrying
Kinnor. Tel walked boldly forward. "Tel Tellai, sir." He bowed
to Master Dabarrah. "Well, actually, it's Tellai-Angelo, Your
Honor."

"You are welcome at Hesed, Your Highness," said Master
Dabarrah, "as a member of Mistress Caldwell's family." He
extended an arm toward his mistress. "My wife, Anna."

Anna inclined her head toward Tellai, and her deep brown hair
touched with silver slipped forward over her shoulder, covering
Kiel. Casually she tossed it back.

"Master." Firebird caught Dabarrah's eye and expressed silent
thanks for allowing Tel to pass the perimeter at Procyel II. Under
normal circumstances, he would have been turned away like any
other non-Sentinel.

"Mistress Firebird." Anna Dabarrah nodded again. "Are you
and the children well?"

"Yes." Firebird inhaled the free air of Procyel. "But I could
sleep away a dekia. Master Dabarrah, what *has* happened to Carradee's little Iarlet and Kessaree? Are they all right? We understood they were to come here."

The lanky Master Sentinel addressed Brennen. "The little ones'
transport left Naetai two months ago. It has not arrived."

Brennen's stare remained steady on Dabarrah. Firebird groaned.
Out of the corner of her eye, she saw Tellai raise one hand in a
gesture of helpless protest.

"No word at all?"

"None. Malfunction, perhaps."

Perhaps not. Firebird held down the first shock of grief. What
would Tel be feeling?

"Come in." Dabarrah gestured toward the House's elevator.
"Please."

"Let me take the children while you bathe and eat," offered
Anna. "Brennen, come to our rooms to freshen; Firebird, you
know the way to your own."

Down the white stone walkway Firebird followed a blue-skirted
sekiyr. Beside her, past its white latticework railing, rippled a
vast underground reflecting pool, its blue-green underwater lights
reflecting asymmetric patterns off a high white ceiling and darkened skylights. Paths of stepping stones showed like square shadows floating on bright water.

In the suite where she had spent her wedding night, she gladly
shed the skyff and trousers she had worn since dinner at Shanneman's. Then she bathed quickly and slipped into a cool blue gown

she found laid out on the bed, near the wall of water that cascaded down the room's south side. Water flowed everywhere at Hesed, it seemed. *Of course,* she mused as she smoothed the long waves of her hair. *Men from watery Thyrica built this sanctuary.*

As her thirsty ears drank in the liquid sounds, she caught a faint breath of the scent of Soldane, sweet and pungent. *So those are kirka trees on the islands.*

Such a lovely prison. Will they ever let us leave?

Yet the depth of her relief to have reached sanctuary awed her. Had the hormones of pregnancy and motherhood done this? Had she lost her hunger for adventure, or had the allure of this garden world enthralled her, so that she would never be a callow warrior again?

Her children were safe. That was enough.

Brennen waited on the walkway with Tel, whose plain gray jumpsuit lent him a new aura of understated maturity. "Dabarrah's office." Brennen extended an arm, and as she took it, he stepped out down the walkway. "We are expected."

Dabarrah stood inside, waiting, like a white-and-gold statue. "Your Highness," he said, "forgive me a moment's necessary rudeness. May I speak alone with the Caldwells? Briefly?"

"Oh. Certainly." Tel retreated out the arch toward the pool.

Dabarrah nodded to Brennen, who looked serious and felt troubled. "You have to know, Mari."

She sat down on a white stone bench, the serenity of Hesed ebbing.

". . . Why Dickin has told us to keep apart."

"All right," she said. "I see. Here, we're safe. Before, the Shuhr might have . . . heard . . . what the trouble is."

"Exactly," he said. "Mari, somehow—and this is the danger, we're not sure how—you killed Bosk Terrell."

She sat stunned. "What?"

"We found his body in the house's security entry. No sign of injury, no poison." He flicked at a blemish in the white stone wall. "No other explanation."

Firebird glanced from Brennen to Dabarrah. The elder Master pressed his palms together.

"Do you remember what you did to him?" Brennen asked.

"No. I didn't try to do any— No, wait. I tried to fight back, it's true. But I didn't know how. I got no farther than Turning. After that—nothing."

"After that, your mental strength was so totally exhausted that you nearly died. I had to lend you beta strength to keep your autonomous systems functioning, while your own energy rebuilt.'' Shifting his feet, he fingered his cuff tab. ''The images of death you told me about: If they're truly bound by the carrier, as you envision them, they might have caused his death. But we don't know. And we don't know what to do. You only Turned?''

''That's . . . all I remember.''

''If we—Dickin and Dabarrah and I—understand it correctly, his epsilon control over his own life centers could have convinced him he *was* dying . . . killing him. If so, only the starbred face any danger from contact with you, and those of higher potential would be in greater danger. It would take the mental strength of two, at least, to kill this way—''

''Or so we believe,'' Dabarrah said, carefully, as if correcting an overconfident student.

''No Sentinel has ever been able to do this,'' said Brennen. ''You have no control, no training. I think you see the potential danger . . .''

Wide-eyed, she nodded. ''To you, Brenn. And . . .'' She paused, horrified. ''The babies?'' She turned to Dabarrah. ''Is there anything you can do?''

''That is why you were sent here.'' Dabarrah spoke gently. ''My degree is in psi medicine. It is likely I can help and guide you, where others could not.''

And the other reason I was sent here was for isolation, she thought miserably. *To keep other Sentinels safe . . . from me. Oh, squill.*

And is that why they put the babies in tardema-sleep? So I couldn't harm them?

Footsteps approached on the waterside walkway. A young sekiyr entered, followed by a gliding cart crowded with earthenware dishes. The sekiyr extended the cart's legs and carefully set out dinner as Master Dabarrah pulled stools to a wooden sideboard.

Brennen stepped to the arch. ''Tellai?'' he called.

Firebird took the thick stew Brennen served, filled with chunks of vegetables so bright they must have been carried on the run from garden to kettle; coarse-textured brown bread with a seductive aroma; and berries—colored and faceted like garnets, they were the size of eggs but smelled like melons.

After the first few mouthfuls, however, she hardly tasted them. *I killed a man. Using only . . . I didn't mean to. . . .*

Brennen and Tel ate with more enthusiasm, discussing the battles at Thyrica and Echo Six with Dabarrah, though Firebird saw and sensed occasional glances Brennen sent her way.

I'll be all right, she kept thinking at him.

When Brennen explained how they had tried to draw off the Shuhr blockading Hesed, the elder Master nodded solemnly. "They vanished two days ago, without preliminaries," said Dabarrah. Firebird pricked up her ears. They had not met the Hesed fleet at Echo Six, after all. How many ships did those renegades own? "In the respite," Dabarrah continued, "we have run messengers everywhere our people live in numbers. We have also had long words with Alta, who passed news to the High Council at Elysia. No action is being taken yet, and we are fully self-sufficient should they reinstate the blockade, but plans of several sorts are being discussed—as is your RIA work, although only among ourselves."

RIA? Nibbling at a chunk of brown bread, Firebird attended again. Immediately she felt a cautionary surge from Brennen. Tel, examining a four-bite garnetberry, seemed not to hear.

Brennen set down his cup and fingered its rim. "And you can help Mari? The Masters from College did what they could, quickly, for the alpha tampering, but she needs deeper healing of that sort, too."

She flushed.

Dabarrah stretched out his long legs beneath the cart. "Yes," he said. "But I will need to research and observe carefully before acting. You will be somewhat vulnerable, my lady, particularly if the blockaders return, and turn an attack downward. But you will be here, and we will see that you are cared for."

Firebird sighed, surrendering to lethargy, and then yawned mightily.

Brennen rose. "I'll see you back to the rooms. Then I wish to talk to Tel and Master Dabarrah a little longer."

She pushed back her stool. "I can find my way. Good night, gentlemen."

Dabarrah stood as Brennen sank back onto his stool. "Let me walk with you, Mistress Firebird."

Firebird accepted Dabarrah's arm, wondering if he wished to begin his assessment already.

Brennen watched them go. Through the arch, the central expanse glowed, turquoise rippled with dusky blue shadows.

Hesed: He *had* feared he would never stand here again. He had returned, but neither at peace nor in triumph.

"I have loved Master Jenner," he said softly to Tel, "since I served as a sekiyr under him. He shows the power of gentleness more clearly than any other."

"I see what you mean." Tel tipped his head back, cracked his neck, and then met Brennen's gaze. "It's not Dabarrah's authority that gives him such strength of spirit, but the other way around."

Brennen nodded, surprised. "You're stronger yourself than anyone realized. Until you came up against real adversity, you had no chance to show it."

"Thank you." Tel slid from his stool onto the long stone bench, gazed slowly across the office's bank of communications terminals, then out toward the vast pool. "This is an impressive place, Caldwell."

"It's a far cry from the Angelo palace."

"It's more serene. Quieter. But there's more power at work. Even I can feel it."

"Hesed is probably the most heavily protected enclave in this region of the Federate Whorl."

"Then Firebird and the babies are finally out of danger."

Another sekiyr came in. After laying his mug on the bench, Brennen transferred dishes from the sideboard into the cart's shelves as she retracted the grounding legs. She steered it out.

Yes. Out of danger, he thought, surprised by his bitterness. *From the Shuhr and from the Federacy's threats. And, perhaps, from herself.* He stirred, unable to ease a heavy new sense of mortality, and followed the sekiyr with his stare, recalling his own days of sanctuary service. "We should never have left."

"If you hadn't, would I have been able to contact you?"

"No."

"Then I'm glad you did."

Brennen shifted uncomfortably and ignored Tel's comment. "At Hesed, we live close to the soil. We do without weather control, grow food the old ways, and keep animals—to refresh the spirit and remind us of our kinship with the rest of creation. That is one of our oldest definitions of the Word, Tel: the created universe, all that fills it, and the expressed laws that keep it functioning."

Tel nodded slowly.

Brennen laced his fingers around one knee and went on. "Everyone at the Sentinel College spends at least one rotation here as a sekiyr, relearning the relationship between creativity and authority—our role in the Word—and mankind's old ways of matching basic living skills with self-expression. Relearning the satisfaction of meeting our own survival needs and of adding beauty where necessity has been satisfied." He fingered the repeating corn-sheaf pattern on his earthenware mug. "We are not evolving gods, but servants. Many of our elderly return to spend their last years in defensive fielding service. The sekiyrra perform most manual labor, but everyone must work to maintain the retreat and keep it as natural as possible. Firebird will probably be excused from the heaviest labor because of Kinnor and Kiel, but you and I will enter the task rotation tomorrow morning."

Tel flexed his slender arms, almost smiling. "That's where you built the shoulders, Caldwell?"

"It's a good life, which serves a profound need in the starbred. Even on Thyrica we are a people apart. Hesed is our sanctuary, and in time of need it would be our last retreat. You'll be content."

"No. Never content, so long as Phoena is a prisoner. I came for your help." Tel drummed his fingers on the bench beside him. "I don't know that I would have the audacity to ask again, now that I understand your situation. But every day she's there, I can't help thinking it will be worse for her."

Brennen sensed Tellai's ache, his fear and desperate hope. "If I stay here for Firebird's sake, you'll try to go yourself."

The dark eyes met his again, welcoming scrutiny. "Yes," Tel said.

Brennen commanded his muscles to release, his unaccustomed self-doubt to let him go. "You haven't a chance."

"I know."

Numbly he rubbed his face. Phoena's person had become a nexus of attention, regardless of her personality. The words of the Federate summons rose in his memory: Regional's offer, its ultimatum, and the threat—veiled, to be sure, but there—against Firebird's citizenship, and therefore her life. Compared with the N'Taian regime, the Federacy was a paragon of ideals—but as ever, the bureaucracy spawned by implicit trust in a few officials sometimes failed. There was a need for ethical men and women on the High Command, a need a Sentinel could fill.

And undoubtedly the Shuhr were subjecting Phoena to inquiries that daily increased the risk to them all. Certainly Terrell and other Shuhr agents had drawn on such research.

Terrell had been Shuhr. That hurt.

"The two of us might succeed. She'd come away for me." Tellai began confidently, then faltered. "I think."

One more echo of Brennen's inner argument insisted on being

heard. *Firebird has never hesitated to offer her life honorably. Never.*

"I don't mean to be unkind, Tel," Brennen said aloud, "but you would be a hindrance. You saw how they worked at Firebird's subconscious. If I have to protect you, I'll never be able to work against their surveillance. If anyone goes for Phoena, I will. Alone."

Tel's expression wrenched at him.

"I'll think it over," Brennen said gruffly, unsure of his voice and mind. "I said I would help you if I could, and I intend to keep my word."

The autumn morning broke fresh. Bursts of wind cooled sekiyrra who labored in Hesed's gardens, east of the hill where Firebird picked her way down the grassy slope with Brennen. Her pale blue gown trailed the last of the summer flowers, and tears chilled her cheeks. Last night, with infinite sympathy, Master and Mistress Dabarrah had refused to give the twins back, fearing her unknown power over their unformed minds. And now . . .

"I understand." Firebird pushed the words out as evenly as she could. "Of course. I see what's at stake. You've done this kind of thing all your life. But won't you wait until Master Dabarrah has my problem in hand? He might need your help. Kiel and Kinnor need you."

"My training is in other specialties." He said it with deep regret. "Dabarrah is well trained and equipped for his work, Mari. And the children have Dabarrah and Mistress Anna and every teacher and sekiyr at the sanctuary to care for them, until . . . Dabarrah feels certain you have . . . learned to control that wild talent."

She felt betrayed by fate and her own heart, which had given her love to this man and the children she'd never hoped for, only to demand death and separation. "It's a trap, Brenn! It's not Phoena they want, it's you!"

He walked on down the grassy hill without answering.

"Not even Danton wants Phoena, Brennen," she insisted, lengthening her steps.

"No." He turned his head so she could hear his whisper. "There, you're wrong. The Federacy contacted me weeks ago."

"And . . . ?" She halted in midstride.

"If attempting to save your sister is a matter of Federate security, as they claim, I would be free to use all my abilities without breaking the laws of our people, even if I had to take her against her will. And if I succeed, the Federacy wants me back. Do those things comfort you?"

She stared out over the river into the red stone of Hesed Valley. At the corner of her eye she saw him take several more steps down the meadow, then turn back.

"Is Phoena worth it, Brennen? —Is the Federacy?"

He looked up at her, and she devoured the sight of him standing with the wind in his hair. She felt his heart at peace, for danger did not turn him from his resolve.

Her own heart keened with the fear of losing him. *Your fame is assured,* she wanted to cry. *Must you be a hero a hundred times over?*

"Mari," he answered, "where would we be, if Tel hadn't been there to help you at Trinn Hill?"

Silently she shook her head.

"And at Echo Six, when you came under attack again?"

Firebird brushed away another icy tear.

He reached out and closed his fingers around her hand, and they walked on, down toward the House. "Remember why Tel came to us, and what I promised him. It has been as hard for him to change his thinking as it was for you."

"Harder, maybe." She stepped over the burrow of some small creature and lengthened her stride to match Brennen's, watching the ground, where leaves were reddening on red stones. "He has a secure position on Naetai, and he could still return to it. I had nothing left to live for."

"I'm glad you see that." He stopped again. "Now that your sister has seen the enemy, maybe she too has found enough wisdom to realize what they are."

"Brennen." As her eyes filled with tears, he drew her into his arms. It was on the tip of her tongue to beg him not to go alone to Three Zed, not to risk himself when she needed his support more than ever.

She spoke slowly and emphatically. "You *don't . . . need . . . to go.*"

But for Tel's sake he wanted to go, folly though it seemed. Tel's shifting attitudes hung in the balance, and even Phoena was not beyond redemption. Firebird had been ready to die for far less over the red sands of VeeRon.

"If you forbid me," he said softly, "I'll stay. I have never before saved my life by sheltering it, but I have no right to demand a sacrifice you're unable to make."

"It's the wrong time. And the wrong reason." She let her chin droop. His arms tightened their circle.

He didn't answer, but she read his willful numbing of

emotion—not a shielding, but careful affective control. He ached beneath it, for her and for the timing. She felt, too, his awe of the shamah and his reserved paternal pride.

And did he fear her mysterious ability?

"I won't forbid you," she said at last.

He nearly crushed her against himself. "Your strength," he whispered beside her ear, "has always been greater than your fear. Be strong for Tel when I am gone. If I can win Phoena's trust and her freedom, it will be a victory for all of us."

She drew on his calmness to gather herself together, and when she had mastered her grief, she tangled her fingers with his. They walked on down.

At the hilltop fielding station, he had shown her the system that protected Hesed from unauthorized approach, as Thyrica would be if isolated for defense. Now they stepped into the musty underground hangar where the HF-117s had been parked. To her surprise, one craft had been partially gutted, and portions of its electronic heart were being transferred onto a smaller craft. As she watched, a thin sekiyr walked across the bay with a large cylindrical object hovering several inches above his outspread hands.

"That's a toroidal juncture," Brennen whispered. "Does it look familiar?"

"I saw several up at the fielding station."

He beckoned her outside. On the grassy breakaway strip, new growth glistened in the scars of their landing.

"We progressed far enough with the RIA equipment to mount two systems into HFs when the emergency arose, and we brought one along," Brennen said as he walked. "Dardy tested it at Echo Six. The power is still very low, but it should give a Sentinel the remote capability to pass through a fielding net undetected. I'll take it to Three Zed."

She sighed.

"I would take you along if I could. At any other time, your skills would have been invaluable."

"Thank you." She didn't look up. "You can't wait? You're certain?"

He shook his head. "The Shuhr are as unbalanced as they have ever been. We've disabled their fleet and virtually wiped out their larger colony, and any Echo Six elements that survived will be as eager for Three Zed blood as for ours, if their defenses had been cut to gather that fleet. Now is the time to go, before they reach a new balance and the blockaders return to Hesed."

"I see that. If only it weren't Phoena."

"Phoena and Tel."

"Yes," she whispered.

"Two hundred ships!" thundered Juddis Adiyn. Phoena nearly put her hands to her ears to mute his roar.

Adiyn wore black, as did the other forty men and women in the long central office, for he had declared a day of mourning. The Shuhr fleet commander, a tall man of charismatic features, stood before Adiyn's desk, flanked by his subordinates and surrounded by the staff of Three Zed.

"And they had how many?" purred Dru Polar, who sat between Adiyn and Phoena at one end of the ebony desk top. Polar's satiny orange sash was the brightest flash of color in the room. Phoena liked that, though she distrusted his hasty glances toward Cassia Tulleman, ripe and supple in tight black shipboards.

"Eleven, Mine Eldest."

"What was that? I don't think I heard you correctly." Mockingly, Adiyn touched one ear.

The fleet commander raised hopeless eyes that hardened into acceptance of his fate. "Eleven ships," he repeated distinctly. "Eleven reached Echo Six. Heavy-fighter class, trained to fight as a unit, and solidly led. And something else, too, some disruptor field we have never encountered before. We had more guns, Eldest, it is true, but many of my pilots had not flown warships before last month."

Adiyn rose from his chair and strolled around the projection tank. "Do you have any idea how much work went into collecting that fleet?"

Phoena compressed her lips as the graying Eldest paced before his line of officers. The idiots. She couldn't believe it herself. Her N'Taian contact, Penn Baker, and a quarter of the Shuhr's fighters had died, and Firebird had eluded them again. Those in charge would not make the mistake another time, if she had anything to say about it.

"I do, Mine Eldest. I hijacked twenty of them."

"Do you think that excuses you?" Adiyn's pacing brought him before Phoena and Dru Polar, and he turned again. "We cannot afford to lose more men. Your staff will have another chance. But, Commander, I don't think we can afford to keep you."

Phoena glanced sidelong at Dru.

Adiyn lowered himself back into his desk chair. "Do you remember why this battle was fought? The real reason, please, as you see it.''

The commander took several deep breaths before speaking. "The old shamah spoke of our death, Eldest. A pyre. At the hands of a—a union of Thyrica with a lost outbred Aurian line."

"One of those lost, outbred Aurians stands before you." Adiyn stared down his nose at the commander.

Phoena glared but did not otherwise express her irritation. That ridiculous prophecy again. Dru had alluded to it several times. His belief in such a primitive notion confirmed what Phoena had known all along: N'Taians were intellectually superior to both Sentinels and Shuhr, powers or no powers. She disliked humoring anyone, but Dru was a titillating lover. Fascinating, frightening. Thrilling.

"And you will die at her hands. Polar. Show Her Highness how to operate the striker."

Polar slid a weapon from the vermillion sash. The fleet commander went pale.

Eagerly Phoena stood to examine it, as Polar rolled it between his hands. It had the look of a baron's baton of office, a silver rod with a row of buttons within finger's reach of its knurled handle. Dru touched one, and a needlelike probe sprang from its far end.

"If you'd like to see what it can do, use a low charge and avoid the nervous system. You'll have to be cautious if you don't want to kill too quickly." He slid a black stud toward the pommel. "The farther up the shaft you set this, the more power to the probe. Activate here." He stroked an orange button below the thumb cradle.

Phoena snatched the baton. If only she'd had one of these at Hunter Height! For a minute she retracted and extended the probe: to get the feel of holding it, and entertain her audience and victim a little longer.

She stepped out between the desk and the commander, faced Adiyn, and inclined her head. "Sir, this Angelo is at your service. Shall I demonstrate the consequences of failing our cause?"

Benignly, Adiyn smiled. "Please."

Phoena looked the fleet commander up and down, ordering herself to stay calm. In a fit of frustration she had strangled her pruupa, but she had never personally killed a human, not even a Wastling, and she did not want Polar nor the others to know that. She guessed she was the only person in the room without that distinction. She considered the commander, who outweighed her by half.

"You. And you." She flicked a graceful finger at two of the commander's subalterns. "Hold him for me."

The commander flinched but did not cry out when she touched the probe to his elbow at very low power. She crossed behind him, considering, then pierced the back of his knee. When again she pressed the orange thumb stud, his weight shifted instantly, and his involuntary back kick missed her by centimeters.

Lovely, she gloated. Lovely.

Then she began to experiment in earnest.

Later, Dru Polar escorted her to her rooms. "What was your hurry?" he asked as they rounded a corner of the brown-walled inner corridor. "We were all enjoying ourselves."

"I certainly didn't expect the highest power level to kill him from a finger touch. That's a long way from the brain."

"Effective use is very complex. At that power, if you'd even approached a major nerve, he'd have gone instantly. As it was, he took a while to die."

"He did." Phoena stepped regally, heady with the omnipotent sensation of having ended a human life.

At her door, they stopped. She slipped into his arms, but not too close, and lowered her eyes seductively. "If I get a chance at Firebird, will you lend it to me again?"

"I think that can be arranged."

"What's the absolute worst you could do with it? I'd want to know I was giving her the very slowest way out."

"Lowest power, throat pressure point." His eyes seemed to crackle as he reached for the side of her neck and caressed at the hinge of her jaw, below her ear. "Here," he breathed. "Very, very slow it will be."

She pulled away in momentary fright, then pressed against his hard, muscular body. No man had ever drawn her so intensely.

"Shall I stay tonight?" he whispered.

"No." She wriggled free and palmed the lock. "I'm worn out. Too much excitement for one day." Slipping in, she gave him a kittenish smile, then pushed closed the door she could open from the passway—but not from inside.

Brennen allowed no one but Firebird to see him off.

He gripped her hands as they stood on the grassy breakway

strip beside the RIA-modified DS-220. Dawn and her heart were breaking.

"No regrets." He kissed her cheek. "This is my life. You knew this risk when you married me. I would do it again, if you'd have me. Would you?"

She felt one of his legs pressing against her own, smelled his warm breath. "You'd do it again, knowing that in taking me, you got an obstinate woman who *had* to learn to Turn—and Phoena in the bargain?"

"Yes." Tenderly he pressed his lips to her other cheek. "Be patient."

"I love you," she answered. "I'll always love you."

His surge of love and gratitude burned as he covered her lips with his own, held tight, then pulled away. From the pocket of his belt he drew the bird-of-prey medallion on a gold chain. "Keep this for me, Mari." Her hand closed on the memento of his childhood. "Stay close to Dabarrah until you're healed. There are those whose association I cannot avoid, such as Shamarr Dickin, but Master Jenner I trust of my own love and volition. He will do all for you that can be done."

Brennen swung up into the cockpit with the briefest glance over his shoulder. Clutching the golden bird, Firebird backed away. The dawn sky was thickening to rain, as it had on the spring morning two days after their wedding, when they had lain in a stone shelter just upriver.

She felt his anguish, tangibly distinguishable from her own, gradually disappearing under attention to procedure as the generators' howl modulated into the purring sublight engines. The silvery craft rose, hovered a moment, and then streaked off. She clung to the awareness of his presence as it slipped from her like oilweed.

It flickered and went out.

Firebird set her tear-streaked face toward the House. Half blind, she stumbled to the lift.

Chapter 15

Well Rewarded

allegro malinconico
quickly, melancholy

Just outside Three Zed's fielding net, Brennen eased the ship into a long orbit matching the planet's and activated RIA. All its circuits checked. Relaxing in the pilot's chair, he tentatively extended his awareness forward, and as in practice at Thyrica, the sensations that reached him through the imperfect RIA relays became slightly blurred. He sifted space above the planet's surface cautiously for satellites and orbiting ships.

Several hours later, satisfied that he had located each one, he asked his computer to correlate data. A pattern sprang up promptly on the six screens: portions of the fielding net double-covered the planet, but over some areas only a single satellite projected epsilon energy. He chose the single-covered area nearest the colony and turned RIA toward its satellite, shielding himself from the barrage of Shuhr energies the satellite broadcast. Against that outwelling he felt inward, into the physical form of the satellite itself. Tracing its circuitry, he found similarities with Hesed's fielding design: resonal circuits, a toroidal juncture. Once he understood the differences, he nudged the energy in one line across a gap to another, simulating a disruptive meteor pass. It shorted dead.

Quickly, knowing the groundside fielding team's checks could find and reset the malfunctioning circuit at any moment, he pulled off the RIA headset, engaged the main drive, and eased forward, alert for any challenge. His ship was armed well enough to survive a chase outsystem into slip, but his goal lay planetside.

He *could* have used Firebird's help. An empty place was beside him where she should be, her intense, alert gaze framed by highlights in auburn waves, reflected from the panel lights. After waiting all his life for a connatural woman, to lose her would be anguish like that when he had lost his father. Why had she awakened that wild talent?

She insisted on trying to become all she could. He could not begrudge her that.

And little wild-hearted Kinnor, and Kiel—with a burst of epsilon static, he ended the emotional distraction. His life was worth risking now *because* of that family, a microcosm of humanity.

Still wishing he were at Hesed, he dropped through the breach, slipped again into the RIA system, and probed ahead for Three Zed's mass detector. Nothing yet. He was still untracked. He set an autopilot course, then again took up the RIA accord. With his attention finely focused he brought the ship nearer, and at last sensed the mass detector's outer field as it began to echo with his craft's presence. His extended consciousness rode a wave downward to the main complex. The part of his mind that remained free of RIA directed his left hand to the slip-shields. Power to the mass detector dipped as groundside energy guns fired automatically on the threatening object. He might still be unnoticed, however, for occasional bits of meteoric debris would pass any fielding system. At the next moment his slip-shields deflected energy, but he had already nudged the mass detector's circuits. On the ground display, the blip vanished.

Once again he turned his attention to guiding the DS-220, with occasional checks through the RIA unit to see if his presence was yet monitored. On minimal power he glided between black boulders to a small clear space, fired braking rockets to set down, then secured the ship and waited.

When an hour's watch left him unchallenged and still apparently unnoticed, he packed uniform and belt pockets and prepared to approach the dome. From a hollow in the RIA bank he slid a small metal ring that was actually two rings, joined around their circumferences: a detonator mechanism for the ship's inbuilt explosive system, easier to conceal than a touchcard. Now that RIA had passed two real tests, its value to each side had tripled. The Shuhr must not capture its secrets. The ring felt cold on his finger and a little too large, an oddly familiar sensation. After a moment's reflection, he remembered that he had last worn a ring as a sekiyr. On his left side, opposite his blazer, he hooked a shock pistol.

He activated another security cycle, which would stun anyone but himself who tried to gain entry, worked into a vacuum suit and helmet, sealed and pressurized them, and stepped off the ship.

Phoena sat beside Polar in the lowest level of a circular theater, watching Juddis Adiyn lead four young, dark-haired Shuhr down a triple flight of broad steps to the stage. Phoena would have taken them for full adults, but she knew better. Dru promised blood tonight. Her pulse pounded with anticipation, but the uncanny stillness unnerved her; she suspected she would never adjust to these people and their silent way of communicating. Somewhere near her seat, someone was wearing a stout, unpleasant perfume.

She nudged Polar's arm. "Will Adiyn speak aloud?"

"Of course. It's traditional at Final Confirmation." He sounded wistful, a rather amazing display of emotion, for Polar. She made a mental note to ask later why he let himself feel so sentimental about these—"Wastlings" seemed a good term—then glanced again at the stage. The two girl-women had tied back their hair, and all four wore skin-fitting white shipboards. It looked like a paupers' double wedding.

Adiyn strutted to center stage. "Sig, Lerra, Care, Torin, you stand at the edge of full adulthood. Thirty-three were born in your year and you four remain, the most fit to be called Unbound, to rule your lives as we will one day rule humanity, by only one law: the rule of power. May you prove worthy to wield that power. But you wait upon the judgment of your elders. Do any of you wish to leave the floor?"

Phoena poked Polar. "What?" she whispered.

"If they're afraid to go through with this, he'll kill them cleanly now."

"Ah."

"Then, adults . . ." Adiyn smiled benevolently. "I call you forward to leave the mark of your witnessing on each candidate."

Dru bent for his bootknife. "Well?" Phoena asked querulously. "Now will you tell me what this is about?"

"The Elders have judged these four, and every full adult is to draw blood on each candidate to confirm him. Some, however, have orders to cull one. None of the candidates knows if, or when, or by whose hand he will die, or if he will be momentarily initiated a Full Adult."

Phoena strangled her flash of sympathy. "Do you kill tonight?"

"Perhaps. Watch and see."

He went through this, she realized, as the first cluster of Shuhr adults stepped forward with their dirks. *They've all been through it and survived.* Only half conscious that she was licking her upper lip, she watched as tiny red streaks budded on white fabric and other men and women took the places of the knife wielders.

"May I?" she whispered.

"No."

Brennen checked the charge on his blazer, holstered it, and stepped softly to the inner door of the dome's small-craft bay.

Interesting. The little knot of machinery at the edge of the open door had an epsilon lock, hardened against mental tampering. Brennen would have liked to study it, but he crept out into the corridor, surrounding himself with a shielding cloud of epsilon static so no Shuhr would sense his presence. He remembered Phoena's aura vividly, but he dared not extend a quest-pulse through any door lest someone notice him. Instead, he dropped to the bottom of the nearest lift shaft and began to search for some file or record of where Phoena was being kept.

When Polar stepped down to the stage, one girl already lay dead, struck through the heart. The taller of the two boys looked almost N'Taian in stance and feature, and against her determination, Phoena hoped he would be spared. Polar grasped the surviving girl close to his body and held his knife at her throat for several heartbeats before grinning, drawing back, and scratching her scalp.

Phoena clenched the arms of her seat. She had seen him like this. He had undoubtedly focused his mind inward on one terrorized candidate, all his sentimentality forgotten.

When all the adult Shuhr had returned to their seats, that girl and Phoena's boy remained standing, visions of bloody triumph. Phoena sighed, glad for the tall youth and finally free to admit it. Polar remained intent on the stage, rubbing a knuckle against his chin.

Adiyn stepped down again. "Care Scurrly, I welcome you." He presented the shaking girl an ornate silver dirk. "Before your initiation, I ask one thing more."

"Eldest?" The girl stood baffled and exhausted, like the boy beside her. Phoena glanced around the theater's bowl.

Adiyn swept out an arm. "Kill him," he ordered.

Victory faded from the boy's eyes. Phoena inhaled softly. "That's cruel! He thought he had made it!"

Although trembling violently, the girl hesitated only a moment before driving the blade into her age-mate's chest. Polar's stare followed as one more body fell on the bloody stage. Then he shut his eyes tight and exhaled slowly, as the girl cleaned her new knife. "Did you say something?" Polar asked at last.

"No." Phoena slumped in her seat.

Polar shifted full around to face her, and he looked amused. "Didn't you enjoy that?"

"Yes. Your people may be few, but they will never be weak."

"Good." He straightened suddenly in his seat, as if hearing a distant voice. His glance flickered toward Adiyn, and a slow smile spread across his long face. "Go back to your rooms," he said. "Something has come up."

She wanted to protest. Her legs, however, stood her and turned her up the stairs before her mouth would open, just as Polar Commanded.

Brennen found quarters that carried Phoena's presence, but they stood vacant, dimly lit by a tiny bathing room luma. A ruffled nightgown lay on the floor, so he leaned against the bedroom wall and waited, fully alert but fully shielded.

In time he grew drowsy. He swallowed a stim capsule and called up in mnemonic sequence all his dealings with Phoena, searching each encounter for a clue that might constrain her hostility. Unfortunately, he had never had occasion to access her alpha matrix. The puzzle plagued him. If he had not yet solved it, it might have no answer at all.

At last, the outer door slid open and the overhead lumipanels glimmered on. Brennen shrank deeper into darkness, strengthening the epsilon static around him.

But she came alone. Light, clicking footfalls approached as the outer door swung home. Through the blue arch Phoena walked, waving on the bedroom light as she passed. She wore yellow, a gown of more color than substance, and on her loose, shoulder-length chestnut hair lay a circlet of amber stones.

He stepped away from the wall.

Phoena gasped and spun on one sandaled foot, hair and arms flying. She would have run shouting back the way she came, except that Brennen anticipated precisely that reaction. Energy flickered through his arm. "*T'sa.*" He immobilized her just short of the arch.

Watching her dark eyes, he touched her alpha matrix, barely stroking, gently reassuring her. "Phoena," he whispered, using his voice to channel calming overtones. "No fear." Again he was struck by the intensity of her will. It resisted his as powerfully as Firebird once had done, but her savor, fatally flawed by an unswervingly selfish focus, resonated with startling blood lust. He counted ten slowly before dropping his hand.

"I'm sorry, Your Highness. I would rather not have done that."

Phoena turned to face him, eyes narrow and defiant now, hands clenched at her sides. "Brennen Caldwell," she seethed. "You alien *filth*. This time, you two have gone too far." She glared around the bedroom. "Where is she?"

" 'She,' Phoena?"

"Firebird," sneered Phoena, and she took a step backward. "Do you really think you can destroy Three Zed the way you took Hunter Height? Are you letting her lay in the explosives this time? Only this time it's not going to work. You'll never leave this place alive, either of you."

"She's not here, Phoena," he answered levelly, stroking again to calm her. "I've come alone. But not to destroy this facility, Your Highness. I've come for you."

"To do what to me, Caldwell?"

"To get you away from the Shuhr before they murder you."

Her body relaxed, though she laughed shrilly. "Murder? Me? Caldwell, your hyperactive mind has created a flattering little fantasy. Let me inform you, General, that I am the personal guest of Testing Commander Dru Polar—who, I assure you, is ten times your equal. I have been accepted among these people. I will leave this colony only as Queen of Naetai."

As he listened, his probe found the discontinuity indicative of repeated, incautious breaching. She was no longer herself; only deep access healing would restore her personality. He projected understanding and respect into her subconscious—cautiously, lest anyone sense his activity. "I've come on behalf of your husband, Phoena. Prince Tel came for my help, hoping to rescue you himself. I would not let him try."

"Tel!" She half laughed, half spat the name.

Brennen stood quietly.

"For your information," she snarled, "I only married Tel to get Carradee off my elbow." She whirled again, led back out into the sitting room, and then draped herself on the lounger.

"Carradee," she continued as Brennen walked nearer, "is a

simpering idiot with no feel for the dignity of the throne. And Tel—''

"He loves you." Brennen stared down at her. She looked so much like Firebird—taller, fuller figured, but just as beautiful.

"That's his privilege. But there are others. Even here."

"The Shuhr have lulled your defenses. You cannot see the danger."

She tossed her head and gave a short, unpleasant laugh. "I'm no longer the innocent you tricked at Hunter Height, Brennen Caldwell. I've learned a lot about you people since I came here. I know what abilities they have—you, in particular. It pleases me to inform you that the Unbound have a superb intelligence cadre on Thyrica, and that there is far too much power here for you to overcome. Just try to destroy us and you'll see."

"I've come for your sake, Madame. Not to try to destroy the colony." Brennen took one step closer and diverted all the effort he could spare from concealing his presence into supporting his words. "You are in terrible peril. I'm not leaving without you."

She looked up and met his stare, hating him. "Then you were stupid to come. I'm not leaving. The second you're gone from here, I intend to call for Dru."

He probed. Through Phoena's eye of memory he saw "Dru" holding a knife at the throat of a dark-haired girl who was already wounded in baffling ways. This then was the Testing Commander, who had tampered with Phoena's mind—and body. He recognized a keen sensual shading to that memory. She would not leave Polar willingly.

"Then for the sake of your family, I must take you." He angled one hand slightly and modulated his voice into Command. "You will come with me. You will come silently."

She opened her mouth to protest, but no sound came. He slowly lowered the hand. Still she did not move. Satisfied with his hold on her, he stepped toward the outer door.

"Come," he ordered.

Phoena's sandals clicked as she walked forward.

"Take off your shoes."

Awkwardly she knelt and obeyed. Beneath the compliant exterior her fury flamed, and for an instant he wondered how in all the habitable worlds Tellai would regain her confidence.

That, he told himself, *is Tel's problem. Mine is to escape with her. Quickly.* "Your Highness, if we are caught they will destroy us both. You must believe me. Even Commander Polar has no affection for you. Give me your help.'' He searched her eyes for warmth but found none. Even after all his subtle stroking, he expected none.

Nudging the door's opening circuits, he stole through. He sensed Phoena's surprise; could she not have opened it? He amplified her uneasiness. A chance—perhaps a last chance to win her.

Down a level he led, through a darkened maintenance area far from the feel of living presences, toward the hatchway where he had entered.

The inner door had been shut.

He pressed the palmpanel: nothing. With all the skill a Master Sentinel could focus, he nudged for the locking circuits. Nothing. Fielding technology impenetrable.

They must contain their own children, he told himself firmly. *Particularly if they breed for talent.* ''Where did *you* come in?'' he asked Phoena, then forced the knowledge from her memory. ''All right. Go.'' He turned her back toward the heart of the facility and made her run.

Shuhr. Ahead. He felt the flickering energy of their epsilon matrices, heard their voices. He shielded himself.

The muttering stopped. Brennen backed into Phoena, drew his blazer, and modulated his carrier for access, to Command the breach deep into her alpha matrix to hide her. Leaning against the wall beside him, gasping and panting, she shook her head defiantly and squeezed her eyes tightly closed.

He could not afford a concentrated effort. He unhooked his shock pistol and fired; he would have to carry her. Phoena crumpled quietly to the floor, unconscious and undetectable—now. As he lifted her, slow, measured footsteps came closer, halted, then drew away again.

Perhaps, then, they had not felt her presence. Perhaps they knew of some poorly guarded exitway. If he scanned skillfully, they might not sense—

A foreign probe brushed past him. Instantly he withdrew his own. Balancing Phoena over one shoulder to keep his blazer arm free, he ran back the way they had come, down a long ramp. He paused and risked another probe.

The counterblow nearly stunned him.

Down toward the maintenance area he pelted at a dead run. At every corner he raised his arm to fire, then let it fall and pump. Phoena was not light. He had to leave the complex *now,* or they would seal it before he could breach a lock.

Abruptly he felt what he had feared: the presence of another, close behind. He shielded himself heavily, with all the static he could raise.

It was not enough.

Never had he felt such power as this presence carried, coming closer, effused with the assurance that he could not escape. He blocked pain and exhaustion from his awareness, and still he ran with Phoena bumping on his shoulder, aware that the presence followed without tiring. He passed a series of rooms, all closed. Around one bend farther, out of sight, he sensed other Shuhr before him. Breathing heavily, he drew the blazer, dropped Phoena into a doorway, and then pressed in to stand over her.

Footsteps echoed at his back. He felt it again: the pursuer, the power. One figure rounded the bend behind him, then another. Which was it? He stepped without hesitation across the hall and fired. A horrible howl ripped through his subconscious. More figures appeared ahead.

He whirled again, stepping across the corridor as he fired to keep the Shuhr at each end of the straightaway. He hadn't time to draw his crystace.

He—

Brennen woke curled on a dark red-gray carpet, his left shoulder aching dully where a shock pistol had connected, his left cheek stinging. Automatically he blocked the pain. Presences, strong and foreign, pulsed all around him, and he shielded himself, not only from their probing, but also from any awareness of the she-biyl. To know without doubt that he would momentarily die for Phoena Angelo would end the hope that kept him moving. He ran his right hand down his forearm. The crystace was gone, but the ring remained. Hastily he twisted its halves to join the contacts that would blast his escape ship apart.

Then he stood—slowly, searching the long office with his inner eye for weak links in the chain of strength that surrounded him, hoping to find one mind open enough to voice-command.

He found only Phoena, glowing with triumph. Before a massive black desk, she stood between two men with tangible darkness in their eyes. *Dru Polar and Juddis Adiyn,* he understood without spoken word.

Polar. Brennen could not deny a compelling confidence in that dark-browed face, a magnetic aura in the lashless eyes. Beside Polar, Adiyn seemed a shadow, although Adiyn wore his authority like a broadsword. Subdued resentment sparked between them. If the circle had a weakness, it was that rivalry.

Brennen pulled his heels together and straightened his back. Phoena sidled closer to Polar.

"Phoena," Brennen rebuked her.

"Brennen," she mocked in syrupy tones, and she extended an arm toward him with a twisting motion, as if flinging dirt away. "You'll never kidnap *me* again. Do you believe me now? Dru tells me he and Adiyn, together, can Command you. It's your turn at last.

"Dru?" Phoena pressed her palms together and struck a graceful pose. "I want to see him crawl."

"Naturally." Polar turned to Adiyn. Slowly he raised a hand. Brennen felt him halt, savoring the moment, and as Brennen waited under absolute affective control, the doubled entity condensed before him that had chased him down Three Zed's halls. At the deepest level Polar's energy began to flow, but Adiyn's epsilon aura barely flickered. They were *not* linking, although clearly Polar intended to give that appearance and even Adiyn thought it was the case. Polar bore the touch of some other hand. Only Brennen's talent and training enabled him to sense it.

The pressure of Command fell on him, like wires that first circled his limbs and then possessed them, slithering into his bones to move them at another's will. "Crawl to her, Caldwell," Polar sneered. Brennen's body buckled to the floor, and his arms dragged it across the room to Phoena's feet.

They were no longer bare. Savagely she kicked him, full in the face. He sprawled at the center of the circle, counting rapidly to clear the haze of shock as he automatically blocked sharp pain in cheek and chin. Thirty-two of them stood there, focusing probes and shields against him and waiting—for something, something very specific. He let his outer cloud of static down, but still could not catch it. He recognized one man from a raid he had coordinated against the Shuhr at Mazra, three years back: thin, bony-limbed Astrig Tulleman, staring vengefully as Brennen met his eye. Three Tulleman half-brothers had died in that incident.

But what about Polar? He rolled onto his stomach to scrutinize Polar again. What absent other empowered the Testing Commander?

His shoulder throbbed as he pressed again to his feet. He wiped the blood from his cheek; then, steadily, he walked back toward the desk, halting three meters from Phoena. Even here she stood like a queen, suffused with satisfaction and the pride that was her heritage.

Juddis Adiyn took her hand. She turned to him and smiled with coyness that nauseated Brennen. Adiyn raised her fingers to his lips. "Your Highness. You have served us well."

She curtsied.

Brennen felt the circle tighten expectantly. He touched a hand to his cheek. It came away bloody. He wiped it again.

Adiyn dropped Phoena's hand and bowed. "You may take that knowledge with you," Adiyn said, "to whatever afterlife you expect. Polar?"

Instantly, Brennen understood. The Shuhr anticipated death: but not his, not yet. Movement behind Phoena caught his eye. Dru Polar reached into the folds of his crimson sash and drew out an arm-length rod, glossy silver that momentarily reflected the blood red of his sash, with only a thumb-cradle and several control buttons interrupting the length between its pommel and distal end.

Phoena saw him a second later, and at her flash of terror there rose a pleasured flush from every mind in the chain around.

"Dru!" The outrage of long habit heated her voice, but she stared terrified at his hand, the whites of her eyes showing all around the pupils. "He doesn't mean it! Dru . . . !"

Dendric striker. No. Not even for Phoena. No world calling itself civilized participated in this weapon's manufacture. Obviously Phoena, body stiff, her emotions humming with terror and fury, knew precisely what it would do.

"Don't toy with her." Stepping toward the holo tank full of stars, Adiyn wiped one corner of his mouth. "We've had enough play for one day. Just get her out of our way."

Phoena took a tiny step backward. The auburn hair skimming her yellow-gowned shoulders glistened under office lights.

"Ordinarily, I'd agree. She has been helpful, Jude." Polar seized Phoena's hand. As she tried to shrink farther away, he coiled his fingers around her wrist. "But she wanted to know about this, for her sister's sake, Caldwell. What were your words, little Phoena? Tell Master Brennen." His dark brows barely lowered. Brennen sensed a controlling thrust of epsilon energy leave Polar.

"If I—" Phoena squeaked to a halt. Polar barely strengthened his effort, and her voice became smooth and sultry. "If I get a chance at Firebird, will you lend it to me again?"

Polar's hand slid up Phoena's arm, his Control of her never

flickering. "I think that can be arranged," he said quietly, as if repeating old lines of his own.

Phoena blinked in lazy contentment. "What's the absolute worst you could do with it?" she murmured, oblivious to the circle of leering Shuhr. "I'd want to know I was giving her the very slowest way out."

Brennen pressed his lips together. Phoena *would* have spoken this way. But how to free her?

"Lowest power." With a long finger, Polar slid a control all the way back into his palm. "Throat pressure point." He stroked the angle of Phoena's jaw with the striker's needlelike probe, and slowly, he relinquished Control. "Here. Very, very slow it will seem."

He jabbed the contact into the side of her throat.

Brennen tensed: trained instinct urged him to step forward before Polar could activate the weapon, but he dared not tempt Polar to finish her. Phoena croaked a tiny protest. Her hands crept up toward the striker. Polar shook his head sharply. "Put them down."

Phoena obeyed, drawing a long, husky breath. "I am, Dru. I did."

Behind a layer of static Brennen modulated his carrier. Perhaps, even through those shields, Polar could be Commanded.

Polar slid his hand around her shoulder, pressing his lower body against hers. "Poor little Phoena. I haven't done a thing, though. Maybe I won't. You know how we play."

His thumb shifted to poise over the orange stud.

"You don't need to do this, Dru. I—" Her voice took a new note, one Brennen had never thought to hear. "Please, Dru . . . Please?"

Polar paused a moment, then pressed his lips against hers. Brennen held his breath until Polar pulled away.

Her shoulders slumped. "Dru? Don't—kill me." Phoena glanced toward Brennen. From her stricken brown eyes, hope had vanished—but though her dignity had gone with it, they glittered defiance. He saw Firebird in those eyes. Infuriated by Polar's hands on that vision, he flung a burst of disruptive energy.

Polar flung it back. "Down!" his voice cracked.

Again Brennen tumbled to the floor. He lay still, momentarily dazed, while his carrier rebuilt. Polar caressed the small of Phoena's back.

"Even now Caldwell would save you if he could." Adiyn leaned against the glossy surface of the holo tank. "You know that, don't you? Isn't it touching, Your Highness?"

Polar's epsilon aura flickered as he eased the lulling, deep-level discontinuity off Phoena's consciousness. Brennen felt her moment of confusion—of hesitancy—and then her mental shriek as suddenly, finally, she understood that she had never used Polar; that Polar had used her from beginning to end and let her live only long enough to trap Brennen; and that he was about to use her for the final time. Brennen guessed, too, Polar's reason for removing all anesthetic tampering from Phoena's affective sense: to let her terror rise to its fullest. It *was* rising, uncontrollably, fuel for Polar's hunger.

Brennen struggled to his feet. "Phoena," he whispered as he inched toward the desk. He sent calm, now: peace, for the Crossing.

She refused it. In an instant Phoena turned ferocious, like a cornered animal done with cowering. "You were going to make me *Queen!*" she shrieked. She flexed her hand into a claw, pulled it back to strike for Polar's face—

And Polar's hand tightened on the silver rod.

Phoena collapsed, wailing in a voice that was only half human, and Polar followed her down, holding the striker at the angle of her jaw until her head thumped on the carpeted floor.

A wave of neural contraction spread slowly down her arms, her writhing torso, her legs . . . upward, across her face . . . until in his epsilon senses only an explosion of pain burned where a woman had been. He shifted his weight to spring.

"Hold him!" Adiyn shouted as he stepped away from the tank. Four Shuhr broke the circle and seized Brennen by his shoulders and arms, too engrossed in the spectacle of Phoena's agony to divert epsilon energy into Command.

As her nervous system battled to override wildly sparking receptors, Phoena clawed at her throat and arms, her cries echoing from the ceiling and resounding in his mind. Polar stood motionless, hands pressed together around the striker, eyes fixed and unseeing, mouth barely open, his tongue touched to his upper lip.

Revolted, Brennen leaned hard forward. His captors held him fast, as a second wave of neural contraction began to wash back up Phoena's body toward her contorted face. Her limbs flailed on the dark carpet.

If it were too late to save her, then, could he shorten this?

Standing close to Brennen, Adiyn sent laughter into his awareness. *Put her out of her misery? No, Caldwell.*

Brennen thickened his shields. Phoena began to moan. A third wave was building, rippling back down her body, but this time no flailing went with it.

His hands tightened to fists. He glanced from Adiyn to Polar and then away, repelled by Polar's rapture.

"And if you put her into tardema-sleep, she'd live a little longer," Adiyn continued calmly, softly. "But the damage to the neural sheath is irreversible. As soon as you brought her out of tardema she would finish dying."

Brennen watched in silent, sick horror. The third wave crept down her body, slowly diffusing. Her body pulled into a fetal curl. A slow minute later, she gave a single long gasp. Like claws, her twitching fingers still reached for Polar; her lips had pulled back in a taut grimace, and a trickle of blood stained her cheek where she had bit her lip. She could no longer move, but Brennen felt her agonized hatred, fully conscious—and fully aware she was dying.

He dropped his epsilon cloud and inner shielding. If he could do nothing else for Phoena, he could force the engrossed Shuhr to feel how deeply he pitied her. Perhaps it would be the only compassion any of them ever experienced.

Polar's lashless eyes lost their glazed look and focused on Brennen. "Release him," he rasped.

The gripping hands dropped his arms. Brennen sprang forward and gathered Phoena into his arms, questing with a last pitying, calming touch for her awareness. But even as he held her, it ebbed away. Her eyelids fluttered. The echoes of her agony faded.

And she was consumed.

Brennen knelt helplessly, cradling her lifeless yellow-gowned body against his own. What incredible irony, he groaned. He was her only mourner.

At least Tel had not seen this.

Adiyn flicked a finger, and the men who had held Brennen stepped forward again. Before they took Phoena's body from him, he gently closed her eyes, uncurled her clenched fingers, and straightened the amber circlet on her hair.

Then he wiped blood from his own cheek, stood, and turned to face Adiyn.

Very chivalrous. Adiyn folded his hands across his middle, and his "voice" rumbled in Brennen's alpha matrix. *But you are a fool. You face a similar fate.*

That is not in my hands.

True, Polar projected, walking closer. A sated smile played at his lips and gave his eyes a sleepy gleam. *It is in our hands. We have had time to plan for your coming. Read me and see.*

Instead of probing as invited, Brennen shielded himself and took two steps backward.

Polar laughed. *Coward.* He readjusted the power control of the striking rod. Then he raised his left hand. "Come."

The swollen entity that was Polar and something else buffeted Brennen. Adiyn added his own effort. Brennen planted his feet and threw his strength into resistance. The compulsion to move battered him, growing steadily as they matched his resistance in kind. Step by slow step he approached Polar.

The contact bit his forearm. Anguish crippled his senses and lashed his body, too strong to override. From the circle eager probes licked forward to strip his memory. Too distracted by pain to shield, he turned to his last defense, and willing himself unconscious, he crumpled to the floor.

He came to himself lying down, in a cell that made no pretense of being a guest suite. The black ceiling rose far over his cot, which was a narrow strip as hard as some floors, and a bare luminescent strip shed little light on rough black stone walls. Ghost echoes of neural pain flickered through his body, his shoulder throbbed, his cheek burned. Over him stood Dru Polar, with Adiyn and a buxom, black-haired young woman in a pale blue coverall whom he recognized from the circle in the office. *Cassia Tulleman*, she was silently telling him, and how she would love to rip him apart for the smashing of Echo Six, her home. As he dropped his feet over the cot's edge to sit up, he glanced at her hands. With those nails, she could probably do it.

Then he started. When she stopped sending he no longer felt her presence, nor the others': only pain, pain that did not fade when he willed it away.

Turning with deliberate care to link with his carrier, he felt nothing.

They had dosed him with blocking drugs. For ten days at least, he would be an epsilon cripple.

"As I was saying," Polar began aloud as though the conversation had only begun, "we have made our plans. They are half fulfilled, Caldwell. We have enough of your blood now to clone fresh chromosomal material for our gene pool. And I promise that before we finish with you we will take at least one other victim. Your wife, and hopefully your children."

You haven't the power to break the perimeter at Hesed, he

subvocalized, then realized he could not send. Brennen glanced around again, forcing himself to concentrate on the single factor evidently working in his favor: They intended to hold him alive and out of stasis. "You haven't the power to break the perimeter at Hesed," he repeated aloud.

"That's true." Adiyn's head bobbed once. "But we won't need to attack Hesed to take her. She'll come to us."

"No."

"You know she will, Caldwell. We know her, too, you're forgetting. We know her . . . like a sister."

Phoena. They had taken that knowledge from Phoena, and it was true. When he did not return to Hesed, Firebird would try to come for him, cost her what it may. He had allowed himself to become scent for a second trap.

"Ah, you agree," Adiyn observed. "Good."

Infuriated by his shieldless transparency, Brennen tried to close all information from his thoughts, to express only feelings. "Even if you kill us both, the children will be safe."

"Those children won't be able to threaten us for a long, long time, and by then we will have won. Oh, and another thing. We'll not actually kill her."

Brennen resisted the baiting until an image sprang into his senses from outside. He shrank against the coarse wall. They had shown himself and Firebird and . . .

Cassia Tulleman threw back her head and laughed enthusiastically. "Oh, that was classic!" Then, apparently catching an undercurrent Brennen could no longer touch, she stepped away from Polar. She looked fearful—and if Polar fed on fear, what did Cassia expect from him?

Polar reached into his crimson sash, obviously just as pleased with Brennen's helplessness, but controlling himself more effectively. "That is right, Sentinel. Unless the Chad-negiyl has other plans for her, you will kill her yourself."

He flourished the striker. "With this."

Chapter 16

The Call

accelerando poco a poco
gradually faster

The day after Brennen's departure, Master Dabarrah called Firebird to the private study adjoining his com center. Motioning her to a chair near his desk, the lanky blond Master seated himself. "Are you all right, Mistress Firebird?"

Firebird crossed her ankles under her chair. "Not really," she said softly.

Dabarrah extended one hand across the desk. "It is normal for the pair bonded to feel this grieving when separated. We all have to learn to deal with the sensation. Unquestionably, Brennen is feeling the same."

You're trained, she protested silently. *And so is he.*

"He warned you to expect this, did he not?"

"Yes." Miserably, she curled her fingers together. "Months ago. We've been separated before. Just . . ." she trailed off, "never so far."

"I remember the feeling," he said, and when she glanced up, he was smiling sadly.

She tried to rally her spirits.

"So." He drew back his hand and leaned toward her. "Are you prepared to see what can be done? Specifically, before I can initiate evaluation of the alpha tampering, we must begin to know what caused the death of Bosk Terrell. It is possible that you had less to do with it than we have had to assume for our own safety."

"For Kiel and Kinnor's safety, too. Yes."

"I would like you to Turn again, now. I shall observe from a distance, well shielded."

She pressed her lips together. "I'm on A-status, Master. Is it allowed?"

"For me, it is allowed. Have you forgotten my training?"

"Psi medicine," she murmured. "I see." Feeling frightened —of what his pronouncement might be—and sheepish, wondering if she'd be able to repeat the action at all, Firebird sat still. She had to make the effort and forget the anguish.

"Now, my lady?"

"All right." She steeled herself against what she knew she would find and pressed inward. No sense of a probe followed: Dabarrah had to be shielding heavily. Twice she called up the vision of the wall, and twice she recoiled. She sat resting. Then, forcing herself to focus, she pressed through. Again she entered the roiling mass of vision bound by glimmering cords of energy, flung her will toward one cord, and touched it. It stabbed, it strangled, it burned. Humbled and horrified by this scar of her Wastling years, she shuddered as she opened her eyes.

Dabarrah stood across the room already, pacing rapidly. It was so unlike him—unlike any Sentinel—to show such agitation, that Firebird stared, speechless. At last he returned to her side. "Fascinating. Firebird, that was not at all what I expected to find." He shook his head. Firebird wondered if he realized how rapidly he was speaking. "How odd. How—I'm sorry, Firebird, I am not feeling myself. Go. Thank you. Oh," he added as she stood to leave. "*Very* well done, your Turn. A remarkable feat for one of your age and background. But odd. Very odd."

Firebird paused just short of the archway. "Master? What *is* that, in there?"

"Many sekiyrra find their first experience unsettling." He paced closer to her and laid a quivering hand on her shoulder. "Frequently, one's personality is less an extension of the core of identity than a cover for it. And you, long past the usual age to begin training, must expect to find contrast in a greater degree."

She looked up into his gray eyes. "Is there a chance that I could learn to train it? If it proves . . . nonmalignant? And, Master, what about Kinnor and Kiel?"

Dabarrah pressed his palms together and touched his fingertips

to his chin. "With the carrier convolved inward, I fear you will
be ever unable to direct energy. But there are other skills. We
will see." He nodded vigorously. "We will see about the shilyaha,
too. There is time, my lady. They will not grow and be gone this
winter."

She spent the rest of that day working beside the sekiyrra,
pulling spent garnetberry canes in the gardens, and she dined that
night with Tel. He had learned to groom vell, Hesed's long-legged
riding animals, but his heart, like hers, was at Three Zed, and
conversation dragged.

The following morning, she stood at the quiet waterside edge
of Hesed's commons. It was deserted, except for a white-haired
couple sharing ching tea at a dining table. Something warm and
sugary was baking in the kitchen; in Dabarrah's study, a meeting
had been called—a RIA evaluation, she guessed—but she was
not invited.

Anna Dabarrah stood close by. Dabarrah and Mistress Anna,
alone at Hesed, knew why Firebird had been placed on A-status;
the others knew only that she was not to be "approached
closely"—accessed. The sekiyrra with whom she had worked kept
their distance, though; the wise and the careful shunned her, and
all maintained static shields so as not to read her feelings.

Except Tel, and Anna, now guardian to the twins.

Firebird reached up to her throat and touched Brennen's bird-
of-prey medallion. She wore it, now, a small comfort in her sol-
itude. Early this morning, Anna reported, Kinnor had changed
from an alert if difficult baby to the very embodiment of tension.
Suddenly he could not keep still at all, except in sleep; he de-
manded constant touching, comforting, stroking. "The problem
seems to lie in his epsilon center," Anna said, "but it is not a
dysfunction. We will see if he learns to comfort himself."

"He needs his father." Firebird glanced over her left shoulder
at the retired Sentinels sitting peacefully at their tea. "Brennen
knows Kin's makeup. Brennen could help him."

Anna's hands stroked the white rail, out and together, as Firebird
studied her profile. Childless at forty Standard years, the Mistress
of Hesed had become mother to eight sekiyrra at any time, year
in and year out. Not a typical motherly face: deep, intelligent eyes
and a nose almost jewellike in symmetry, a little too long for
beauty on another woman, but on Anna part of the whole.

"Master Dabarrah," she said, "will help Kinnor. You cannot
panic. Too many small things go wrong with every child. Most
problems vanish with time and tenderness."

"I hope the Master hurries." Firebird stared down into the water. *And I must stay away,* she mourned.

But she feared more for Brennen than for Kinnor. It had been only three days since he left—and she hoped to see him in seven—yet all this morning, she had not been able to shake the sensation that something had gone terribly wrong. A forgotten dream, perhaps, and perhaps not.

Anna flicked long, silvered brown hair behind her shoulder and gazed up at the gleaming skylights. Perhaps Anna's heart saw children she had never borne, who might be sekiyrra now. "Babies of strong epsilon potential can be difficult because they have no way of telling you what's disturbing them—and it could be some other's influence. I was ten when your Brennen was born, and my family lived near his, in Peak. . . ."

If she had lost Brennen, how could she hope to deal with her twins' problems?

Anna tossed her head. "I don't think you're listening," she said. "Firebird Mari, how may I help you?"

Firebird wondered if this close surveillance was merely the woman's nature, or if Anna was under orders. "I think I'd like to return to the garden, Anna." *He'll come back to us. He must.*

Anna reached for her hand.

Firebird pulled it back. "Don't touch me, Anna. Please. I'll crack."

"Firebird," the Sentinel woman said gently. "You should not stray too far from call, should there be a blockade emergency."

"I *know.*" Firebird spread her hands on the railing. "And I must stay close for fear of mental attack until the alpha tampering is healed, despite the fact that the blockaders are thirty-five hundred kilos out, only a hundred-fifty times Brennen's range. Who knows, perhaps the Shuhr have . . ." She found she could not say "RIA" even to Anna. ". . . projectors of their own." *He can't die there. It's not possible.*

With a hand-lifting gesture, Anna caught her gaze. "Firebird, you must control your emotions. You are disrupting the sanctuary. Brennen will return. He will save your sister if anyone can."

Firebird drew back a step. "Don't comfort me with platitudes." Her wistful depression turned to unreasonable anger, and she didn't care if the elderly couple sensed it. "Brennen has taken a virtually untested craft against an enemy that represents all he despises. He is outnumbered by hundreds, and his only ally will be stealth. He has gone for the sake of my wretched, scheming sister, who he last saw trying to execute him by disintegration. And the shamah is no help, no assurance at all of his survival. Brennen is the finest Thyrica could send against the Shuhr and was probably the best intelligence officer the Federacy ever had, and if he succeeds it will not be because of platitudes, but because of skill—and hard training—and perseverance—and prayer.''

Without letting Anna reply, she fled down the pavement to the golden double-doors of the groundside lift. If only she could *fly* —get into a fightercraft and push it to its limits—get *off* the *ground*—

When she stepped off onto the lawn she stopped in surprise, hearing music. She followed the haunting melody up onto the hillside. It sounded . . . like a kinnora, beautifully played.

Kinnor, she moaned silently. *What's wrong, little Kin? Do you miss him, too?*

Halfway to the top, she found the sekiyr. He sat cross-legged, black hair falling unheeded into his face, and he was playing a kinnora. Firebird had a sudden, heart-wrenching flash of memory. Corey Bowman of Naetai had waved jauntily from the stepstand of his own tagwing fightercraft the last time she had ever seen him, and black hair tumbled into his eyes, too, before he tipped head into helmet for battle. He had died that day; instantly, she hoped, and painlessly, his fighter turned to fusion fire under the lasers of Brennen's Delta Squadron. Her more-than-brother, black-eyed and rebellious, wildest of the Wastlings . . .

She blinked hard, stepping slowly so not to disturb the sekiyr and shatter the dear illusion.

He laid down the instrument, though, sensing her approach, and looked up with solemn blue eyes in a clear oval face that dispelled all imagery of Corey Bowman. ''You're Mistress Caldwell.''

''And you're . . . ?'' Firebird winced. ''Forgive me.''

''Labeth Kinsman.'' He fingered his narrow gold sekiyr's ring.

Inwardly she groaned: a relative of Ellet's. A cumulus cloud passed in front of the sun, raising prickles on her arm. ''Please finish, Labeth. That piece was lovely.''

As he plucked another intricate melody, she sank onto the soft, cropped grass. At any moment he would leave, avoiding her, but offering some gracious excuse.

To her surprise, he finished the piece and then lifted the instrument from his lap. ''You play, don't you?''

''A . . . similar instrument. And I've dabbled with the kinnora.''

"I thought so, from the kind of attention you pay." He held it out to her.

She wanted the comfort of the clairsa so badly . . . but on kinnora, she'd make such an amateurish fool of herself . . .

Firebird. He's offering friendship. Take it!

She accepted the little harp, balanced the dark wooden soundbox on her thigh, and picked out a simple tune.

He smiled. "Self-taught?"

"On kinnora, yes."

He reached for the upper arch. "Let me show you the proper position."

For an hour she listened, watched, and tried to imitate Labeth Kinsman, joyously confused by his direct gaze and gentle fearlessness. That afternoon, when Labeth was called for work, they harvested the last snow-apples together, Firebird at ground level and Labeth in the treetops.

The round, white fruit felt heavy in her hands, and the rapidly filling basket promised food for months to come. *The Sentinels are right, it is good for the spirit here . . . whoops!* She bent to retrieve a dropped fruit, but just before her fingers closed it flew to the basket, apparently of its own accord.

"I'm sorry," Labeth called down. "I should've seen that sooner."

"It's all right." Gazing out over the valley, she leaned against the rough trunk and finally asked, "Labeth? Are you related to Ellet Kinsman?"

Crisping brown leaves fluttered as he laughed, rising from tenor to counter-tenor. With a rattle of branches, he dropped down to land beside her. "I am her brother." He regained the mature timbre. "Not her favorite, I'm afraid. It's not easy, being the youngest in the shadow of such a grand lady. . . ."

Firebird thought of Carradee and Phoena. "Believe me, I know."

He flicked a long-winged insect off the basket. "But we correspond, and I'd heard of you a year ago. She never mentioned the clairsa, only Caldwell. Ellet is a raptor, Firebird, with a sharp eye for the quarry. She'll do well for herself." Hefting a snow-apple, he bit into it noisily and then grinned.

Remembering Ellet on her lounger, pressed against Air Master Damalcon Dardy, Firebird smiled, too. But when Labeth rose again up the trunk, she closed her eyes, letting her heart cry in longing and anguish.

Brennen!

• • •

Ellet Kinsman flung down a pile of papers and addressed the ceiling of her close little cubicle. "Any deadhead with the Second Division could have done this!" Brennen had gone to Hesed, and here she sat, on the Special Operations floor of the MaxSec Tower, at Regional Headquarters on Alta. Stuck on a halfwit's job.

But Orders were Orders, and Ellet had been called. Sighing, she sent a flicker of epsilon energy at the scattered papers on her small square desktop and swept them together. Daylight streamed in the tiny window on her left; through the open door in front of her, she could hear secretaries' voices.

Once, the cubicle two-to-her-right had been assigned to Brennen. *And will be again,* she fumed. *He may have been dismissed, but . . .* She finger-pressed a wrinkle from her uniform. Only yesterday, she had discovered and initiated an appeal procedure. High Command might see things a little differently from Regional.

There is compensation in being on Alta. She undoubtedly knew more now about the current N'Taian situation than Firebird herself. The Electorate's secessionist element was coming very close to trying to dethrone the Angelos—ostensibly a long-term regency —because of Carradee's familial problems, but evidently the "alien blood" was a factor, too.

That would change Firebird's attitudes. Ordering the papers on her desk top and drawing a deep breath, she rescanned the top page.

It was a policy review, regarding the status of the Carolinian mining colony, VeeRon. That explained why she'd been called to assist. She had watched the N'Taian invasion of VeeRon, witnessed the horror of "dirty" weapons that sterilized a world for centuries. Apparently, the last colonists were struggling to keep VeeRon's irradium mines open—it was a skeleton crew, men without families, only enough to maintain the mining robots— *bedim them,* Ellet observed. Then, *No, it was their home.*

But the N'Taian attack had left so much radiation in the atmosphere that the Federacy was drafting a recommendation that Caroli evacuate it permanently. No dome, no matter how well shielded, would block all radiation. No wonder the use of those weapons was forbidden by all known treaties.

Scorch those N'Taians! All of them! *Particularly—*

A shadow passed in front of her door and hovered at its edge, then tapped against it.

"Come in," Ellet said.

A young woman with silver hair slipped through, wearing Thyrian blue and a four-rayed rank star. Ellet quickly scrolled through memory and located the woman, a second-year commissioned Sentinel. The name was Kyr—

"Kyrie Spieth." The girl saluted, and added subvocally, *Hello, Sentinel Kinsman.*

Ellet, she sent, *is fine privately. Welcome to Alta.*

Thank you. Kyrie handed her a message cylinder. *From Caroli; probably relevant to your policy review.*

Excellent. You've been there?

Just got in.

Ellet motioned Kyrie to fold down the extra seat from the wall of her small cubicle. Kyrie sat sideways, resting some of her weight on one foot.

What's the mood on Caroli?

The silver-haired girl leaned one arm against the wall. *To be honest, the VeeRon review isn't getting much public attention. They're more concerned about the series of reports on the fact that Three Zed is helping rebuild Echo Six.*

Fact of life: The Shuhr don't cooperate, returned Ellet. *People don't like having their assumptions shaken.*

Kyrie nodded soberly. *The morning I left, I heard that the recruiting for Carolinian Home Guard is up forty percent over this time last year.*

Dropping her pile of papers into a filing slot on the right side of her desk, Ellet considered.

Ellet?

She raised her head to look directly at the younger Sentinel, alerted by the cautious tone of that address.

Is it true, Kyrie sent, *that there's research afoot that would give us a new advantage over the Shuhr?*

Ellet began to strengthen her shields, then hastily aborted the gesture. She could not afford to alarm the young Sentinel by acting too sensitive.

But what had initiated this speculation?

She'd have loved to access the curious girl, to see if RIA had slipped out into general Sentinel gossip, but she knew her Privacy and Priority Codes. She could not justify using force here. Minor deception, however, was allowable.

Not to my knowledge, she answered, holding her inner shields firmly in place. Unless the younger Sentinel actively probed, she would not sense Ellet's epsilon activity. *What have you heard?*

Hopeful speculation, probably. Kyrie shifted into vocal speech. "What's the shamev like?"

"Lady Firebird?" Ellet leaned back against her desk chair and once more spoke upward, toward the ceiling. "Strong. Strange. Foreign."

"Not one of us."

Ellet grimaced. "Close enough." *Spieth*. She suddenly remembered a matter that had been kept quiet in the Starbred Families. A Spieth had married out of the Families two generations back. That would account for Kyrie's unusual hair—and, come to think of it, for Master Aldana Spieth's unusually sympathetic acceptance of Lady Firebird.

"Why has the College put her on A-status?"

Why, indeed? Ellet thought without sending. "I'm sorry," she answered. "I'm not at liberty to say." Barely, she strengthened her shields in a refusal gesture.

"Oh. I'm sorry." Kyrie's emotional state, which had relaxed during the conversation, returned to that of a respectful subordinate.

"Nothing scorched." Ellet leaned forward again.

"A pleasure to meet you." Kyrie stood and refolded her seat.

And you, Ellet sent. Kyrie palmed the door shut behind her.

Ellet pulled the Review Board hardcopy from its slot, reconsidered it, then dropped it in again. Carefully slipping finger and thumb into the opening surfaces of the Carolinian message cylinder, she broke its seal. The papers dropped flat on her desk. Ellet gave them a quick once-over, confirmed that they dealt with her assignment, and then slipped them with the Review Board papers into the filing slot. Time for lunch. Another day, and she'd be done.

She rested her arms and head on her desktop. Hesed. How to get to Hesed, then, quickly?—and once there, how to convince Firebird to try to rescue her sister Phoena? The notion had been strengthening at the back of Ellet's mind for two days, along with the certainty that Ellet could somehow make it work.

Ellet wasn't due for fielding rotation for years, though. And she wasn't sick, in need of sanctuary. The only legitimate excuse she could think of, that would necessitate a trip to the sanctuary, would be pair bonding, and despite Damalcon Dardy's hints and meaningful epsilon touches, she was not a candidate for that state.

Not while Firebird Angelo lived.

Ellet pressed a single panel on her desk top, darkening the window glass, and shut her eyes to think.

Brennen lay in his cell, too exhausted to sleep. All day, the Shuhr had worked at breaking him, and now he knew the misery of resistance without epsilon shields. He hoped Adiyn's staff had gleaned only trivia, for he had kept his mind focused on trifles. He understood their methods and so dealt with them even without his epsilon abilities, but he would not outlast them.

Aching, he rolled over on his cot. Too many years had passed since he had endured pain without the ability to block it. He willed himself unconscious; Polar shot him full of stimulants and continued.

At least he retained affective control and he could forget the pain afterward. He shifted again and turned to other thoughts.

Unless he could prevent Mari's coming, her death seemed as certain as his own. But how to warn her away? Any day, they might break his defenses. What if they knew Firebird could kill . . . *had* killed? If they knew, and she came, what kind of "research" would she endure?

And what if they gained knowledge of RIA?

He shut his eyes against the grim cell and a buzzing headache. The blocking drug had begun to wear off early, a fact he desperately hoped to hide from his captors. They must have underestimated their dosage.

If only he could touch some other mind, reach across space to call someone in. (*Impossible,* his inner voice insisted.) If the Federacy would attack this bedimmed colony and destroy it, Mari might be spared the consequences of their rashness, though he would die with the Shuhr. But whom among the Federates could he call on? (*There, you see?* it taunted.) He would have to reach someone near Regional Command, a Sentinel sensitive enough to him to catch the faintest, most distant cry, if with returning strength he could launch one so far. Who . . . ?

Ellet.

He sat up and stared through darkness toward the ceiling. Ellet's mind would be open to him. His slightest touch would stir her to action. (*But what kind of action? He could easily lure her to her death, too.*) He must make it clear that she must not come alone into the trap, that she must bring others, convince Regional to attack.

(*Not the fleet!* He had been forced from Federate service and would not cry to them for help.)

Who am I fooling? he groaned. The Federacy could justify attacking from its own ends. *If I can touch Ellet at all from this distance, that will be beyond anything I have undertaken before.*

He formulated a terse message of mental images: *Ellet, RIA, Fleet, soon.* He shaped and integrated it into a single form and imbued it with urgency. Recalling the sense of hugeness he had experienced while linked to RIA, he called that sensation to mind and drew himself inward, focusing all his returning strength on the call. Then he flung it outward in all directions and dropped exhausted into sleep.

The following evening, Cassia Tulleman stepped through the black cell door. At each shoulder of her sleeveless jumpsuit a streamer scarf fluttered, white below her shimmering dark hair. He rose off his cot and warily greeted her.

"I'm not staying," she answered. "But if you want to eat tonight, I'd suggest you come with me to Polar's quarters. He's asked us to dinner."

"Us?"

She turned half away from him, displaying her provocative silhouette, brown beneath white gauze. "He has asked me. But I'd rather not go alone. I am choosing to bring you. Come, if you're coming." She inclined her head toward him. "Are you?"

He fingered the cuff of his tunic. "You do fear him. What has he done?"

Cassia drew a silver shock pistol. "After you," she purred, and she followed him down the passways, directing him at each corner.

As he stepped into Polar's apartment with Cassia's hand arched on his arm, he blinked, visually hammered by the riot of color in the outer room, each chair and lounger apparently chosen to clash with the shade of its nearest neighbor, the stretch of flooring just underneath, and the walls behind. Above a long mirrored cabinet built of red-and-black grained wood, there hung the trophy head of some huge catlike beast, its lips curled back to show six upper fangs. Though the room's opulent spaciousness relieved his cramped kinesthetic senses, its harlequin brightness crowded him. Could Polar be color blind, or was this his taste?

Polar wore a long shimmering shirt of deep magenta belted in black and very tight black pants; his hair, combed in waves, glistened with matching magenta flecks. *Not color blind, then, unless someone dresses him*. Brennen saw resentment in his eyes as he greeted them, as if he had said, "Cassia. What's this?"

She caressed Brennen's arm. "A change of scenery will stimulate the memory—yes?"

Polar's glance returned to Brennen. "Certainly, Cassia, if it will entertain you." He poured a glass of ruby-colored liquor. "Steen, my friends?"

"Naturally." Cassia took the cordial.

Polar raised one eyebrow toward Brennen as he handed Cassia

her drink, and Brennen shook his head. Even if the liquor was not laced with killcare or some other hypnotic, he had good reason to stay alert, shieldless in this company.

The doors opened soundlessly as Brennen took a fan-backed chair beside Cassia in the dining alcove. Hurriedly a youngster set before them a dinner that looked and smelled very different from the subsistence food Brennen had eaten the previous night. He dispatched the delicately spiced dishes quickly, without trying to conceal his enjoyment. Cassia watched him, amused, but he refused to take notice. Even if kindness had not been her intention, tonight he moved unfettered among the Shuhr, watching them. If he ever escaped, he would have knowledge no other had reported.

As he sipped excellent, fresh kaffa, a second boy removed platters. Even stripped of probing ability, Brennen could see that the child radiated fear in Polar's presence, almost dropping a goblet in his haste to be gone. Brennen thought of Firebird, his Wastling, who like this child had expected to die young, of Hesed and his own children.

Polar pushed back his chair, strolled to a wall unit, and opened a cabinet. "A fascinating thing." He shifted and twisted his hand just so. Brennen heard the familiar singing note of his crystace as Polar turned. His first, unshieldable impulse was to try to wrest it from Polar's hands. Cassia laughed, while Polar's expression broadcast taunting superiority. He swung the shimmering, virtually invisible blade of the Sentinels' ceremonial weapon around his head. "I've tested it on a few substances: permastone, durasteel, subadults—I haven't been able to shatter it, but I suppose I haven't tried with all my strength. I would rather keep it for my collection." Fingering off the sonic activator to return the Aurite crystal's molecular bonds to their stable length, Polar tucked it into his black sash, then half smiled. Brennen sidestepped toward another pair of loungers. When he committed himself to one, Cassia pointedly joined him.

Polar watched them. "Caldwell, I came across a rather cluttered compartment in your surface memory of knife-fighting skills. Have you been studying recently?"

"Not recently."

"Of course." Opening one hand, Polar gestured knowingly. "It's more likely that you've been teaching."

"Not recently . . ."

"Cassia has been tutoring my son Jerric." Polar glanced from Brennen to Cassia, and Brennen sensed a slightly tipsy undercurrent in Polar's superficial tone. "Here we are with an hour to spare, and I've had too little lighthearted sport for weeks on end. If the two of you would enjoy a practice match, I would find that both novel and entertaining.''

"Not him, Dru. He's too likely to hold back and waste my efforts," she said, but she plucked the scarves from her shoulders.

"All right." Polar flexed his arms. "I'll take you, Cassia, if you're willing. Too long without practice leaves one's edge rusty. Our pet Sentinel can referee."

Cassia and Dru reached for their boots, and each came up with a triangle-bladed dirk half the length of a Carolinian dagger. Observing no preliminaries, they simply went at each other, Polar from his stance and Cassia out of the lounger. Their litheness did not surprise Brennen. At Three Zed and Echo Six only the fittest would survive.

Before Cassia had fully risen out of her crouch, Polar's blade flickered. "Score," Brennen called. "Polar." Cassia's bare arm bled just below the elbow.

Polar led her to the cabinet and drew out a medical kit. In a minute, they returned to center floor.

"We'll try that again." Polar poured and drained another cordial. "There. Perhaps now we are more evenly matched."

"Ready." Cassia's tone defied him.

"Begin."

Polar's early strike, evidently meant to intimidate, seemed to anger Cassia. She slashed randomly. Polar hung back in a casual stance, all his weight on one foot. Suddenly she stepped in close, tripped him, and swung her dirk down. He twisted as he fell. The blade sliced only shirt and skin, but it was a near miss of a major artery.

"Score," Brennen said softly, sensing Polar's freely broadcast anger and surprise. "Tulleman."

Cassia nursed Polar this time and then ignored him, walking instead to Brennen's lounger. Polar stayed behind, leaning on the cabinet with yet another goblet, from which he sipped more delicately.

"Now, Sentinel?" she asked. "Now that you know I can hold my own?"

He rose uneasily. "All right, Cassia. Polar, will you lend me a blade? Mine is elsewhere."

Polar chose another slender dirk from the cabinet. In the moment both men held it their eyes met, and Brennen glimpsed hatred flickering there, not the least blunted by liquor. "That one's an alien design." A corner of Polar's mouth twitched. "Watch your grip."

He followed Cassia to the center of the room. Polar turned to watch, clenching his blazer in his right hand and a knife in his left, on guard.

Cassia crouched, eyeing Brennen hungrily, arms glistening. Brennen adjusted his hand around the unfamiliar grip. Its hold was perpendicular to those to which he was accustomed, and he would swat with the flat and not cut unless he paid as careful attention to his hold as to Cassia. He did not dare harm her—he did not even want to blood her—but he could see in the smile lines around her eyes that she would thoroughly enjoy slicing him for sport.

She sprang. He ducked and dodged but did not counterattack.

"Come on." She planted clenched fists on her hips, black hair quivering with the shake of her shoulders. "If you're not going to cooperate, give the knife back to Dru."

He nodded and stepped out counterclockwise to lead in with a glaring feint, then parried her counterstroke with the flat of his blade. Metal rang.

She pulled back, wringing her hand. "What are you trying to do, disarm me? We don't play that way."

"So you won't fight, Sentinel?" Brennen spun in time to see Polar drop the blazer, shift knife to his right hand, and lunge.

Swiftly Brennen backed out of the Shuhr's reach. "No, Polar."

"You'd best defend yourself. You could serve my purposes just as well with one—less—arm!"

Polar lunged again, closer this time. Brennen sprang away, watching for the slightest opening. Polar offered none but crouched closer yet, steady on his feet: barely, dangerously drunk.

Brennen prepared to leap in any direction as he Turned, seeking his carrier across the gap that continued to narrow as the drug wore off.

There! He quenched his jubilation. The P'nah felt tenuous, but he would be able to use resources Polar expected him to lack.

And what of Polar's resources? In Adiyn's absence Polar would not call up that power-gorged imitation link, would he? The thought blazed across Brennen's mind before he could blank it: *Does Polar guess that I know?*

Polar's attention flashed to Cassia for approval. Brennen attacked.

Polar responded with astonishing reflexes. Brennen felt fire on his chest. Automatically blocking the pain with familiar epsilon energy, he aimed a cut at Polar's withdrawing knife arm. Polar laughed as he sprang away. Brennen's hold on the grip had shifted, and what might have been an effective slice was a comical swipe.

The black-haired Shuhr returned to his crouch, gloating with his lashless black eyes. "We'll tape your rents later, all at once. Say it, Cassia. Score. Polar. And here's a better." He charged again.

"Dru!" Cassia shouted. Brennen saw the knife homing for his shoulder. "Cool down!" He twisted aside. "Adiyn will have your head if you maim him!"

"He'll have no such thing." Polar spun and stabbed again from well within Brennen's guard.

Brennen's backward leap saved his arm but betrayed him.

Transparently flinging fury away, Polar abandoned his attack and stood very still, eyeing Brennen.

Brennen felt Polar's probe lick at his epsilon matrix. He relinquished the Turn too late.

"Cassia," Polar said icily, "our guest is in need of his medication. Would you be so kind as to administer it?"

Cassia stopped circling. Her face clouded for an instant, then she tossed her head. "I would enjoy that. Of course, Dru. I don't suppose you keep any in here?"

"Ah, but I do." He gestured toward a black carryall on the floor.

Brennen tensed, wondering if he dared fight, as Cassia sorted through ampules.

"I wouldn't," Polar said quietly, very sober now.

Brennen fingered the thumbguard of the dirk and Turned again. The carrier flickered; he had not regained solid enough linkage to depend on it.

Cassia filled a long-needled venous syringe and flicked its barrel almost casually. Brennen could feel her crowing at him. *You'll hold him, Dru?*

Polar lifted a hand in casual Command stance, strode forward, and took the alien knife from Brennen.

"I'm ready." Cassia stepped up. "Kneel."

Kneel? Brennen sent, hoping only to gain a little time.

There are other positions. But this is the best for the spinal fluid. She let a droplet fall from the needle.

Brennen swallowed hard. *Nonsense.*

On your knees, Caldwell. Polar's hand shifted.

Chapter 17

The Dreams

con molto affetto
with deep feeling

Brennen's head tilted inexorably under Cassia's taloned push, and a UV beamer kissed the hairline at the base of his skull. A cold bite of pain mocked his hopes; he felt a moment of dizziness. Then Polar released him.

He scrambled to his feet, fighting to retain contact with the carrier, although he knew they watched and laughed. The pain of the knife slash across his chest increased steadily as his control slipped. He wiped salt water from his eyes.

Cassia flicked a fingernail across his shoulder. "I'll tend you. But you'd better get back to your room. You'll be asleep in a few minutes."

She shoved him onto the steel-hard cot. "Lie still."

"It will heal, Cassia," he protested as he begged aching muscles to relax. "I've had worse."

"Oh, have you?" Her smile widened greedily. She pulled off his shirt and began to work at the crusting wound with a damp, warm handcloth from the kit. He pulled away and rolled toward the wall, barking a knee on black stone.

Suddenly fire crawled over every centimeter of his skin. Gasping, he twisted to face Cassia.

She smirked. The burning sensation ceased without leaving even a sense of warmth. He shivered.

"What was that?"

Cassia laughed. "My wild talent. Synthesizing a heat response at the nerve endings. Shall I call it up again?"

He groaned. "No."

"Then lie still," she hissed.

He grew warm, limp, and drowsy as Cassia checked the slash with a 'scanner, then dressed it with a strip of biotape. She touched his left cheek, near his ear, where he had cut it falling in the corridor, then been kicked by Phoena. "You're going to have a scar. I like it."

When she finished, she laid the kit on the floor and began to massage his body. Her hands were strong on his shoulders, and when she worked deep into the inner layers of muscle, his chest lost all pain; there, her touch became gentler, avoiding the taped knife stroke. Somehow she kept her claws out of his flesh. He sighed shallowly.

She lay down on him. Like perfume, a thread of epsilon energy slipped past shields he no longer could raise, and her stroking became an inner caress, wickedly sweet as she kneaded his shoulders.

Exhausted and drugged, Brennen could no longer muster the strength to resist her gently. With vehemence he had not used in Polar's quarters, he threw her off, and she fell to the floor. The access dissipated.

Grimacing as she rose, she reached for the shock pistol on her belt. "All right, Sentinel. How will you please me?—stunned?"

He pushed up to sit, blinking slowly, hoping she would believe him even more deeply drugged than he felt. His weary body sagged forward. As she stepped closer, he reached out a hand.

"That's better," she whispered.

He lunged forward and closed his hand over hers on her weapon. She laughed.

Groggily he considered his choices. He could not shoot her down. Cassia could open the cell door from inside and he could not, and plainly if he continued to resist, he would only excite her to more repellent demands.

Still he gripped her hand, and the pistol.

A second delicate tendril slithered into his consciousness. Its texture had Firebird's fierce pride but a heavy "otherness": he could never have bonded Cassia. He knew he could please her, though, and she would know it, too.

She stood motionless, eyes half closed, guiding her stroking probe deeper.

It was not easy to ignore that sensation. "Please go." He dropped her hand.

"Mm." She straightened and withdrew. "That's a start. I could develop a taste for your kind, Sentinel—when you're awake."

"No, Cassia."

"You think, 'No.' " The sound of her retreating footsteps gave him little comfort.

Tel sat in Firebird's rooms late at night, dressed like her in a long nightrobe. As on the past four nights, they shared hopes: Brennen and Phoena ought to have returned a day before, might return momentarily. But Firebird's sense of disaster had not diminished, and tonight, when Tel mentioned Kinnor and Kiel—two Standard months old, today—she began to cry: long, racking sobs that shamed her.

Unexpectedly he reached out and pulled her head to his shoulder. He was not Brenn, but the gesture was comforting, his arms warm, and his shoulder already becoming too firm for an aristocrat's. When she stopped shaking, he kept one arm around her waist.

"I should be shot, Firebird." He whispered so softly she could barely hear him above the unending cascade down the wall. "I wish I had never left Naetai. Brennen would still be here, if not for me."

She groaned at the guilt lined on his forehead and brought herself under shaky control. "Don't talk that way, Tel. We made our choices, and not in ignorance."

"Firebird, they'll be back. I'm sure. But if—if—Brennen . . . doesn't return, then neither will . . . I mean, if Phoena is . . . gone—then you're no Wastling any longer. And if you ever wanted to go home—"

The tears gathered again. "It will be a very long time before I stop hoping he'll be back."

"Let me finish." Tel laid his other hand on her arm. "Please. I couldn't bear to see you left a widow because of me. I'd owe you—well, anything I could give. If you wanted it."

Firebird saw that he, too, wavered near tears. "Thank you, Tel. I'll remember that."

That night Firebird's dreams began. The visions of death seeped up into her sleep, robbing her of the little peace she hoped to find. One recurred: Calmly she leaned against a wall, facing an amphitheater full of N'Taian nobles with a cloth target laid over her chest. She stood patiently, discussing ballistics with a single guard, slowly losing that uncaring calm until she realized it was death— the end of all hope and victory—she awaited so passively.

Then she began to run, chased closely by—by what? She did not dare turn to look, she must escape! For Brennen faced some terrible danger. Only if she could reach him in time did he stand a chance of survival. She could even hear him, pleading in a kind of desperation she had thought her capable husband incapable of feeling. She must bring RIA. She must bring help. The Fleet— even, illogically, Ellet Kinsman.

After two nights of this and a frustrating first attempt at throwing pottery, she begged an appointment with Dabarrah.

"What can I do?" she asked forlornly after describing the dreams. "Is this what Brennen feared, the first symptoms of losing my mind?"

He steepled his fingers and eyed her across the desk. "Perhaps the recurrence of these dreams is a better sign than you think," he said calmly.

She rubbed a sore arm. "How can that be?"

"I believe that you have begun to sense the core layer of re-pressed imagination. Perhaps the carrier, now stirred, is beginning to work free. If so, it will increasingly dominate your thinking and dreams for a period."

"Is that good?"

"In your case, I cannot say. The horrors will lessen, the more you understand and face them."

"I see. But I . . . hope . . . ." She halted. She didn't know what to hope. She passed the back of her hand over her eyes. "I am defeated by my own fantasies. I thought that by facing death in my mind I could cure myself of fear. I thought I had learned courage, Master. But I merely bound up my fear of death with cords of epsilon energy."

"Do not deal too harshly with yourself," he answered. "You suffered much as a child, and indeed only your courage allows you to touch that carrier at all. You do not know how this crisis may resolve itself."

"Brennen," she whispered. "I've lost him."

"Not necessarily, Mistress. He *is* alive; one can tell from ob-serving you that the pair bond remains intact. But this separation, at this time, is wise, however difficult for you to endure. I should hear back from the College within a week, with word regarding how I— *we*—might proceed with your evaluation and training. Then, my lady, it could well be that you will be allowed his touch again."

"And our sons?"

"Perhaps. They are defenseless, Firebird Mari, and very, very vulnerable to you."

Later that day, a trio of Sentinels ran the blockade with messages, foiling the Shuhr's jamming of DeepScan transmissions. Firebird heard most of the news over lunch, from Labeth. Hearing of Rattela's attempts to strengthen his regency left her in a choking fury. She and Rattela had detested one another for years. Also, Ellet sent word of a Shuhr attack on a colony world near Alta.

But Labeth brought no word of Brennen.

Master Dabarrah called Firebird to his office immediately after the meal. Uneasily she seated herself before his desk, flicking the hem of a soft red gown closer to her ankles.

"I have had other news from the blockade runners that you must hear, Mistress."

"Yes?" she asked, her voice barely a quaver.

"Not what you fear. But a word has been put in my ear from sources very close to the Federacy's Regional Council. You heard about the Shuhr attack at Kerramour City?"

She nodded. *Sources close to the Regional Council. That must mean Ellet*, she thought.

"The circuits of command close slowly, but apparently the Federate fleet is preparing a counterstrike. One reason for delay has been the need for absolute secrecy, to gain every possible advantage against the Shuhr, whom they fear with an even deeper, more superstitious dread than we do."

She glanced away, catching Dabarrah's implication. The Federates dreaded the Sentinel kindred, too, reluctant though both sides were to admit it. How different the interrelation from her old view as a N'Taian outsider!

"In the unity of the Shuhr worlds, which have feuded for so long, the High Command sees both a threat and a target. The Shuhr forces are gathering again near Echo Six. The planned counterstrike entails simultaneous attacks on both known localities."

"And—will anything be done first . . . ?"

"If anything is officially known of Master Brennen's whereabouts, or planned for his aid, my messenger brought no word." He laid one hand on the desk. "I think we must assume not. You must not speak of this to anyone—except Prince Tel, should you wish that, since his wife is probably still at Three Zed as well. Even here, we must maintain security."

"Officially known?" Firebird cried. "Where else could he be?"

"Mistress Firebird." Dabarrah raised his brows. "Be still."

Ellet. Firebird stared ahead, unseeing. *She's got to do something!*

Tel leaned away from the white railing and watched Firebird hurry from Dabarrah's office. He could tell from her long, jerky strides that she was badly upset. He did not feel entirely stable himself; tonight, he could think of nothing but Phoena.

These two weeks at Hesed had changed him. He was stronger, both physically and emotionally. The pastoral setting strengthened the link he had always felt with nature, and his work with breeding animals—for which, he'd been assured, he showed a real talent —heightened his sense of identity as a man, a step above the beasts.

And Phoena had left him.

She had always acted as if she needed him, as if she treasured what he could give her . . . .

And she had gone to the Shuhr.

When Firebird retreated through the arch of her rooms, Tel stepped out across the stones. Firebird hadn't noticed his growing agitation, these last two days. He hadn't mentioned it. She was too full of her own concerns—and this matter hurt his pride too badly. This was not something one shared with a woman.

So he would go to Dabarrah, the healer.

When he rapped lightly at the door of the Master's office, he was not surprised to hear the Master's voice call softly, "Come in, Your Highness."

He passed inside. The Master sat on the long, white stone bench carved into the left wall. Tel sank into a still-warm wooden chair. He half expected, half dreaded that Dabarrah would ask, "What can I do for you?" And how would he say it? How would he humble himself a second time to a Sentinel, as he had done before Brennen Caldwell, to ask for the kind of help only they could give? He glanced around the office, at banks of silent equipment, white stone—and the serene Master.

"I have news for you," said Dabarrah. "Bad news, perhaps." Slowly, carefully, he told of the impending Federate strike.

Tel waved the news away. "Surely they'll be out by then. They're probably on their way, will be back tomorrow."

Dabarrah's hair shone white-gold in the lamplight. "So we all hope," the Master said. "And I sense you have come to me for something else. Relating, perhaps, to Princess Phoena? Something you wish to settle in yourself before her return?"

"What can you do?" Tel asked. "I have to know all you would do, before I consent."

"I know you have been abandoned." Dabarrah turned aside, pulling his lanky legs up onto the bench in front of him. "I will not—I cannot—eliminate your hurt. You would not wish that; it would diminish you as a feeling person. But you have now built the strength to deal with it. I can go back with you, and refresh your memories of your times with Phoena. If you recall her more accurately, knowing now what she has done, you may gain a deeper understanding of her motives, and your own. That is a kind of access healing. Is it something you feel can help you?"

Tel curled his fingers around the sides of the chair. "Yes, Master. I think . . . I understand my own motives better now than I did when I left Naetai."

Dabarrah gave him a questioning look.

Tel reached for his sash ends—but he wore no sash now, only simple gray shipboards. "I . . . remained in correspondence with the Duke of Claighbro—Rattela—while I resided on Thyrica . . . as I suppose you know."

"We knew, though nothing was said to Mistress Firebird."

"Yes. I . . . have come to expect that of you. Well. Muirnen Rattela and I were very good friends, before. Before the invasion, before Hunter Height. You have only recently had word of Rattela's attempts to take power on Naetai. I had heard of his intent already. I . . . encouraged him, especially when he wrote of Phoena's nobility and sacrifice as a leader in the Loyalist cause. I assumed he meant to encourage Carradee to abdicate in Phoena's favor. I dreamed, once, of sitting beside Phoena's throne. I'm not so certain I believe that any more. Rattela is hinting at disbarring the entire Angelo family. He wants the crown!"

In the silence of the room, Tel heard water running beyond the arch. He shifted on the hardwood chair, relieved to have confessed his old ambition.

Dabarrah turned to lean forward again. "All this will affect the N'Taian people less than you think, Tel. Our primary concern is for the safety of the Angelo women—all three, if at all possible. Should the situation arise when you deem it appropriate, I would appreciate your conveying to Her Majesty and her husband the Prince that they would be welcome to join you here in safety."

"Oh." Tel stared, considering. "Daithi—could he be healed here, perhaps? So that Carradee could have another daught—another heir?" He pressed his lips together. "Though, if the Angelo genes are your concern, you should know that Carradee will not marry again.''

"Prince Daithi would be welcome, of course. Do you think the Queen and her consort would be happy here?''

"Absolutely. Oh, Master, absolutely. But only if Carradee felt she had discharged her duty to Naetai, done her utmost, and been sent away. . . . She *would* seek to fulfill that priority first, yet . . ." He pushed upright in the seat again. "Either Phoena or Firebird would have made a stronger Queen.''

Dabarrah smiled wryly. "I will not argue that, Tel. Will you send to Her Majesty?''

"By the next blockade runner out.''

Dabarrah stood. "You would be more comfortable in the inner room, then, if you wish to go through with the healing.''

Tel pushed up out of his chair. "I am ready," he said. "My conscience is clean, now.''

Brennen struggled apprehensively to consciousness, fearing at any moment to be assailed again by the probe Polar had flung repeatedly through his alpha matrix. The lights had been brought up, and—he tested cautiously—his body had been released from voice-command.

Then Polar had finished once again.

It was the fourth day of interrogation. Polar was toying with him, going slowly, prolonging his struggle, savoring his fear. On the third, Polar had claimed he'd broken, presenting him a sheet of data. But Brennen saw nothing Polar's agents could not have learned from Bosk Terrell's cohorts on Thyrica, and he said as much. This time he was told nothing: a different kind of torment, because he *had* begun to weaken. Eventually, Polar would stop dallying and call up the power of that Other whose energy provided the imitation link with Adiyn. And then?

The sound of footsteps alerted him to Polar's return; no sense of approaching mind, he observed dully. Only his outer senses remained.

He pulled himself upright and opened his eyes, then sat at the edge of the steely slab, gripping its rim with both hands. That last defense, willing himself unconscious, had returned to his control when he discovered a way to counter Polar's stimulants. He had used that defense relentlessly at each inkling of slippage. In time, however, it would exhaust him beyond the ability to use it.

Polar stepped up close beside him. "Very interesting, Caldwell.

Next time we shall 'discuss' your Ree-a project in closer detail. And why should P'nah be so heavy on *your* mind?''

Brennen barely kept himself from reacting with bald emotional violence. Had he come that close to his breaking point?

"But not today. Tomorrow. Come. I have something to show you."

In a second laboratory, two Shuhr carried a thin, dark-haired boy between them and forced him onto the metal table. As Brennen took a stool, double-guarded himself, Polar rolled his own stool close.

The boy groaned.

"Be still," Polar said. "I will ease this for you if I can. And be comforted by the fact that Caldwell watches this time."

The boy turned dark eyes on Brennen, who saw mingled with his fear an awful hatred.

"Better." Polar reached for the boy's chest and let his hand lie there. "My real hopes are built on this, Caldwell. Today I think you will see how timely and fortuitous your arrival among us has been.

"Sadly, this boy has failed in his testings. As a cull, he was chosen for this demonstration."

"I can see he's no volunteer." Brennen clenched his stool.

The boy shot him a baleful glance.

"Manners, Caldwell. He's unhappy enough as matters stand."

"Now, let me explain the procedure. With electromagnetic disruption probes here . . ." He slipped a hand under the small of the boy's back and taped on a wire. ". . . and here . . ." He repeated the act at a pale, sweaty temple. "I will be able to bring about a momentary reversal of polarity of his epsilon wave. The subject's automatic reaction to the reversal is to Turn—he can't help it—and if at that instant I can link mentally with him, the superimposition of antipodal waves should release a surge of wave-synchronous energy. It will be mine permanently, if I can fuse it with my own . . . all the experimental evidence points that way, anyway. It will leave him little more than a vegetable, unfortunately, but hypothetically able to move at my will."

"Hypothetically?" Brennen repeated dully.

"Yes. Thus far, all such attempts have failed. We have been unable to proceed past this point, for reasons you will see."

Abruptly Brennen felt he understood why Polar owned power that reeked of duplicity. The "research" had proven more successful than Polar would publicly acknowledge. "You are anxious to have me observe, then," he said, to mask his suspicion.

"Oh, yes."

Brennen understood. He wished he did not. "But—Polar, this boy is too young to have begun to exercise—"

"Does age affect potential?" Polar turned away. "Proceed." As two techs hurried to carry out the order, Polar leaned over the boy's body. "Now," he barked.

Polar's energy thrust outward, surged, and then faded into the epsilon silence in which Brennen now lived.

The boy lay without breathing, his face gray and contorted.

Sighing, Polar whirled the stool. "As you see, none of my subjects have survived the reversal process. I feel certain that their epsilon strength has proven too slight to maintain mental function. A strong enough subject, though, might survive long enough for me to accomplish fusion. Possibly." Polar smiled, showing a row of perfect yellow-cream teeth. He saluted mockingly and then spoke to Brennen's guards. "Take the General Coordinator back to await further . . . debriefing."

Keeping all thought silenced, Brennen walked with the pair back to his quarters. The door shut behind him without a sound, and this time Brennen was glad to see it close, grateful to be left alone, to think.

He dropped onto his cot. *What had really happened in that laboratory?*

Had Polar devoured the boy's potential, made it his own, as Brennen suspected? Or had the "demonstration" failed, as Polar claimed?

Reversed polarity.

Could that be Firebird's wild talent? Through some mutation over twenty generations in the isolated Angelo line, had she inherited a naturally reversed-polarity epsilon wave?

He sat up straight, imagining Firebird's vivid visions of death, bound up with her epsilon carrier and empowered by Polar's notion of "wave-synchronous antipodal fusion." If both Terrell and Firebird had been Turning at the moment of contact, all Terrell's native energy and that of the fusion would have been diverted into making the visualizations real . . . into convincing him *he* was dying . . . into killing him.

Could it be true? Or could that power surge Polar sought so eagerly simply prove fatal in all cases? If that were so, then she *was* a deadly danger to all Sentinels.

He couldn't begin to understand.

One thing, however, he understood perfectly.

Brain death or "fusion," Polar intended this fate for him.

Chapter 18

The Holy Tale

> *lucernarium*
> song for Vespers, or evening worship;
> its texts most often refer to light

Evening lay gentle on Hesed's commons. Firebird sat alone at a wooden table near the kitchens, staring out over the water. Around its edge, dim lights shone pale turquoise. The water shimmered, and in her memory she saw Brennen, in white and gold, prepared to take her forever as his wife. A tear pooled on the underside of her chin.

Across the water, a dark figure hurried along its edge, a folder under one arm. Tall and slender, it looked like Ellet's brother Labeth. Solemnly she watched him stride along—

And stop, and knock at the door of her room.

She did not move. Today, after leaving Master Dabarrah's office, she had caught a glimpse of Kiel and Kinnor: Anna and a sekiyr had been sitting on a blanket on the hillside with them. Firebird had run the other way.

She wished now she had tried to get closer. Another tear coursed down her cheek as Labeth walked toward the commons.

She wiped her face dry and tilted her head to look up at him. "Good evening, Labeth. Are my babies well?"

His dark eyes blinked once in an expression that might have been carefully modulated concern. "Firebird. I'm glad I found you. Yes, they are well. May I join you?"

Firebird laid a hand on the chair next to her own.

Setting his folio on the table, Labeth seated himself. For a few seconds, he gazed at the water with her.

"How go your studies?" she asked.

He turned his large blue eyes toward her. "I've been commended on access penetration. So they go well. But I came to show you something I've found."

"Oh?"

Labeth laid a hand on the folder. "You're all right?" he asked solemnly.

"I'm all right, Labeth." She rested her forearms on the table. "What have you brought?"

"Well." He too leaned forward. "Master Bendict has been working on a new translation of *Olami Auria*, a collection of Aurian holy tales. They were never used as sacred writ, but as teaching stories for the Aurian children. There's a Colonial translation that's commonly used in study, but it's incomplete, and Master Bendict has been translating the lost stories. He read me this today—" Labeth drew two sheets of fresh, pale parchment from the folder. "It brought tears to my eyes. I know you're having a difficult time, Firebird. I thought. . . . You find comfort in your music, as I do. Do you ever write? Have you ever tried setting a ballad?"

"I finished one not long after I first arrived at Hesed, based on a character from N'Taian history."

Labeth's lips formed an *o*. "Then this is yours, Firebird." He touched the top sheet of parchment. "This is the story of Ahriyth of Metsura, and I'd like to hear it some day, if you can make it a ballad."

"Who was she?"

He leaned away, and his long, oval face became serious again. "I'd like you to read it yourself. Tell me what you think tomorrow." Sliding the parchment back into its protective folder, he eyed her. "You *are* all right?"

A delicate touch of "otherness" at the edge of her perception told Firebird that despite A-status and orders, he wanted to know for himself.

"Things aren't good, Labeth," she said. "But Master Dabarrah has seen me daily for a week. He says, now, my alpha matrix is definitely conducive to training. Perhaps he's simply acknowledging the Angelo stubbornness, but I expect things to reach a crisis point soon enough."

"This may help." He stood, looked once slowly around the

high, blue-lit underground hall, and then slipped the folder under her elbow. "Tell me what you think of it tomorrow, if you can."

"No one can write a ballad that quickly."

"Just tell me what you think of it. Good night."

"Good night," she murmured, and as he retreated past the kitchens toward the sekiyrra's quarters on the pool's north side, she drew the parchment out again and skimmed the boldly lettered first lines of paragraphs.

Ahriyth, the wealthiest woman in Metsura . . .

In her was death. . . .

What? Firebird felt a cold shiver pass down her spine, and she read on quickly.

Three men had set out to win her. Three had died. . . .

Grimacing, Firebird turned to the second freshly calligraphed page.

Yet there was a wise young man of pure heart . . .

And their children grew strong in Metsura. . . .

She started. Could it be that she had killed Bosk Terrell because there was evil in *him*?—That he had brought death with him, and so suffered it himself?

If that were true, then despite the terrors inside her, she posed no danger to Brennen—to Kiel, nor Kinnor—only to those who meant her harm.

With wild hope in her heart, Firebird flung paeans of thanks toward Labeth. She knew he would not sense them, but she needed to shout or dance or do *something*—

Something wild and joyful, like the Firebird she once had been.

Brennen.

Caught short with her hands in the air, she glanced around and carefully lowered them.

Their children needed a blood parent, someone who could nurture them in Sentinel ways, understanding and sharing their hereditary synaptic patterns. If the effort to bring him back cost her life, it was worth it still, for Kiel and Kinnor's sake.

RIA. Fleet, soon. The memory of that dream was so strong.

The parking bay beside the House held several non-RIA-equipped spacecraft, some of which could possibly pass the Shuhr blockade, if manned by a skillful pilot.

Better to wait for a RIA ship.

Bless Labeth. Bless him!

She tucked the folder under one arm and hurried to her rooms. The following day, she was less sure. No one had drawn that interpretation from "Ahriyth of Metsura" before, she guessed, only Labeth, a sekiyr, and Firebird, an outsider. If the tale had been lost, few had seen it at all. Yet perhaps an "Ahriyth" with this killing ability appeared only once a millennium; how, then, would anyone know if she were that woman? She didn't dare ask Master Dabarrah. Weary and dissatisfied and unsure of herself, she was still determined.

She would go for Brennen as soon as she could find a way, to die with him in the Federate raid, if she could accomplish nothing else.

Late that afternoon, another group of blockade runners reached Hesed's perimeter. After watching the little ships glide in on the grassy strip, Firebird seated herself in the commons for dinner with Tel. She was midway through the soup course when a sandy-blond man and a tall, slender, black-haired woman approached across the stepping stones. Firebird set down her spoon, stared, then scrambled to her feet.

"Ellet!" She hastily extended a hand. "And Air Master Dardy. Welcome!"

"Mistress Caldwell," Ellet Kinsman returned smoothly.

Tel stood. Firebird laid a hand on his shoulder. "My sister's husband, Ellet: Prince Tel Tellai-Angelo. Tel, this is Captain Ellet Kinsman of the Federate forces, and Air Master Damalcon Dardy of Thyrica."

"Yes," said Ellet. "We know of you, Prince Tel. We have just come from Master Dabarrah's rooms."

Firebird sat back down. Dardy seated Ellet, then walked off to find a sekiyr to bring two more bowls. Firebird could hardly speak, her mind echoed so loudly with the ethereal, desperate voice of Brennen. *RIA, fleet, soon . . . Ellet.*

"I've had the news," Ellet said quietly, "from Master Dabarrah. I'm sorry. For all of us."

Firebird met her stare. Which news? Did Ellet condemn her for letting Brennen go to Three Zed, as she sometimes blamed herself? And did Ellet know, now, why Sentinels had been told to shun her?

Tel checked the silvery pitcher. "I'll get more kaffa." He hurried off toward the servo, leaving Firebird alone with Ellet.

Firebird took a deep breath. "I'm glad to see you."

Ellet Kinsman glanced darkly in Tel's direction, as he bowed gracefully to a sekiyr and then turned back to the table. "Tonight," she whispered. "We need to talk."

Firebird answered with a nod and gravely allowed Tel to pour her another cup of kaffa.

"He's alive, then," Ellet remarked as confidently as Master Dabarrah had done. "And since he hasn't returned empty-handed, we can assume his RIA unit took him past their fielding. The RIA ships run the blockade here well enough. He's there."

"A prisoner."

Ellet had hinted that she wondered about Firebird's A-status, but Firebird, relieved to learn Ellet did not yet know the full reason for it, turned the conversation to Brennen. Easily.

The constant cascade poured down the long wall of Firebird and Brennen's room, and beside the wide bed, a luma globe shone dimly.

"I must do something, Ellet." Firebird clenched a slick red and blue audio rod in frustration. "Kiel and Kinnor need their father. *I* need their father. If I thought I could break out of Hesed's perimeter and pass the fielding at Three Zed, nothing could keep me here. You've seen Mistress Anna, and everyone else, with the twins. Even if I failed, Kiel and Kin would be raised as lords— or princes."

"I know."

Firebird sighed. "What can you tell me about the situation at Three Zed? Have the plans changed?"

"No. The fleet means to destroy every square meter of both colonies."

"That's what I feared." Firebird bowed her head, and auburn hair tumbled over her shoulder.

"They suspect he's alive, too, but they won't authorize a raid on his behalf. Their attack must be a surprise—only Regional Command knows when it will come, and few of us know it's being planned at all. A raid would alert the Shuhr, and according to Regional, the stakes are too high now to gamble for his sake." Ellet grimaced.

Firebird frowned. "The Council . . . are they still angry with him?"

"They've said nothing."

Absently tapping the audio rod against her bedside table, Firebird let her stare wander around the room. "What kind of ship do you have?"

"Our group came with two 212 *Brumbees* and one J46 transport with a RIA system."

Firebird came as alert as if she had been handed an armed missile. "You have . . ." she pushed the word out through the lingering counter-compulsion, "RIA?"

Ellet barely smiled. "One RIA craft. We've found a way to make RIA *catch* a carrier, to ease the effort of modulation and spare epsilon strength for finer work. There are five RIA ships now, still concealed from the Federacy. As we were coming to Hesed through the blockade, we were allowed one."

"Why . . . ?" Firebird stifled her curiosity. Ellet Kinsman's business was her own.

But Ellet answered. "Damalcon wishes Master Dabarrah's blessing for our bonding. I have not given my consent, but for his advice, and for news of you and Brennen, the run to Hesed was worth the risk. Dabarrah is mighty in the Word."

Of course. A detached portion of Firebird's mind absorbed and accepted the news. Dardy, Brennen's friend; Ellet, with whom Brennen had admitted marginal connaturality. *It fits.*

As does Ellet's reluctance to take anyone but Brennen, bedim her!

"Might I be allowed to look at your ship, Ellet?" she asked without turning to meet the tall Sentinel's eyes.

"I'd have been surprised if you hadn't asked. You've undoubtedly been too busy these days with important matters for much flying."

Firebird flushed, and she spun to see Ellet's face, solemn and knowing. A hint of an understanding crept into her mind. Ellet meant to give Firebird her chance to run to Three Zed, knowing it would probably cause her death—in a worthy cause, as before: this time, a chance Brennen might escape alone. Firebird slid a finger up and down the audio rod's gleaming surface.

Undoubtedly Ellet, too, suffered from visions of Brennen in Shuhr hands.

Ellet's cheek barely twitched. "I would not even be surprised to find Damalcon willing to check you out in it tomorrow morning. There will be time before we meet with Dabarrah."

Ellet strode out across the stepping stones, barely controlling her satisfaction. Although untrainable and unstable, Firebird was now determined to go—and would unquestionably fail at Three Zed.

Dardy had arrived at Alta with the RIA ship, never suspecting Ellet hoped to send Firebird after Phoena. Dabarrah's news that Brennen already had left nearly crushed Ellet—temporarily.

Ellet was no sekiyr to be thwarted by bad news.

Tomorrow, Firebird would be gone. To keep a RIA craft from falling into Shuhr hands, she and Dardy would be justified in taking a *Brumbee* and chasing her (and thereby avoiding the question of forging a pair bond tomorrow—although Dardy was a good man, attractive enough for pleasure, and certainly connatural).

(But he was not Brennen Caldwell.)

Since they'd never be able to intercept her in slip, they would arrive within hours of her at Three Zed. The *Brumbee* was far faster than a J46. The two trained Sentinels would make an effort to free Brennen. Assisting another Sentinel in danger was expressly allowed by the Privacy and Priority Codes, regardless of risk or expense. Ellet and Brennen—and, hopefully, Dardy—would return with both ships. That was how she would justify it to Dabarrah.

But if Firebird's ship is destroyed by the Shuhr before we can arrive there . . .

Ellet smiled. *We save the RIA secret. And return with Brennen.*

Firebird found Dardy willing to check her out, although her cautious attempt to run up the RIA unit was less than encouraging.

When she returned to her chamber, however, she found not Ellet but Mistress Anna—holding fair little Kiel. Red-faced and shaking, for a full minute Anna stood cradling Kiel, silently challenging Firebird to try rationalizing that RIA flight.

Firebird stepped into the room. Kiel . . .

"This is your son," Anna said hoarsely. "The heir of your body and the image of your husband. How dare you consider leaving him? How dare you, Firebird?"

She ached to touch him. Would Anna let her?

Let her? She was his mother! "You have taken him from me already, Anna." Firebird's voice shook. "He's more yours than mine, now."

"Do you consider yourself more equal to the challenge than Brennen? Do you wish these children orphaned? Never to know mother or father?"

Firebird crossed to the cascade and parted the watery curtain with one finger, but she could not take her eyes off little Kiel. Image of his father! Gently squared chin, sapphire eyes . . . "Never to know the horror their mother found inside herself?"

Mistress Anna caressed Kiel's round cheek with her nose, then looked up, her emotions controlled once again, her expression softer.

"If," Firebird said hurriedly, "anything were to happen to me, Anna, please don't let them know—"

"You are *safe* here. But Firebird, you are so frightened. That's why you anger so easily nowadays." Anna appeared to relax further, though Firebird was never certain of most Sentinels' true feelings. They controlled so blessed well. "Would it comfort you to write a testament—now? Perhaps if you knew Kiel and Kinnor would remain safe at Hesed regardless of circumstances, it would ease your heart. Master Jenner and I would be more than willing to stand as their guardians. In the morning, when you can think clearly again, that will bring peace."

Firebird sank onto the bedside, keeping all her own emotions firmly in check. She must bring Brennen back. No second thoughts. She pressed her palms together, hard. "Yes, Anna. I think it would." Then she stared up at the Sentinel woman. "Let me hold him."

"I cannot."

"I am his mother, Anna Dabarrah, and you brought him to my room, using him, using me. I have never—" Her voice rose steadily. "—Never broken your prohibition, as unnatural as it is. I would never harm him." And here, now, she felt certain it was true. "Give him to me."

Slowly, Anna stepped closer. She laid the sleeping child in Firebird's arms.

He felt heavier than she expected, with a faint, milky smell about him. "Oh, Kiel," she whispered.

Squirming, he gave a short cry. Anna reached down.

"I am not hurting him." Firebird sat stiffly for a moment, then lifted him up to Anna.

Anna took him and strode with him toward the door. "Come to Master Jenner's rooms this evening."

Brennen. Firebird sat a little longer on the bedside, staring through the curtain of water, across space. *I'm coming.*

The testament was made and witnessed. Standing at one edge of his office, Master Dabarrah watched Firebird stride away, down the poolside. Mistress Anna stood beside his desk, her head bowed, reading the paper carefully one more time.

She means to go, Anna subvocalized. Her tightly guarded expression said nothing, but on the resonance of the pair bond Dabarrah felt intense reproof. *I thought her heart would change, when she saw this on paper. That's why I offered it.*

Closing the outer door and dimming the office lights, Dabarrah barely shook his head, displeased with himself. He should have told Anna the news from College the moment it arrived. He had waited for an opportune and private moment, and that only made this day difficult: for Anna and for Firebird.

Anna laid down the parchment and folded her hands against the skirt of her long silver gown. *I will send a sekiyr to watch her rooms. Guard her. Keep her here, under gentle restraint.*

No, he answered.

Dabarrah felt her momentary confusion, then it turned to waiting steadiness. She would not protest while uninformed. How he loved this woman!

The College sent a word I received only today, Anna; those who want her banished from Thyrica have gained support. They are all but ready to pronounce the sentence and never let her return. Yes, we could keep Firebird here. She would be welcome. But would she be happy?

Yes. In time—

Happy with us? Feeling, as she would, that we had denied her the final chance to try to bring back Brennen, for their children's sake?

And her own, sent Anna, but without condemnation. *Yet you are right. Kept here against her will, she taints the Sanctuary with her misery.*

Dabarrah felt her mood change, and answered, *It would slowly tear her apart if that bond were broken by his death. I don't feel certain she would survive long. I wish he had considered that before he left her.*

But . . . She flexed her fingers. *The last we heard, the College Masters were going to let you train her.*

Dabarrah shrugged. *They have been evenly divided for some time. Perhaps I let my own hope for the outcome cloud the issue.*

Sadness, sympathy, and pain flooded the bonding resonance.

Are you ready to be a mother, then, Anna? he asked, laying an arm across her shoulder. *I can think of two teaching Sentinels here who would join Firebird in her effort if they understood the situation. Tomorrow morning, I will speak to them, choose one, and send Firebird on her way with our help and blessings.* He sank with Anna onto the white stone bench, careful not to sit on her long, straight hair.

You know her strength, Anna sent. *She will bring him back or die.*

Yes. Yet I think either of them, given the choice, would rather make the Crossing together.

Instead of alone.

He covered her hand with his own and wrapped her in his shielding cloud, pressing comfort through her. Together they sat quietly, until he added, *There is the matter of Sentinel Kinsman.*

How does that follow, Jenner? Does she guess what Firebird means to do with the RIA craft she brought?

Ellet came to Hesed precisely for that purpose: to lure Firebird away to her death, hoping to precipitate a rescue effort aimed at Brennen. Dabarrah showed her the sum of Ellet's actions that had led him to this conclusion.

Indignant, Anna stared at him. *So now, because Ellet has precipitated the situation, we must send one more Sentinel into the trap at Three Zed, to assist Firebird and help protect the RIA secret.* Anna brought her emotions under complete affective control. *I would not have thought it of Ellet. She is the responsible one, Mistress Firebird the volatile one.*

Neither is so simple as that, he sent in return. *Ellet's sense of responsibility has showed serious gaps.*

Is she trying to regain a chance at Brennen for herself, then? Why did she come here with Sentinel Dardy? Is she deceiving him as to their compatibility?

No, no. They are deeply connatural. In denying him, Ellet is resisting what is probably her only chance for bonded happiness within the ethical system.

Anna slipped out from under his arm and stood. *You should discipline her, then, Master Dabarrah.*

Yes. Would you bring her—and Air Master Dardy—to the office, my love?

Anna stood silently for a few seconds, fingering her skirt. Then, smiling, she nodded. *Indeed.* She turned to the door.

The moment Firebird got back to her rooms, she called Tel in and detailed her intentions.

"Fuel banks are charged? And there's room for four, to make our escape?" he asked.

Sitting on the head of her bed, she nodded. "Easily—although it cuts the psychological volume below minimal. The question is whether I can learn to control that projection module well enough to matter before we reach Three Zed. It's only a three-day slip, and I have no training. I'll have to do it on instinct."

"I have every confidence in your instincts, Firebird." He paced to the other side of the bed. "I can practice piloting in slip on the override sims, so I'll be able to help if you need it."

She thought for a moment. "Are we crazy, Tel?"

Pursing his soft, sensitive lips, he exhaled sharply. "Maybe. It doesn't matter. You're right; they probably didn't manage to get away. If that is so, they'll be caught in the Federate attack. So we must go. It's simple."

"We'll have to leave quickly. I can't keep secrets from these people, and they already suspect." Firebird leaned back against the wall. "They'd just as soon be rid of me, I think. But you needn't go, unless you want to as badly as I do."

Tel smacked his palms together. "Can you be ready in an hour?"

"Half an hour would be better, if you can manage it. I don't think even Anna would be watching for me so soon."

"Good," he said, and he strode toward the door.

"Meet me here," she said softly.

Ten minutes later, Anna Dabarrah stood against the office doorway. Inside, Ellet Kinsman and Damalcon Dardy occupied all her husband's attention—and half of hers. She should call a sekiyr to attend Kinnor and Kiel. Yet she had just checked their alpha rhythms, and they were sleeping deeply. For half an hour, they would not need her.

Only half an hour. That much time, I can offer to Ellet and Damalcon. Closing the office door behind her, she went in.

For the only time since the prohibition had been lain on her, Firebird stole into the Dabarrahs' private rooms and found them empty of adults. She stood in the dim light, gazing down at two tiny warming cots, then bent and kissed each child, heart aching. *Little sons of destiny,* she crooned silently. *I'm sorry.* One tear splattered on a tiny cheek, but fortunately it was Kiel's. He wriggled but did not cry out. Firebird wrenched away from her sons' cribside, crept along the pool, and slipped back into her rooms to finish packing.

"I'll fly it out." Firebird slip-sealed the craft. Inside it, the air smelled of damp earth and kirka trees. "But once the blockaders come on screen, you'd better take it and leave me the guns." At the edge of her vision, Tel stowed and secured their satchels. She worked through the preflight sequence, sinking her maternal depression deep. "We're going to alert someone no matter what we do, so we'll make this fast. It's a straight shot out the hollow. I'll accelerate the second we hit the bay's main aisle. Ready?"

"Ready." On his face she saw hard determination, and though she despised the object of his affections, in that moment she knew she loved Tel.

They blasted into a starry sky and soared on full impulse. Firebird noted a single blip on the fore sensors. Shuhr blockader ahead. Hurriedly she punched in the fielding drop code she had seen Dardy use.

But the interlink came alive. "RIA Eight," spoke Master Dabarrah's voice over the headset. "You have no clearance. Identify yourself and your intended destination."

Tel's long-lashed eyes grew wide and worried. Ignoring her sensor screens, Firebird took a deep breath. "Three Zed," she answered evenly.

For three long breaths, she heard only the engines.

At Dabarrah's elbow, elderly Master Keeson spoke urgently. "Two—three other blockaders, now, closing on them from south and west."

Dabarrah stared helplessly at his main communications board. "The volatile one": Anna's label had proven true. Firebird had moved too quickly, this time. Touching one finger to the glowing surveillance screen, he considered two options: to use the fielding system to Command Firebird back to ground, so she might leave Hesed tomorrow with at least one experienced Sentinel on board, or to let her go on, now, alone.

Those Shuhr were closing quickly. She might not be able to land in safety.

No one's near the parking bay—he asked Keeson, head of his fielding team, *who could get a support ship up, quickly?*

The elderly Master's white head shook. *She took the only RIA craft in the bay.*

Frowning, Dabarrah leaned toward his pickup mike.

The onboard link spoke again. "Are you alone, Lady Firebird?"

"No," she said. "Prince Tel has come with me." The controls vibrated under her hands. On the board, Tel crossed his fingers.

The Shuhr ship they had been tracking centered on the fore screen. "Take the controls, Tel." She reached for the ordnance board. Unless Dabarrah allowed it, they could go no farther. But she would see one Shuhr blockader dead. Tel set the craft into a rolling turn while she armed a missile, and the moment the ship began to level out, she fired.

Master Dabarrah spoke again, his voice firm and gentle. "Go, daughter of courage. Go with all the blessing we can give. And His Highness as well. But hurry. Three more craft are closing with you."

"Thank you, Master." Silently scolding herself for inattentiveness, she extended the resolution of the aft screens. "Yes. I see them. Thank you, Master," she repeated, and shut off the link.

"Got him!" Tel cried. The blip ahead vanished.

"I'll take it now." Firebird diverted her thrusters and set in a vertical course, and the speedy little transport ship responded as designed. The push put them out of range, first of the following blockaders and then of the planet's gravitational interference. She fed the ship's computer the celestial coordinates she had surreptitiously researched from Hesed's database, and the navcomputer translated the coordinates into a heading for Three Zed. Firebird took a confirming readout and then pressed the jump bar. The slip-shield activated, the translight drive pressed her spine against the seat's frame, and they were away.

"Just like that?" Tel asked.

Firebird smiled down the console, wishing she could kiss him but not daring to offend his sensibilities. She sighed and stretched, then sat fingering Brennen's medallion on its chain at her throat. "Just like that. Now, the work begins. Unless I can learn to ride this RIA unit in three days, we'll do just as well ringing the bell and asking the Shuhr to take us in."

In his bed beneath Three Zed's dome, Juddis Adiyn lay staring at light threads dancing projected on his ceiling. Blues and purples, yellow and pale red, against the black of night—

. . . the young woman he knew to be Firebird Caldwell, sleeping in a spacecraft near a strange young man, dreams of deadly fear and deadly purpose filling her mind . . .

(Excellent! She was on her way, then!)

He felt it fading, this glimmer of the shebiyl. Of all his acquaintances, he alone could see it with such clarity, and for this long. Adiyn closed his eyes—

The path branched. He pressed his awareness upward—

. . . she lay at his feet, writhing out her life. Nearby, Caldwell, holding the dendric striker: anguish hammered him to his knees. . . .

Excellent. And probable, then. Polar will want to Share this. But only probable.

Feeling smug despite his self-warning, he pressed across the gap to another branch of gleaming vision—

. . . an explosion in his brain, fire and blinding light . . . and then darkness. . . .

Too far along! Go back!

But he could not. Adiyn cursed the shebiyl that afforded such clear glimpses but would not yield to manipulation. What lay further back on that path? Where the nexus point, how to prevent disaster?

He quieted his pounding pulse. Many times, he had seen his own death—sometimes as a high probability, sometimes even at Dru Polar's hands—so he could not let that chance rule his expectations. He sent signals through his body to stop it from perspiring. Then, though the shebiyl faded, he pressed his point of focus across, toward yet another dim branch—

. . . she lay at his feet, writhing . . .

Yes. An attractive woman, in death. Very much like the sister. Two of the line accounted for. Next, the children.

As the shebiyl faded, he drifted toward sleep.

Chapter 19

Three Zed

sempre crescendo
always becoming louder

Carradee Angelo gripped the arms of her gilt chair and stared up and down both branches of the U-shaped Electoral table, unable to internalize the debate going on around her, able only to realize that fate was about to play a cruel, cruel trick.

Close on her left, Wellan Bowman stood. He cut a fine figure in black, tall and white-faced, leaning on a diamond-crusted walking stick. "'. . . but under Federate supervision, the Assembly has received more and more power. Before the Electorate loses all authority, we must consolidate behind a strong ruler. I wish to express my support for the Duke of Claighbro's motion."

Carradee kept her eyes open, her back straight. That made seven of them. Seven of the highest-ranking nobles of Naetai, asking with a single voice that she step off the throne. Seven Electors out of twenty-seven.

Beside her, Rattela shuffled his legs under his bulk and stood ponderously but regally. "Madame." With one satin-swathed arm, he made a sweeping motion that took in both sides of the table. "Your service to Naetai in this most trying of times shall never be forgotten, never diminished in respect, no matter what course taken from this juncture. You alone, perhaps, could have led us through the adjustment to the Federates' temporary overlordship.

"Yet the situation is changing." He pressed his palms together.

Her Electorate. She had chosen several of these men and women specifically for their respect for the Federates, to ease the transition into occupation—and then, one day, Federate covenance. How were they taking this?

One commoner, a professor in a scarlet robe, nodded solemnly at the Duke.

Rattela leaned one arm on the table, knitting his sculpted brows. "Madame, we sympathize deeply with you. We know how strong is your concern for His Highness, and your preference for remaining with him." Rattela glanced at the empty chair at Carradee's right side. "And Madame, you cannot keep the truth of his condition from the N'Taian people much longer."

Carradee blinked. It was true; gladly she would give up the throne, if it meant she could have Daithi whole again—gladly!

"Without an heiress, Your Majesty, the line is in grave jeopardy." Rattela smoothed the ends of his blue nobleman's sash. "Naetai must have a strong, single ruler—even if only a regent-designate, acting on behalf of the Crown. There is a precedent, as you well know, early in the second century of the Angelo dynasty . . ."

Carradee let him talk. She knew the story of Grand Duke Tarrega Erwin. Everyone in the room should have known it. Regent for the infant Queen Bobri, Erwin had guided Naetai safely through the Coper Rebellion. Her left foot began to itch, but she dared not move to ease it. That would look weak.

Rattela stopped speaking. Regents. They were speaking of a long-term regency. Unlike her mother, Carradee had never been happy with power. *Would* it be best for Naetai?

The stiff fabric of her skirt rustled in the silence as she straightened under the Chamber's high dome. "Should a regency prove desirable, there is the matter of rank. First Lord Baron Erwin, Baron Parkai. As the highest nobles of the land, have you considered the weight that would be thrust upon you, should one of you be chosen to serve as regent for our daughter, Iarlet?"

As she sat down, she saw whispers pass around the table. They had assumed Rattela, leader of the secessionist movement since Phoena's defection and temporary regent while she cared for Daithi, would take on any regency left by her absence. And as for Iarlet—most of them thought her dead. Carradee knew procedural justice. Presenting Iarlet as her heiress would slow the proceedings to a fuddbug's crawl.

Bualin Erwin stood on her left. A vigorous man in his seventies kept implant-young in appearance, he cocked one eyebrow at her.

"Madame, my father's removal from this body after the VeeRon War has left somewhat of a stain on our family. At present, if called upon to serve as Regent, I shall decline for the sake of maintaining good relations with the Federate governor."

"Oh," Carradee murmured softly. It made sense, but she was surprised to hear him pass by the honor so quickly.

Beside Rattela, young Reshn Parkai rose. "For the same reason, Madame, my father's involvement in and death at the Hunter Height debacle would preclude me from accepting the rod."

And that left His Grace, Muirnen Rattela, Duke of Claighbro, sitting beside her, smug in his dignity. She wondered briefly if the Barons had truly stood down out of honor, or if Muirnen Rattela had made offers.

Carradee felt lightheaded, as if she were floating away from the world she had always known. Where would she go? What would she do?

She would continue to care for Daithi. Governor Danton's words came back to her, and those of Tellai's recent message—the offer of sanctuary, where Firebird now lived. And, perhaps, her daughters, too, hidden and safe.

She hesitated in midthought. No one had contested her nomination of Iarlet as her successor.

Rattela meant to have a long rule.

Carradee rose again. "Noble Electors, this body is now recessed. We shall meet tomorrow morning at nine hundred. At that time, we . . . I shall lay before you certain documents. That is all."

Her touch deactivated the recording microphone at her place on the table. She stepped back from her chair and walked toward the gilded doors. Slowly—they could wait. The heels of her leather pumps clicked on the gold-shot black marble floor; the high white ellipse of the ceiling echoed. Other than that sound, the chamber lay absolutely still. She imagined she could feel the stare of Rattela's soft green eyes, following her down. Two red-jacketed guards stood beside the gilt doors, reached simultaneously for handles, and pushed outward, letting her through. The doors shut behind her: *boom*.

Numbly she stood in place, listening to the faint scraping of chairs and a sudden rise in voices.

Carradee fled up the long, curving stairs to Daithi's room.

Solicitor Merriam, whose forefathers had been legal counsel to queens for two centuries, came to her an hour later, all the tools of his trade in his papercase: data terminal, parchment, long black pens. He spread them on a spiral-legged table and pulled up a chair.

"I wish two documents made." Carradee sat stiffly on the other side of the table in the dim light of the sitting room. After a good cry under Daithi's limp arm, she had bathed, put on fresh clothes, and made up her mind. She was ready, now, to face the changes in her life.

Perhaps she was not strong enough to make a Queen, but Muirnen Rattela could steer the course of Naetai's future without the Angelo fortune. That belonged to her and to her family—not the Electorate.

"Two documents," she repeated. "A document of abdication. And a new will."

The red stone of a broad, glacial valley poking in places through long winter-browned grass, and graceful, man-high brown riding animals cantering on low hills: These, and a cold blue sky veiled by wisps of high cloud, framed Carradee's first vision of the Hesed Valley.

When the lanky Master Sentinel who introduced himself as Jenner Dabarrah took her underground and she saw the vast pool rippling under the skylights, her grieving eased. Iarlet and Kessaree *had* vanished, despite her hopes—but that was months ago, now. Firebird had gone only yesterday.

She would weep later.

She saw Daithi revived from travel sedation and safely bedded in a warm, impressively modern special-care cubicle in Hesed's medical center before she followed the young man assigned as her guide—Labeth was his name—to the waterside commons. At Master Dabarrah's circular table she met his long-haired wife, and a smiling young couple he introduced as Sentinel Dardy and his bride, Ellet. The young woman's dazed, joyous stare never left the man's boyish face, and he waited on her with constant tenderness and deference.

"Bonding shock." Dabarrah leaned toward Carradee and spoke gently, with a smile full of warmth. "It lasts only a few days. It is good for the Sanctuary to have them here. All of us feel their love and wonder, and they do not mind our company. They scarcely notice us."

Carradee stared a little longer at the tall, oval-faced woman. She certainly seemed happy. Was that what had happened to Firebird?

These were good people. Governor Danton had been right.

She spooned the last drops of rich brown broth from the bottom of her bowl, then tidily refolded her napkin. "Now, Master," she said. "May I see my nephews?"

The computer brought Firebird's RIA craft out of slip-state at a wide margin from Three Zed. As Firebird expected, it seemed all too soon. After grasping Tel's hand in unspeaking understanding, she relinquished the ship to him and slid on the splayed-finger headset.

Edging inward toward P'nah, she felt strangely composed by the realization that this time she dared not fail. The terrors of a hundred deaths did not touch her; perhaps Dabarrah was right, and she was coming to terms with them. She passed through the horror-storm, secured the carrier, and then reached back out for the RIA harmonic.

Instantaneously she became a huge presence, able to send her point of consciousness wherever she chose. She exhaled gently in relief and let that point drop toward Three Zed, alert for signs of motion in high orbit.

"There," she murmured to Tel. "I've found their net. But don't go in yet."

To her altered perception the satellites felt like queer, disembodied intelligences, glaring into space in their rotations. How to blind one of those eyes? She could rely only on instinct, on this crude sense of visualization, and a remark made long ago by her traitorous old instructor at the Planetary Naval Academy, Vultor Korda, deprecating a Sentinel who could only "push a few electrons along." If phase control were truly among the simplest skills, perhaps in concert with the powerful RIA unit she could kill a satellite.

She extended her probe a little farther, to touch one solar-sailed cylinder. Passing within its metal walls, her changed senses registered a cacophony of electrical activity, hissing and buzzing in staccato rhythms. Like the visualization that allowed her to Turn, this sparked an idea. Perhaps if the "RIA sense" told her she could hear, she could also sing.

Imagining a note at utter, tritonal disharmony from the satellite's fundamental pitch, she willed that note to sound, using the satellite's circuitry as her instrument. It vibrated at the frequency she commanded. The satellite howled around her, every surface a sounding board. A series of harmonics began to build, tone on shattering tone, that made her cringe and almost flee. Then it fell absolutely silent.

Across a vast vacuum she wrenched her awareness back into the pilot's seat of the RIA ship. "I got one, Tel," she gasped. At last she appreciated how exhausting the outlay of mental energy could be. "There." With the computer's light wand she set a spark onto the fore screen and covered one smoothly moving point of light.

"It's too far from us now." He pulled one hand off the controls. "We've fallen back in orbit."

"Chase it! I'll listen for others!"

The transport shuddered as he accelerated in pursuit of the dead surveillance satellite and its corridor of marginal safety. Firebird snugged her harness, leaned back with her eyes closed, and forced herself again into accord with RIA. Pressing the RIA sense forward, she scouted for the weird music of those satellite eyes. It seemed she waited forever for the ship to drop, all the while trying to hold blinders before the sickening visions that rose with her carrier. They roiled more vividly than ever, and she wondered if the RIA circuits fed them. She hummed softly to distract herself: a melody she'd composed in slip for Labeth, and Ahriyth of Metsura.

"We're through their orbital altitude," Tel said in a loud whisper. His voice broke the RIA accord. "Where do we set down?"

She too wanted to whisper, eyeing the sensor screens. "Squill, Tel, I don't know." Extending the RIA probe once more, she began to scrutinize the black sphere for "sounds" of life. "Take us as low as you can," she murmured, and she swept the point of awareness along the planet's distant surface. "We don't know if those other satellites see down as well as upward. This could take a while."

For an hour she searched, and she finally spotted the colony by its cackle of enharmonic voices. "That dome, Tel. Don't get too close."

He cut speed and dropped lower yet, into the shadow of a black peak. "Here, Firebird?"

He set down with a jolt Firebird chose to ignore. Gladly she pulled off the headset and shook out her hair, shaking free, too, of a sickening dread at the pit of her stomach. For a while she would be very glad to avoid contact with that epsilon carrier.

Tel rose first. "Hurry, Firebird."

"You still—"

"Go. I'll guard the ship."

"You're sure?"

"I'd only trip you up." He looked away, and she knew how badly he wished to go in, despite his determination to help where he best could.

"Thank you, Tel." She unclasped her flight harness and stood. Working quickly but deliberately so not to unnerve herself, she checked through the gear she'd scavenged from the ship's emergency supplies: food concentrates and painkiller jellies, two recharges for the Federate-issue blazer she'd found under the pilot's chair, a pair of doorbreaker charges that would send their pulse to a panel's edge and detonate there, and a little electronic tap circuit. She unclasped her web belt and slid the pouch around to ride on her left hip opposite the blazer. *Doesn't look like much,* she observed. She hoped, however, to depend not on gear but the bond link to find Brennen, and then on his abilities to escape.

Just before she left the ship, she embraced Tel awkwardly through the gawky pressure suit. "Give me one day," she warned as she opened the helmet's clasps, preparing to don it. "I probably won't survive even that long if I don't find Brennen, but give me a Standard day. If I'm not back, or if you see any sign they've found you, get offworld fast."

"Firebird." He sniggered, a most uncharacteristic, ungentlemanly laugh. "Do you think I could do that?"

"Tel," she growled, knowing she could threaten him no longer. He only shrugged.

Ruefully she smiled. "You're right. I can't order you away either. Be careful, then, if you come in. Chances are, we'll be dead together."

Then he did kiss her. Firebird stood a moment with her head bowed, searching for words to apologize for the hatred she once had nurtured for him and his kind. She couldn't. She could only hope he understood, when ten minutes later she turned back and saluted him, near the edge of the craft's visual range.

Struggling against the too-large vacuum suit, she crossed the boulder field between ship and dome under a firmament of sense-deafening, silent blackness. As she skirted the dome's perimeter, a minor airlock came into view, guarded by a single man.

Firebird stole nearer, keeping to the shadows. When she felt she could inch no closer without being seen, she steadied her blazer on the dome and shot the dark figure. It folded and fell silently. She crept in, closed the small side 'lock, and brought the air pressure up. Once inside the entry bay, she hurriedly unsuited.

The bay vibrated with the creation of auxiliary power. Firebird tiptoed across and then peered down a long inbound corridor, twitching at the safety stud on her blazer with a tense forefinger. The way seemed clear. She began her search.

It was not difficult to sense the layout of the dome; the curving passages ran parallel to the outside, straight ones led in or changed level. She halted at the first junction. Now, where? And how to stay hidden?

A powerful hunch, vaguely like the bonding resonance, told her Brennen would be much nearer if she took the left straightaway.

But was it a trap? A defense invented by the Shuhr to lure any intruder to his death?

Resolutely she turned left and hurried inward, straining to hear footsteps. The dome remained uncannily quiet.

At every junction and lift shaft the sensation repeated, until ten minutes later she stood before a blackened, forbidding metal door, its lockpanel arrayed with colored tabs and an alphanumerical coder. She hesitated, fighting the panicky sensation of being one minute too late, and the auditory hallucination of bootsteps approaching.

Placing a hand on the door, she tried to relax. Once her panic submitted to control, she kicked the door rapidly three times with a metal-tipped boot, then waited—then did it again. After another second she felt a faint, thrilling surge of awareness as if she had awakened—Brennen!

The first instant's joyous welcome turned suddenly to ice. Firebird gasped as if sliced by the painful, inexplicably faint but frozen touch. In it she felt a wordless cry: to flee—to seek out the Fleet—to go back to Heséd. For help he would have been grateful, but Firebird he wished anywhere else in the galaxy.

That, too, passed. She relaxed into the contact, loosening her right hand to let it rise in his control. Surely he had been able to observe the unlocking sequence on that panel.

Nothing happened. Confused now and badly frightened, she took matters in hand. From the gear pocket at her belt she pulled out one of the little charges and pressed it to the door. It seized hold with a soft *chunk* she hoped Brennen recognized.

She set the delay for three seconds and stepped up the corridor as far as she dared. A wild crackling noise filled the hall, and then the panel fell outward with the clang of a huge gong. She gathered herself to spring into the cell.

Brennen was faster. He leaped through the frame, over the door that lay in the passway.

Whole—she felt whole again! Firebird stood dazed, bathing in the sensation, letting it flow over her and through her and—

Brennen seized her hand and pulled her up the corridor, heels pounding. At the corner of the hall he palmed a panel and pushed her into a tiny service room. He pressed in, palmed the uncoded lock panel, and then clutched her. Gasping in the dim orange half-dark she kissed and caressed him, rising to the urgent press of his lips, despite the desperate need to escape and the certainty that others heard the fall of that massive door.

She laid her head against his chest and circled his waist with her arms, then pulled back to see him. His face looked thinner than she remembered; a dark scar crossed his left cheek near his ear, where some wound had gone untreated, and they had taken his Master's star. But under the tiny orange luma his eyes gleamed, windows to the soul she loved. Her hands tightened at his waist, and she might have sung for joy, but she felt no need to speak. The touch of resonance pulsed faintly in the depth of her mind.

It did not deepen, though. She drew away, confused. Was he shielding—did he fear her?

"Blocked, Mari," he whispered. He touched the medallion hanging over her shirt front. "Drugs. They injected me again only an hour ago—I can't even touch my potential. How in all the worlds did you get here?"

"In one of the RIA ships. With Tel."

"You what?" Brennen breathed, and he pulled away. He shook his head slightly and touched two fingers to the corners of her eyes. "I can't believe it. But here you are, and I see truth in your eyes. Mari!" He slid his arms back around her shoulders and pressed against her. "But, RIA. The Shuhr—"

How she wished she could sense his feelings! "Tel's guarding the ship," she said. "I won't . . . Turn. I won't do anything to harm you."

He drew a ragged breath, and her doubts fled. Keen on that breath had come the intensity of uncompromising pride and approval. Even without the bonding resonance she could read *that*. Together they sank to a sitting position in the tiny, cramped cubicle.

"Brenn. I'm not so sure any more that I would harm you if you—touched me. I read an Aurian story—"

"Nor am I," he whispered quickly. "I've seen research, here. Can you Turn now?"

"Now?"

"I've been blocked," he went on, "but if another could Turn

and open completely to me, I think his epsilon energy might take me across that blocking to my own carrier, for as long as I could hold the Turn myself. If we can't make it work, we have very little chance of escape. If it harms either of us, nothing is really changed. Don't worry about what happened to Bosk Terrell: try.''

"Of course." Firebird took several deep breaths and shut her eyes. Did she really believe Ahriyth's story applied to her? She was relaxing against Brennen's shoulder, envisioning the wall and all that lay behind it, when passing footsteps brought her alert.

"Easy," whispered Brennen. He slipped her blazer from the holster and trained it on the door's edge.

The footfalls passed.

"Try once more. It's worth the delay." He closed his arms around her again, one hand at her waist and the other arm across her shoulders, the loosely held blazer tickling her spine.

Several minutes later she still sat there, tears streaking down her cheeks. Brennen helped her to her feet. "I suspect you're trying too hard," he whispered. "It ought to be like falling asleep."

"I know. I'm out of practice—by decree." She wiped her face. "Where's Phoena?"

"She is dead, Mari," he said softly. "The Shuhr executed her the day I arrived."

"No! Oh—poor Tel!"

"Poor Tel, indeed." He shook his head, and faintly, like an echo of the resonance they had known, she felt his regret. Somehow it did not seem possible for Phoena to be dead. She could not grieve for her—later, perhaps, though nothing guaranteed she would live that long.

"Tel is waiting with the ship," she said, "about a half-kilo off. Do you know a way outside?"

He smiled faintly. "I have a feel for the layout here. First, though, we should see if we can sabotage their power source. With the distraction of a power-down, we would probably stand the best chance of escape. They know what RIA is, now, I'm afraid." In the dim orange light he grimaced. " From me. I wish we had another blazer."

"Keep mine. Generator, then. That would kill their fielding and energy guns, too, so we could take off. But what about the airlocks? They use power."

"Auxiliary." He reached for the door's edge.

She shook off sympathy. There wasn't time for it. "All right. Let's go."

With two fingers he pried the sliding door open. He peered

through and then swept her into the passway ahead of him. "Drop shaft," he whispered. "End of this hall, turn right. It will be on the left. I'll cover behind."

She stretched back to plant a last kiss on his throat for luck, then sprinted down the brightly lit yellow corridor. Her heart started to pound; exhilarated, she began to believe they would escape.

But careening around the corner, she flew practically into the arms of a tall stranger in black. She recoiled, flailing wildly for balance. This was a Shuhr, a renegade! His hand angled upward: "T'sa," he hissed. Her body froze in a wide-armed stance.

He smiled with his mouth, but his dark eyes narrowed. "Mistress Caldwell! Oh, don't be afraid." He took a step forward. "I won't harm you. Standing orders: alive and unhurt. Have you found him?"

Brennen rounded the corner, Firebird's blazer at the ready. The Shuhr's glance darted away, his hand changed angle, and Firebird felt the Command shift from her. Caught off balance, Brennen sprawled on the slick yellow floor. Firebird pulled her black dagger from its hidden sheath and lunged.

Chapter 20

. . . A Pyre for the Enemies of Thyrica

stretto con fuoco
climactic, concluding section
in faster tempo; with fire

The stranger grabbed for Firebird's arm. She twisted away, her reactions appallingly slow, dulled by days of inactivity. She wished she *could* kill again, consciously, as she had killed Bosk Terrell —*if* she had killed him. *Don't overextend!* she admonished herself, and she thrust short with the night-black blade. He struck her elbow aside, but he was slow—much slower than Brennen, even when Brennen had "matched" in training her—and insistently he kept one hand at a peculiar angle. That was his difficulty! He was still holding Brennen under voice-command!

He swung and seized her. Firebird wriggled out of a half head-lock, escaping the rank smell of his sweat, and sprang in behind him. Abruptly he shifted his weight to fall backward. Brennen had pinned her that way several times, in training, but Brennen had never fallen with all his weight, nor had she held a live blade. She clenched the beaded grip two-fisted over her ribs, planted the point in the Shuhr's back, and let him fall.

His agonized shriek tore at her ears. Her head hit the floor, and they rolled together. Skull ringing, she pushed away and pressed shakily to her feet. Her ribs hurt. A blankly staring corpse lay on black stone. She shuddered violently.

Released from Command by his captor's death, Brennen hurried up, knelt, rolled the body over, and drew out the dagger. From point to hilt the black blade shone wetly red. Firebird retched again, surprised after all she'd been through to find herself sickened by a bloody knife.

Wiping it clean on the stranger's stained tunic, Brennen gently said, "First knife kill, Mari, quick and clean. Well done." He handed up the dagger, hilt first.

With quivering hands she fumbled it into its sheath. "Good training," she answered lightly, but she did not meet his eyes.

Brennen still bent low, searching at the dead man's belt. "He wasn't armed. Pity. Here." He gave her blazer back. "We'll get another." He broke into a run again, leading up the passway toward the drop shaft.

Firebird came close behind, running hard to smother her shock, and jumped down the shaft after him. Knees bent, she landed; then, like racers from a block, they pounded down the stone-floored lower hallway.

Brennen vanished around a corner. Firebird felt the sudden surge of his alarm. Despite his blocking, the fear grew painful and loud. She skidded to a halt barely around the bend.

In the wide access to the stone-lined generator chamber stood two men and a woman, each angling a hand in such a way that Firebird knew she was caught, even before she felt the invisible cords draw tight on her body.

They looked so ordinarily human, and yet—yet—their eyes, like Terrell's hands, betrayed them. Quick-moving and suspicious, those eyes trusted no one.

She dared not try to Turn, dared not even think of trying to use her Turn as a weapon against them. They watched her like hunting kiel.

First one stepped closer, then another. Then the third. All wore battle gray, except for the younger man's wide, sulfur-yellow sash belt.

"What's this, Caldwell?" The older man came another careful pace on stocky legs. Behind him, a huge complex of generating machinery hummed softly.

The younger pair, lean, dark-haired and agile-looking, stepped close to Firebird, separating her from Brennen. She stood panting and did not try to flee.

"Mistress Caldwell." The elder's voice flowed like honey. "We heard you had arrived. We have been expecting you."

The younger, larger man gave a rasping laugh she supposed was meant to imitate a polite chuckle. "My lady, you are surprised? Certainly you didn't think you arrived without our notice.

Your strike at our satellite lacked all subtlety. Indeed, you dis-appointed me badly. I thought surely the woman of Brennen Cald-well's choosing would deal with our mass detectors." He sniffed softly. "No, yours is a delightfully transparent, freely broadcasting mind. As is that of your friend outside—or shall I say, 'was,' in his case?"

Tel—*no*! she wanted to cry, but the Shuhr spoke on. "In fact, I had to call a special training session under my lieutenant, just to keep the entire security division from interfering with the little drama we are about to play."

Drugged an hour ago—had everyone watched her come in, then, but Brennen? Firebird's hand tightened convulsively on the grip of her blazer, useless down at her side. Her finger rested far from the firing stud and would not move.

"Forgive our lack of manners." The older man who had spoken first stood back. "I am Eldest Juddis Adiyn. My colleagues, Test-ing Commander Dru Polar and Cassia Tulleman. Polar, in partic-ular, has anticipated meeting you. He and your sister were very close."

"Very close." Polar touched a hand to his forehead and bowed. "To the depths of her subconscious, to the very moment of her death. So you see, I know you well also—as she knew you."

Firebird's hackles rose. What little pity she felt for Phoena died in that instant, and the old rancor returned.

Cassia Tulleman stepped closer, her fluid movements unham-pered by her military-cut shipboards, and ran a finger down the line of Firebird's nose. "Mistress of the faithful Master." She turned the fingernail to scratch. Caught in Command, Firebird could not pull back. Her eyes teared with pain as she glanced from Cassia to Brennen and back again. Brennen's expression, closed and hostile, told her that Cassia, like Ellet, had tried and failed. Firebird felt the faint, drug-fogged touch of Brennen's emotions vanish, as he shielded them from her. Was there more to fear here than death?

"Yes, Mistress." Polar kept his dark, lashless eyes toward her. "Much more. We will show you how she died."

Indignant, Firebird silenced her thoughts. These were no Sen-tinels to respect her mind's privacy.

Polar approached Brennen. From the shimmering yellow sash he pulled a silver rod as long as her forearm. "Take it!" he barked. Brennen's hand jerked out. Firebird stood terrified by the sight of Brennen voice-commanded. "You remember, don't you? Throat pressure point . . ." As Brennen gripped the haft beside the orange thumb stud, Polar's hand slipped along the surface, touching and sliding controls. A long needle thrust from the other end. Firebird recoiled.

"Ooh," breathed Cassia. "She's phobic!"

"So I see." The corners of Polar's mouth twitched, and Firebird groaned. Brennen had tried to help her fight that irrational fear. If only she had persisted!

"Mistress." Adiyn hitched his thumbs into the pockets of his shipboards. "Anticipation is frequently six-tenths of pleasure. Let me explain precisely what Master Caldwell will do with that dendric striker."

She glanced again at the silvery rod. Polar brandished it as Adiyn spoke.

"Neuromuscular ultracontraction is invariably fatal, and it will take what will seem to be a very long time before sensation ends. When you have died, this honored guest will be taken to his own more public fate. Is that right, Polar? You are prepared?"

At Polar's slow smile, she glanced at Brennen. He stood visibly shaken; the scar along his cheek looked dark and angry on his fair skin. Horrified, she tried at last to break the Command. She could not.

"First, the pleasure at hand." Polar touched Brennen's shoulder with the striker. "Bonded as he is to you, he will experience—ah, yes, your imagination responds. I shall see that he senses your emotional state, since at present he is less than fully able."

Firebird gritted her teeth, trying to project to Brennen—through her fearful defiance—trust and forgiveness and the hope he'd escape.

"Acch," Cassia hissed. "That's vulgar! You can do better than that, woman! Don't you believe Adiyn? Give this murderer the end of your blazer!"

Firebird's right hand came up, still holding the weapon. Automatically her forefinger slid off the safety circuit and took up the slack on the firing stud. Several meters down her sights she saw the glacial-ice blue of Brennen's eyes. If only she could swing her arm and sight on Polar instead!

"Maybe I'll let you do it," Cassia said hastily. "Save your Sentinel from what he fears the most. We could bargain. Perhaps you'd like to hear what happened to your nieces."

"I would *not*," gasped Firebird.

"But my brother Astrig was there. He said they were such pretty little girls."

"No!" Firebird cried. She would trust nothing the Shuhr woman told her.

Cassia shrugged and stepped away. "Fine. You're as ungrateful as the rest of them."

"Caldwell," Polar barked. "Go to her."

Firebird felt Brennen raise total resistance, but it had as much effect as that of a fragile mira lily trying to cling in a hailstorm. He approached step by unwilling step, holding the rod low and stiff-armed. Her blazer, like a creature she could not control, followed his eyes. When he had crossed the distance, it touched the bridge of his nose. Still Cassia left her forefinger free.

Apparently Polar sensed that. He bristled. "Cassia!" The two young Shuhr glowered at each other.

"Can you?" Firebird read on Brennen's lips.

Turn? Firebird quailed. The visions inside had never hinted at *this* end. Drawing a deep, shaking breath, she tried to blank out her surroundings: the humming generators, the Shuhr hungering for her agony, the promise of death in Brennen's hand. To pass the wall would multiply the terrors. Her faith had fled. Guessing she would kill Brennen if he were caught in those horrors, she hesitated.

Then she tried, praying the bickering Shuhr would not sense her effort.

Beyond all else, Brennen's nearness distracted her. She could ignore everything but the presence she had longed for so desperately. Everything but Brennen, powerless though he stood.

Gasping, she let her eyelids fly open. Her blazer still rested on Brennen's nose, and down at her side, his hand held the silvery horror.

"I can't," she mouthed.

"Try," he breathed.

Polar gestured angrily, turned away from Cassia, and stepped close. "Now."

Even Firebird could sense the huge, engorged unity of power that seemed to be Polar and Adiyn in link, exerting their strength together, though Adiyn hung back. Her terror rose fresh as Brennen's arm lifted. The contact jabbed the angle of her throat, and panic seized her. She already stood unable to move; now, she could scarcely think.

"Do it, woman," Cassia urged from the other side. "Kill him! Kill him before he can kill you, and save him the watching!"

"Cassia!" Polar shouted. "Follow orders or stay out of this!"

"You   low-blooded—empty-headed—half-watt!"   Cassia

shrieked, and Firebird's hand remained free to fire. "You don't rule the Tullemans!"

"And you have no right to kill Caldwell!" bellowed Adiyn. Polar's hand twisted violently. Cassia fell away from Firebird, crashed against a corner of the corridor, and dropped to the floor.

Firebird stood motionless, released from Command but held helpless by the terror piercing the skin at her throat. Although Brennen kept his hand steady, the pulse pounding in her carotid artery made the needle quiver horribly.

Polar laid one hand on Brennen's shoulder and one on hers, and dreamily shut his eyes.

Again Firebird felt Brennen's love pressing into her: a benediction, a till-we-meet he meant with all his heart.

Here then, for the last time, she would touch him at the core of their souls. If that touch killed him, she would at least cheat the Shuhr of their pleasure. Reconciled to her destiny and flushed with a queer excitement, she bowed her head to receive his last blessing.

—And Turned.

A flicker of terrorized strength licked up through her. Back upon it flowed an incredible surge of energy. It must be Brennen's carrier, resonating with her own—

The skin of her throat tore. Roused by pain, she let go of the Turn, wheeled, and fired. She wanted Polar, but Adiyn was there. He fell backward, eyes wide in surprise.

Something landed on her back. Firebird felt her head seized, her neck twisted by hands that tangled into her hair and gouged her scalp with long, cutting nails.

"Brennen?" she choked. Had she killed him? Where was he?

Cassia's voice seethed unintelligible words into her ear. Flaming anguish erupted through her body. Hate and horror and nauseating "otherness" pounded into her, throttling her awareness with a mental stranglehold. Pinned, burning, and unable to do anything else, Firebird groped back down toward the terror and energy she could not control. Cassia clung snakelike to her point of awareness, tightening her arms as well, while searing, crippling heat licked deep into Firebird. As Firebird's imagination absorbed Cassia's fiery attack, a new glimmer of blue-orange flame joined and illuminated the miasma of unreal death. She could almost smell smothering smoke.

Abruptly Cassia's psionic coils loosened. Firebird sensed sudden fear, heavy with otherness.

She exulted. This was how Bosk Terrell had died! Defiantly

she flung herself inward, heedless of her own peril. The Turn became a wrenching dive into extinction, and she took Cassia with her. Immaterial smoke thickened as they plummeted. Firebird struggled for a last cool breath. Cassia's terror grew in her senses; she thought she heard a long, quavering scream. Fiercely she accelerated the fall. For an instant the vision shifted: In a N'Taian tagwing fighter, they plunged toward the black mountains of VeeRon.

Impact: an instant of terror. It was done in a heartbeat. Then she felt nothing at all.

The moment Firebird caught her epsilon carrier, Brennen seized the spark: a vicious strength that startled him in its desperate, haunted intensity. He drove that spark across the drug-induced chasm between control and his own carrier—it was there! Crowing triumph, he grabbed hold. Access-linked with Firebird across a doubled carrier, he glimpsed her blazing core of energy—and anguish.

Then a swell of power rose through him, shock waves blasting through his trained checks and controls: so much energy he could not direct it, but he dared not stop its flow lest he return to the helpless, blocked state. Throwing both hands wide in bewilderment, he sent the striker flying and stood stupefied.

Antipodal fusion—Polar's research—surely this was it!

Bodily, Polar flung him to the ground. Brennen rolled automatically to break the fall, struggling to bring the inward explosion under control. From too little epsilon strength he had passed suddenly to far, far too much!

From Adiyn's loose, lifeless hand, a blazer flew to Polar.

Forcing back the energy storm to keep it from overpowering his control, Brennen willed its tiniest wisp into his voice. He pressed up from the floor, stretched out a hand, and Commanded Polar.

"Down!"

The Shuhr fell sideways. His blazer glanced against stone, momentarily knocked loose of his hand. Still minimizing the frenzy of power, Brennen directed the excess inward on itself, holding energy with energy, and let free a kinetic burst to call that blazer.

It slid past him, out of control across the stone floor. He groaned. In all his memories of training, no instruction lingered to help him channel this eruption.

Polar staggered to his feet and reached into the air before him to gather and focus power. Again, energy coalesced with Polar's that was not his own. In front of the black-haired Shuhr condensed the thickest epsilon shield Brennen had ever sensed. He loosed the torrent that filled him in a desperate strike at Polar's mental centers, but the static shield held unbreached.

Brennen gasped, fighting despair. What *was* this entity? Against such an adversary no mental attack had any hope. Its only weakness was Polar's human body. He must strike Polar physically, cut him down.

But Brennen had nothing to throw, no weapon of any kind.

From his sash, Polar pulled Brennen's own crystace—Polar's trophy. Its familiar whine cut through Polar's shout. "Know, Sentinel, that you die by the will of the Chad-negiyl." He held his arm high over his head, poised to throw.

Chad-negiyl—the Shuhr overlord empowered Polar! Roused by fury, Brennen sent a last word of Command, backed by the torrent of energy bursting its gates—not at Polar, invulnerable behind his shield, but at the crystace.

"Down!" he Commanded it. Energy flowed up, and through him, and was gone.

Polar vanished with a crash. The chamber fell silent except for the piercing note of the crystace and the generators' hum.

Brennen struggled to his feet and lurched to the spot where Polar had stood. An impact crater two-foot wide and half a meter deep, bisected by a slender trench a full meter long, had been blown into stone. The crystace lay in the trench, but burying most of the blade's length . . .

Turning away, Brennen swallowed hard. Beneath a reddish-gray, smashed object that looked only vaguely as though it had been a human head, he had glimpsed a width of gray sleeve darkening with moisture. Under that, in the crater's depths, lay an unrecognizable mass.

The crystace had crushed pommel first through bone and flesh into the stony floor, the shock waves of its passing reducing Polar's body to the jelly that lined the crater.

That's a new use for a crystace. Brennen exhaled with shaky relief and relinquished the Turn.

Then he saw Firebird lying near the chamber's back wall, her limbs tangled on black stone with Cassia's, auburn hair and black twisted like silken rope around both their throats.

Aghast, he stumbled toward them. Had Firebird killed again? The first time, he'd barely saved her. He rolled her onto her back to quest for echoes of consciousness.

He felt nothing.

She was gone: her deadly P'nah had taken her at last.

He inhaled to scream denial, not caring who would hear. Let them come; he would bury her body under corpses, and—

Realization slapped down his anguish. He had lost the carrier again and was blocked; of course, he would feel nothing! Cradling Firebird's head, he fumbled, searching for a pulse.

There! At the side of her throat it barely throbbed, as when she'd killed Terrell. Desperate with relief, he searched her body for other injuries, but found only scratches and the crusting cut at her throat where the probe had torn free.

He reached for Cassia. At no angle could he find a pulse, either in wrist or throat.

The Shuhr woman was dead, then.

He straightened and eyed all corners of the chamber. The right kind of mental touch might revive Firebird, but because she lay stunned, she could not lend him the bridging spark to his own carrier. He was helpless.

But not yet beaten. From the crater, he carefully plucked his crystace. He staggered across the chamber. The "special training session" called by Polar might keep the rest of the Shuhr away, might give him a chance to get Firebird to that RIA ship. Tel— what had they done to Tellai? With shaking arms he pulled himself up a long ladder onto the metal grate platform high on the generator. Under normal circumstances, he could have jumped it. He glared for a minute at a glasteel cover curving protectively over the row of relays, bolted and locked in place.

Activating the crystace once more, he sliced the cover away, then reversed every switch on the board with a sweep of his arm, plunging the chamber into blackness. When he touched off the humming crystace, the silence seemed to roar.

Toeing gingerly for each rung, he descended to the smoothed basalt floor, then dropped to his knees. Cautiously he crawled back. The notion of pitching headlong across Polar's crater made him extremely cautious.

Another minute's groping in darkness brought him to the sound of Firebird's shallow breathing. Gently he lifted her over his shoulder, but when he tried to step, his legs buckled, light though she was. He let her fall again. Infuriated by his exhaustion and impotence, but still too full of adrenaline for the sleepiness of the blocking injection to touch him, he took her by both shoulders and shook, first cautiously and then harder. "Mari," he pressed. "Mari."

She did not rouse. "Mari," he whispered. "Get up!"

Sliding his hands down her arms, he found her wrists and began to drag her up the passway.

Chapter 21

Beyond the Wall

delicatamente
delicately

Tellai groaned, pressing the heels of his hands into his eyes and folding forward over the instrument panel. She was dead—Phoena was dead . . .

"Help her, Tel. Please," gasped Brennen. Firebird lay where he had let her drop, on the deck of the spacecraft's cabin. Through her helmet's faceplate Tel saw her dark eyes open but blank. Hastily he unlatched the helmet and twisted it free. Brennen fell against the airlock, slip-sealing it with one hand, then released his own suit's clasps along chest and waist.

"She's alive? What happened to me—and her?" Numbly Tel stripped Firebird's heavy metal-and-fabric suit away.

Brennen stepped out of his own pirated outer garment. "You were put into tardema-sleep by a fielding team that's temporarily without generator power. That's why you're free of it now. And she—she's been through another psionic attack."

"Will she—live?"

"I don't know," Brennen whispered. Her eyes closed and her mouth relaxed open, uncontrolled.

"How long has Phoena been . . . ?" Tel shoved the bulky suits under the bench.

Brennen knelt to slip an arm around Firebird, but stopped and looked at Tel. "Three weeks," he whispered. "I'm sorry."

Tel nodded. His lip quivered, but he frowned hard and controlled it.

Brennen lifted Firebird onto the rear bench and strapped her down with black acceleration webbing. "Do you think—"

"Don't talk, Caldwell." Tel lifted one of Firebird's limp hands and pressed it to his cheek where he'd bruised himself falling unconscious. "Just get us out of here."

"I don't think I have the energy left to fly this. Can you?"

"Oh." Tel hurried toward the pilot's chair. "Yes. I can."

Dabarrah sat up straight in bed. For an instant, he hoped he'd not wakened Anna; then he saw her vacant pillow and heard her in the adjoining room, softly crooning a lullaby.

What? Brennen? Is that you?

The voice spoke again in his alpha matrix, quietly, as from a great distance. *It is, Master. I'm on RIA link, about two hours out.*

Dabarrah covered his eyes with his hands, the better to focus on that faint subvocalization. *Brennen! We had all but given up hope!*

Mari hadn't. She's with me, in deep psychic shock. She has killed again—but she controlled it, Jenner. She and I have touched, and I am unharmed. I saw her wall. In fact—

Dabarrah sat motionless as Brennen opened his memory, revealing a montage of days in the hands of the Shuhr, of research, and antipodal fusion—and his guesses regarding Firebird's frightening talent. *We know so little about her bloodline. Who's to say if the mutation might have occurred before her progenitress reached Naetai? Master, she is not a danger to us—though maybe, some day, to the Shuhr. Remember the shamah. I am certain of it. I will prove it, when we arrive.*

Dabarrah formed his thoughts with care. *I am glad to hear you speak so, Brennen, but there will remain testing.*

Bring her out of shock and I will do the testing myself. There was a pause. *Kinnor—and Kiel. Have they changed?* Dabarrah clearly felt the longing that rode that wave of epsilon energy. The new RIA unit's accuracy had been greatly improved.

Of course, Brennen. They change daily. Two hours, you estimate? He ordered the words in his mind but did not attempt to send. *Queen Carradee has come here, to sanctuary. What of Prince Tel, and the sister, Phoena?*

My regards to Carradee, if you speak with her before I can. Tellai is unharmed—but—Phoena is dead.

■ ■ ■

Tel stepped through the hatchway out into the predawn wind.
Just beyond Master Dabarrah, under the lights of Hesed's grassy
landing strip, a small figure in dark green waited at the foot
of the boarding ladder. Brennen had warned him to anticipate
Carradee. Tel glanced back over his shoulder into the ship's
darkness.

"Go ahead," said Brennen Caldwell's voice. "I've got her."

Squaring his shoulders, he stepped down the ladder. Hesitantly,
Carradee waved.

He hurried toward her. "Carradee. Majesty." Kneeling on the
soft grass, he took her hand and kissed it.

"Prince Tel. It *is* you. You look so different." Beneath loose
blonde curls, her forehead wrinkled deeply. "Are you all right,
Tel? Phoena . . . They tell me . . ."

He sighed relief. They had spared him having to tell her himself.
"You know, then." She watched him, waiting. He saw pity in
her gray eyes. "Yes, I'll be all right. Caldwell and I have . . .
talked. Give me time to mourn her, Carradee. Please—"

Abruptly Carradee gave a little gasp and clutched his hand. Tel
got to his feet. Brennen had emerged, carrying Firebird. She lay
in his arms, her legs dangling lifelessly and her hair hanging in
auburn waves over his elbow. Carradee shivered, dropped his
hand, and pulled her woolen coat close.

With a grave nod to Carradee, Brennen passed them, Dabarrah
at his elbow. Tel stepped out behind them, leading Carradee. An
image of Phoena exploded into his mind: Phoena, as he had known
her. Beautiful, powerful, noble.

No. That noble image was Phoena, as he had *imagined* her,
and she had never existed.

Tel covered Carradee's hand with his own. Carradee needed
him here, now. A sekiyr strode toward him, carrying a warm
jacket. Tel slipped it on. "General Caldwell seems certain Firebird
will live," he said. They walked slowly, falling farther and farther
behind the others. "At least, he's more certain than he was two
days ago." Tel paused. Caldwell, the invulnerable, implacable
Sentinel: *He* existed only as a facade, a beautifully controlled
image that concealed the real man behind his role. "I don't think
we begin to understand the kind of love these pair-bonded people
have for one another. But—" He pressed Carradee's hand, and
she smiled. She, too, who had been Queen of Naetai, was a
woman. "I am glad you came, Carradee," he said. "This is a
good place." He stared up at the shadowed red rock of the Hesed

valley. "A good place. But what of Naetai? Was Rattela unkind to you?"

Haltingly, Carradee explained all that had transpired. He nodded as she spoke, and as the sky lightened, the breeze blew strands of dark hair into his face. Carradee Angelo Second, whom he had never seen happy since her accession, looked content here.

"And Firebird," she finished. "She *must* recover. You see, the Assembly would not let the Electorate disbar our line, not permanently. I was allowed to abdicate in Iarlet's favor, and for that time, Rattela serves as regent. But once—if . . ." Her voice quivered, and at the golden double-doors of the groundside lift, he paused to hear her out. "Master Dabarrah has promised to send a team looking for Iarlet and Kessaree. But if Naetai declares my princesses legally dead . . ." She trailed off again and glanced down at the grass, then looked directly at him, her brows arching in sincere anguish. "Unless Daithi and I have other children, the Crown passes to Firebird. And her sons."

Tel almost laughed, imagining petite, straight-backed Firebird, her chin tilted as obstinately as ever, wearing the jeweled N'Taian crown. *Firebird. The proud, capable little Wastling . . .*

Soberly, he dismissed the image. Firebird had chosen a new road. Could she go back up it, back to Naetai?

And could Caldwell go along?

Smiling at that thought, Tel stood aside for Carradee to step onto the lift. She slipped her hand through his arm again. "It's peaceful here," she said, looking once all around her. "And Daithi is . . . he seems . . ."

The lift began to drop. *And what of the twins? Where do they belong?*

". . . he's better. Happier. Come with me, Tel. Come see him. Would you?"

Firebird and Brennen will straighten it out. They're capable. Suddenly content, Tel made a half-bow to Carradee as the lift doors opened. "Of course, Majesty. It will be good to see Prince Daithi again."

There had been fire, and terror, flooding the region between dreaming and waking, but Firebird was ready to wake, now. A warm weight lay on her chest. She raised a hand to touch it and felt silky hair on a firm skull. She threaded her fingers into it.

Then something warmer yet invaded the recesses of her awareness: the sensation of a tropical sea that smelled of incense . . .

"Brennen," she murmured.

The drowsiness let her go. She opened her eyes. Brennen pulled up to a sitting position. White stone shone overhead.

"Where . . . ?" She rolled her head to either side. Beyond white walls, water whispered and splashed, and she caught a breath of damp kirka trees.

"Yes. Hesed," he said softly. He took her hand. "How do you feel?"

That delicate touch remained at the fringe of her consciousness. He shouldn't be inside her alpha matrix, but he was. "Whole." She shut her eyes. "Brenn. You're here. Where are Kiel and Kinnor?"

"Close." He squeezed her fingers. "Dabarrah let me waken you in private. He and I shared memory a number of times while you slept, Mari. It's been days since he brought you out of shock paralysis. He thought it best to let your mental energy regroup before rousing you. Then, he said, you could be tested."

"Tested?" she asked sleepily. "When? For what?"

He touched her chin, leaned close, and kissed her. When he drew away, he whispered, "I am testing now, Mari."

The touch at the back of her mind grew stronger and began to stroke. Closing her eyes again, she trembled. Was everything terrible going to come untrue, all at once?

"Brenn," she said. It was difficult to concentrate on speaking, with sensation rising in every niche of her body and mind. "The blocking drugs they gave you, at Three Zed. Just before I reached you. You beat them."

"There's medical equipment, shipboard, on all our transport craft," he murmured. "Blood cleansing. You remember. We did it to you, once."

"A long time ago." She opened her eyes. He was staring into them. The sensation of penetration intensified. She breathed deeply.

"Don't Turn," Brennen whispered. "Let me. And we will see if all this A-status has been necessary."

Despite his warning, his words cued an immediate visualization of the wall—but the power behind it held no allure. "Do you remember that explosion of energy?" he asked as he stroked and caressed, all without touching her. "In the generator chamber?"

"It's nearly the last thing I do remember. Did I kill—her?"

"You Turned," he said, "as I did. I think *that's* what we'd better not try when we're alone. And yes, Cassia is dead." While he spoke, the probe stirred her memory: days alone at Hesed, her anguish over giving up the twins, her determination to go to him, whatever the consequences. "We will have to repeat the doubled

Turn for Dabarrah. Another day. When you are strong again.'' He began to slowly pull the tendril free. ''We believe we have identified the cause of that psiclysm, and why you can kill. Your carrier is different, apparently, and amplifies any of ours beyond control.

''But that will come later,'' he said, and he withdrew. ''We're safe,'' he whispered. ''You pass.'' Straightening, he touched a panel on the wall. ''Done, Master,'' he said. ''She controls beautifully. I think—'' He glanced back down at her. ''It's the family stubbornness.''

Lazily, Firebird shook her head. ''Which family?''

''The Aurian family. Dabarrah is sending down some people who want to see you.'' He shifted and arranged her hair on her shoulders. ''There's a message roll waiting in our room, from Regional Command.''

Something was about to happen. She could feel Brennen's anticipation; yet she lay still, willing to play along with him. ''They want you back on Alta, do they?'' she asked.

He rubbed the short, dark scar on his cheek. ''Perhaps. I haven't opened it. But I have fulfilled their conditions for reinstatement. That would be my guess, too.''

''It would do me good to see them ask you back.'' In contentment she closed her eyes again. A minute passed, then another. ''All those fantasies were wasted, Brenn.''

His thoughts must have been focused on something distant. ''Hmm?''

''Beyond that wall, I tried to conquer my own death. But facing death is nothing like imagining it, and the strength I needed came from . . . elsewhere. Strange, that it should have worked out this way. That wall,'' she repeated. ''It became a wall between us.''

She felt him take her hand.

''Did we accomplish anything, really, Brenn?''

After a short pause, he said, ''Yes. Our strike at Echo Six, and the death of two of Three Zed's colonial commanders, give Alta's attack a better chance of succeeding. And, Mari, think of what we've learned, of the possibilities . . . between us.''

She heard footsteps and opened her eyes.

Anna Dabarrah glided through the arch, followed by a slender sekiyr. A kicking, blond baby gazed at her from Anna's shoulder. The sekiyr came from behind Anna to lay dark-haired Kin on Firebird's lap, while Brennen watched. Kinnor didn't stir. ''He's been so content since you both returned, Firebird,'' Anna said, as Firebird fingered Kinnor's tight little fist. ''Apparently he does need his father. They seem to be linked at such a depth that Kin sensed Brennen's trials at Three Zed.'' Glancing aside at Brennen, whose intensifying radiance warmed Firebird with unconcealed intensity, Anna held out Kiel. "I apologize, Lady Firebird." She looked at Brennen again, as if apologizing to him, too. "We were only trying to protect them. You must know that."

"I do." Careful not to jostle and wake Kinnor on her lap, Firebird accepted Kiel as carefully as she might take a crystal goblet. He hiccupped, stared a little longer, and then broke into a broad smile. "Kiel," she whispered, cradling him with both arms, and then she reached down to touch Kinnor's dark curls. "You know me, don't you? You know your mother."

"Ghh," said Kiel.

irebird shut her eyes, her cheek pressed to her son's, and silently rejoiced. "Anna, is it over?" she asked. Then, swept through by sympathy for Carradee's grief for her own babies, she opened her eyes. She must ask about—

But Anna and the girl had left the room. Brennen folded Firebird, Kiel, and Kinnor together into his arms. "You will have much to learn, Mari. But there are no more walls between us." His voice came muffled through her hair as he rested his head on her shoulder. She struggled to reach for him, but he trapped her arms inside his own, and he was too strong. Holding tightly, he said again, "No more walls."

About the Author

Kathy Tyers, a California native, settled in Montana chiefly to see if she would find wilderness as inspiring in reality as in J.R.R. Tolkien's works (she did, and she stayed). She has earned degrees in microbiology and education, an amateur radio license and a SCUBA certificate, and has worked as an immunobiology tech and a primary teacher in a private school—but as the daughter of a flutist and a brassman, she has always considered music a necessity of life. A classical flutist turned semiprofessional folk artist, Kathy performs on flute and Irish harp with her guitarist–music teacher husband, Mark, and they have released two successful folk albums. They have one son, two cats, and about thirty assorted musical instruments.

Fusion Fire continues the story of Firebird, begun in the novel by the same name. Ms. Tyers is currently at work on her third novel, *Crystal Witness*.